D0201815

GASLIT NIGHTMARES

Stories by
Robert W. Chambers,
Charles Dickens, Richard Marsh,
and Others

Edited by Hugh Lamb

DOVER PUBLICATIONS, INC.
Mineola, New York

Copyright

Copyright © 1988 by Hugh Lamb
All rights reserved.

Bibliographical Note

This Dover edition, first published in 2006, is a new anthology of sixteen stories reprinted from the work *Gaslit Nightmares: An Anthology of Victorian Tales of Terror,* edited by Hugh Lamb, originally published by Futura Publications, London, in 1988.

International Standard Book Number: 0-486-44924-6

Manufactured in the United States of America
Dover Publications, Inc., 31 East 2nd Street, Mineola, N.Y. 11501

To Tamar and Zara

Contents

ACKNOWLEDGEMENTS

There are many sources of inspiration for the discovery of material for such a book as this, ranging from booksellers' catalogues to the casual mention of a name in another work. Victorian publishers themselves were most helpful; they often printed catalogues of their entire output in the backs of their books, a practice which has long since died out, alas. I must acknowledge the help I've received from the following people: the staff of Sutton Public Library (who turn up book after book I've given up for lost); Mike Ashley, for help with biographical details; similarly, Bob Hadji in Canada for help with Lady Dilke; and grateful thanks for help received from that expert researcher, Richard Dalby.

GASLIT
NIGHTMARES

The Undying Thing

BARRY PAIN

Journalist and humorist Barry Pain (1864–1928) was a prolific writer of short stories, many in comic mood but a lot in grim and macabre vein. Beyond one story ('The Moon Slave') he is very seldom reprinted, which is a pity; his work repays study and his several volumes of short stories are well worth acquiring. I recommend these titles (but you'll have to search hard): STORIES IN THE DARK *(1901),* STORIES IN GREY *(1911),* THREE FANTASIES *(1904),* DEALS *(1904) and* INNOCENT AMUSEMENTS *(1918). Also worth finding is his novel of witchcraft and the supernatural* THE SHADOW OF THE UNSEEN *(1907), written in collaboration with James Blyth.*

'The Undying Thing' comes from STORIES IN THE DARK *and I hope will show you what I mean. Why this long fantasy has been overlooked for three-quarters of a century is a mystery, for it is streets ahead of many similar stories written in those days and still reprinted now. Barry Pain also reveals one of the rare gifts of the true humorist: knowing when* not *to put your tongue in your cheek.*

1

The Undying Thing

I

Up and down the oak-panelled dining-hall of Mansteth the master of the house walked restlessly. At formal intervals down the long severe table were placed four silver candlesticks, but the light from these did not serve to illuminate the whole of the surroundings. It just touched the portrait of a fair-haired boy with a sad and wistful expression that hung at one end of the room; it sparkled on the lid of a silver tankard. As Sir Edric passed to and fro it lit up his face and figure. It was a bold and resolute face with a firm chin and passionate, dominant eyes. A bad past was written in the lines of it. And yet every now and then there came over it a strange look of very anxious gentleness that gave it some resemblance to the portrait of the fair-haired boy. Sir Edric paused for a moment before the portrait and surveyed it carefully, his strong brown hands locked behind him, his gigantic shoulders thrust a little forward.

'Ah, what I was!' he murmured to himself – 'what I was!'

Once more he commenced pacing up and down. The candles, mirrored in the polished wood of the table, had burnt low. For hours Sir Edric had been waiting, listening intently for some sound from the room above or from the broad staircase outside. There had been sounds – the wailing of a woman, a quick abrupt voice, the moving of rapid feet. But for the last hour he had heard nothing. Quite suddenly he stopped and dropped on his knees against the table:

'God, I have never thought of Thee. Thou knowest that – Thou knowest that by my devilish behaviour and cruelty I did veritably murder Alice, my first wife, albeit the physicians did maintain that she died of a decline – a wasting sickness. Thou knowest that all here in Mansteth do hate me, and that rightly. They say, too, that I am mad; but that they say not rightly, seeing that I know how wicked I am. I always knew it, but I never cared until I loved – Oh, God, I never cared!

His fierce eyes opened for a minute, glared round the room, and closed again tightly. He went on:

'God, for myself I ask nothing; I make no bargaining with Thee. Whatsoever punishment Thou givest me to bear I will bear it; whatsoever Thou givest me to do I will do it. Whether Thou killest Eve or whether Thou keepest her in life – and never have I loved but her – I will from this night be good. In due penitence will I receive the holy Sacrament of Thy Body and Blood. And my son, the one child that I had by Alice, I will fetch back again from Challonsea, where I kept him in order that I might not look upon him, and I will be to him a father in deed and very truth. And in all things, so far as in me lieth, I will make restitution and atonement. Whether Thou hearest me or whether Thou hearest me not, these things shall be. And for my prayer, it is but this: of Thy loving kindness, most merciful God, be Thou with Eve and make her happy; and after these great pains and perils of childbirth send her Thy peace. Of Thy loving-kindness, Thy merciful loving-kindness, O God!'

Perhaps the prayer that is offered when the time for praying is over is more terribly pathetic than any other. Yet one might hesitate to say that this prayer was unanswered.

Sir Edric rose to his feet. Once more he paced the room. There was a strange simplicity about him, the simplicity that scorns an incongruity. He felt that his lips and throat were parched and dry. He lifted the heavy silver tankard from the table and raised the lid; there was still a good draught of mulled wine in it with the burnt toast, cut heart-shape, floating on the top.

'To the health of Eve and her child,' he said aloud, and drained it to the last drop.

Click, click! As he put the tankard down he heard distinctly two doors opened and shut quickly, one after the other. And then slowly down the stairs came a hesitating step. Sir Edric could bear the suspense no longer. He opened the dining-room door, and the dim light strayed out into the dark hall beyond.

'Dennison,' he said, in a low, sharp whisper, 'is that you?'

'Yes, yes. I am coming, Sir Edric.'

A moment afterwards Dr. Dennison entered the room. He was very pale; perspiration streamed from his forehead; his cravat was disarranged. He was an old man, thin, with the air of proud humility. Sir Edric watched him narrowly.

'Then she is dead,' he said, with a quiet that Dr. Dennison had not expected.

'Twenty physicians – a hundred physicians could not have saved her, Sir Edric. She was —' He gave some details of medical interest.

'Dennison,' said Sir Edric, still speaking with calm and restraint, 'why do you seem thus indisposed and panic-stricken? You are a physician; have you never looked upon the face of death before? The soul of my wife is with God —'

'Yes,' murmured Dennison, 'a good woman, a perfect, saintly woman.'

'And,' Sir Edric went on, raising his eyes to the ceiling as though he could see through it, 'her body lies in great dignity and beauty upon the bed, and there is no horror in it. Why are you afraid?'

'I do not fear death, Sir Edric.'

'But your hands – they are not steady. You are evidently overcome. Does the child live?'

'Yes, it lives.'

'Another boy – a brother for young Edric, the child that Alice bore me?'

'There – there is something wrong. I do not know what to do. I want you to come upstairs. And, Sir Edric, I must tell you, you will need your self-command.'

'Dennison, the hand of God is heavy upon me; but from this time forth until the day of my death I am submissive to it, and God send that that day may come quickly! I will follow you and I will endure.'

He took one of the high silver candlesticks from the table and stepped towards the door. He strode quickly up the staircase, Dr. Dennison following a little way behind him.

As Sir Edric waited at the top of the staircase he heard suddenly from the room before him a low cry. He put down the candlestick on the floor and leaned back against the wall listening. The cry came again, a vibrating monotone ending in a growl.

'Dennison, Dennison!'

His voice choked; he could not go on.

'Yes,' said the doctor, 'it is in there. I had the two women out of the room, and got it here. No one but myself has seen it. But you must see it, too.'

He raised the candle and the two men entered the room – one of the spare bedrooms. On the bed there was something moving under cover of a blanket. Dr. Dennison paused for a moment and then flung the blanket partially back.

They did not remain in the room for more than a few seconds. The moment they got outside, Dr. Dennison began to speak.

'Sir Edric, I would fain suggest somewhat to you. There is no evil, as Sophocles hath it in his "Antigone," for which man hath not found a remedy, except it be death, and here –'

Sir Edric interrupted him in a husky voice.

'Downstairs, Dennison. This is too near.'

It was, indeed, passing strange. When once the novelty of this – this occurrence had worn off, Dr. Dennison seemed no longer frightened. He was calm, academic, interested in an unusual phenomenon. But Sir Edric, who was said in the village to fear nothing in earth, or heaven, or hell, was obviously much moved.

When they had got back to the dining-room, Sir Edric motioned the doctors to a seat.

'Now, then,' he said, 'I will hear you. Something must be done – and to-night.'

'Exceptional cases,' said Dr. Dennison, 'demand exceptional remedies. Well, it lies there upstairs and is at our mercy. We can let it live, or, placing one hand over the mouth and nostrils, we can –'

'Stop,' said Sir Edric. 'This thing has so crushed and humiliated me that I can scarcely think. But I recall that while I waited for you I fell upon my knees and prayed that God would save Eve. And, as I confessed unto Him more than I will ever confess unto man, it seemed to me that it were ignoble to offer a price for His favour. And I said that whatsoever punishment I had to bear, I would bear it; and whatsoever He called upon me to do, I would do it; and I made no conditions.'

'Well?'

'Now my punishment is of two kinds. Firstly, my wife, Eve, is dead. And this I bear more easily because I know that now she is numbered with the company of God's saints, and with them her pure spirit finds happier communion than with me; I was not worthy of her. And yet she would call my roughness by gentle, pretty names. She gloried, Dennison, in the mere strength of my body, and in the greatness of my stature. And I am thankful that she never saw this – this shame that has come upon the house. For she was a proud woman, with all her gentleness, even as I was proud and bad until it pleased God this night to break me even to the dust. And for my second punishment, that, too, I must bear. This thing that lies upstairs, I will take and rear; it is bone of my bone and flesh of my flesh; only, if it be possible, I will hide my shame so that no man but you shall know of it.'

'This is not possible. You cannot keep a living being in this house unless it be known. Will not these women say, "Where is the child?"'

Sir Edric stood upright, his powerful hands linked before him, his face working in agony; but he was still resolute.

'Then if it must be known, it shall be known. The fault is mine. If I had but done sooner what Eve asked, this would not have happened. I will bear it.'

'Sir Edric, do not be angry with me, for if I did not say this, then I should be but an ill counsellor. And, firstly, do not use the word shame. The ways of nature are past all explaining; if a woman be frail and easily impressed, and other circumstances concur, then in some few rare cases a thing of this sort does happen. If there be shame, it is not upon you but upon nature – to whom one would not lightly impute shame. Yet it is true that common and uninformed people might think that this shame was yours. And herein lies the great trouble – the shame would rest also on her memory.'

'Then,' said Sir Edric, in a low, unfaltering voice, 'this night for the sake of Eve I will break my word, and lose my own soul eternally.'

About an hour afterwards Sir Edric and Dr. Dennison left the house together. The doctor carried a stable lantern in his hand. Sir Edric bore in his arms something wrapped in a blanket. They went through the long garden, out into the orchard that skirts the north side of the park, and then across a field to a small dark plantation known as Hal's Planting. In the very heart of Hal's Planting there are some curious caves: access to the innermost chamber of them is exceedingly difficult and dangerous, and only possible to a climber of exceptional skill and courage. As they returned from these caves, Sir Edric no longer carried his burden. The dawn was breaking and the birds began to sing.

'Could not they be quiet just for this morning?' said Sir Edric wearily.

There were but few people who were asked to attend the funeral of Lady Vanquerest and of the baby which, it was said, had only survived her by a few hours. There were but three people who knew that only one body – the body of Lady Vanquerest – was really interred on that occasion. These three were Sir Edric Vanquerest, Dr. Dennison, and a nurse whom it had been found expedient to take into their confidence.

During the next six years Sir Edric lived, almost in solitude, a life of great sanctity, devoting much of his time to the education of the younger Edric, the child that he had by his first wife. In the course of this time some strange stories began to be told and believed in the neighbourhood with reference to Hal's Planting, and the place was generally avoided.

When Sir Edric lay on his deathbed the windows of the chamber were open, and suddenly through them came a low cry. The doctor in attendance hardly regarded it, supposing that it came from one of the owls in the trees outside. But Sir Edric, at the sound of it, rose right up in bed before anyone could stay him, and flinging up his arms cried, 'Wolves! wolves! wolves!' Then he fell forward on his face, dead.

And four generations passed away.

II

Towards the latter end of the nineteenth century, John Marsh, who was the oldest man in the village of Mansteth, could be prevailed upon to state what he recollected. His two sons supported him in his old age; he never felt the pinch of poverty, and he always had money in his pocket; but it was a settled principle with him that he would not pay for the pint of beer which he drank occasionally in the parlour of The Stag.

Sometimes farmer Wynthwaite paid for the beer; sometimes it
was Mr. Spicer from the post-office; sometimes the landlord of
The Stag himself would finance the old man's evening
dissipation. In return, John Marsh was prevailed upon to state
what he recollected; this he would do with great heartiness and
strict impartiality, recalling the intemperance of a former
Wynthwaite and the dishonesty of some ancestral Spicer while
he drank the beer of their direct descendants. He would tell you,
with two tough old fingers crooked round the handle of the
pewter that you had provided, how your grandfather was a poor
thing, 'fit for nowt but to brak steeans by ta rord-side.' He was so
disrespectful that it was believed that he spoke truth. He was
particularly disrespectful when he spoke of the most devilish
family, the Vanquerests; and he never tired of recounting the
stories that from generation to generation had grown up about
them. It would be objected, sometimes, that the present Sir
Edric, the last surviving member of the race, was a pleasant-
spoken young man, with none of the family wildness and hot
temper. It was for no sin of his that Hal's Planting was haunted –
a thing which everyone in Mansteth, and many beyond it, most
devoutly believed. John Marsh would hear no apology for him,
nor for any of his ancestors; he recounted the prophecy that an
old mad woman had made of the family before her strange death,
and hoped, fervently, that he might live to see it fulfilled.

The third baronet, as has already been told, had lived the
latter part of his life, after his second wife's death, in peace and
quietness. Of him John Marsh remembered nothing, of course,
and could only recall the few fragments of information that had
been handed down to him. He had been told that this Sir Edric,
who had travelled a good deal, at one time kept wolves, intending
to train them to serve as dogs; these wolves were not kept under
proper restraint, and became a kind of terror to the neighbourhood. Lady Vanquerest, his second wife, had asked him
frequently to destroy these beasts; but Sir Edric, although it was
said that he loved his second wife even more than he hated the
first, was obstinate when any of his whims were crossed, and put
her off with promises. Then one day Lady Vanquerest herself
was attacked by the wolves; she was not bitten, but she was badly
frightened. That filled Sir Edric with remorse, and, when it was

too late, he went out into the yard where the wolves were kept and shot them all. A few months afterwards Lady Vanquerest died in childbirth. It was a queer thing, John Marsh noted, that it was just at this time that Hal's Planting began to get such a bad name. The fourth baronet was, John Marsh considered, the worst of the race; it was to him that the old mad woman had made her prophecy, an incident that Marsh himself had witnessed in his childhood and still vividly remembered.

The baronet, in his old age, had been cast up by his vices on the shores of melancholy; heavy-eyed, grey-haired, bent, he seemed to pass through life as in a dream. Every day he would go out on horseback, always at a walking pace, as though he were following the funeral of his past self. One night he was riding up the village street as this old woman came down it. Her name was Ann Ruthers; she had a kind of reputation in the village, and although all said that she was mad, many of her utterances were remembered, and she was treated with respect. It was growing dark, and the village street was almost empty; but just at the lower end was the usual group of men by the door of The Stag, dimly illuminated by the light that came through the quaint windows of the old inn. They glanced at Sir Edric as he rode slowly past them, taking no notice of their respectful salutes. At the upper end of the street there were two persons. One was Ann Ruthers, a tall, gaunt old woman, her head wrapped in a shawl; the other was John Marsh. He was then a boy of eight, and he was feeling somewhat frightened. He had been on an expedition to a distant and fœtid pond, and in the black mud and clay about its borders he had discovered live newts; he had three of them in his pocket, and this was to some extent a joy to him, but his joy was damped by his knowledge that he was coming home much too late, and would probably be chastised in consequence. He was unable to walk fast or to run, because Ann Ruthers was immediately in front of him, and he dared not pass her, especially at night. She walked on until she met Sir Edric, and then, standing still, she called him by name. He pulled in his horse and raised his heavy eyes to look at her. Then in clear tones she spoke to him, and John Marsh heard and remembered every word that she said; it was her prophecy of the end of the Vanquerests. Sir Edric never answered a word. When she had finished, he rode on, while she remained standing there, her eyes fixed on the stars above her. John Marsh dared not pass the mad woman; he turned round and walked back, keeping close to Sir Edric's horse. Quite suddenly, without a word of warning, as if in a moment of ungovernable irritation, Sir Edric wheeled his horse round and struck the boy across the face with his switch.

On the following morning John Marsh – or rather, his parents – received a handsome solatium in coin of the realm; but sixty-five years afterwards he had not forgiven that blow, and still spoke of the Vanquerests as a most devilish family, still hoped and prayed that he might see the prophecy fulfilled. He would relate, too, the death of Ann Ruthers, which occurred either later on the night of her prophecy or early on the following day. She would often roam about the country all night, and on this particular night over the Vanquerest lands, where trespassers, especially at night, were not welcomed. But no one saw her, and it seemed that she had made her way to a part where no one was likely to see her; for none of the keepers would have entered Hal's Planting by night. Her body was found there at noon on the following day, lying under the tall bracken, dead, but without any mark of violence upon it. It was considered that she had died in a fit. This naturally added to the ill-repute of Hal's Planting. The woman's death caused considerable sensation in the village. Sir Edric sent a messenger to the married sister with whom she had lived, saying that he wished to pay all the funeral expenses. This offer, as John Marsh recalled with satisfaction, was refused.

Of the last two baronets he had but little to tell. The fifth baronet was credited with the family temper, but he conducted himself in a perfectly conventional way, and did not seem in the least to belong to romance. He was good man of business, and devoted himself to making up, as far as he could, for the very extravagant expenditure of his predecessors. His son, the present Sir Edric, was a fine young fellow and popular in the village. Even John Marsh could find nothing to say against him; other people in the village were interested in him. It was said that he had chosen a wife in London – a Miss Guerdon – and would shortly be back to see that Mansteth Hall was put in proper order for her before his marriage at the close of the season. Modernity kills ghostly romance. It was difficult to associate this modern and handsome Sir Edric, bright and spirited, a good sportsman and a good fellow, with the doom that had been foretold for the Vanquerest family. He himself knew the tradition and laughed at it. He wore clothes made by a London tailor, looked healthy, smiled cheerfully, and, in a vain attempt to shame his own head-keeper, had himself spent a night alone in Hal's Planting. This last was used by Mr. Spicer in argument, who would ask John Marsh what he made of it. John Marsh replied, contemptuously, that it was 'nowt'. It was not so that the Vanquerest family was to end; but when the thing, whatever it was, that lived in Hal's Planting, left it and came up to the house, to Mansteth Hall itself, then one would see the end of the Vanquerests. So Ann Ruthers had prophesied. Sometimes Mr. Spicer would ask the pertinent question, how did John Marsh know that there really was anything in Hal's Planting? This he asked, less because he disbelieved, than because he wished to draw forth an account of John's personal experiences. These were given in great detail, but they did not amount to very much. One night John Marsh had been taken by business – Sir Edric's keepers would have called the business by hard names – into the neighbourhood of Hal's Planting. He had there been suddenly startled by a cry, and had run away as though he were running for his life. That was all he could tell about the cry – it was the kind of cry to make a man lose his head and run. And then it always happened that John Marsh was urged by his companions to enter Hal's Planting himself, and discover what was there. John pursed his thin lips together, and hinted that that also might be done one of these days. Whereupon Mr. Spicer looked across his pipe to Farmer Wynthwaite, and smiled significantly.

Shortly before Sir Edric's return from London, the attention of Mansteth was once more directed to Hal's Planting, but not by any supernatural occurrence. Quite suddenly, on a calm day, two trees there fell with a crash; there were caves in the centre of the plantation, and it seemed as if the roof of some big chamber in these caves had given way.

They talked it over one night in the parlour of The Stag. There was water in these caves, Farmer Wynthwaite knew it; and he expected a further subsidence. If the whole thing collapsed, what then?

'Ay,' said John Marsh. He rose from his chair, and pointed in
the direction of the Hall with his thumb. 'What then?'

He walked across to the fire, looked at it meditatively for a
moment, and then spat in it.

'A trewly wun'ful owd mon,' said Farmer Wynthwaite as he
watched him.

III

In the smoking-room at Mansteth Hall sat Sir Edric with his
friend and intended brother-in-law, Dr. Andrew Guerdon. Both
men were on the verge of middle-age; there was hardly a year's
difference between them. Yet Guerdon looked much the older
man; that was, perhaps, because he wore a short, black beard,
while Sir Edric was clean shaven. Guerdon was thought to be an
enviable man. His father had made a fortune in the firm of
Guerdon, Guerdon and Bird; the old style was still retained at
the bank, although there was no longer a Guerdon in the firm.
Andrew Guerdon had a handsome allowance from his father,
and had also inherited money through his mother. He had taken
the degree of Doctor of Medicine; he did not practise but he was
still interested in science, especially in out-of-the-way science.
He was unmarried, gifted with perpetually good health, interested in life, popular. His friendship with Sir Edric dated
from their college days. It had for some years been almost certain
that Sir Edric would marry his friend's sister, Ray Guerdon,
although the actual betrothal had only been announced that
season.

On a bureau in one corner of the room were spread a couple
of plans and various slips of paper. Sir Edric was wrinkling his
brows over them, dropping cigar-ash over them, and finally
getting angry over them. He pushed back his chair irritably, and
turned towards Guerdon.

'Look here, old man!' he said. 'I desire to curse the original
architect of this house – to curse him in his down-sitting and his
uprising.'

'Seeing that the original architect had gone to where beyond
these voices there is peace, he won't be offended. Neither shall I.
But why worry yourself? You've been rooted to that blessed

bureau all day, and now, after dinner, when every self-respecting man chucks business, you return to it again – even as a sow returns to her wallowing in the mire.'

'Now, my good Andrew, do be reasonable. How on earth can I bring Ray to such a place as this? And it's built with such ingrained malice and vexatiousness that one can't live in it as it is, and can't alter it without having the whole shanty tumble down about one's ears. Look at this plan now. That thing's what they're pleased to call a morning room. If the window had been *here* there would have been an uninterrupted view of open country. So what does this forsaken fool of an architect do? He sticks it *there*, where you see it on the plan, looking straight on to a blank wall with a stable yard on the other side of it. But that's a trifle. Look here again —'

'I won't look any more. This place is all right. It was good enough for your father and mother and several generations before them until you arose to improve the world; it was good enough for you until you started to get married. It's a picturesque place, and if you begin to alter it you'll spoil it.' Guerdon looked round the room critically. 'Upon my word,' he said, 'I don't know of any house where I like the smoking-room as well as I like this. It's not too big, and yet it's fairly lofty; it's got those comfortable-looking oak-panelled walls. That's the right kind of fireplace, too, and these corner cupboards are handy.'

'Of course this won't *remain* the smoking-room. It has the morning sun, and Ray likes that, so I shall make it into her boudoir. It *is* a nice room, as you say.'

'That's it, Ted, my boy,' said Guerdon bitterly; 'take a room which is designed by nature and art to be a smoking-room and turn it into a boudoir. Turn it into the very deuce of a boudoir with the morning sun laid on for ever and ever. Waste the twelfth of August by getting married on it. Spend the winter in foreign parts, and write letters that you can breakfast out of doors, just as if you'd created the mildness of the climate yourself. Come back in the spring and spend the London season in the country in order to avoid seeing anybody who wants to see you. That's the way to do it; that's the way to get yourself generally loved and admired!'

'That's chiefly imagination,' said Sir Edric. 'I'm blest if I can see why I should not make this house fit for Ray to live in.'

'It's a queer thing: Ray was a good girl, and you weren't a bad sort yourself. You prepare to go into partnership, and you both straightway turn into despicable lunatics. I'll have a word or two with Ray. But I'm serious about this house. Don't go tinkering it; it's got a character of its own, and you'd better leave it. Turn half Tottenham Court Road and the culture thereof – Heaven help it! – into your town house if you like, but leave this alone.'

'Haven't got a town house – yet. Anyway I'm not going to be unsuitable; I'm not going to feel myself at the mercy of a big firm. I shall supervise the whole thing myself. I shall drive over to Challonsea tomorrow afternoon and see if I can't find some intelligent and fairly conscientious workmen.'

'That's all right; you supervise them and I'll supervise you. You'll be much too new if I don't look after you. You've got an old legend, I believe, that the family's coming to a bad end; you must be consistent with it. As you are bad, be beautiful. By the way, what do you yourself think of the legend?'

'It's nothing,' said Sir Edric, speaking, however, rather seriously. 'They say that Hal's Planting is haunted by something that will not die. Certainly an old woman, who for some godless reason of her own made her way there by night, was found there dead on the following morning; but her death could be, and was, accounted for by natural causes. Certainly, too, I haven't a man in my employ who'll go there by night now.'

'Why not?'

'How should I know? I fancy that a few of the villagers sit boozing at The Stag in the evening, and like to scare themselves by swopping lies about Hal's Planting. I've done my best to stop it. I once, as you know, took a rug, a revolver and a flask of whisky and spent the night there myself. But even that didn't convince them.'

'Yes, you told me. By the way, did you hear or see anything?'

Sir Edric hesitated before he answered. Finally he said:

'Look here, old man, I wouldn't tell this to anyone but yourself. I did think that I heard something. About the middle of the night I was awakened by a cry; I can only say that it was the kind of cry that frightened me. I sat up, and at that moment I heard some great, heavy thing go swishing through the bracken behind me at a great rate. Then all was still; I looked about, but I could find nothing. At last I argued as I would argue now that a man who is just awake is only half awake, and that his powers of observation, by hearing or any other sense, are not to be trusted. I even persuaded myself to go to sleep again, and there was no more disturbance. However, there's a real danger there now. In the heart of the plantation there are some caves and a subterranean spring; lately there has been some slight subsidence there, and the same sort of thing will happen again in all probability. I wired today to an expert to come and look at the place; he has replied that he will come on Monday. The legend says that when the thing that lives in Hal's Planting comes up to the Hall the Vanquerests will be ended. If I cut down the trees and then break up the place with a charge of dynamite I shouldn't wonder if I spoiled that legend.'

Guerdon smiled.

'I'm inclined to agree with you all through. It's absurd to trust the immediate impressions of a man just awakened; what you heard was probably a stray cow.'

'No cow,' said Sir Edric impartially. 'There's a low wall all round the place – not much of a wall, but too much for a cow.'

'Well, something else – some equally obvious explanation. In dealing with such questions, never forget that you're in the nineteenth century. By the way, your man's coming on Monday. That reminds me today's Friday, and as an indisputable consequence tomorrow's Saturday, therefore, if you want to find your intelligent workmen it will be of no use to go in the afternoon.'

'True,' said Sir Edric, 'I'll go in the morning.' He walked to a tray on a side table and poured a little whisky into a tumbler. 'They don't seem to have brought any seltzer water,' he remarked in a grumbling voice.

He rang the bell impatiently.

'Now why don't you use those corner cupboards for that kind of thing? If you kept a supply there, it would be handy in case of accidents.'

'They're full up already.'

He opened one of them and showed that it was filled with old account-books and yellow documents tied up in bundles. The servant entered.

'Oh, I say, there isn't any seltzer. Bring it, please.'

He turned again to Guerdon.

'You might do me a favour when I'm away tomorrow, if there's nothing else that you want to do. I wish you'd look through all these papers for me. They're all old. Possibly some of them ought to go to my solicitor, and I know that a lot of them ought to be destroyed. Some few may be of family interest. It's not the kind of thing that I could ask a stranger or a servant to do for me, and I've so much on hand just now before my marriage —'

'But of course, my dear fellow, I'll do it with pleasure.'

'I'm ashamed to give you all this bother. However, you said that you were coming here to help me, and I take you at your word. By the way, I think you'd better not say anything to Ray about the Hal's Planting story.'

'I may be some of the things that you take me for, but really I am not a common ass. Of course I shouldn't tell her.'

'I'll tell her myself, and I'd sooner do it when I've got the whole thing cleared up. Well, I'm really obliged to you.'

'I needn't remind you that I hope to receive as much again. I believe in compensation. Nature always gives it and always requires it. One finds it everywhere, in philology and onwards.'

'I could mention omissions.'

'They are few, and make a belief in a hereafter to supply them logical.'

'Lunatics, for instance?'

'Their delusions are often their compensation. They argue correctly from false premises. A lunatic believing himself to be a millionaire has as much delight as money can give.'

'How about deformities or monstrosities?'

'The principle is there, although I don't pretend that the compensation is always adequate. A man who is deprived of one sense generally has another developed with unusual acuteness. As for monstrosities of at all a human type one sees none; the things exhibited in fairs are, almost without exception, frauds. They occur rarely, and one does not know enough about them. A really good text-book on the subject would be interesting. Still, such stories as I have heard would bear out my theory – stories of their superhuman strength and cunning, and of the extraordinary prolongation of life that has been noted, or is said to have been noted, in them. But it is hardly fair to test my principle by exceptional cases. Besides, anyone can prove anything except that anything's worth proving.'

'That's a cheerful thing to say. I wouldn't like to swear that I could prove how the Hal's Planting legend started; but I fancy, do you know, that I could make a very good shot at it.'

'Well?'

'My great-grandfather kept wolves – I can't say why. Do you remember the portrait of him? – not the one when he was a boy, the other. It hangs on the staircase. There's now a group of wolves in one corner of the picture. I was looking carefully at the picture one day and thought that I detected some over-painting in that corner; indeed, it was done so roughly that a child would have noticed it if the picture had been hung in a better light. I had the over-painting removed by a good man, and underneath there was that group of wolves depicted. Well, one of these wolves must have escaped, got into Hal's Planting, and scared an old woman or two; that would start a story, and human mendacity would do the rest.'

'Yes,' said Guerdon meditatively, 'that doesn't sound improbable. But why did your great-grandfather have the wolves painted out?'

IV

Saturday morning was fine, but very hot and sultry. After breakfast, when Sir Edric had driven off to Challonsea, Andrew Guerdon settled himself in a comfortable chair in the smoking-room. The contents of the corner cupboard were piled up on a table by his side. He lit his pipe and began to go through the papers and put them in order. He had been at work almost a quarter of an hour when the butler entered rather abruptly, looking pale and disturbed.

'In Sir Edric's absence, sir, it was thought that I had better come to you for advice. There's been an awful thing happened.'

'Well?'

'They've found a corpse in Hal's Planting about half an hour ago. It's the body of an old man, John Marsh, who used to live in the village. He seems to have died in some kind of a fit. They were bringing it here, but I had it taken down to the village where his cottage is. Then I sent to the police and to a doctor.'

There was a moment or two's silence before Guerdon answered.

'This is a terrible thing. I don't know of anything else that you could do. Stop; if the police want to see the spot where the body was found, I think that Sir Edric would like them to have every facility.'

'Quite so, sir.'

'And no one else must be allowed there.'

'No, sir. Thank you.'

The butler withdrew.

Guerdon arose from his chair and began to pace up and down the room.

'What an impressive thing a coincidence is!' he thought to himself. 'Last night the whole of the Hal's Planting story seemed to me not worth consideration. But this second death there – it can be only coincidence. What else could it be?'

The question would not leave him. What else could it be? Had that dead man seen something there and died in sheer terror of it? Had Sir Edric really heard something when he spent that night there alone? He returned to his work, but he found that he got on with it but slowly. Every now and then his mind wandered back to the subject of Hal's Planting. His doubts annoyed him. It was unscientific and unmodern of him to feel any perplexity, because a natural and rational explanation was possible; he was annoyed with himself for being perplexed.

After luncheon he strolled round the grounds and smoked a cigar. He noticed that a thick bank of dark, slate-coloured clouds was gathering in the west. The air was very still. In a remote corner of the garden a big heap of weeds was burning; the smoke went up perfectly straight. On the top of the heap light flames danced; they were like the ghosts of flames in the strange light. A few big drops of rain fell. The small shower did not last for five seconds. Guerdon glanced at his watch. Sir Edric would be back in an hour, and he wanted to finish his work with the papers before Sir Edric's return, so he went back into the house once more.

He picked up the first document that came to hand. As he did so, another, smaller, and written on parchment, which had been folded in with it, dropped out. He began to read the parchment; it was written in faded ink, and the parchment itself was yellow and in many places stained. It was the confession of the third baronet – he could tell that by the date upon it. It told the story of that night when he and Dr. Dennison went together carrying a burden through the long garden out into the orchard that skirts the north side of the park, and then across a field to a small, dark plantation. It told how he made a vow to God and did not keep it. These were the last words of the confession:

'Already upon me has the punishment fallen, and the devil's wolves do seem to hunt me in my sleep nightly. But I know that there is worse to come. The thing that I took to Hal's Planting is dead. Yet it will come back again to the Hall, and then will the Vanquerests be at an end. This writing I have committed to chance, neither showing it nor hiding it, and leaving it to chance if any man shall read it.'

Underneath there was a line written in darker ink, and in quite a different handwriting. It was dated fifteen years later, and the initials R.D. were appended to it:

'It is not dead. I do not think that it will ever die.'

When Andrew Guerdon had finished reading this document, he looked slowly round the room. The subject had got on his nerves, and he was almost expecting to see something. Then he did his best to pull himself together. The first question he put to himself was this: 'Has Ted ever seen this?' Obviously he had not. If he had, he could not have taken the tradition of Hal's Planting so lightly, nor have spoken of it so freely. Besides, he would either have mentioned the document to Guerdon, or he would have kept it carefully concealed. He would not have allowed him to come across it casually in that way. 'Ted must never see it,' thought Guerdon to himself. He then remembered the pile of weeds he had seen burning in the garden. He put the parchment in his pocket, and hurried out. There was no one about. He spread the parchment on the top of the pile, and waited until it was entirely consumed. Then he went back to the smoking-room; he felt easier now.

'Yes,' thought Guerdon, 'if Ted had first of all heard of the finding of that body, and then had read that document, I believe that he would have gone mad. Things that come near us affect us deeply.'

Guerdon himself was much moved. He clung steadily to reason; he felt himself able to give a natural explanation all through, and yet he was nervous. The net of coincidence had closed in around him; the mention of Sir Edric's confession of the prophecy which had subsequently become traditional in the village alarmed him. And what did that last line mean? He supposed that R.D. must be the initials of Dr. Dennison. What did he mean by saying that the thing was not dead? Did he mean that it had been gifted with some preternatural strength and vitality and had survived, though Sir Edric did not know it? He recalled what he had said about the prolongation of the lives of such things. If it still survived, why had it never been seen? Had it joined to the wild hardiness of the beast a cunning that was human – or more than human? How could it have lived? There was water in the caves, he reflected, and food could have been secured – a wild beast's food. Or did Dr. Dennison mean that though the thing itself was dead, its wraith survived and haunted the place? He wondered how the doctor had found Sir Edric's confession, and why he had written that line at the end of it. As he sat thinking, a low rumble of thunder in the distance startled him. He felt a touch of panic – a sudden impulse to leave Mansteth at once and, if possible, to take Ted with him. Ray could never live there. He went over the whole thing in his mind again and again, at one time calm and argumentative about it, and at another shaken by blind horror.

Sir Edric, on his return from Challonsea a few minutes afterwards, came straight to the smoking-room where Guerdon was. He looked tired and depressed. He began to speak at once:

'You needn't tell me about it – about John Marsh. I heard about it in the village.'

'Did you? It's a painful occurrence, although, of course —'

'Stop. Don't go into it. Anything can be explained – I know that.'

'I went through those papers and account-books while you were away. Most of them may just as well be destroyed; but there are a few – I put them aside there – which might be kept. There was nothing of any interest.'

'Thanks; I'm much obliged to you.'

'Oh, and look here, I've got an idea. I've been examining the plans of the house, and I'm coming round to your opinion. There are some alterations which should be made, and yet I'm afraid that they'd make the place look patched and renovated. It wouldn't be a bad thing to know what Ray thought about it.'

'That's impossible. The workmen come on Monday, and we can't consult her before then. Besides, I have a general notion what she would like.'

'We could catch the night express to town at Challonsea, and —'

Sir Edric rose from his seat angrily and hit the table.

'Good God! don't sit there hunting up excuses to cover my cowardice, and making it easy for me to bolt. What do you suppose the villagers would say, and what would my own servants say, if I ran away tonight? I am a coward – I know it. I'm horribly afraid. But I'm not going to act like a coward if I can help it.'

'Now, my dear chap, don't excite yourself. If you are going to care at all – to care as much as the conventional damn – for what people say, you'll have no peace in life. And I don't believe you're afraid. What are you afraid of?'

Sir Edric paced once or twice up and down the room, and then sat down again before replying.

'Look here, Andrew, I'll make a clean breast of it. I've always laughed at the tradition; I forced myself, as it seemed at least, to disprove it by spending a night in Hal's Planting; I took the pains even to make a theory which would account for its origin. All the time I had a sneaking, stifled belief in it. With the help of my reason I crushed that; but now my reason has thrown up the job, and I'm afraid. I'm afraid of the Undying Thing that is in Hal's Planting. I heard it last night. John Marsh saw it last night – they took me to see the body, and the face was awful; and I believe that one day it will come from Hal's Planting —'

'Yes,' interrupted Guerdon, 'I know. And at present I believe as much. Last night we laughed at the whole thing, and we shall live to laugh at it again, and be ashamed of ourselves for a couple of superstitious old women. I fancy that beliefs are affected by weather – there's thunder in the air.'

'No,' said Sir Edric, 'my belief has come to stay.'

'And what are you going to do?'

'I'm going to test it. On Monday I can begin to get to work, and then I'll blow up Hal's Planting with dynamite. After that we shan't need to believe – we shall *know*. And now let's dismiss the subject. Come down into the billiard-room and have a game. Until Monday I won't think of the thing again.'

Long before dinner, Sir Edric's depression seemed to have completely vanished. At dinner he was boisterous and amused. Afterwards he told stories and was interesting.

It was late at night; the terrific storm that was raging outside had awoke Guerdon from sleep. Hopeless of getting to sleep again, he had arisen and dressed, and now sat in the window-seat watching the storm. He had never seen anything like it before; and every now and then the sky seemed to be torn across as if by hands of white fire. Suddenly he heard a tap at his door, and looked round. Sir Edric had already entered; he also had dressed. He spoke in a curious, subdued voice.

'I thought you wouldn't be able to sleep through this. Do you remember that I shut and fastened the dining-room window?'

'Yes, I remember it.'

'Well, come in here.'

Sir Edric led the way to his room, which was immediately over the dining-room. By leaning out of the window they could see that the dining-room window was open wide.

'Burglar,' said Guerdon meditatively.

'No,' Sir Edric answered, still speaking in a hushed voice. 'It is the Undying Thing – it has come for me.'

He snatched up the candle, and made towards the staircase; Guerdon caught up the loaded revolver which always lay on the table beside Sir Edric's bed and followed him. Both men ran down the staircase as though there were not another moment to lose. Sir Edric rushed at the dining-room door, opened it a little, and looked in. Then he turned to Guerdon, who was just behind him.

'Go back to your room,' he said authoritatively.

'I won't,' said Guerdon. 'Why? What is it?'

Suddenly the corners of Sir Edric's mouth shot outward into the hideous grin of terror.

'It's there! It's there!' he gasped.

'Then I come in with you.'

'Go back!'

With a sudden movement, Sir Edric thrust Guerdon away from the door, and then, quick as light, darted in, and locked the door behind him.

Guerdon bent down and listened. He heard Sir Edric say in a firm voice:

'Who are you? What are you?'

Then followed a heavy, snorting breathing, a low, vibrating growl, an awful cry, a scuffle.

Then Guerdon flung himself at the door. He kicked at the lock, but it would not give way. At last he fired his revolver at it. Then he managed to force his way into the room. It was perfectly empty. Overhead he could hear footsteps; the noise had awakened the servants; they were standing, tremulous, on the upper landing.

Through the open window access to the garden was easy. Guerdon did not wait to get help; and in all probability none of the servants could have been persuaded to come with him. He climbed out alone, and, as if by some blind impulse, started to run as hard as he could in the direction of Hal's Planting. He knew that Sir Edric would be found there.

But when he got within a hundred yards of the plantation, he stopped. There had been a great flash of lightning, and he saw that it had struck one of the trees. Flames darted about the plantation as the dry bracken caught. Suddenly, in the light of another flash, he saw the whole of the trees fling their heads upwards; then came a deafening crash, and the ground slipped under him, and he was flung forward on his face. The plantation had collapsed, fallen through into the caves beneath it. Guerdon slowly regained his feet; he was surprised to find that he was unhurt. He walked on a few steps, and then fell again; this time he had fainted away.

The Serpent's Head

LADY DILKE

'The fates which dog the heels of men through life, and bring them to the gates of hell, most often twist some trivial mistake of ours into the scourge they bear in their avenging hands.' Thus Lady Dilke (1840–1904) introduced her first book of short stories THE SHRINE OF DEATH (1886). An ironic statement, perhaps carrying more than its superficial meaning in Lady Dilke's case, for she was involved in one of Victorian society's most notorious scandals.

In 1861, Emilia Strong married the clergyman Mark Pattison. He died in 1884 and the following year she met and fell in love with the Liberal statesman Sir Charles Wentworth Dilke. He was deputy leader of his party, a member of Gladstone's Cabinet, and regarded by no less an observer than Disraeli as a future Prime Minister. His relationship with Emilia led to a sensational divorce case and the ruin of his political career.

In the same year that THE SHRINE OF DEATH appeared, Emilia married Sir Charles Dilke and this obviously sparked off an interest in politics in her own writing. Such books as TRADE UNIONISM AMONG WOMEN (1893) and ART IN THE MODERN STATE (1888) followed, and her volume of reminiscences and philosophy THE BOOK OF THE SPIRITUAL LIFE appeared posthumously in 1905.

The tales in THE SHRINE OF DEATH are strange stories indeed. 'The Serpent's Head' repays close reading; it is a florid drama of passion and madness wherein a lonely castle is the setting for Lady Dilke's 'gates of hell'.

24

LADY DILKE

The Serpent's Head

In a castle by the Northern Sea two women, a girl and her mother, dwelt alone; nor, had they wished for friends and neighbours, were there any to find in that desolate country. All the space which was not covered by water was spread with sand, for the hills near the coast, mined by the stealthy advances of the sea, were for ever falling over and strewing the shore with ruin. The only feature of this mournful landscape was a black reef of rocks to the north, the position of which was marked, even at the highest tides, by a crag called 'The Serpent's Head.'

The castle itself, which was on an eminence completely isolated from the surrounding country, showed but the scanty remains of its ancient glories; the great tower yet stood on the north proudly intact within the inner series of fortifications, but facing it on the south and east were nought but ruins, whilst on the west a disused building called 'The Chamber on the Wall' presented a gloomy and deserted aspect. Such life as yet lingered within a fortress meant to contain a thousand men was apparently confined to the tower, and centred on the existence of two women.

In a vast and vaulted chamber, the sides of which were riddled with strange closets, and mantled with books, the mother constantly sat; but her gaze was more often on the deserted courts below than on the pages before her, and oftenest of all her eyes would seek the black reef on the north, and spy out the antics of her daughter, diving and swimming about the Serpent's Head.

The girl, in her childish days, had been content, finding infinite amusement, as the fisher children did, in the wonders of the sands; in the hollows of the great drifts she had built for herself many a fairy chamber; but as she grew older these sports were all outworn, and of all her delights one only remained to her, for she was a fearless swimmer, and to dive into the deep

25

waters off the Serpent's Head was ever a pleasure to her.

There, too, she would sit for hours gazing seawards. No tiniest speck of sail that crossed the waters could escape her watchful eyes, and as she watched she dreamed that some day one of these distant sails should bear down towards her, and one should come, in whose hand she would lay her own, and they two would flee to the far East. But as the changeless years went by and brought him not, the girl grew sullen, and a sense of wrong possessed her, for the older she grew, the clearer became her consciousness of a world beyond her, and the greater her longing to seek it.

So the sea, with its journeying ships, appeared to her as the path of deliverance, and the way of escape, and the castle in which she dwelt was a prison to her; and sometimes sudden fits of gusty passion would overtake her, for weariness grew to hate, and hate to wrath, and rising to her feet she would clench and shake her impotent hands at the grey walls above her, frowning motionless at the ever-moving sea. Then her mother, if by chance she saw these demoniacal gestures, would smile a bitter smile, and when they met her eyes would have a challenge in them, so that the girl's passion, which the moment before had risen high with questioning, fell before her gaze, nor did it ever seem possible to her to speak her thoughts, and there was never any confidence between them.

Thus it was that the girl went always alone, and one morning in the late autumn, having risen from a bed fevered with evil dreams, she betook herself, as was her wont, to the Serpent's Head. It was low water, and stepping lightly from point to point, she soon reached the utmost projecting crag, and sat herself down upon it. Now as she sat, she looked into the waters below, and her eyes fastened on two long ribands of seaweed which floated out of a cave beneath, or were sucked back as the tide ebbed or flowed. As she looked on them, these ribands of weed seemed to her like two long arms stretching and reaching out to her. Then suddenly she remembered her dream, for in her dream it had seemed to her that her own heart lay in her hands, and as she held it before her, lo! two arms had stretched themselves out of the darkness, and her heart lay no longer in her own hands, but in those of her mother, and she heard her mother's voice saying, 'It is mine!' and a great anguish had come upon her, as she felt her mother's fingers in her heart-strings, and she awoke.

Now when the girl remembered her dream, the fever of the night ran yet in her veins, and she continued to watch the witch-like movements of the weeds upon the water, until it was as though she felt the clasp of their slimy tendrils drawing her downwards, and yielding to a sudden impulse, she sprang to her feet, cast her garments from her, and hastily girding on a little blue gown which she had brought with her, she threw herself into the sea. Once she had touched the water her dream faded, and she forgot her meaning to enter the cave below, and struck out from the land. Nor was it long before all the blackness in her heart vanished, and she began to laugh, joying and sporting in the boundless waters. But soon there arose a sea fog such as afflict those coasts, and in a moment the shore and the sea were as one, for on all sides the impenetrable mist had fallen.

At this the girl made, as she thought, for the point whence she had come, and she did not discover that she had utterly lost her bearings till the sound of the signal, fired from the castle walls, rolled past her through the waves of shivering mist. She was now weary, but the sound was no sure guide, for, having reached the shore, she found herself still so far out of her course that her feet were in the quicksands which lay to the south of the Serpent's Head. Now anger and fear laid hold upon her, for the tide was coming in fast, and she knew that no man might land at that point with his life; so, turning to the north, she struck out again for the rocks, and the old fever mounted to her brain, and she fancied that the hand of her mother lay heavy on her life, and her thought was, 'I will not die, but live. I will be stronger than thou!' And even when, in her extremity, the end seemed very close to her, the fog began to lift, and before her she saw the black shape of the Serpent's Head. Then, with a desperate effort, she drew near it, and the fog lifted altogether, and she saw that no other part of the reef was visible; but though she laid her hands upon it, the numbness of her body was such that she could get no footing, nor by any means could she raise herself on to the rock.

There was one, however, who now watched her, one who had ridden from afar, and caught by the fog and the rising tide had

tarried near the rocks. When this one saw the girl clinging to the
Serpent's Head, he rode his horse a little way up the shore, till
he could put him in the curve of the breakers, and thus, like one
who had often done the same, he strove to reach her; but by this
means he could not, so next, letting go his horse, he made
himself ready, and fetching a wide circle, he reached her and
brought her safely to land.

   When he touched the shore he laid her on the sands and knelt
beside her, and she, half conscious only, opening her eyes and
seeing him thus close, made one of her dreams and of her escape
from death, and putting her arms about him said, 'I have saved
my heart, and it is yours;' and she thrust her mouth to his and
she kissed him. After this she lay still as in a swoon, and he was
amazed; but the girl was very beautiful, and great pity and
tenderness possessed him as he saw her thus. Then he looked
about for help, and so looking he espied a narrow path
embedded in the grass-grown sand, and leading to the postern
gate of the castle. Taking her then in his arms, he bore her slowly
thither, for the way was steep, and pausing now and again he felt
that the pressure of her arms about him tightened until she held
him so close that when he had brought her into the presence of
her mother scarcely might her stiffened fingers be unclasped
from about his neck.

   Now when at last she opened her eyes, she lay in her own
room, and her mother stood near, and she heard her mother say,
'Would God that she had perished in the sea!' and she saw her
mother's face that it was very stern as she said this. But the heart
of the girl was glad; she felt neither fear nor anger, and hate
seemed harmless, so great a love within an hour past had leapt
up within her. And, though no word had passed, she knew that
he who had fetched her from the sea was her lover, and that even
as it was with her so it was with him.

   Next day, and each day after, they met again by the Serpent's
Head; but her mother watched her, and looking towards the
rocks at sunset she saw them together. Then neither that night
nor the next did she take any rest, and on the morning of the
second day, when the girl would have gone forth, her mother met
her and said, 'I have somewhat to say unto you.' And the girl,
suspecting her purpose, stood still before her, and folding her

arms across her breast she answered, 'He is my lover, and shall be my husband.' And the mother at this cried, 'Are you hot so soon? But I have that to tell you which shall put out your fires. There is a curse on you, even the curse of your accursed father and his race. O God!' she continued, 'shall not one life suffice, and shall his seed drag yet another and another down into the abyss? Shall a son born of your body live to rivet these devil's chains on another life as fair as mine?'

And a great shiver passed over her, and she closed her eyes a space before she spoke again, and then it was in a different tone, a tone of pitiful pleading, that she said, 'Child! for the sake of your love, put him from you; die sooner than bring this death to his soul;' and in so saying she averted her eyes, for she knew that if she looked upon the girl and saw in her her father's features, the dregs of hate, grown cold, would be as gall within her, and turn her words to bitter. So laying her hands on the hangings of the wall her lips moved silently as in prayer, and she went on, as one in a trance, 'I gave my soul to him who was your father, and here for years I served him, but by no service could his spirit be appeased, and the hour came that I knew him to be mad, and he knew it also, but the world knew it not, and a great fear came upon him that I who knew it should betray him. Day and night he watched me, nor could I by any means elude his cunning, till at the last he had me at his will.'

Here her voice dropped and her lips were white, as thrusting aside the folds she pointed to the stains on the floor beneath. 'There,' she said, 'is my blood;' and letting go the curtains she loosened her gown and showed a deep and ugly scar upon her breast, and even as she did so, a dagger, dislodged by her sudden action from among the weapons on the wall above, slipped from its holdings and fell between them with a terrible rattling sound. So she stooped, and picking it up looked steadfastly upon it. 'It is the same,' she said. 'Ah, God! that night, and the long days that went before, and the long years that have followed after! Is there any mercy or any justice in Heaven?'

But the girl put no faith in her, and the thoughts which had been in her mind that day when the fog had fallen on the waters returned to her, so that she gave no heed to threats or pleadings, and the anguish of the other's soul moved her to scorn only and laughter, for the story of her house was as a fable to her, and when her mother called on her to stay the curse, and stretched out her hands in her praying, she called to mind the witchlike moving weeds below the Serpent's Head, and she remembered her dream, and how she had felt the fingers of her mother on her heart. Then too she remembered how she had been delivered in her need, and turning to go she answered, 'I will not die, but live. I will be stronger than thou.'

But the mother said, 'Not so; yet if you will do this deed you shall first ask your father's blessing;' and as she said this she laughed, and the girl felt that her laughter was more to be dreaded than any threats.

So now they two went forth, and crossing the court, came to the broken flight of steps which led up to the Chamber on the Wall. When they had mounted these they stood before an ancient door heavily bound with iron. Then the mother knocked, and was answered, and entered, and the girl, though she was stricken with fear, followed her in silence. But when she had come into the presence of her father a great compassion filled her heart, and her eyes were drawn to the subtle appeal of his. 'Has she told you,' he said, 'that I am mad? I am not mad, my little child, it is she;' and here his voice took on an accent of infinite pathos; 'it is she, who was once all the world to me, who has abandoned me and left me desolate. Ah! for God's sake take me home! Come back to me, my wife! Give me love! Yet, how should any love such as I am?'

And as he pleaded thus, turning from one to the other, the girl, seeing his chains, thought shame of her mother, and with reproach on her tongue she made to go forward as though she would have embraced him. But her words died on her lips, for looking on her mother's face she saw that it was as the face of one inspired, and even as she was about to advance towards him, her mother put her on one side, and saying, 'Lord God! take my life if by this means it is Thy will that this plague be stayed,' she put herself within his reach, and kneeling down close to him folded her arms on her breast. Then, before the girl was aware of his purpose, he had her mother in his grip, and before any aid could come near she was dead.

All that night long the girl watched alone by the body of her mother in the tower, and a great struggle went on in her mind as she began to see the meaning of her mother's act, and at daybreak the spell upon her was so strong, that as she saw the grey light of dawn she rose, and falling on her knees beside the bed she folded her arms on her breast, and it seemed as if she, too, were about to dedicate her life that so the curse of her house might be stayed. But the chamber windows fronted the east, and even as she lifted her face to heaven the first rays of the morning sun flushed the sky, and caught the crests of the waves, and the path of light on the waters went by the Serpent's Head and changed its black to gold. At this sight the girl started to her feet, and throwing wide the windows, 'I will not die!' she said. 'Is there no other way?' Even as she asked this question she answered it with another. 'Why should my seed live?' and as she spoke thus, turning to leave the room she saw her own face in the glass, and it was as the face of her father. Then her gaze became fixed, and presently she whispered to herself and smiled. And turning her back upon the corpse she went swiftly to seek her lover on the rocks.

Not long after this the father died, and the girl married her lover, and the castle, which had so long seemed like a vast and empty shell, overflowed with life. And all things prospered with her, only of all the children born to her not one lived. And many said it was best so, seeing that their inheritance, all fair to outward seeming, had so dark a spot within; but the husband was ill content, for most of all he desired a son that should bear his name, and his wife was angered at this, for she thought, 'Why should not I be sufficient for him? What need has he of child or heir when I am near?' And her passion for him was spiced with jealousy, and when once more she became with child and saw the hope in his eyes, she set herself to cheat it. Nor by any means could she be persuaded to value rest, or to live in such wise as was deemed fitting; and now at dusk the hoofs of her horses would be heard in mad gallop along the causeway, or at early dawn she would be seen battling with the crested waters off the Serpent's Head.

Between her and her husband there were high words, and he reproached her, and swore there was purpose in her folly; then she caught him and held him, crying, 'Why should this devil's brat come between us! You are all the world to me. Am I less to you?' and she would have kissed him, but there was that in her passion which filled him with loathing, and thrusting her from him he said, 'Are you mad?' After he had said this he repented himself, but she answered him nothing, only her face blanched. And from this day forward she was very gentle, nor did she cross his will in any way, nor even once did she return to the Serpent's Head; only sitting in the tower chamber there, where her mother had so often sat before her, she watched the waves beating on the rocks. And her husband, wishing to feel her mind, said 'The day will come when you will be there again;' and she smiled as she answered, 'Ay! the day will come.'

Yet, though she was so gentle, he felt that there was wrong between them, and when the child was born his great joy was poisoned by fear lest it should displease her, and he watched to see if there should be any change in her manner or in her look; but he could find none, till one day he, having taken the child in his arms, looked up suddenly, and thought he saw a gleam of malice in her eyes, yet this faded into smiles so swiftly, that after, when he recalled her look, he misdoubted that which he had seen.

Shortly after this she and her child were missed from the castle, and it was late evening; so fearing he knew not what, the husband looked from the windows to the rocks, and there he descried her, seated on the Serpent's Head, with her little one on her knee. The tide was coming in fast, and dumb with anguish and terror, he made haste to reach the shore; but the way seemed long to him, and even when he drew near to her he scarce dared to approach her, for his fears shaped themselves as he ran, and became one agony of terror for his child's life, and he thought, 'If I come upon her unawares, she may cast him into the sea.' But she, though her back was turned to him, was aware of his coming, and she rose to her feet and faced him, still holding her child in her arms, whilst he, wading, and often slipping and stumbling, made his way slowly to her.

And as he drew close he saw that she wore the little blue gown in which she was wont to bathe, and her golden hair was loose about her neck as when he had seen her first, and her feet were bare, and a smile was on her face as she kissed the child in her arms as if it were very dear. Then calling and moaning out to him she cried, 'My mother's hand is heavy on me; oh! my love, save me! Her hand is heavy on the child, and her arms are stretching from the waves to seize us. Ah! my love, save us!' And now he had almost laid his hands upon her, when she, thrusting the little one from her, shrieked, 'Take your devil's brat, I will have none of it!' And he saw that his child was dead.

At this, he made as though he would have seized her, but before he could lay hands on her she had him by the throat, nor could any strength of his avail to unloose her fingers; as he struggled with her thus, he felt the crag rock beneath his feet, and between his teeth he cursed the day that had brought him thither to mix his blood with that of her demon blood.

But neither to curse nor to pray could then avail him. The tide came on, nor was there any help from land or sea. And the great waves leapt high above them, and her fingers tightened on him, and her lips clung to his mouth, so that gasping for breath he stamped in his fury with his foot. Then was the great crag loosened utterly from its hold; for a moment it hung above the abyss below; next, with a steady roll and a sound as of thunder, it plunged into the seething waters. In the gathering night a cloud of spray arose to heaven; then the waves rolled on to the shore, and neither in ebb nor flow can any man find where the Serpent's Head has made the grave of its ghastly burden. But the plague of that house was stayed in the land.

The Phantom Model

HUME NISBET

If the introduction to his book of macabre tales is anything to go by, Hume Nisbet (1849–c. 1920) was a midnight worker: '(these stories were) thought out during hours of solitude when the bustling world was hushed in slumber, and solemn midnight granted to the mind the true conditions for the reception of the occult mysteries.' The results are certainly worth reading, as you'll see.

Hume Nisbet was born in Stirling, Scotland. He left home at the age of sixteen to spend the next seven years travelling around Australia. When he returned to Scotland, he got a job as art master in an Edinburgh college, and after eight years, went back to Australia, where he took up writing for a living after a brief spell as a publisher's agent.

During his frequent visits back to Britain, he took the time to put together and introduce THE HAUNTED STATION *(1894), from which comes 'The Phantom Model'. In his introduction, Nisbet hinted strongly at the real-life origins of his literary phantoms. They were, he said, 'gleaned from reliable sources or personal experience . . . malignant influences I have attempted to define in such sketches as "The Phantom Model".' If Nisbet's art career ever brought him up against anything like the following story, small wonder he gave it up! It contains an interesting description of London's poverty-stricken areas as potent as any by Charles Dickens; note the contemporary reference to Jack the Ripper.*

HUME NISBET

The Phantom Model

A WAPPING ROMANCE

I

The Studio

'Rhoda is a very nice girl in her way, Algy, my boy, and poses wonderfully, considering the hundreds of times she has had to do it; but she isn't the model for that Beatrice of yours, and if you want to make a hit of it, you must go further afield, and hook a face not quite so familiar to the British Public.'

It was a large apartment, one of a set of studios in the artistic barrack off the Fulham Road, which the landlord, himself a theatrical Bohemian of the first class, has rushed up for the accommodation of youthful luminaries who are yet in the nebulous stage of their Art-course. Each of these hazy specks hopes to shine out a full-lustred star in good time; they have all a proper contempt also for those servile daubsters who consent to the indignity of having R.A. added to their own proper, or assumed, names. Most of them belong to the advanced school of Impressionists, and allow, with reservations, that Jimmy Whitetuft has genius, as they know that he is the most generous, as well as the most epigrammatical, of painters, while Rhoda, the model, also knows that he is the kindest and most chivalrous of patrons, who stands more of her caprices than most of her other masters do, allows her more frequent as well as longer rests in the two hours' sitting, and can always be depended upon for a half-crown on an emergency; good-natured, sardonic Jimmy Whitetuft, who can well appreciate the caprices of any woman, or butterfly of the hour, seeing that he has so many of them himself.

Rhoda Prettyman is occupied at the present moment in what she likes best, warming her young, lithe, Greek-like figure at the

35

stove, while she puffs out vigorous wreaths of smoke from the cigarette she has picked up at the table, in the passing from the daïs to the stove. She is perfect in face, hair, figure and colour, not yet sixteen, and greatly in demand by artists and sculptors; a good girl and a merry one, who prefers bitter beer to champagne, a night in the pit to the ceremony of a private box, with a dozen or so of oysters afterwards at a little shop, rather than run her entertainer into the awful expense of a supper at the Criterion or Gatti's. Her father and mother having served as models before her, she has been accustomed to the disporting of her charms *à la vue* on raised daïses from her tenderest years, and to the *patois* of the studios since she could lisp, so that she is as unconscious as a Solomon Island young lady in the bosom of her own family, and can patter 'Art' as fluently as any picture dealer in the land.

They are all smoking hard, while they criticize the unfinished Exhibition picture of their host, Algar Gray, during this rest time of the model; Rhoda has not been posing for that picture now, for at the present time the studio is devoted to a life-club, and Rhoda has been hired for this purpose by those hard-working students, who form the young school. Jimmy Whitetuft is the visitor who drops in to cut them up; a marvellous eye for colour and effect Jimmy has, and they are happy in his friendly censorship.

All round the room the easels are set up, with their canvases, in a half-moon range, and on these canvases Rhoda can see herself as in half-a-dozen mirrors, reflected in the same number of different styles as well as postures, for these students aim at originality. But the picture which now occupies their attention is a bishop, half-length, in the second working upon which the well-known features and figure of Rhoda are depicted in thirteenth-century costume as the Beatrice of Dante, and while the young painter looks at his stale design with discontented eyes, his friends act the part of Job's comforters.

'There isn't a professional model in London who can stand for Beatrice, if you want to make her live. They have all been in too many characters already. You must have something fresh.'

'Yes, I know,' muttered Algar Gray. 'But where the deuce shall I find her?'

'Go to the country. You may see something there,' suggested

Jack Brunton, the landscapist. 'I always manage to pick up something fresh in the country.'

'The country be blowed for character,' growled Will Murray. 'Go to the East End of London, if you want a proper Beatrice; to the half-starved crew, with their big eyes and thin cheeks. That's the sort of thing to produce the spiritual longing, wistful look you want. I saw one the other day, near the Thames Tunnel, while I was on the prowl, who would have done exactly.'

'What was she?' asked Algar eagerly.

'A Ratcliff Highway stroller, I should say. At any rate, I met her in one of the lowest pubs, pouring down Irish whiskey by the tumbler, with never a wink, and using the homespun in a most delectable fashion. Her mate might have served for Semiramis, and she took four ale from the quart pot, but the other, the Beatrice, swallowed her dose neat, and as if it had been cold water from one of the springs of Paradise where, in olden times, she was wont to gather flowers.'

'Good Heavens! Will, you are atrocious. The sentiment of Dante would be killed by such a woman.'

'Realistic, dear boy, that's all. You will find very exquisite flowers sometimes even on a dust-heap, as well as where humanity grows thickest and rankest. We have all to go through the different stages of earthly experience, according to Blavatsky. This Beatrice may have been the original of Dante in the thirteenth century, now going through her Wapping experience. It seems nasty, yet it may be necessary.'

'What like was she?'

'What sort of an ideal had you when you first dreamt of that picture, Algy?'

'A tall, slender woman, of about twenty or twenty-two, graceful and refined, with pale face blue-veined and clear, with dark hair and eyes indifferent as to shade, yet out-looking — a soulful gaze from a classical, passive and passionless face.'

'That is exactly the Beatrice of the East End shanty and the Irish whiskey, the sort of holy after-death calm pervading her, the alabaster-lamp-like complexion lit up by pure spirits undiluted, the general dreamy, indifferent pose — it was all there when I first saw her, only a battle royal afterwards occurred between her and the Amazon over a sailor, during which the alabaster lamp flamed up and Semiramis came off second best; for commend me to your spiritual demons when claws and teeth are wanted. No matter, I have found your model for you; take a turn with me this evening and I'll perhaps be able to point her out to you, the after negotiations I leave in your own romantic hands.'

II

Dante in the Inferno

It is a considerable distance from the Fulham Road to Wapping even going by 'bus, but as the two artist friends went, it was still farther and decidedly more picturesque.

They were both young men under thirty. Art is not so precocious as literature, and does not send quite so many early potatoes into the market, so that the age of thirty is considered young enough for a painter to have learnt his business sufficiently to be marketable from the picture-dealing point of view.

Will Murray was the younger of the two by a couple of years, but as he had been sent early to fish in the troubled waters of illustration, and forced to provide for himself while studying, he looked much the elder; of a more realistic and energetic turn, he did not indulge in dreams of painting any single *magnum opus*, with which he would burst upon an astonished and enthusiastic world, he could not afford to dream, for he had to work hard or go fasting, and so the height of his aspirations was to paint well enough to win a note of approval from his own particular school, and keep the pot boiling with black and white work.

Algar Gray was a dreamer on five hundred per year, the income beneficent Fortune had endowed him with by reason of his lucky birth; he did not require to work for his daily bread, and as he had about as much prospect of selling his paint-creations, or imitations, as the other members of this new school, he spent the time he was not painting in dreaming about a possible future.

It wasn't a higher ideal, this brooding over fame, than the circumscribed ideal of Will Murray; each member of that young school was too staunch to his principles, and idealized his art as represented by canvas and paints too highly to care one jot about

the pecuniary side of it; they painted their pictures as the true
poet writes his poems, because it was right in their eyes; they
held exhibitions, and preached their canons to a blinded public;
the blinded public did not purchase, or even admire; but all that
did not matter to the exhibitors so long as they had enough left to
pay for more canvases and frames.

Will Murray was keen sighted and blue-eyed, robust in body
and for ever on the alert for fresh material to fill his sketch book.
Algar Gray was dark to swarthiness, with long, thin face, rich-
toned, melancholy eyes, and slender figure; he did not jot down
trifles as did his friend, he absorbed the general effect and
seldom produced his sketching-block.

Having time on their hands and a glorious October evening
before them, they walked to Fulham Wharf and, hiring a wherry
there, resolved to go by the old water way to the Tower, and after
that begin their search for the Spiritual, through the Inferno of
the East.

There is no river in the world to be compared for majesty and
the witchery of association, to the Thames; it impresses even the
unreading and unimaginative watcher with a solemnity which he
cannot account for, as it rolls under his feet and swirls past the
buttresses of its many bridges; he may think, as he experiences
the unusual effect, that it is the multiplicity of buildings which
line its banks, or the crowd of sea-craft which floats upon its
surface, or its own extensive spread. In reality he feels, although
he cannot explain it, the countless memories which hang for ever
like a spiritual fog over its rushing current.

This unseen fog closes in upon the two friends as they take up
their oars and pull out into mid-stream; it is a human fog which
depresses and prepares them for the scenes into which they must
shortly add their humanity; there is no breaking away from it, for
it reaches up to Oxford and down to Sheppey, the voiceless
thrilling of past voices, the haunting chill of dead tragedies, the
momentous hush of acted history.

It wafts towards them on the brown sails of the gliding barges
where the solitary figures stand upright at the stern like so many
Charons steering their hopeless freights; it shapes the fantastic
clouds of dying day overhead, from the fumes of countless fires,
and the breaths from countless lips, it is the overpowering

absorption of a single soul composed of many parts; the soul of a great city, past and present, of a mighty nation with its crowded events, crushing down upon the heart of a responsive stream, and this is the mystic power of the pulsating, eternal Thames.

They bear down upon Westminster, the ghost-consecrated Abbey, and the history-crammed Hall, through the arches of the bridge with a rush as the tide swelters round them; the city is buried in a dusky gloom save where the lights begin to gleam and trail with lurid reflections past black velvety-looking hulls — a dusky city of golden gleams. St. Paul's looms up like an immense bowl reversed, squat, un-English, and undignified in spite of its great size; they dart within the sombre shadows of the Bridge of Sighs, and pass the Tower of London, with the rising moon making the sky behind it luminous, and the crowd of shipping in front appear like a dense forest of withered pines, and then mooring their boat at the steps beyond, with a shuddering farewell look at the eel-like shadows and the glittering lights of that writhing river, with its burthen seen and invisible, they plunge into the purlieus of Wapping.

Through silent alleys where dark shadows fleeted past them like forest beasts on the prowl; through bustling market-places where bloaters predominated, into crammed gin-palaces where the gas flashed over faces whereon was stamped the indelible impression of a protest against creation; brushing tatters which were in gruesome harmony with the haggard or bloated features.

Will Murray was used to this medley and pushed on with a definite purpose, treating as burlesque what made the dreamer groan with impotent fury that so dire a poverty, so unspeakable a degradation, could laugh and seem hilarious even under the fugitive influence of Old Tom. They were not human beings these breathing and roaring masses, they were an appalling army of spectres grinning at an abashed Maker.

'Here we are at last, Algy,' observed Will, cheerily, as the pair pushed through the swinging doors of a crammed bar and approached the counter, 'and there is your Beatrice.'

III

The Picture

The impressionists of Fulham Road knew Algy Gray no more, after that first glimpse which he had of Beatrice. His studio was once again to let, for he had removed his baggage and tent eastward, so as to be near the woman who would not and could not come West.

His first impressions of her might have cured many a man less refined or sensitive; — a tall young woman with pallid face leaning against the bar and standing treat to some others of her kind; drinking furiously, while from her lips flowed a husky torrent of foulness, unrepeatable; she was in luck when he met her, and enjoying a holiday with some of her own sex, and therefore wanted no male interference for that night, so she repulsed his advances with frank brutality, and forced him to retire from her side baffled.

Yet, if she offended his refined ears, there was nothing about her to offend his artistic eyes; she had no ostrich feathers in her hat, and no discordancy about the colours of her shabby costume; it was plain and easy-fitting, showing the grace of her willowy shape; her features were statuesque, and as Will had said, alabaster-like in their pure pallor.

That night Algar Gray followed her about, from place to place, watching her beauty hungrily even while he wondered at the unholy thirst that possessed her, and which seemed to be sateless, a quenchless desire which gave her no rest, but drove her from bar to bar, while her money lasted; she appeared to him like a soulless being, on whom neither fatigue nor debauchery could take effect.

At length, as midnight neared, she turned to him with a half smile and beckoned him towards her; she had ignored him hitherto, although she knew he was hunting her down.

'I say, matey, I'm stumped up, so you can stand me some drink if you like.'

She laughed scornfully when she saw him take soda water for his share, it was a weakness which she could neither understand nor appreciate.

'You ain't Jacky the Terror, are you?' she enquired carelessly
as she asked him for another drink.

'Certainly not, why do you ask?'

"Cos you stick so close to me. I thought perhaps you had
spotted me out for the next one, not that I care much whether
you are or not, now that my money is done.'

His heart thrilled at the passivity of her loneliness as he looked
at her; she had accepted his companionship with indifference,
unconscious of her own perfection, utterly apathetic to everything; she a woman that nothing could warm up.

She led him to the home which she rented, a single attic
devoid of furniture, with the exception of a broken chair and
dilapidated table, and a mattress which was spread out in the
corner, a wretched nest for such a matchless Beatrice.

And as she reclined on the mattress and drank herself to sleep
from the bottle which she had made him buy for her, he sat at the
table, and while the tallow candle lasted, he watched her, and
sketched her in his pocket-book, after which, when the candle
had dropped to the bottom of the bottle which served as a candle
stick, and the white moonlight fell through the broken window
upon that pure white slumbering face, so still and death-like, he
crept softly down the stairs, thralled with but one idea.

Next day when he came again she greeted him almost
affectionately, for she remembered his lavishness the night
before and was grateful for the refreshment which he sent out for
her. Yes, she had no objections to let him paint her if he paid
well for it, and came to her, but she wasn't going out of her beat
for any man; so finding that there was another attic in the same
house to let, he hired it, got the window altered to suit him and
set to work on his picture.

The model, although untrained, was a patient enough sitter to
Algar Gray when the mood took her, but she was very variable in
her moods, and uncertain in her temper, as spirit-drunkards
mostly are. Sometimes she was reticent and sullen, and would
not be coaxed or bribed into obedience to his wishes, at other
times she was lazy and would not stir from her own mattress,
where she lay like a lovely savage, letting him admire her
transparent skin, with the blue veins intersecting it, and a
luminous glow pervading it, until his spirit melted within him,

and he grew almost as purposeless as she was.

Under these conditions the picture did not advance very fast, for now November was upon them with its fogs. Very often on the days when she felt amiable enough to sit, he had no light to take advantage of her mood, while at other times she was either away drinking with her own kind or else sulking in her bleak den.

If he wondered at first how she could keep the purity of her complexion with the life she led or how she never appeared overcome with the quantity of spirits she consumed, he no longer did so since she had given him her confidence.

She was a child of the slums in spite of her refinement of face, figure and neatness of attire; who, six years before had been given up by the doctors for consumption, and informed that she had not four months of life left. Previous to this medical verdict she had worked at a match factory, and been fairly well conducted, but with the recklessness of her kind, who resemble sailors closely, she had pitched aside caution, resolved to make the most of her four months left, and so abandoned herself to the life she was still leading.

She had existed almost entirely upon raw spirits for the past six years, surprised herself that she had lived so long past her time, yet expecting death constantly; she was as one set apart by Death, and no power could reclaim her from that doom, a reckless, condemned prisoner, living under a very uncertain reprieve, and without an emotion or a desire left except the vain craving to deaden thought, and be able to die *game*, a craving which would not be satisfied.

Algar Gray, for the sake of an ideal, had linked himself to a soul already damned, which still held on to its fragile casement, a soul which was dragging him down to her own hell; her very cold indifference to him drew him after her, and enslaved him, her unholy transparent loveliness bewitched him, and the foulness of her lips and language no longer caused him a shudder, since it could not alter her exquisite lines or those pearly tints which defied his palette; and yet he did not love the woman; his whole desire was to transfer her perfection to his canvas before grim Death came to snatch her clay from the vileness of its surroundings.

IV

A Lost Soul

December and January had passed with clear, frosty skies, and the picture of Beatrice was at length ready for the Exhibition.

When a man devotes himself body and spirit to a single object, if he has training and aptitude, no matter how mediocre he may be in ordinary affairs, he will produce something so nearly akin to a work of genius as to deceive half the judges who think themselves competent to decide between genius and talent.

Algar Gray had studied drawing at a good training-school, and was acknowledged by competent critics to be a true colourist, and for the last three months he had lived for the picture which he had just completed, therefore the result was satisfactory even to him. Beatrice, the ideal love of Dante, looked out from his canvas in the one attic of this Wapping slum, while Beatrice, the model, lay dead on her old mattress in the other.

He had attempted to make her home more home-like and comfortable for her, but without success; what he ordered from the upholsterer she disposed of promptly to the brokers, laughing scornfully at his efforts to redeem her, and mocking coarsely at his remonstrances, as she always had done at his temperate habits. He was not of her kind, and she had no sympathy with him, or in any of his ways; she had tolerated him only for the money he was able to give her and so had burnt herself out of life without a kindly word or thought about him.

She had died as she wished to do, that is, she had passed away silently and in the darkness leaving him to discover what was left of her, in the chill of a winter morning, a corpse not whiter or less luminous than she had been in life, with the transparent neck and delicate arms, blue-veined and beautiful, and the face composed with the immortal air of quiet which it had always possessed.

She had lasted just long enough to enable him to put the finishing touches upon her replica, and now that the undertakers had taken away the matchless original, he thought that he might return to his own people, and take with him the object which he had coveted and won. The woman herself seemed nothing to him while she lay waiting upon her last removal in the room next to his, but now that it was empty, and only her image remained before him, he was strangely dissatisfied and restless.

He had caught the false appearance of purity which was about her, but all unaware to himself, this constant communication of the more natural part had been absorbed into his being, until now the picture looked like a body waiting for the return of its own mocking spirit, and for the first time, regretful wishes began to tug at his heart-strings; it was no longer the Beatrice of Dante that he wanted, but the Beatrice who had mockingly enslaved him with her vileness, and whom he had permitted to escape from him for an ideal, she who had never tempted him in life, was now tormenting him past endurance with hopeless longings.

He had gone out that afternoon with the intention of returning to his studio in the West End, and making arrangements for bringing his picture there, but after wandering aimlessly about the evil haunts where he had so often followed his late model, he found that he could not tear himself from that dismal round. A shadowy form seemed to glide before him from one gin-palace to another as she had done in life; the places where she had leaned against the bars seemed still to be occupied by her cold and mocking presence, no longer passive, but repulsing him as she had done in the early part of the first night, while he grew hungry and eager for her friendship.

She was before him on the pavement as he turned towards his attic; her husky, oath-clogged voice sounded in his ears as he passed an alley, and when he rushed forward to seize her, two other women fled from him out of the gloom with shrieks of fear. All the voices of these unfortunates are alike, and he had made a mistake.

The ice had given way on the morning of her death, and the streets were now slushy and wet, with a drizzling fog obscuring objects, so that only an instinct led him back to his temporary studio; he would draw down his blind and light his lamp, and spend the last evening of the slums in looking at his work.

It appeared almost a perfect piece of painting, and likely to attract much notice when it was exhibited. The dress which Beatrice had worn still lay over the back of the chair near the door, where she had carelessly flung it when last she took it off.

He turned his back to the dress-covered chair and looked at the picture. Yes, it was the Beatrice whom Dante yearned over all his life – as she appeared to him at the bridge, with the same pure face and pathetic eyes, but not the Beatrice whom he, Algar Gray, passed over while she lived, and now longed for with such unutterable longing when it was too late.

He flung himself down before his *magnum opus,* and buried his face in his hands with passionate and hopeless regret.

Was that a husky laugh down in the court below, on the stairs, or in the room beside him? – her devil's laugh when she would go her own way in spite of his remonstrances.

He raised his head and looked behind him to where the dress had been lying crumpled and away from his picture. God of Heaven! his dead model had returned and now stood at the open door beckoning upon him to come to her, with her lovely transparent arm bare to the elbow, and once more dressed in the costume which she had cast aside.

He looked no more at his replica, but followed the mocking spirit down the stairs, into the fog-wrapped alley, and onwards where she led him.

Down towards Wapping Old Stairs, where the shapeless hulks of the ships and barges loomed out from the swirling, rushing black river like ghosts, as she was, who floated towards them, luring him downwards, amongst the slime, to the abyss from which her lost soul had been recalled by his evil longings.

The Accursed Cordonnier

BERNARD CAPES

Bernard Capes wrote five collections of strange stories in the late 1890s and early 1900s and was ignored by anthologists from then on. If you think it may have been because of the quality of his work, read these two and be amazed.

Capes, who was born in London in 1854, died in 1918 of heart failure compounding influenza. His writing career, as far as books were concerned, spanned only twenty years, yet he was one of the era's most prolific authors. He contributed stories to at least twenty-one of the magazines then prevalent, very often with a dozen appearances in the same journal over the years. His most popular work was probably the novel THE LAKE OF WINE (1898) and all told he produced over thirty-five books, the last being the posthumous THE SKELETON KEY (1919).

Bernard Capes was undoubtedly one of the Victorian age's great fantasists and I think it hard that he has not been given the recognition due him. I hope these two stories will help. Not the least strange thing about Capes' work is the startling similarity it bears to later writers' plots. His tale 'The Moon Stricken' is almost identical to a later work from M.P. Shiel, 'The Place of Pain'. I think it likely Shiel was influenced by Capes, but what of the strange likeness between Capes' 'The Black Reaper' (which appeared in his AT A WINTER'S FIRE in 1899) and Ray Bradbury's classic story 'The Scythe'? And while there have been many works on the legendary figure featured in his story 'The Accursed Cordonnier' (from the June 1900 issue of The Dome*) hardly any have approached Capes' imaginative treatment of the theme.*

BERNARD CAPES

The Accursed Cordonnier

'Poor Chrymelus, I remember, arose from the diversion of a card-table, and dropped into the dwellings of darkness.' – HERVEY

It must be confessed that Amos Rose was considerably out of his element in the smoking-room off Portland Place. All the hour he remained there he was conscious of a vague rising nausea, due not in the least to the visible atmosphere – to which, indeed, he himself contributed languorously from a crackling spilliken of South American tobacco rolled in a maize leaf and strongly tinctured with opium – but to the almost brutal post-prandial facundity of its occupants.

Rose was patently a degenerate. Nature, in scheduling his characteristics, had pruned all superlatives. The rude armour of the flesh, under which the spiritual, like a hide-bound chrysalis, should develop secret and self-contained, was perished in his case, as it were, to a semi-opaque suit, through which his soul gazed dimly and fearfully on its monstrous arbitrary surroundings. Not the mantle of the poet, philosopher, or artist fallen upon such, can still its shiverings, or give the comfort that Nature denies.

Yet he was a little bit of each – poet, philosopher, and artist; a nerveless and self-deprecatory stalker of ideals, in the pursuit of which he would wear patent leather shoes and all the apologetic graces. The grandson of a 'three-bottle' J.P., who had upheld the dignity of the State constitution while abusing his own in the best spirit of squirearchy; the son of a petulant dyspeptic, who alternated seizures of long moroseness with fits of abject moral helplessness, Amos found his inheritance in the reversion of a dissipated constitution, and an imagination as sensitive as an exposed nerve. Before he was thirty he was a neurasthenic so practised, as to have learned a sense of luxury in the very consciousness of his own suffering.

It was a negative evolution from the instinct of self-protection – self-protection, as designed in this case, against the attacks of the unspeakable. Another evolution, only less negative, was of a certain desperate pugnacity, that derived from a sense of the inhuman injustice conveyed in the fact that temperamental debility not only debarred him from that bold and healthy expression of self that it was his nature to wish, but made him actually appear to act in contradiction to his own really sweet and sound predilections.

So he sat (in the present instance, listening and revolting) in a travesty of resignation between the stools of submission and defiance.

The neurotic youth of to-day renews no ante-existent type. You will look in vain for a face like Amos's amongst the busts of the recovered past. The same weakness of outline you may point to – the sheep-like features falling to a blunt prow; the lax jaw and pinched temples – but not to that which expresses a consciousness that combative effort in a world of fruitless results is a lost desire.

Superficially, the figure in the smoking-room was that of a long, weedy young man – hairless as to his face; scalped with a fine lank fleece of neutral tint; pale-eyed, and slave to a bored and languid expression, over which he had little control, though it frequently misrepresented his mood. He was dressed scrupulously, though not obtrusively, in the mode, and was smoking a pungent cigarette with an air that seemed balanced between a genuine effort at self-abstraction and a fear of giving offence by a too pronounced show of it. In this state, flying bubbles of conversation broke upon him as he sat a little apart and alone.

'Johnny, here's Callander preaching a divine egotism.'

'Is he? Tell him to beg a lock of the Henbery's hair. Ain't she the dog that bit him?'

'Once bit, twice shy.'

'Rot! – In the case of a woman? I'm covered with their scars.'

'What,' thought Rose, 'induced me to accept an invitation to this person's house?'

'A divine egotism, eh? It jumps with the dear Sarah's humour. The beggar is an imitative beggar.'

'Let the beggar speak for himself. He's in earnest. Haven't we been bred on the principle of self-sacrifice, till we've come to think a man's self is his uncleanest possession?'

'There's no thinking about it. We've long been alarmed on your account, I can assure you.'

'Oh! I'm no saint.'

'Not you. *Your* ecstasies are all of the flesh.'

'Don't be gross. I —'

'Oh! take a whisky and seltzer.'

'If I could escape without exciting observation,' thought Rose.

Lady Sarah Henbery was his hostess, and the inspired projector of a new scheme of existence (that was, in effect, the repudiation of any scheme) that had become quite the 'thing.' She had found life an arbitrary design – a coil of days (like fancy pebbles, dull or sparkling) set in the form of a mainspring, and each gem responsible to the design. Then she had said, 'To-day shall not follow yesterday or precede to-morrow'; and she had taken her pebbles from their setting and mixed them higgledy-piggledy, and so was in the way to wear or spend one or the other as caprice moved her. And she became without design and responsibility, and was thus able to indulge a natural bent towards capriciousness to the extent that – having a face for each and every form of social hypocrisy and licence – she was presently hardly to be put out of countenance by the extremist expression of either.

It followed that her reunions were popular with worldlings of a certain order.

By-and-by Amos saw his opportunity, and slipped out into a cold and foggy night.

II

'De savoir votr' grand âge,
Nous serions curieux;
A voir votre visage,
Vous paraissez fort vieux;
Vous avez bien cent ans,
Vous montrez bien autant?'

A stranger, tall, closely wrapped and buttoned to the chin, had issued from the house at the same moment, and now followed in Rose's footsteps as he hurried away over the frozen pavement.

Suddenly this individual overtook and accosted him.

'Pardon,' he said. 'This fog baffles. We have been fellow-guests, it seems. You are walking? May I be your companion? You look a little lost yourself.'

He spoke in a rather high, mellow voice – too frank for irony.

At another time Rose might have met such a request with some slightly agitated temporising. Now, fevered with disgust of his late company, the astringency of nerve that came to him at odd moments, in the exaltation of which he felt himself ordinarily manly and human, braced him to an attitude at once modest and collected.

'I shall be quite happy,' he said. 'Only, don't blame me if you find you are entertaining a fool unawares.'

'You were out of your element, and are piqued. I saw you there, but wasn't introduced.'

'The loss is mine. I didn't observe you – yes, I did!'

He shot the last words out hurriedly – as they came within the radiance of a street lamp – and his pace lessened a moment with a little bewildered jerk.

He had noticed this person, indeed – his presence and his manner. They had arrested his languid review of the frivolous forces about him. He had seen a figure, strange and lofty, pass from group to group; exchange with one a word or two, with another a grave smile; move on and listen; move on and speak; always statelily restless; never anything but an incongruous apparition in a company of which every individual was eager to assert and expound the doctrines of self.

This man had been of curious expression, too – so curious that Amos remembered to have marvelled at the little comment his presence seemed to excite. His face was absolutely hairless – as, to all evidence, was his head, upon which he wore a brown silk handkerchief loosely rolled and knotted. The features were presumably of a Jewish type – though their entire lack of accent in the form of beard or eyebrow made identification difficult – and were minutely covered, like delicate cracklin, with a network of flattened wrinkles. Ludicrous though the description, the lofty individuality of the man so surmounted all disadvantages of appearance as to overawe frivolous criticism. Partly, also, the full transparent olive of his complexion, and the pools of purple shadow in which his eyes seemed to swim like blots of resin, neutralised the superficial barrenness of his face. Forcibly, he impelled the conviction that here was one who ruled his own being arbitrarily through entire fearlessness of death.

'You saw me?' he said, noticing with a smile his companion's involuntary hesitation. 'Then let us consider the introduction made, without further words. We will even expand to the familiarity of old acquaintanceship, if you like to fall in with the momentary humour.'

'I can see,' said Rose, 'that years are nothing to you.'

'No more than this gold piece, which I fling into the night. They are made and lost and made again.'

'You have knowledge and the gift of tongues.'

The young man spoke bewildered, but with a strange warm feeling of confidence flushing up through his habitual reserve. He had no thought why, nor did he choose his words or inquire of himself their source of inspiration.

'I have these,' said the stranger. 'The first is my excuse for addressing you.'

'You are going to ask me something.'

'What attraction —'

'Drew me to Lady Sarah's house? I am young, rich, presumably a desirable *parti*. Also, I am neurotic, and without the nerve to resist.'

'Yet you knew your taste would take alarm – as it did.'

'I have an acute sense of delicacy. Naturally I am prejudiced in favour of virtue.'

'Then – excuse me – why put yours to a demoralising test?'

'I am not my own master. Any formless apprehension – any shadowy fear enslaves my will. I go to many places from the simple dread of being called upon to explain my reasons for refusing. For the same cause I may appear to acquiesce in indecencies my soul abhors; to give countenance to opinions innately distasteful to me. I am a quite colourless personality.'

'Without force or object in life?'

'Life, I think, I live for its isolated moments – the first half-dozen pulls at a cigarette, for instance, after a generous meal.'

'You take the view, then —'

'Pardon me. I take no views. I am not strong enough to take anything – not even myself – seriously.'

'Yet you know that the trail of such volitionary ineptitude reaches backwards under and beyond the closed door you once issued from?'

'Do I? I know at least that the ineptitude intensifies with every step of constitutional decadence. It may be that I am wearing down to the nerve of life. How shall I find that? diseased? Then it is no happiness to me to think it imperishable.'

'Young man, do you believe in a creative divinity?'

'Yes.'

'And believe without resentment?'

'I think God hands over to His apprentices the moulding of vessels that don't interest Him.'

The stranger twitched himself erect.

'I beg you not to be profane,' he said.

'I am not,' said Rose. 'I don't know why I confide in you, or what concern I have to know. I can only say my instincts, through bewildering mental suffering, remain religious. You take me out of myself and judge me unfairly on the result.'

'Stay. You argue that a perishing of the bodily veil reveals the soul. Then the outlook of the latter should be the cleaner.'

'It gazes through a blind of corruption. It was never designed to stand naked in the world's market-places.'

'And whose the fault that it does?'

'I don't know. I only feel that I am utterly lonely and helpless.'

The stranger laughed scornfully.

'You can feel no sympathy with my state?' said Rose.

'Not a grain. To be conscious of a soul, yet to remain a craven under the temporal tyranny of the flesh; fearful of revolting, though the least imaginative flight of the spirit carries it at once beyond any bodily influence! Oh, sir! Fortune favours the brave.'

'She favours the fortunate,' said the young man, with a melancholy smile. 'Like a banker, she charges a commission on small accounts. At trifling deposits she turns up her nose. If you would escape her tax, you must keep a fine large balance at her house.'

'I dislike parables,' said the stranger drily.

'Then, here is a fact in illustration. I have an acquaintance, an impoverished author, who anchored his ark of hope on Mount Olympus twenty years ago. During all that time he has never ceased to send forth his doves; only to have them return empty-beaked with persistent regularity. Three days ago the olive branch – a mere sprouting twig – came home. For the first time a magazine – an indifferent one – accepted a story of his and offered him a pound for it. He acquiesced; and the same night was returned to him from an important American firm an under-stamped MS., on which he had to pay excess postage, half a crown. That was Fortune's commission.'

'Bully the jade, and she will love you.'

'Your wisdom has not learned to confute that barbarism?'

The stranger glanced at his companion with some expression of dislike.

'The sex figures in your ideals, I see,' said he. 'Believe my long experience that its mere animal fools constitute its only excuse for existing – though' (he added under his breath) 'even they annoy one by their monogamous prejudices.'

'I won't hear that with patience,' said Rose. 'Each sex in its degree. Each is wearifully peevish over the hateful rivalry between mind and matter; but the male only has the advantage of distractions.'

'This,' said the stranger softly, as if to himself, 'is the woeful proof, indeed, of decadence. Man waives his prerogative of lordship over the irreclaimable savagery of earth. He has warmed his temperate house of clay to be a hot-house to his imagination, till the very walls are frail and eaten with fever.'

'Christ spoke of no spiritual division between the sexes.'

There followed a brief silence. Preoccupied, the two moved slowly through the fog, that was dashed ever and anon with cloudy blooms of lamplight.

'I wish to ask you,' said the stranger at length, 'in what has the teaching of Christ proved otherwise than so impotent to reform mankind, as to make one sceptical as to the divinity of the teacher?'

'Why, what is your age?' asked Rose in a tone of surprise.

'I am a hundred to-night.'

The astounded young man jumped in his walk.

'A hundred!' he exclaimed. 'And you cannot answer that question yourself?'

'I asked you to answer it. But never mind. I see faith in you like a garden of everlastings – as it should be – as of course it should be. Yet disbelievers point to inconsistencies. There was a reviling Jew, for instance, to whom Christ is reported to have shown resentment quite incompatible with His teaching.'

'Whom do you mean?'

'Cartaphilus; who was said to be condemned to perpetual wandering.'

'A legend,' cried Amos scornfully. 'Bracket it with Nero's fiddling and the hymning of Memnon.'

A second silence fell. They seemed to move in a dead and stagnant world. Presently said the stranger suddenly –

'I am quite lost; and so, I suppose, are you?'

'I haven't an idea where we are.'

'It is two o'clock. There isn't a soul or a mark to guide us. We had best part and each seek his own way.'

He stopped and held out his hand.

'Two pieces of advice I should like to give you before we separate. Fall in love and take plenty of exercise.'

'Must we part?' said Amos. 'Frankly, I don't think I like you. That sounds strange and discourteous after my ingenuous confidences. But you exhale an odd atmosphere of witchery; and your scorn braces me like a tonic. The pupils of your eyes, when I got a glimpse of them, looked like the heads of little black devils peeping out of windows. But you can't touch my soul on the raw when my nerves are quiescent; and then I would strike any man that called me coward.'

The stranger uttered a quick, chirping laugh, like the sound of a stone on ice.

'What do you propose?' he said.

'I have an idea you are not so lost as you pretend. If we are anywhere near shelter that you know, take me in and I will be a good listener. It is one of my negative virtues.'

'I don't know that any addition to my last good counsel would not be an anti-climax.'

He stood musing and rubbing his hairless chin.

'Exercise – certainly. It is the golden demephitizer of the mind. I am seldom off my feet.'

'You walk much – and alone?'

'Not always alone. Periodically I am accompanied by one or another. At this time I have a companion who has tramped with me for some nine months.'

Again he pondered apart. The darkness and the fog hid his face, but he spoke his thoughts aloud.

'What matter if it does come about? To-morrow I have the world – the mother of many daughters. And to redeem this soul – a dog of a Christian – a friend at Court!'

He turned quickly to the young man.

'Come!' he said. 'It shall be as you wish.'

'Do you know where we are?'

'We are at the entrance to Wardour Street.'

He gave a gesture of impatience, whipped a hand at his companion's sleeve, and once more they trod down the icy echoes, going onwards.

The narrow lane reverberated to their footsteps; the drooping fog swayed sluggishly; the dead blank windows and high-shouldered doors frowned in stubborn progression and vanished behind them.

The stranger stopped in a moment where a screen of iron bars protected a shop front. From behind them shot leaden glints from old clasped bookcovers, hanging tongues of Toledo steel, croziers rich in nielli – innumerable and antique curios gathered from the lumber-rooms of history.

A door to one side he opened with a latch-key. A pillar of light, seeming to smoke as the fog obscured it, was formed of the aperture.

Obeying a gesture, Rose set foot on the threshold. As he was entering, he found himself unable to forbear a thrill of effrontery.

'Tell me,' said he. 'It was not only to point a moral that you flung away that coin?'

The stranger, going before, grinned back sourly over his shoulder.

'Not only,' he said. 'It was a bad one.'

III

> ... 'La Belle Dame sans merci
> Hath thee in thrall!'

All down the dimly luminous passage that led from the door straight into the heart of the building, Amos was aware, as he followed his companion over the densely piled carpet, of the floating sweet scent of amber-seed. Still his own latter exaltation of nerve burned with a steady radiance. He seemed to himself bewitched – translated; a consciousness apart from yesterday; its material fibres responsive to the least or utmost shock of adventure. As he trod in the other's footsteps, he marvelled that so lavish a display of force, so elastic a gait, could be in a centenarian.

'Are you ever tired?' he whispered curiously.

'Never. Sometimes I long for weariness as other men desire rest.'

As the stranger spoke, he pulled aside a curtain of stately black velvet, and softly opening a door in a recess, beckoned the young man into the room beyond.

He saw a chamber, broad and low, designed, in its every rich stain of picture and slumberous hanging, to appeal to the sensuous. And here the scent was thick and motionless. Costly marqueterie; Palissy candlesticks reflected in half-concealed mirrors framed in embossed silver; antique Nankin vases brimming with pot-pourri; in one corner a suit of Milanese armour, fluted, damasquinée, by Felippo Negroli; in another a tripod table of porphyry, spectrally repeating in its polished surface the opal hues of a vessel of old Venetian glass half filled with some topaz-coloured liqueur - such and many more tokens of a luxurious aestheticism wrought in the observer an immediate sense of pleasurable enervation. He noticed, with a swaying thrill of delight, that his feet were on a padded rug of Astrakhan – one of many, disposed eccentrically about the yellow tassellated-marble floor; and he noticed that the sole light in the chamber came from an iridescent globed lamp, fed with some fragrant oil, that hung near an alcove traversed by a veil of dark violet silk.

The door behind him swung gently to: his eyes half closed in a dreamy surrender of will: the voice of the stranger speaking to him sounded far away as the cry of some lost unhappiness.

'Welcome!' it said only.

Amos broke through his trance with a cry.

'What does it mean – all this? We step out of the fog, and here – I think it is the guest-parlour of Hell!'

'You flatter me,' said the stranger, smiling. 'Its rarest antiquity goes no further back, I think, than the eighth century. The skeleton of the place is Jacobite and comparatively modern.'

'But you – the shop!'

'Contains a little of the fruit of my wanderings.'

'You are a dealer?'

'A casual collector only. If through a representative I work my accumulations of costly lumber to a profit – say thousands per cent – it is only because utility is the first principle of Art. As to myself, here I but pitch my tent – periodically, and at long intervals.'

'An unsupervised agent must find it a lucrative post.'

'Come – there shows a little knowledge of human nature. For the first time I applaud you. But the appointment is conditional on many things. At the moment the berth is vacant. Would you like it?'

'My (paradoxically) Christian name was bestowed in compliment to a godfather, sir. I am no Jew. I have already enough to know the curse of having more.'

'I have no idea how you are called. I spoke jestingly, of course; but your answer quenches the flicker of respect I felt for you. As a matter of fact, the other's successor is not only nominated, but is actually present in this room.'

'Indeed? You propose to fill the post yourself?'

'Not by any means. The mere suggestion is an insult to one who can trace his descent backwards at least two thousand years.'

'Yes, indeed. I meant no disparagement, but —'

'I tell you, sir,' interrupted the stranger irritably, 'my visits are periodic. I could not live in a town. I could not settle anywhere. I must always be moving. A prolonged constitutional – that is my theory of health.'

'You are always on your feet – at your age —'

'I am a hundred to-night. But – mark you – *I have eaten of the Tree of Life.*'

As the stranger uttered these words, he seized Rose by the wrist in a soft, firm grasp. His captive, staring at him amazed, gave out a little involuntary shriek.

'Hadn't I better leave? There is something – nameless – I don't know; but I should never have come in here. Let me go!'

The other, heedless, half pulled the troubled and bewildered young man across the room, and drew him to within a foot of the curtain closing the alcove.

'Here,' he said quietly, 'is my fellow-traveller of the last nine months, fast, I believe, in sleep – unless your jarring outcry has broken it.'

Rose struggled feebly.

'Not anything shameful,' he whimpered – 'I have a dread of your manifestations.'

For answer, the other put out a hand, and swiftly and silently withdrew the curtain. A deepish recess was revealed, into which the soft glow of the lamp penetrated like moonlight. It fell in the first instance upon a couch littered with pale, uncertain shadows, and upon a crucifix that hung upon the wall within.

In the throb of his emotions, it was something of a relief to Amos to see his companion, releasing his hold of him, clasp his hands and bow his head reverently to this pathetic symbol. The cross on which the Christ hung was of ebony a foot high; the figure itself was chryselephantine and purely exquisite as a work of art.

'It is early seventeenth century,' said the stranger suddenly, after a moment of devout silence, seeing the other's eyes absorbed in contemplation. 'It is by Duquesnoy.' (Then, behind the back of his hand) 'The rogue couldn't forget his bacchanals even here.'

'It is a Christ of infidels,' said Amos, with repugnance. He was adding involuntarily (his *savoir faire* seemed suddenly to have deserted him) – 'But fit for an unbelieving —' when his host took him up with fury —

'Dog of a Gentile! – if you dare to call me Jew!'

The dismayed start of the young man at this outburst blinded him to its paradoxical absurdity. He fell back with his heart thumping. The eyes of the stranger flickered, but in an instant he had recovered his urbanity.

'Look!' he whispered impatiently. 'The Calvary is not alone in the alcove.'

Mechanically Rose's glance shifted to the couch; and in that moment shame and apprehension and the sickness of being were precipitated in him as in golden flakes of rapture.

Something, that in the instant of revelation had seemed part only of the soft tinted shadows, resolved itself into a presentment of loveliness so pure, and so pathetic in its innocent self-surrender to the passionate tyranny of his gaze, that the manhood in him was abashed in the very flood of its exaltation. He put a hand to his face before he looked a second time, to discipline his dazzled eyes. They were turned only upon his soul, and found it a reflected glory. Had the vision passed? His eyes, in a panic, leaped for it once more.

Yes, it was there – dreaming upon its silken pillow; a grotesque carved dragon in ivory looking down, from a corner of the fluted couch, upon its supernal beauty – a face that, at a glance, could fill the vague desire of a suffering, lonely heart – spirit informing matter with all the flush and essence of some flower of the lost garden of Eden.

And this expressed in the form of one simple slumbering girl; in its stately sweet curves of cheek and mouth and throat; in its drifted heap of hair, bronze as copper-beech leaves in spring; in the very pulsing of its half-hidden bosom, and in its happy morning lips, like Psyche's, night-parted by Love and so remaining entranced.

A long light robe, sulphur-coloured, clung to the sleeper from low throat to ankle; bands of narrow nolana-blue ribbon crossed her breast and were brought together in a loose cincture about her waist; her white, smooth feet were sandalled; one arm was curved beneath her lustrous head; the other lay relaxed and drooping. Chrysoberyls, the sea-virgins of stones, sparkled in her hair and lay in the bosom of her gown like dewdrops in an evening primrose.

The gazer turned with a deep sigh, and then a sputter of fury –

'Why do you show me this? You cruel beast, was not my life barren enough before?'

'Can it ever be so henceforward? Look again.'

'Does the devil enter? Something roars in me! Have you no fear that I shall kill you?'

'None. I cannot die.'

Amos broke into a mocking, fierce laugh. Then, his blood shooting in his veins, he seized the sleeper roughly by her hand.

'Wake!' he cried, 'and end it!'

With a sigh she lifted her head. Drowsiness and startled wonderment struggled in her eyes; but in a moment they caught the vision of the stranger standing aside, and smiled and softened. She held out her long, white arms to him.

'You have come, dear love,' she said, in a happy, low voice, 'and I was not awake to greet you.'

Rose fell on his knees.

'Oh, God in Heaven!' he cried, 'bear witness that this is monstrous and unnatural! Let me die rather than see it.'

The stranger moved forward.

'Do honour, Adnah, to this our guest; and minister to him of thy pleasure.'

The white arms dropped. The girl's face was turned, and her eyes, solemn and witch-like, looked into Amos's. He saw them, their irises golden-brown shot with little spars of blue; and the soul in his own seemed to rush towards them and to recoil, baffled and sobbing.

Could she have understood? He thought he saw a faint smile, a gentle shake of the head, as she slid from the couch and her sandals tapped on the marble floor.

She stooped and took him by the hand.

'Rise, I pray you,' she said, 'and I will be your handmaiden.'

She led him unresisting to a chair, and bade him sweetly to be seated. She took from him his hat and overcoat, and brought him rare wine in a cup of crystal.

'My lord will drink,' she murmured, 'and forget all but the night and Adnah.'

'You I can never forget,' said the young man, in a broken voice.

As he drank, half choking, the girl turned to the other, who still stood apart, silent and watchful.

'Was this wise?' she breathed. 'To summon a witness on this night of all – was this wise, beloved?'

Amos dashed the cup on the floor. The red liquid stained the marble like blood.

'No, no!' he shrieked, springing to his feet. 'Not that! it cannot be!'

In an ecstasy of passion he flung his arms about the girl, and crushed all her warm loveliness against his breast. She remained quite passive – unstartled even. Only she turned her head and whispered: 'Is this thy will?'

Amos fell back, drooping, as if he had received a blow.

'Be merciful and kill me,' he muttered. 'I – even I can feel at last the nobility of death.'

Then the voice of the stranger broke, lofty and passionless.

'Tell him what you see in me.'

She answered, low and without pause, like one repeating a cherished lesson –

'I see – I have seen it for the nine months I have wandered with you – the supreme triumph of the living will. I see that this triumph, of its very essence, could not be unless you had surmounted the tyranny of any, the least, gross desire. I see that it is incompatible with sin; with offence given to oneself or others; that passion cannot live in its serene atmosphere; that it illustrates the enchantment of the flesh by the intellect; that it is happiness for evermore redeemed.'

'How do you feel this?'

'I see it reflected in myself – I, the poor visionary you took from the Northern Island. Week by week I have known it sweetening and refining in my nature. None can taste the bliss of happiness that has not you for master – none can teach it save you, whose composure is unshadowed by any terror of death.'

'And love that is passion, Adnah?'

'I hear it spoken as in a dream. It is a wicked whisper from far away. You, the lord of time and of tongues, I worship – you, only you, who are my God.'

'Hush! But the man of Nazareth?'

'Ah! His name is an echo. What divine egotism taught He?'

Where lately had Amos heard this phrase? His memory of all things real seemed suspended.

'He was a man, and He died,' said Adnah simply.,

The stranger threw back his head, with an odd expression of

triumph; and almost in the same moment abased it to the crucifix on the wall.

Amos stood breathing quickly, his ears drinking in every accent of the low musical voice. Now, as she paused, he moved forward a hurried step, and addressed himself to the shadowy figure by the couch –

'Who are you, in the name of the Christ you mock and adore in a breath, that has wrought this miracle of high worship in a breathing woman?'

'I am he that has eaten of the Tree of Life.'

'Oh, forego your fables! I am not a child.'

'It could not of its nature perish' (the voice went on evenly, ignoring the interruption). 'It breathes its immortal fragrance in no transplanted garden, invisible to sinful eyes, as some suppose. When the curse fell, the angel of the flaming sword bore it to the central desert; and the garden withered, for its soul was withdrawn. Now, in the heart of the waste place that is called Tiah-Bani-Israïl, it waits in its loveliness the coming of the Son of God.'

'He has come and passed.'

It might have been an imperceptible shrug of the shoulders that twitched the tall figure by the couch. If so, it converted the gesture into a bow of reverence.

'Is He not to be revealed again in His glory? But there, set as in the crater of a mountain of sand, and inaccessible to mortal footstep, stands unperishing the glory of the earth. And its fragrance is drawn up to heaven, as through a wide chimney; and from its branches hangs the undying fruit, lustrous and opalescent; and in each shining globe the world and its starry system are reflected in miniature, moving westwards; but at night they glow, a cluster of tender moons.'

'And whence came *your* power to scale that which is inaccessible?'

'From Death, that, still denying me immortality, is unable to encompass my destruction.'

The young man burst into a harsh and grating laugh.

'Here is some inconsistency!' he cried. 'By your own showing you were not immortal till you ate of the fruit!'

Could it be that this simple deductive snip cut the thread of

coherence? A scowl appeared to contract the lofty brow for an
instant. The next, a gay chirrup intervened, like a little spark
struck from the cloud.

'The pounding logic of the steam engine!' cried the stranger,
coming forward at last with an open smile. 'But we pace in an
altitude refined above sensuous comprehension. Perhaps before
long you will see and believe. In the meantime let us be men and
women enjoying the warm gifts of Fortune!'

IV

'Nous pensions comme un songe
Le récrit de vos maux;
Nous traitions de mensonge
Tous vos plus grands travaux!'

In that one night of an unreality that seemed either an enchanted
dream or a wilfully fantastic travesty of conventions, Amos
alternated between fits of delirious self-surrender and a rage of
resignation, from which now and again he would awake to
flourish an angry little bodkin of irony.

Now, at this stage, it appeared a matter for passive acquiesc-
ence that he should be one of a trio seated at a bronze table, that
might have been recovered from Herculaneum, playing three-
handed cribbage with a pack of fifteenth-century cards – limned,
perhaps by some Franceso Bachiacca – and an ivory board inlaid
with gold and mother-of-pearl. To one side a smaller 'occasional' table held the wine, to which the young man resorted at the
least invitation from Adnah.

In this connexion (of cards), it would fitfully perturb him to
find that he who had renounced sin with mortality, had not only a
proneness to avail himself of every oversight on the part of his
adversaries, but frequently to peg-up more holes than his hand
entitled him to. Moreover, at such times, when the culprit's
attention was drawn to this by his guest – at first gently; later,
with a little scorn – he justified his action on the assumption that
it was an essential interest of all games to attempt abuse of the
confidence of one's antagonist, whose skill in checkmating any
movement of this nature was in right ratio with his capacity as a
player; and finally he rose, the sole winner of a sum respectable
enough to allow him some ingenuous expression of satisfaction.

Thereafter conversation ensued; and it must be remarked that nothing was further from Rose's mind than to apologize for his long intrusion and make a decent exit. Indeed, there seemed some thrill of vague expectation in the air, to the realisation of which his presence sought to contribute; and already – so rapidly grows the assurance of love – his heart claimed some protective right over the pure, beautiful creature at his feet.

For there, at a gesture from the other, had Adnah seated herself, leaning her elbow, quite innocently and simply, on the young man's knee.

The sweet strong Moldavian wine buzzed in his head; love and sorrow and intense yearning went with flow and shock through his veins. At one moment elated by the thought that, whatever his understanding of the ethical sympathy existing between these two, their connexion was, by their own acknowledgment, platonic; at another, cruelly conscious of the icy crevasse that must gape between so perfectly proportioned an organism and his own atrabilarious personality, he dreaded to avail himself of a situation that was at once an invitation and a trust; and ended by subsiding, with characteristic lameness, into mere conversational commonplace.

'You must have got over a great deal of ground,' said he to his host, 'on that constitutional hobby-horse of yours?'

'A great deal of ground.'

'In all weathers?'

'In all weathers; at all times; in every country.'

'How do you manage – pardon my inquisitiveness – the little necessities of dress and boots and such things?'

'Adnah,' said the stranger, 'go fetch my walking suit and show it to our guest.'

The girl rose, went silently from the room, and returned in a moment with a single garment, which she laid in Rose's hands.

He examined it curiously. It was a marvel of sartorial tact and ingenuity; so fashioned that it would have appeared scarcely a solecism on taste in any age. Built in one piece to resemble many, and of the most particularly chosen material, it was contrived and ventilated for any exigencies of weather and of climate, and could be doffed or assumed at the shortest notice. About it were cunningly distributed a number of strong pockets or purses for the reception of divers articles, from a comb to a sandwich-box; and the position of these was so calculated as not to interfere with the symmetry of the whole.

'It is indeed an excellent piece of work,' said Amos, with considerable appreciation; for he held no contempt for the art which sometimes alone seemed to justify his right of existence.

'Your praise is deserved,' said the stranger, smiling, 'seeing that it was contrived for me by one whose portrait, by Giambattista Moroni, now hangs in your National Gallery.'

'I have heard of it, I think. Is the fellow still in business?'

'The tailor or the artist? The first died in bankrupt in prison – about the year 1560, it must have been. It was fortunate for me, inasmuch as I acquired the garment for nothing, the man disappearing before I had settled his claim.'

Rose's jaw dropped. He looked at the beautiful face reclining against him. It expressed no doubt, no surprise, no least sense of the ludicrous.

'Oh, my God!' he muttered, and ploughed his forehead with his hands. Then he looked up again with a pallid grin.

'I see,' he said. 'You play upon my fancied credulity. And how did the garment serve you in the central desert?'

'I had it not then, by many centuries. No garment would avail against the wicked Samiel – the poisonous wind that is the breath of the eternal dead sand. Who faces that feels, pace by pace, his body wither and stiffen. His clothes crackle like paper, and so fall to fragments. From his eyeballs the moist vision flakes and flies in powder. His tongue shrinks into his throat, as though fire had writhed and consumed it to a little scarlet spur. His furrowed skin peels like the cerements of an ancient mummy. He falls, breaking in his fall – there is a puff of acrid dust, dissipated in a moment – and he is gone.'

'And this you met unscathed?'

'Yes; for it was preordained that Death should hunt, but never overtake me – that I might testify to the truth of the first Scriptures.'

Even as he spoke, Rose sprang to his feet with a gesture of uncontrollable repulsion; and in the same instant was aware of a horrible change that was taking place in the features of the man before him.

V

'Trahentibus autem Judaeis Jesum extra praetorium cum venisset ad ostium, Cartaphilus praetorii ostiarius et Pontii Pilati, cum per ostium exiret Jesus, pepulit Eum pugno contemptibiliter post tergum, et irridens dixit, 'Vade, Jesu citius, vade, quid moraris?" Et Jesus severo vultu et oculo respiciens in eum, dixit: 'Ego vado, et expectabis donec veniam!" Itaque juxta verbum Domini expectat adhuc Cartaphilus ille, qui tempore Dominicae passionis – erat quasi triginta annorum, et semper cum usque ad centum attigerit aetatem redeuntium annorum redit redivivus ad illum aetatis statum, quo fuit anno quand passus est Dominus.' – MATTHEW OF PARIS, Historia Major.

The girl – from whose cheek Rose, in his rough rising, had seemed to brush the bloom, so keenly had its colour deepened – sank from the stool upon her knees, her hands pressed to her bosom, her lungs working quickly under the pressure of some powerful excitement.

'It comes, beloved!' she said, in a voice half terror, half ecstasy.

'It comes, Adnah,' the stranger echoed, struggling – 'this periodic self-renewal – this sloughing of the veil of flesh that I warned you of.'

His soul seemed to pant grey from his lips; his face was bloodless and like stone; the devils in his eyes were awake and busy as maggots in a wound. Amos knew him now for wickedness personified and immortal, and fell upon his knees beside the girl and seized one of her hands in both his.

'Look!' he shrieked. 'Can you believe in him longer? believe that any code or system of his can profit you in the end?'

She made no resistance, but her eyes still dwelt on the contorted face with an expression of divine pity.

'Oh, thou sufferest!' she breathed; 'but thy reward is near!'

'Adnah!' wailed the young man, in a heartbroken voice. 'Turn from him to me! Take refuge in my love. Oh, it is natural, I swear. It asks nothing of you but to accept the gift – to renew yourself in it, if you will; to deny it, if you will, and chain it for your slave. Only to save you and die for you, Adnah!'

He felt the hand in his shudder slightly; but no least knowledge of him did she otherwise evince.

He clasped her convulsively, released her, mumbled her slack white fingers with his lips. He might have addressed the dead.

In the midst, the figure before them swayed with a rising throe

– turned – staggered across to the couch, and cast itself down before the crucifix on the wall.

'Jesu, Son of God,' it implored, through a hurry of piercing groans, 'forbear Thy hand: Christ, register my atonement! My punishment – eternal – and oh, my mortal feet already weary to death! Jesu, spare me! Thy justice, Lawgiver – let it not be vindictive, oh, in Thy sacred name! lest men proclaim it for a baser thing than theirs. For a fault of ignorance – for a word of scorn where all reviled, would *they* have singled *one* out, have made him, most wretched, the scapegoat of the ages? Ah, most holy, forgive me! In mine agony I know not what I say. A moment ago I could have pronounced it something seeming less than divine that Thou couldst so have stultified with a curse Thy supreme hour of self-sacrifice – a moment ago, when the rising madness prevailed. Now, sane once more – Nazarene, oh, Nazarene! not only retribution for my deserts, but pity for my suffering – Nazarene, that Thy slanderers, the men of little schisms, be refuted, hearing me, the very witness to Thy mercy, testify how the justice of the Lord triumphs supreme through that His superhuman prerogative – that they may not say, He can destroy, even as we; but can He redeem? The sacrifice – the yearling lamb – it awaits Thee, Master, the proof of my abjectness and my sincerity. I, more curst than Abraham, lift my eyes to Heaven, the terror in my heart, the knife in my hand. Jesu – Jesu!'

He cried and grovelled. His words were frenzied, his abasement fulsome to look upon. Yet it was impressed upon one of the listeners, with a great horror, how unspeakable blasphemy breathed between the lines of the prayer – the blasphemy of secret disbelief in the Power it invoked, and sought, with its tongue in its cheek, to conciliate.

Bitter indignation in the face of nameless outrage transfigured Rose at this moment into something nobler than himself. He feared, but he upheld his manhood. Conscious that the monstrous situation was none of his choosing, he had no thought to evade its consequences so long as the unquestioning credulity of his co-witness seemed to call for his protection. Nerveless, sensitive natures, such as his, not infrequently give the lie to themselves by accesses of an altruism that is little less than self-effacement.

'This is all bad,' he struggled to articulate. 'You are hipped by some devilish cantrip. Oh, come – come! – in Christ's name I dare to implore you – and learn the truth of love!'

As he spoke, he saw that the apparition was on its feet again – that it had returned, and was standing, its face ghastly and inhuman, with one hand leaned upon the marble table.

'Adnah!' it cried, in a strained and hollow voice. 'The moment for which I prepared you approaches. Even now I labour. I had thought to take up the thread on the further side; but it is ordained otherwise, and we must part.'

'Part!' The word burst from her in a sigh of lost amazement.

'The holocaust, Adnah!' he groaned – 'the holocaust with which every seventieth year my expiation must be punctuated! This time the cross is on thy breast, beloved; and to-morrow – oh! thou must be content to tread on lowlier altitudes than those I have striven to guide thee by.'

'I cannot – I cannot. I should die in the mists. Oh, heart of my heart, forsake me not!'

'Adnah – my selma, my beautiful – to propitiate –'

'Whom? Thou hast eaten of the Tree, and art a God!'

'Hush!' He glanced round with an awed visage at the dim hanging Calvary; then went on in a harsher tone, 'It is enough – it must be.' (His shifting face, addressed to Rose, was convulsed into an expression of bitter scorn.) 'I command thee, go with him. The sacrifice – oh, my heart, the sacrifice! And I cry to Jehovah, and He makes no sign; and into thy sweet breast the knife must enter.'

Amos sprang to his feet with a loud cry.

'I take no gift from you. I will win or lose her by right of manhood!'

The girl's face was white with despair.

'I do not understand,' she cried in a piteous voice.

'Nor I,' said the young man, and he took a threatening step forward. 'We have no part in this – this lady and I. Man or devil you may be; but –'

'Neither!'

The stranger, as he uttered the word, drew himself erect with a tortured smile. The action seemed to kilt the skin of his face into hideous plaits.

'I am Cartaphilus,' he said, 'who denied the Nazarene shelter.'

'The *Wandering Jew!*'

The name of the old strange legend broke involuntarily from Rose's lips.

'Now you know him!' he shrieked then. 'Adnah, I am here! Come to me!'

Tears were running down the girl's cheeks. She lifted her hands with an impassioned gesture; then covered her face with them.

But Cartaphilus, penetrating the veil with eyes no longer human, cried suddenly, so that the room vibrated with his voice, 'Bismillah! Wilt thou dare the Son of Heaven, questioning if His sentence upon the Jew – to renew, with his every hundredth year, his manhood's prime – was not rather a forestalling, through His infinite penetration, of the consequences of that Jew's finding and eating of the Tree of Life? Is it Cartaphilus first, or Christ?'

The girl flung herself forward, crushing her bosom upon the marble floor, and lay blindly groping with her hands.

'He was a God and vindictive!' she moaned. 'He was a man and He died. The cross – the cross!'

The lost cry pierced Rose's breast like a knife. Sorrow, rage, and love inflamed his passion to madness. With one bound he met and grappled with the stranger.

He had no thought of the resistance he should encounter. In a moment the Jew, despite his age and seizure, had him broken and powerless. The fury of blood blazed down upon him from the unearthly eyes.

'Beast! that I might tear you! But the Nameless is your refuge. You must be chained – you must be chained. Come!'

Half dragging, half bearing, he forced his captive across the room to the corner where the flask of topaz liquid stood.

'Sleep!' he shrieked, and caught up the glass vessel and dashed it down upon Rose's mouth.

The blow was a stunning one. A jagged splinter tore the victim's lip and bought a gush of blood; the yellow fluid drowned his eyes and suffocated his throat. Struggling to hold his faculties, a startled shock passed through him, and he dropped insensible on the floor.

VI

'Wandering stars, to whom is reserved the blackness of darkness for ever.'

Where had he read these words before? Now he saw them as scrolled in lightning upon a dead sheet of night.

There was a sound of feet going on and on.

Light soaked into the gloom, faster – faster; and he saw –

The figure of a man moved endlessly forward by town and pasture and the waste places of the world. But though he, the dreamer, longed to outstrip and stay the figure and look searchingly in its face, he could not, following, close upon the intervening space; and its back was ever towards him.

And always as the figure passed by populous places, there rose long murmurs of blasphemy to either side, and bestial cries: 'We are weary! the farce is played out! He reveals Himself not, nor ever will! Lead us – lead us, against Heaven, against hell; against any other, or against ourselves! The cancer of life spreads, and we cannot enjoy nor can we think cleanly. The sins of the fathers have accumulated to one vast mount of putrefaction. Lead us, and we follow!'

And, uttering these cries, swarms of hideous half-human shapes would emerge from holes and corners and rotting burrows, and stumble a little way with the figure, cursing and jangling, and so drop behind, one by one, like glutted flies shaken from a horse.

And the dreamer saw in him, who went ever on before, the sole existent type of a lost racial glory, a marvellous survival, a prince over monstrosities; and he knew him to have reached, through long ages of evil introspection, a terrible belief in his own self-acquired immortality and lordship over all abased peoples that must die and pass; and the seed of his blasphemy he sowed broadcast in triumph as he went; and the ravenous horrors of the earth ran forth in broods and devoured it like birds, and trod one another underfoot in their gluttony.

And he came to a vast desolate plain, and took his stand upon a barren drift of sand; and the face the dreamer longed and feared to see was yet turned from him.

And the figure cried in a voice that grated down the winds of space: 'Lo! I am he that cannot die! Lo! I am he that has eaten of the Tree of Life; who am the Lord of Time and of the races of the earth that shall flock to my standard!'

And again: 'Lo! I am he that God was impotent to destroy because I had eaten of the fruit! He cannot control that which He hath created. He hath builded His temple upon His impotence, and it shall fall and crush Him. The children of his misrule cry out against Him. There is no God but Antichrist!'

Then from all sides came hurrying across the plain vast multitudes of the degenerate children of men, naked and unsightly; and they leaped and mouthed about the figure on the hillock, like hounds baying a dead fox held aloft; and from their swollen throats came one cry:

'There is no God but Antichrist!'

And thereat the figure turned about – and it was Cartaphilus the Jew.

VII

'There is no death! What seems so is transition.'

Uttering an incoherent cry, Rose came to himself with a shock of agony and staggered to his feet. In the act he traversed no neutral ground of insentient purposelessness. He caught the thread of being where he had dropped it – grasped it with an awful and sublime resolve that admitted no least thought of self-interest.

If his senses were for the moment amazed at their surroundings – the silence, the perfumed languor, the beauty and voluptuousness of the room – his soul, notwithstanding, stood intent, unfaltering – waiting merely the physical capacity for action.

The fragments of the broken vessel were scattered at his feet; the blood of his wound had hardened upon his face. He took a dizzy step forward, and another. The girl lay as he had seen her cast herself down – breathing, he could see; her hair in disorder; her hands clenched together in terror or misery beyond words.

Where was the other?

Suddenly his vision cleared. He saw that the silken curtains of the alcove were closed.

A poniard in a jewelled sheath lay, with other costly trifles, on a settle hard by. He seized and, drawing it, cast the scabbard clattering on the floor. His hands would have done; but this would work quicker.

Exhaling a quick sigh of satisfaction, he went forward with a noiseless rush and tore apart the curtains.

Yes – he was there – the Jew – the breathing enormity, stretched silent and motionless. The shadow of the young man's lifted arm ran across his white shirt front like a bar sinister.

To rid the world of something monstrous and abnormal – that was all Rose's purpose and desire. He leaned over to strike. The face, stiff and waxen as a corpse's, looked up into his with a calm impenetrable smile – looked up, for all its eyes were closed. And this was a horrible thing, that, though the features remained fixed in that one inexorable expression, something beneath them seemed alive and moving – something that clouded or revealed them, as when a sheet of paper glowing in the fire wavers between ashes and flame. Almost he could have thought that the soul, detached from its envelope, struggled to burst its way to the light.

An instant he dashed his left palm across his eyes; then shrieking, 'Let the fruit avail you now!' drove the steel deep into its neck with a snarl.

In the act, for all his frenzy, he had a horror of the spurting blood that he knew must foul his hand obscenely, and sprinkle his face, perhaps, as when a finger half plugs a flowing water-tap.

None came! The fearful white wound seemed to suck at the steel, making a puckered mouth of derision.

A thin sound, like the whinny of a dog, issued from Rose's lips. He pulled out the blade – it came with a crackling noise, as if it had been drawn through parchment.

Incredulous – mad – in an ecstasy of horror, he stabbed again and again. He might as fruitfully have struck at water. Then slashed and gaping wounds closed up so soon as he withdrew the steel, leaving not a scar.

With a scream he dashed the unstained weapon on the floor and sprang back into the room. He stumbled and almost fell over the prostrate figure of the girl.

A strength as of delirium stung and prickled in his arms. He stopped and forcibly raised her – held her against his breast – addressed her in a hurried passion of entreaty.

'In the name of God, come with me! In the name of God, divorce yourself from this horror! He is the abnormal – the deathless – the Antichrist!'

Her lids were closed; but she listened.

'Adnah, you have given me myself. My reason cannot endure the gift alone. Have mercy and be pitiful, and share the burden!'

At last she turned on him her swimming gaze.

'Oh! I am numbed and lost! What would you do with me?'

With a sob of triumph he wrapped his arms hard about her, and sought her lips with his. In the very moment of their meeting, she drew herself away, and stood panting and gazing with wide eyes over his shoulder. He turned.

A young man of elegant appearance was standing by the table where *he* had lately leaned.

In the face of the new-comer the animal and the fanatic were mingled, characteristics inseparable in pseudo-revelation.

He was unmistakably a Jew, of the finest primitive type – such as might have existed in preneurotic days. His complexion was of a smooth golden russet; his nose and lips were cut rather in the lines of sensuous cynicism; the look in his polished brown eyes was of defiant self-confidence, capable of the extremes of devotion or of obstinacy. Short curling black hair covered his scalp, and his moustache and small crisp beard were of the same hue.

'Thanks, stranger,' he said, in a somewhat nasal but musical voice. 'Your attack – a little cowardly, perhaps, for all its provocation – has served to release me before my time. Thanks – thanks indeed!'

Amos sent a sick and groping glance towards the alcove. The curtain was pulled back – the couch was empty. His vision returning, caught sight of Adnah still standing motionless.

'No, no!' he screeched in a suffocated voice, and clasped his hands convulsively.

There was an adoring expression in her wet eyes that grew and grew. In another moment she had thrown herself at the stranger's feet.

'Master,' she cried, in a rich and swooning voice: 'O Lord and Master – as blind love foreshadowed thee in these long months!'

He smiled down upon her.

'A tender welcome on the threshold,' he said softly, 'that I had almost renounced. The young spirit is weak to confirm the self-sacrifice of the old. But this ardent modern, Adnah, who, it seems, has slipped his opportunity?'

Passionately clasping the hands of the young Jew, she turned her face reluctant.

'He has blood on him,' she whispered. 'His lip is swollen like a schoolboy's with fighting. He is not a man, sane, self-reliant and glorious – like you, O my heart!'

The Jew gave a high, loud laugh, which he checked in mid-career.

'Sir,' he said derisively, 'we will wish you a very pleasant good-morning.'

How – under what pressure or by what process of self-effacement – he reached the street, Amos could never remember. His first sense of reality was in the stinging cold, which made him feel, by reaction, preposterously human.

It was perhaps six o'clock of a February morning, and the fog had thinned considerably, giving place to a wan and livid glow that was but half-measure of dawn.

He found himself going down the ringing pavement that was talcous with a sooty skin of ice, a single engrossing resolve hammering time in his brain to his footsteps.

The artificial glamour was all past and gone – beaten and frozen out of him. The rest was to do – his plain duty as a Christian, as a citizen – above all, as a gentleman. He was, unhypnotized, a law-abiding young man, with a hatred of notoriety and a detestation of the abnormal. Unquestionably his forebears had made a huge muddle of his inheritance.

About a quarter to seven he walked (rather unsteadily) into Vine Street Police Station and accosted the inspector on duty.

'I want to lay an information.'

The officer scrutinised him, professionally, from the under side, and took up a pen.

'What's the charge?'

'Administering a narcotic, attempted murder, abduction, profanity, trading under false pretences, wandering at large – great heavens! what isn't it?'

'Perhaps you'll say. Name of accused?'

'Cartaphilus.'

'Any other?'

'The Wandering Jew.'

The Inspector laid down his pen and leaned forward, bridging his finger-tips under his chin.

'If you take my advice,' he said, 'you'll go and have a Turkish bath.'

The young man gasped and frowned.

'You won't take my information?'

'Not in that form. Come again by-and-by.'

Amos walked straight out of the building and retraced his steps to Wardour Street.

'I'll watch for his coming out,' he thought, 'and have him arrested, on one charge only, by the constable on the beat. Where's the place?'

Twice he walked the length of the street and back, with dull increasing amazement. The sunlight had edged its way into the fog by this time, and every door and window stood out sleek and self-evident. But amongst them all was none that corresponded to the door or window of his adventure.

He hung about till day was bright in the air, and until it occurred to him that his woeful and bloodstained appearance was beginning to excite unflattering comment. At that he trudged for the third time the entire length to and fro, and so coming out into Oxford Street stood on the edge of the pavement, as though it were the brink of Cocytus.

'Well, she called me a boy,' he muttered; 'what does it matter?'

He hailed an early hansom and jumped in.

The Vengeance Of The Dead

ROBERT BARR

Robert Barr (1850–1912) took up writing after an early career as a schoolmaster and a reporter and it was as an author that he achieved lasting success.

Born in Glasgow, Barr emigrated to Canada with his parents at the age of four. He must have been a bright child; he became headmaster of a public school in Windsor, Ontario, in his teens, and then hopped just over the border to Detroit, America, where he became a reporter on that city's Free Press. *Barr was very successful on the paper, so much so that it sent him to England in 1881 to establish a British edition. Whatever happened to that British edition is uncertain, but one thing is for sure: Barr liked his country of origin so much he decided to stay, and set about building his own publishing concern.*

His first book of stories, STRANGE HAPPENINGS *(1883), appeared under the name Luke Sharp, Barr's journalistic* nom-de-plume, *and from then on he produced many short stories, mostly detective fiction but with the occasional (and welcome) macabre work among them. He founded, with Jerome K. Jerome,* The Idler *magazine in 1892, which ran for over eighteen years, until Barr's retirement.*

Barr's most quoted work is THE TRIUMPHS OF EUGENE VALMONT *(1906), reputed to be the inspiration for Agatha Christie's Hercule Poirot. Certainly, his detective stories have received wider reprinting than his tales of terror. But these lesser-known works were just as good, as this story will show, I hope. It comes from* REVENGE! *(1896), a fine set of stories all amply explained by the book's title. This particular piece of revenge is probably the most peculiar of the book, but neat and enjoyable all the same.*

ROBERT BARR

The Vengeance of the Dead

It is a bad thing for a man to die with an unsatisfied thirst for revenge parching his soul. David Allen died, cursing Bernard Heaton and lawyer Grey; hating the lawyer who had won the case even more than the man who was to gain by the winning. Yet if cursing were to be done, David should rather have cursed his own stubbornness and stupidity.

To go back for some years, this is what had happened. Squire Heaton's only son went wrong. The squire raged, as was natural. He was one of a long line of hard-drinking, hard-riding, hard-swearing squires, and it was maddening to think that his only son should deliberately take to books and cold water, when there was manly sport on the countryside and old wine in the cellar. Yet before now such blows have descended upon deserving men, and they have to be borne as best they may. Squire Heaton bore it badly, and when his son went off on a Government scientific expedition around the world the squire drank harder and swore harder than ever, but never mentioned the boy's name.

Two years after, young Heaton returned, but the doors of the Hall were closed against him. He had no mother to plead for him, although it was not likely that would have made any difference, for the squire was not a man to be appealed to and swayed this way or that. He took his hedges, his drinks, and his course in life straight. The young man went to India, where he was drowned. As there is no mystery in this matter, it may as well be stated here that young Heaton ultimately returned to England, as drowned men have ever been in the habit of doing, when their return will mightily inconvenience innocent persons who have taken their places. It is a disputed question whether the sudden disappearance of a man, or his reappearance after a lapse of years, is the more annoying.

If the old squire felt remorse at the supposed death of his only son he did not show it. The hatred which had been directed against his unnatural offspring redoubled itself and was bestowed on his nephew David Allen, who was now the legal heir to the estate and its income. Allen was the impecunious son of the squire's sister who had married badly. It is hard to starve when one is heir to a fine property, but that is what David did, and it soured him. The Jews would not lend on the security – the son might return – so David Allen waited for a dead man's shoes, impoverished and embittered.

At last the shoes were ready for him to step into. The old squire died as a gentleman should, of apoplexy, in his armchair, with a decanter at his elbow; David Allen entered into his belated inheritance, and his first act was to discharge every servant, male and female, about the place and engage others who owed their situations to him alone. Then were the Jews sorry they had not trusted him.

He was now rich but broken in health, with bent shoulders, without a friend on the earth. He was a man suspicious of all the world, and he had a furtive look over his shoulder as if he expected Fate to deal him a sudden blow – as indeed it did.

It was a beautiful June day, when there passed the porter's lodge and walked up the avenue to the main entrance of the Hall a man whose face was bronzed by a torrid sun. He requested speech with the master and was asked into a room to wait.

At length David Allen shuffled in, with his bent shoulders, glaring at the intruder from under his bushy eyebrows. The stranger rose as he entered and extended his hand.

'You don't know me, of course. I believe we have never met before. I am your cousin.'

Allen ignored the outstretched hand.

'I have no cousin,' he said.

'I am Bernard Heaton, the son of your uncle.'

'Bernard Heaton is dead.'

'I beg your pardon, he is not. I ought to know, for I tell you I am he.'

'You lie!'

Heaton, who had been standing since his cousin's entrance, now sat down again, Allen remaining on his feet.

'Look here,' said the new-comer. 'Civility costs nothing –'

'I cannot be civil to an impostor.'

'Quite so. It *is* difficult. Still, if I am an impostor, civility can do no harm, while if it should turn out that I am not an impostor, then your present tone may make after arrangements all the harder upon you. Now will you oblige me by sitting down? I dislike, while sitting myself, talking to a standing man.'

'Will you oblige me by stating what you want before I order my servants to turn you out?'

'I see you are going to be hard on yourself. I will endeavour to keep my temper, and if I succeed it will be a triumph for a member of our family. I am to state what I want? I will. I want as my own the three rooms on the first floor of the south wing – the rooms communicating with each other. You perceive I at least know the house. I want my meals served there, and I wish to be undisturbed at all hours. Next, I desire that you settle upon me, say, five hundred a year – or six hundred – out of the revenues of the estate. I am engaged in scientific research of a peculiar kind. I can make money, of course, but I wish my mind left entirely free from financial worry. I shall not interfere with your enjoyment of the estate in the least.'

'I'll wager you will not. So you think I am fool enough to harbour and feed the first idle vagabond that comes along and claims to be my dead cousin. Go to the courts with your story and be imprisoned as similar perjurers have been.'

'Of course I don't expect you to take my word for it. If you were any judge of human nature you would see I am not a vagabond. Still that's neither here nor there. Choose three of your own friends. I will lay my proofs before them, and abide by their decision. Come, nothing could be fairer than that, now could it?'

'Go to the courts, I tell you.'

'Oh certainly. But only as a last resort. No wise man goes to law if there is another course open. But what is the use of taking such an absurd position? You *know* I'm your cousin. I'll take you blindfold into every room in the place.'

'Any discharged servant could do that. I have had enough of you. I am not a man to be blackmailed. Will you leave the house yourself, or shall I call the servants to put you out?'

'I should be sorry to trouble you,' said Heaton, rising. 'That is your last word, I take it?'

'Absolutely.'

'Then good-bye. We shall meet at Philippi.'

Allen watched him disappear down the avenue, and it dimly occurred to him that he had not acted diplomatically.

Heaton went directly to lawyer Grey, and laid the case before him. He told the lawyer what his modest demands were, and gave instructions that if, at any time before the suit came off, his cousin would compromise, an arrangement avoiding publicity should be arrived at.

'Excuse me for saying that looks like weakness,' remarked the lawyer.

'I know it does,' answered Heaton. 'But my case is so strong that I can afford to have it appear weak.'

The lawyer shook his head. He knew how uncertain the law was. But he soon discovered that no compromise was possible.

The case came to trial, and the verdict was entirely in favour of Bernard Heaton.

The pallor of death spread over the sallow face of David Allen as he realized that he was once again a man without a penny or a foot of land. He left the court with bowed head, speaking no word to those who had defended him. Heaton hurried after him, overtaking him on the pavement.

'I knew this had to be the result,' he said to the defeated man. 'No other outcome was possible. I have no desire to cast you penniless into the street. What you refused to me I shall be glad to offer you. I will make the annuity a thousand pounds.'

Allen, trembling, darted one look of malignant hate at his cousin.

'You successful scoundrel!' he cried. 'You and your villainous confederate Grey. I tell you — '

The blood rushed to his mouth; he fell upon the pavement and died. One and the same day had robbed him of his land and his life.

Bernard Heaton deeply regretted the tragic issue, but went on with his researches at the Hall, keeping much to himself. Lawyer Grey, who had won renown by his conduct of the celebrated case, was almost his only friend. To him Heaton partially disclosed his hopes, told what he had learned during those years he had been lost to the world in India, and claimed that if he succeeded in combining the occultism of the East with the science of the West, he would make for himself a name of imperishable renown.

The lawyer, a practical man of the world, tried to persuade Heaton to abandon his particular line of research, but without success.

'No good can come of it,' said Grey. 'India has spoiled you. Men who dabble too much in that sort of thing go mad. The brain is a delicate instrument. Do not trifle with it.'

'Nevertheless,' persisted Heaton, 'the great discoveries of the twentieth century are going to be in that line, just as the great discoveries of the nineteenth century have been in the direction of electricity.'

'The cases are not parallel. Electricity is a tangible substance.'

'Is it? Then tell me what it is composed of? We all know how it is generated, and we know partly what it will do, but what *is* it?'

'I shall have to charge you six-and-eightpence for answering that question,' the lawyer had said with a laugh. 'At any rate there is a good deal to be discovered about electricity yet. Turn your attention to that and leave this Indian nonsense alone.'

Yet, astonishing as it may seem, Bernard Heaton, to his undoing, succeeded, after many futile attempts – several times narrowly escaping death. Inventors and discoverers have to risk their lives as often as soldiers, with less chance of worldly glory.

First his invisible excursions were confined to the house and his own grounds, then he went further afield, and to his intense astonishment one day he met the spirit of the man who hated him.

'Ah,' said David Allen, 'you did not live long to enjoy your ill-gotten gains.'

'You are as wrong in this sphere of existence as you were in the other. I am not dead.'

'Then why are you here and in this shape?'

'I suppose there is no harm in telling *you*. What I wanted to discover, at the time you would not give me a hearing, was how to separate the spirit from its servant, the body – that is, temporarily and not finally. My body is at this moment lying apparently asleep in a locked room in my house – one of the rooms I begged from you. In an hour or two I shall return and take possession of it.'

'And how do you take possession of it and quit it?'

Heaton, pleased to notice the absence of that rancour which had formerly been Allen's most prominent characteristic, and feeling that any information given to a disembodied spirit was safe as far as the world was concerned, launched out on the subject that possessed his whole mind.

'It is very interesting,' said Allen, when he had finished.

And so they parted.

David Allen at once proceeded to the Hall, which he had not seen since the day he left it to attend the trial. He passed quickly through the familiar apartments until he entered the locked room on the first floor of the south wing. There on the bed lay the body of Heaton, most of the colour gone from the face, but breathing regularly, if almost imperceptibly, like a mechanical wax-figure.

If a watcher had been in the room, he would have seen the colour slowly return to the face and the sleeper gradually awaken, at last rising from the bed.

Allen, in the body of Heaton, at first felt very uncomfortable, as a man does who puts on an ill-fitting suit of clothes. The limitations caused by the wearing of a body also discommoded him. He looked carefully around the room. It was plainly furnished. A desk in the corner he found contained the MS. of a book prepared for the printer, all executed with the neat accuracy of a scientific man. Above the desk, pasted against the wall, was a sheet of paper headed:

'What to do if I am found here apparently dead.' Underneath were plainly written instructions. It was evident that Heaton had taken no one into his confidence.

It is well if you go in for revenge to make it as complete as possible. Allen gathered up the MS., placed it in the grate, and set a match to it. Thus he at once destroyed his enemy's chances of posthumous renown, and also removed evidence that might, in certain contingencies, prove Heaton's insanity.

Unlocking the door, he proceeded down the stairs, where he met a servant who told him luncheon was ready. He noticed that the servant was one whom he had discharged, so he came to the conclusion that Heaton had taken back all the old retainers who had applied to him when the result of the trial became public.

Before lunch was over he saw that some of his own servants were also there still.

'Send the gamekeeper to me,' said Allen to the servant.

Brown came in, who had been on the estate for twenty years continuously, with the exception of the few months after Allen had packed him off.

'What pistols have I, Brown?'

'Well, sir, there's the old squire's duelling pistols, rather out of date, sir; then your own pair and that American revolver.'

'Is the revolver in working order?'

'Oh yes, sir,'

'Then bring it to me and some cartridges.'

When Brown returned with the revolver his master took it and examined it.

'Be careful, sir,' said Brown anxiously. 'You know it's a self-cocker, sir.'

'A what?'

'A self-cocking revolver, sir' – trying to repress his astonishment at the question his master asked about a weapon with which he should have been familiar.

'Show me what you mean,' said Allen, handing back the revolver.

Brown explained that the mere pulling of the trigger fired the weapon.

'Now shoot at the end window – never mind the glass. Don't stand gaping at me, do as I tell you.'

Brown fired the revolver, and a diamond pane snapped out of the window.

'How many times will that shoot without re-loading?'

'Seven times, sir.'

'Very good. Put in a cartridge for the one you fired and leave the revolver with me. Find out when there is a train to town, and let me know.'

It will be remembered that the dining-room incident was used at the trial, but without effect, as going to show that Bernard Heaton was insane. Brown also testified that there was something queer about his master that day.

David Allen found all the money he needed in the pockets of Bernard Heaton. He caught his train, and took a cab from the station directly to the law offices of Messrs. Grey, Leason, and Grey, anxious to catch the lawyer before he left for the day.

The clerk sent up word that Mr. Heaton wished to see the senior Mr. Grey for a few moments. Allen was asked to walk up.

'You know the way, sir,' said the clerk.

Allen hesitated.

'Announce me, if you please.'

The clerk, being well trained, showed no surprise, but led the visitor to Mr. Grey's door.

'How are you, Heaton?' said the lawyer cordially. 'Take a chair. Where have you been keeping yourself this long time? How are the Indian experiments coming on?'

'Admirably, admirably,' answered Allen.

At the sound of his voice the lawyer looked up quickly, then apparently reassured he said – 'You're not looking quite the same. Been keeping yourself too much indoors, I imagine. You ought to quit research and do some shooting this autumn.'

'I intend to, and I hope then to have your company.'

'I shall be pleased to run down, although I am no great hand at a gun.'

'I want to speak with you a few moments in private. Would you mind locking the door so that we may not be interrupted?'

'We are quite safe from interruption here,' said the lawyer, as he turned the key in the lock; then resuming his seat he added, 'Nothing serious, I hope?'

'It is rather serious. Do you mind my sitting here?' asked Allen, as he drew up his chair so that he was between Grey and the door, with the table separating them. The lawyer was watching him with anxious face, but without, as yet, serious apprehension.

'Now,' said Allen, 'will you answer me a simple question? To whom are you talking?'

'To whom –?' The lawyer in his amazement could get no further.

'Yes. To whom are you talking? Name him.'

'Heaton, what is the matter with you? Are you ill?'

'Well, you have mentioned a name, but, being a villain and a lawyer, you cannot give a direct answer to a very simple question. You think you are talking to that poor fool Bernard Heaton. It is true that the body you are staring at is Heaton's body, but the man you are talking to is me – David Allen – the man you swindled and then murdered. Sit down. If you move you are a dead man. Don't try to edge to the door. There are seven deaths in this revolver and the whole seven can be let loose in less than that many seconds, for this is a self-cocking instrument. Now it will take you at least ten seconds to get to the door, so remain exactly where you are. That advice will strike you as wise, even if, as you think, you have to do with a madman. You asked me a minute ago how the Indian experiments were coming on, and I answered "Admirably." Bernard Heaton left his body this morning, and I, David Allen, am now in possession of it. Do you understand? I admit it is a little difficult for the legal mind to grasp such a situation.'

'Ah, not at all,' said Grey airily. 'I comprehend it perfectly. The man I see before me is the spirit, life, soul, whatever you like to call it – of David Allen in the body of my friend Bernard Heaton. The – ah – essence of my friend is at this moment fruitlessly searching for his missing body. Perhaps he is in this room now, not knowing how to get out a spiritual writ of ejectment against you.'

'You show more quickness than I expected of you,' said Allen.

'Thanks,' rejoined Grey, although he said to himself, 'Heaton has gone mad! stark staring mad, as I expected he would. He is armed. The situation is becoming dangerous. I must humour him.'

'Thanks. And now may I ask what you propose to do? You have not come here for legal advice. You never, unluckily for me, were a client of mine.'

'No. I did not come either to give or take advice. I am here, alone with you – you gave orders that we were not to be disturbed, remember – for the sole purpose of revenging myself on you and on Heaton. Now listen, for the scheme will commend itself to your ingenious mind. I shall murder you in this room. I shall then give myself up. I shall vacate this body in Newgate prison and your friend may then resume his tenancy or not as he chooses. He may allow the unoccupied body to die in the cell or he may take possession of it and be hanged for murder. Do you appreciate the completeness of my vengeance on you both? Do you think your friend will care to put on his body again?'

'It is a nice question,' said the lawyer, as he edged his chair imperceptibly along and tried to grope behind himself, unperceived by his visitor, for the electric button placed against the wall. 'It is a nice question, and I would like to have time to consider it in all its bearings before I gave an answer.'

'You shall have all the time you care to allow yourself. I am in no hurry, and I wish you to realize your situation as completely as possible. Allow me to say that the electric button is a little to the left and slightly above where you are feeling for it. I merely mention this because I must add, in fairness to you, that the moment you touch it, time ends as far as you are concerned. When you press the ivory button, I fire.'

The lawyer rested his arms on the table before him, and for the first time a hunted look of alarm came into his eyes, which died out of them when, after a moment or two of intense fear, he regained possession of himself.

'I would like to ask you a question or two,' he said at last.

'As many as you choose. I am in no hurry, as I said before.'

'I am thankful for your reiteration of that. The first question is then: has a temporary residence in another sphere interfered in any way with your reasoning powers?'

'I think not.'

'Ah, I had hoped that your appreciation of logic might have improved during your – well, let us say absence; you were not very logical – not very amenable to reason, formerly,'

'I know you thought so.'

'I did; so did your own legal adviser, by the way. Well, now let me ask why you are so bitter against me? Why not murder the judge who charged against you, or the jury that unanimously gave a verdict in our favour? I was merely an instrument, as were they.

'It was your devilish trickiness that won the case.'

'That statement is flattering but untrue. The case was its own best advocate. But you haven't answered the question. Why not murder judge and jury?'

'I would gladly do so if I had them in my power. You see, I am perfectly logical.'

'Quite, quite,' said the lawyer. 'I am encouraged to proceed.

Now of what did my devilish trickiness rob you?"

'Of my property, and then of my life.'

'I deny both allegations, but will for the sake of the argument admit them for the moment. First, as to your property. It was a possession that might at any moment be jeopardized by the return of Bernard Heaton.'

'By the *real* Bernard Heaton — yes.'

'Very well then. As you are now repossessed of the property, and as you have the outward semblance of Heaton, your rights cannot be questioned. As far as property is concerned you are now in an unassailable position where formerly you were in an assailable one. Do you follow me?'

'Perfectly.'

'We come (second) to the question of life. You then occupied a body frail, bent, and diseased, a body which, as events showed, gave way under exceptional excitement. You are now in a body strong and healthy, with apparently a long life before it. You admit the truth of all I have said on these two points?'

'I quite admit it.'

'Then to sum up, you are now in a better position – infinitely – both as regards life and property, than the one from which my malignity – ingenuity I think was your word – ah, yes – trickiness – thanks – removed you. Now why cut your career short? Why murder *me?* Why not live out your life, under better conditions, in luxury and health, and thus be completely revenged on Bernard Heaton? If you are logical, now is the time to show it.'

Allen rose slowly, holding the pistol in his right hand.

'You miserable scoundrel!' he cried. 'You pettifogging lawyer – tricky to the last! How gladly you would throw over your friend to prolong your own wretched existence! Do you think you are now talking to a biased judge and a susceptible, brainless jury? Revenged on Heaton? I *am* revenged on him already. But part of my vengeance involves your death. Are you ready for it?'

Allen pointed the revolver at Grey, who had now also risen, his face ashen. He kept his eyes fastened on the man he believed to be mad. His hand crept along the wall. There was intense silence between them. Allen did not fire. Slowly the lawyer's hand moved towards the electric button. At last he felt the ebony rim and his fingers quickly covered it. In the stillness, the vibrating ring of an electric bell somewhere below was audible. Then the sharp crack of the revolver suddenly split the silence. The lawyer dropped on one knee, holding his arm in the air as if to ward off attack. Again the revolver rang out, and Grey plunged forward on his face. The other five shots struck a lifeless body.

A stratum of blue smoke hung breast high in the room as if it were the departing soul of the man who lay motionless on the floor. Outside were excited voices, and someone flung himself ineffectually against the stout locked door.

Allen crossed the room and, turning the key, flung open the door. 'I have murdered your master,' he said, handing the revolver butt forward to the nearest man. 'I give myself up. Go and get an officer.'

The Beckside Boggle

ALICE REA

As always when compiling these Victorian volumes, I come up against authors of whom, at this late date, it is impossible to find out any details. Alice Rea, alas, is one of them. All we know of Miss (or Mrs?) Rea is that she published two books, DALE FOLK, a three-volume novel in 1895, and THE BECKSIDE BOGGLE (1886), of which this is the title story. The latter volume consists of stories of the Lake District, with much local dialect which suggests Miss Rea knew the area. Of the lady herself, we can only judge by the quality of the work and I think you'll like this one. It starts off in leisurely tone but ends in horror. Miss Rea obviously liked her meat with blood in it.

ALICE REA

The Beckside Boggle

But few of the ordinary lake country visitors will be aware of the existence of the small valley which is the scene of this story or tradition. It is a quiet, narrow little dale, situated at the foot of Scawfell, on the west side. Pedestrian tourists, crossing by the mountain track from Eskdale to Wastdale, leave it unnoticed. The black tarn at one side, and the giant fells around, with the treacherous bog beneath their feet, absorb their whole attention. But, to those who do know it, the little dale has an interest all its own.

A quiet hush pervades the place, different from the undisturbed silence of the wild fells above. There is an air of sadness in its solitude, and as you emerge from the narrow gorge, which forms its head, and follow the sheep track by the beckside, where trees and fields and signs of man appear, the riddle is solved. It is no unexplored nook of Nature's own keeping, but a once populous little dale, now forsaken and deserted. Here and there you stumble over heaps of stones – all that remains of what was once a cluster of rude cottages, inhabited, perhaps, in the days when the great peat-bog that surrounds the tarn above was a part of the vast forest of Eskdale and Wastdale.

Further still down the dale a few yards of double walling remain to remind us of the ancient pack-horse road to Kendal.

Between these low walls, when our grandfathers were young, did the gallant bell-horses of nursery lore and their patient followers trot with their heavy packs, eager to rest their weary limbs in the hospitable stable of the 'Nanny Horns.' Of this once busy house of entertainment for man and beast, one gable and a weed-grown garden alone remain.

Before we reach the ruins of the 'Nanny Horns,' however, we come to more hopeful signs of habitation. Here, by the beckside, stands a small farmhouse, with barn, cowhouse, and stable complete. A rude stone bridge spans the stream, and large trees

wave solemnly overhead. But one look at the house, and the
sense of desolation becomes stronger than before. The closed
door, the blank stare of the window-frames, the grass-grown
pavement, tell the same story of desertion.

But here it comes more closely to one's heart. The old dale
folk still speak of the time when this home was alive and busy; we
ourselves can almost remember when the smoke curled from its
wide chimneys; and now it, too, belongs to the past.

Let us push open the creaking door and look around. Before
us is a short passage, ending in a stone staircase; on the left we
see a small ceiled room, evidently the old parlour or bedroom.

It is quite empty and covered with fallen plaster. To the right
is the kitchen. The sun shines brightly through the two glassless
windows. A wide, open fireplace occupies the greater part of the
end of the room opposite the door. Facing the window are the
entrances of the pantry and dairy. In one corner, clearly a fixture
in the wall, there is an old oak cupboard – one shaky door hangs
by a single hinge, and in it we may still see an old brass lock.

The most striking piece of furniture, however, if furniture we
may name it, is a long freestone slab, or sconce, as dale folk call
it, firmly fixed into the wall by the fireplace, which must have
made a comfortable fireside couch in olden times, when a huge
fire burned in the now empty grate, when the good-wife spun in
the opposite corner, and the good-man carded wool in the
armchair by her side.

Let us take our seat now upon the sconce, while I tell you the
story of this last desertion, for around this slab of stone the whole
tradition clings.

We need fear no interruption, for few of our neighbours
would care to take our place, or, indeed, let a setting sun, such as
we now see shining on the opposite fells, find them within a good
quarter of a mile of this spot, for fear that their terror should
suddenly take shape, and reveal to them the form of the
Headless Woman of Beckside. There, the secret is out – the
house is haunted.

Many years ago Beckside was inhabited by a man and his wife of
the name of Southward – Joe and Ann Southward. They had
been farm servants in their youth, and, being in the main sober,

industrious folks, had each saved up a nice little sum of money; so when it just happened that they were both out of situation at the same time, they thought they could not do better than put their two little nest-eggs together. They therefore got married and settled down on this small farm. At this time neither of them was very young, and for several years they had no child; but at last Heaven blessed them with a son, and the whole course of their somewhat monotonous life was changed. I believe there was not to be found in any of the surrounding dales so happy a little family as theirs. They had few wants their farm could not supply, good health, and but one ambition – namely, to save as much money as ever they could to get their son a better start in life than they had had themselves. So they lived on as little as possible, and worked and hoarded until they had a very fair amount put away in an old teapot in the cupboard by the door. Upon the cupboard Joe put a strong lock – a very rare thing in a farm-house in those days – for he was sadly afraid of any harm or loss happening to his little store.

One autumn Joe Southward had to leave home for a whole day, and hardly expected to be back before the next morning, for he was going to Whitehaven on business. Such a thing had never happened before, although they had been married eight years.

'Thu mun cum back heam as seun as thu can, Joe,' his wife said, as he mounted his horse, 'and thu mun mind an' not cau at ower mony public hooses on t' way back' – for though Joe was by no means in the habit of getting drunk, still he had been known to return home now and again from the Eskdale fair, or an occasional sale, just a little more excited than usual, and Ann feared lest in the unwonted dissipation of seeing Whitehaven – a place he had visited only once before, and of which he had told her grand tales – and in the excitement of spending a whole day, and perhaps a night, from home, he might be led on from one extravagance to another.

'Oh, aye, lass, ah'll coom heam as seun as iver ah can git, but thoo mun nut bide up for me efter nine be t' clock. If ah's nut heam be than, ah'll be stoppen feu t'neet at Santon or sum udder spot, maybe t' Crag.'

'Varra weel,' replied his wife, 'ah'll nut waste t' candle biden up for thee – good-bye. Hes thee got tha muny safe? Ah wish thoo wad let me set a stitch in thee breeches pocket to keep folks' hands oot. Ah've heerd tell on a man 'at went t' Whitehebben who had ivery thing 'at ever he had taken oot uv his pocket, an' he kent nowt aboot it whatever.'

'Oh, aye, they're queerish-like folk thear, ah ken, but ah'll nut heve me pockets sowed up. Hoo does te think ah cud pay t' tolls, lass? Gie thee fadder a kiss, Joe, me lad. Noo mind thoo tak's care o' the sell, me lass. Cum up, Charlie,' and he set off at a steady pace on his heavy brown horse over the little stone bridge and down the valley.

Ann, taking her child, a strong little fellow of fifteen months, in her arms, followed her husband as far as the bridge, and stood watching him till he was out of sight, and then, turning back, re-entered the kitchen. There was not much time for her to waste that day, for they had killed a sheep for their winter supply of meat, and Joe had cut it up the day before, ready for salting; so what with that and her ordinary work, and a good many extra things that generally fell to Joe's share, the afternoon was nearly over before she had time to think of her loneliness. But when she had finished cleaning her kitchen and made up the peat fire to boil her kettle she felt a great want of something she could not exactly tell what.

So long as she had been making plenty of noise herself she had never noticed the unusual quiet around her, but now, as she sat to rest for a moment or two in the armchair, not a sound was to be heard but the tick tock of the clock. Joe the younger was asleep. She longed intensely for something other than herself to break the silence.

Just as it was becoming insupportable a little bantam cock in the yard gave a shrill crow, and Ann heaved a great sigh of relief as she heard it.

'Dear, dear,' she thought, 'I dunna ken what's coom ore me, but I do feel lonesome-like someway. Folks 'ud say as I was feelin' t' want o' Joe, but him and me is nut o' that mak' to be sae daft-like. Not but what he's weel enough, an' when yar's lived wi' yan body for seven, going on eight, year, and scarce iver seed any udder body, you, maybe, do feel a bit queer like when they gangs off. I mind when I was servant lass at Crag there was a girt black cat as allus followed me ivery spot where iver I was at, but it got catcht in t' trap wun day. I quite felt t' loss o' it for a bit. I was short o' summut for a day or two, and I's sure 'twas no for love on't, for it hed nowt to crack on in t' way o' leuks. It had lost half on t' tail in t' trap afore, and its ears were maist riven off wi' feetin', yet I quite miste it loike. Now,' she continued, rising, 'I's just wesh me and lash me hair, then when I's had me sup o' milk and bread, and finished t' milking, I's melt down all that sheep fat and git a lock o' seives[1] peeled ready for dipping. I mun mak a lock o' candles this back end.'

By the time the cows were milked and Ann had had her sup of milk and bread (tea of course was not known in these parts in those days), and 'lal Joe' had been put comfortably to sleep in his clumsy wooden cradle, the sun had nearly set, and Ann crossed the yard to the little bridge to see if there was any sign of her husband returning home.

The valley looked very beautiful, lit up by the last rays of the setting sun, which was dipping behind the shoulder of the Screes.

At the head of the dale Scawfell stood out bold and broad, bathed from base to summit in the glowing light, while the purple heather and golden bracken of the surrounding hills gave a warmth of colour to the scene which made it very lovely to behold.

Ann, however, regarded neither gold nor purple, light nor shade, but, turning her back to the king of the valley, Old Father Scawfell, gazed rather longingly (though she would on no account have owned to the feeling) along the rough fell road, which wound by the side of the beck towards the open country. There she stood, her fingers busily engaged knitting a blue wool stocking for her husband, and her eyes fixed upon the road, till the sun, entirely disappearing, left the valley in a hazy shade, and the light, gradually retreating up the fell-sides, robbed the brackens and heather of their glory as it bid them good-night.

Just as she was slowly leaving the bridge she happened to turn her eyes to the Screes side of the valley, and there she was sure she saw some one advancing towards her, yet not quite towards Beckside itself, for the person, whoever it might be, was coming

[1]Rushes

along the old pack-horse road from Keswick, which crossed the dale half way between Beckside and Bakerstead, the next little farm, then without a tenant.

At the point where the old road passes the two houses, stood the 'Nanny Horns,' which was, even at the time I am telling you of, quite a ruin; but the garden belonging to it kept Ann supplied with gooseberries and rhubarb all the summer and spring.

It was when passing this ruin that the person disappeared. For some time Ann stood watching. Presently the figure emerged from the ruin and advanced quickly towards her. She could distinguish now that it was a woman, and that she seemed very tired. As soon as Ann perceived she was making direct for her house she went back and shut the door, for she did not at all like to have a stranger calling at that time of the evening when she was alone.

She had hardly turned from the door and crossed the kitchen towards the fireplace before she felt a shadow pass the window, and, turning suddenly round, she caught a glimpse of a muffled-up face peeping through. It was withdrawn immediately, and at the same moment there was a sharp tap at the door. Going to the window, she could see the woman knocking with a good stout stick. Ann opened the door and asked her what she wanted, rather sharply.

'If you please,' said the woman, 'can you give a poor body a night's lodgings? I's coom a lang way, and I's tired to death. I could na walk another mile to save me life, my feet are that cut wi' t' stones.' And she showed her boots, all burst out and cut, and her swollen feet, which were seen through them.

'Weel, ye ma' coom in,' Ann said at last, though with no very good grace. 'I suppose there's na place else ye could gang til to neet. Where's ta coom fra? Tha' none fra these parts, I reckon.'

'Na,' she answered, seating herself on a bench that ran along by the table under the window. 'Na, I's a Scotchwoman, and I coom fra Penrith. I's going to Ulverstone to see my son; he's got a gude bit o' wark there; I kent some folks in Borrowdale, so I came this way, but I did na ken it wad be sic a road as it is.'

'It's a terrible bad road you've coomt, and ye look real tired out, but draw up to t' fire now ye is here,' Ann said, feeling more kindly disposed when she heard the stranger had friends in

Borrowdale, for her own people came from there. 'Will ye not take yer shawl off, when ye're sae near t' fire?' she asked; for the woman had a small woollen shawl which she kept pinned over her head and the lower part of her face.

'Na, na, if ye'll excuse me,' she answered, 'I's got a bad pain in my teeth, and this warm shawl makes it a wee bit better.'

'It's a nasty loike thing is toothache,' said Ann: 'I niver hed it mysel', but I mind my maister had a spell on't once, and he were fairly driven half daft we' it.'

'Your maister's not at home, maybe,' the woman suggested, looking round the room.

Ann thought her eyes rested longer than they need have done on the cupboard, in the door of which the new lock showed rather conspicuously.

'Oh, yes,' she answered, 'he's been off t'day, but I should nut wonder if he be home gaily seune.'

Ann was very soon busy preparing the fat of the sheep they had killed for melting down to make candles and rushlights for their winter store.

First she brought in a very large three-legged pan and swung it upon the crook in the chimney, then a basket of peat and a good bundle of sticks, which she put down by the hearth, so that she might keep the fire well up under her pan without having to go out again in the dark. She next asked the woman if she would have a 'sup o' poddidge' with her, for she meant to take hers while the fat was melting; but, to her surprise, the woman declined, alleging as a reason that her teeth ached so badly, anything hot would drive her wild.

She took a handful of oat-cake, however, and munched away at that as well as she could under her shawl.

It had now grown quite dark outside – indeed it was after eight o'clock, very nearly nine – but the kitchen looked bright and cheerful by the light of the fire.

'I canna offer ye a bed,' Ann said to her visitor, as she poured out her milk porridge, 'but ye mun choose whether ye had rather sleep in t' barn or t' hayloft.'

'Weel, since ye are sae kind,' she answered, 'wad ye mind if I slept here on this sconce? It will be nice and warm by the fire, and I'm that tired I's niver ken whether it be hard or soft.'

'Aye, weel,' said Ann, 'thee can sleep thear if thee's a mind to, but I's likely keep ye awake a bit. I wants to git all this fat melt down, all what's in t' pan and on this dish too; and, to tell t' truth, I don't think as Joe wad be sae weel pleased to see ony strange body sleeping here when he comes heam.'

'Oh,' she continued, 'I'd sune get up and away into the barn if he came hame; but it's ower late for him to be coming now, is it not?' And she looked keenly over at Ann, who was standing stirring her porridge, to cool it, by the table.

'Ye mun feel lonesome when your guid-man is away. Does he often go off?'

'Noa,' answered Ann, 'we hev been married seven, gaan on eight, year, and he's niver been away a neet afore.'

'Weel, he mun be a steady fellow; you'll be a fine saving couple. I should no wonder if you have a tidy bit of money laid by somewhere for that little chap?' pointing to the cradle where little Joe was sleeping soundly. 'He's as fine a little laddie as iver I saw, and a good one too, or he'd wake up wi' our talking.'

'That is he,' replied Ann, her mother's heart warming at the praise of her son. 'We wad like him to hev a better start in life than we hed oursels.'

'Why you seem to have done varra weel,' said the woman, 'as far as I can see. I wad na mind changing places wi' ye,' she added, with a disagreeable laugh and another look round the room. 'You've a deal o' good furniture, and there's, maybe, summut worth having in that cupboard, that ye lock it up so close. I don't often see a cupboard wi' a lock like that in a farm kitchen.'

'Don't ye?' said Ann, sharply, for she thought the woman was getting rather too familiar. 'We locks our cupboards because we likes to keep our things to oursels. There's no knowing what mak o' folk may come tramping over t' fell.' And she looked significantly at her visitor.

'Weel,' the woman said, 'if you've no objections I'll just lay me down and try to get a bit o' sleep; I mun be off sune in the morning.'

'Well, then,' said Ann, 'I'll git the a bit o' hay to put under thee head.' And she went out to the barn.

Hardly had she left the room, when the woman seized her

half-empty basin and took a good drink of her porridge, and then replaced it as it was on the table.

'Theer,' said Ann, as she returned with a good bundle of hay and spread it on the sconce, 'that'll be a gay bit softer than the freestone.'

She then went to the little parlour where she and her husband slept, and brought thence an old shawl, which she handed to the woman for a covering, saying, 'Mak thysel as comfortable as thee can – ah 'ev gitten t' fat to leuk to, and some seives to peel.'

When Ann returned to her basin of porridge she thought it had gone down a good deal since she had left it, and looked towards the woman as though to ask her if she had taken some.

'Nea,' she thought, 'what wad she want supping my poddidge, when she wadn't have ony hersel? She'll get nea mair, howiver, if it was her,' she added, as she emptied the basin. 'Now I'll just wesh these few things, and thin get to peeling my seives, but first I mun mak t' table straight gin Joe coom heam, though it's gitten ower late now, I fear. I wish he was heam. I don't like the looks o' this woman, she has sic a way si' her o' looking out o' t' corners of her eyes, and peeping all round loike; and she's a terrible girt body too, she must be half a head higher ner I is, and ah's nut sa lal. She's seun fa'n asleep, she mun be tired.'

So it seemed, for almost directly she had lain down she turned her face towards the pantry door, behind the sconce, drew her shawl more closely over her aching face, and was now breathing as regularly as a gigantic baby. And yet, as Ann moved quietly about, putting her things away, she had an uncomfortable feeling that the woman's sharp cunning eyes were following her wherever she went. Once or twice she stopped and looked hard at her visitor, but she was as motionless as could be, and when she spoke to her she received not the slightest answer, but the breathing seemed, if anything, a little heavier. Once, indeed, when she had moved to the little table under the cupboard, she felt convinced the woman was not asleep, and turned suddenly round, for she felt sure she heard a slight rustle of the hay pillow. But no, except a sleepy sort of movement, as though she was covering her aching teeth more warmly from the draughts, the stranger lay as quietly as before.

'Dear, dear, I mun be gettin' silly. I wonder how lang that fat's

gaun to be a-meltin'. When what's in is melt down a bit I'll fill up
t' pan wi' what's on t' dish.'

As the clock in the corner pointed to nine, Ann thought of
what her husband had said about not returning later than that
hour, but still she felt as though she could not go to bed yet.

'He might happen to come.' So she got some rushes, and sat
down on her low chair to peel them, by the side of her child's
cradle, opposite the sconce.

The house was almost as still as it had been in the morning,
only that the ticking of the clock and the snoring of the sleeper
(for the heavy breathing had passed into a regular snore) kept up
a kind of monotonous duet, in which they seemed to be vainly
attempting to keep time with each other; for first one took the
lead and then the other, now they went on for a tick tock or two
quite amicably, and then one would get the start, and the
struggle for precedence would commence again.

It was sleepy work to sit peeling rushes and listening, and poor
Ann grew more and more drowsy. She had had an unusually
hard day's work, and it was now far past her ordinary bed-time,
for the lazy hands of the clock had travelled from nine to half-
past, and thence to ten. Ann's eyelids drooped lower and lower,
the half-finished rush slipped out of her sleepy fingers, her head
sank upon her chest, and there were three sleepers for the clock
to keep time with.

Suddenly Ann started up; she had been roused by the fall of
something, that rung like metal, to the ground. The fire was
glowing low down on the hearth, but was still very hot.

'This willn't dea,' she said to herself, rising from her chair,
and giving herself a shake, 'I mun jest lie down on t' bed a bit. I'll
nut take my things off. I wonder what o'clock it is, and how lang
I've been asleep?'

She took a handful of sticks and threw them on to the fire to
make a blaze by which she might see the time, and in a moment
the kitchen was lighted up from one end to the other. The
fingers of the clock stood at a little after twelve.

'Dear, dear!' thought Ann, 'I hev slept a lang time,' and she
turned to the fire, for she felt chilly. Stooping by it she saw
something bright on the floor near her. It was an open clasp
knife; one of those long, sharp knives that are worn by the blue-

jackets. It must have dropped from the hand or out of the dress of the woman on the sconce.

Instinctively Ann looked towards her; she was lying on her back, the light from the fire fell full upon her face, for the shawl had slipped off; and there, to Ann's horror, she saw it was not that of a woman at all, but of a powerful man. His mouth and chin were adorned with as much of a black bristly beard as would grow during a week's tramp over the fells, out of reach of a razor.

For a moment she stood as though paralyzed with fright, but not longer. He was fast asleep after his long walk; so far she had the advantage, and she was not the woman to let it slip. To catch up her child and run was her first impulse; but where to? The next inhabited house was a mile away, and the slightest noise, such as the opening of the clumsy old door, would wake the man. What should she do? She could not stand still and let herself be certainly robbed of all their hardly earned savings, and possibly murdered with her child. No! a thousand times! she would fight for it! But how? She looked at her child asleep in the cradle, then at the man.

There he lay, his mouth wide open, snoring loudly, one powerful hand closed upon the shawl she had lent him for a covering, while the skirts of his woman's attire hung to the ground.

What was to be done must be done at once.

She looked at the knife lying at her feet; it was sharp and strong; but she might miss her aim, and only wound him. Turning from it she gazed despairingly around the room till her eyes fell upon the pan of boiling fat. In a moment her resolve was taken. With a strength born of desperation, she lifted it off the crook and, without a sound, placed it close to the sconce. Then quietly and stealthily, as Jael crept round the sleeping Syrian captain, the hardy daleswoman reached over to the table, and off it took a large tin dipper with a wooden handle, capable of holding from about five to six quarts. With compressed lips and clenched teeth she approached the sleeper, and, filling her dipper to the brim with the fat, poured it, boiling hot as it was, down his throat and over his face – one, two, three dippers full.

In vain were his struggles. When, at the first great shock he almost started up, she seized him by the throat with one hand,

and pinned him down with the strength of a giantess, regardless
of the scalding fat, which she continued to pour with the other
hand, until the pan was well-nigh empty. Not a cry was heard,
save the first half-chocked scream of agony, but the struggling
and writhing were fearful to behold. Still the woman held on.
She had him in her power, lying on his back so far below her –
and she was a powerful woman. Not a feature quivered, not a
nerve relaxed till her work was done; the struggles and kicks
became weaker, the writhing subsided into an occasional quiver,
and that finally passed into perfect stillness. Not till then, when
all was over, and the fight was ended, did her strength leave her.
She withdrew her hand, the dipper fell from her now nerveless
fingers, and she stood, the victor, indeed, but not triumphant,
transfixed with horror at what she had dared to do, rooted to the
spot, motionless as Lot's wife or the heap on the sconce.

The clock had it all its own way now; there was not another
sound that dare break the silence after that one choked scream
that had not even waked the baby in its cradle. How long she
stood by that sconce, Ann never knew; but presently the clock
struck one, and, as though it broke the spell that held her, Ann
sank upon her chair by the fire; two, three, four o'clock struck,
but still she sat on; five o'clock, and the grey dawn crept in at the
windows; the fire had long since gone out. Still she sat.

At half-past five Joe Southward opened the door of his own
farm-house and entered the kitchen.

'Weel, lass, I's heam at last,' he said. But as his wife turned her
pinched and ashy face towards him he too seemed overpowered
by the spell of silence, though he knew not why. But the child,
hearing his father's voice, set up a cry and shout. His mother
flew to his cradle, lifted him into her uninjured arm, and rushed
with him, folded tightly to her breast, out into the pure dim
daylight, sobbing with great, long, heart-breaking sobs.

'Oh, my lal bairn, I did it for thee – it was not for mysel; thee
mun niver, niver ken as thy mother did it; I did it for thee, my
bairn, my bairn.' And mother and child mingled their sobs and
tears.

Meanwhile Joe had been looking about the kitchen, and now
followed them out.

Bit by bit beneath the trees Joe heard the tale of horror, for

Ann would not re-enter the house, but folded her child in her apron to shield him from the cold morning air.

At length her husband took him from her and carried him into their own bedroom.

'Now, Ann,' he said, 'we mun hide him, thu could deu nowt else, but we mun mind 'at neabody kens owt aboot it for t' sake o' t' bairn.'

So together, ere the day was fairly begun, they dragged the body up the stone stairs, laid it on the wool shelf, which is a kind of ledge between the top of the wall and the roof, in one of the bedrooms, and covered it with the rolled fleeces that were stored there, for they expected several neighbours that day to help in some farm work.

When the neighbours had left, and it was getting dark, Joe took his pick and spade to the ruins of the old public-house, and there he dug as deep a grave as was possible in the stony soil. In one corner of the ruin he found a bundle, done up in a handkerchief, containing the man's male attire, a considerable amount of money, and one or two little things of value which must have been stolen from other farms. After a long consultation they determined to bury these things with him, as they dared not make inquiries concerning them, for they feared lest the manner of his death should become known.

When all was dark and quiet, and 'lal Joe' was fast asleep, Ann and her husband went up the stairs, and entered the little bedroom. Joe pulled away the fleeces, and together they dragged the body from the shelf on to the floor. It was a hideous sight. The fat had now solidified, and formed a hard, white mask, concealing yet indicating the features beneath. At sight of it Ann's face assumed the same ashy hue it had worn the night before; while Joe went about the work with the grim determination of a man upon whom had fallen one of the dirtiest bits of work the Fates could possibly have given. As it had fallen upon him, and what was to be done must be done, why according to his notion the sooner it was over the better. When they had stretched him out on the floor they folded the skirts of his dress about his legs, and then, taking a large corn-sack, carefully drew it over the whole, and stitched up the end.

Joe then went down a few stairs and dragged it upon his back like a sack of flour. It was a great weight, and many were the stops and stumbles before he reached the door of the kitchen, where he propped it up against the wall to take breath, while Ann placed the dip candle she had been holding to light him down in an old horn lantern. When she was ready Joe again hoisted his burden on his back, and stumbled along the passage; then very slowly they crossed the farm-yard, Ann going a little in advance with the lantern. It was a damp, dark night – not a star was to be seen; the branches of the old trees in front of the house, which were dimly visible as the light flickered for a moment across their broad trunks, moaned and creaked in the wind. All the familiar things surrounding them, as they made their way to the ruin, seemed to partake of their horror; even the merry little beck below the fold had changed its every-day chatter with the stones in its bed to a melancholy chant. Not a word did they speak to each other during the frequent pauses which had to be made for breath 'ere they reached the hole that Joe had dug. Once there, they soon lowered their burden into it, and threw in the bundle. Then, seizing his spade, Joe filled up the grave as fast as possible, only pausing now and then to stamp down the earth more firmly.

At length the last spadeful had been thrown in, the last stamp given, and a few loose stones piled up carelessly over the place, to hide any sign of recent digging. Then Joe broke the silence.

'Theer,' he said, wiping his hot brow with his jacket sleeve, 'that's done. He'll do naebody no harm now. Coom, lass, we'll ga heam, we've done a' we can,' and drawing his wife's hand through his arm, as he had never done since the day of their wedding, they left the ruin, re-crossed the field beneath the trees, and entering their house, stood by the fire. Here at last Ann fairly gave way; she drew her hand from her husband's arm, and sank shivering upon her low rocking-chair.

'Oh,' she said, 'I carn't bide it, I canna bide to stop in t' hoose; it will be as if he was allus lyin' there. Thee mun niver gang away agaen, Joe,' and the matter-of-fact, unimpressionable dales-woman clung to her husband like a child.

'Whist, lass,' he said, soothingly, putting his brown hand upon her shoulder, 'thee munna tak on so, thee could not heve done different. If thee hadn't been middlin' sharp wid him, he'd ha'

seun doon for thee an' lal Joe wid his lang knife; thee munna set
sic mich by it. We can do nae mair nor we hev done. Nobbut
keep it til ourrselves, and niver let on' at he iver coomed nar t'
hoose.'

Time passed on, Joe and Ann lived many long years in this
house, for they feared that if they left, some new tenant might dig
about the ruin. Often when the short autumn and winter
afternoons drew to their close, Ann would leave her warm seat by
the fire and cross the yard to speak to Joe in the barn, for she
could bear to stay in the house alone no longer; and later on, at
night, when she sat knitting while her husband was asleep in his
armchair, if she raised her eyes from her work, she could fancy
she saw the long, shapeless figure stretched out on the sconce,
with the fat dropping on to the floor.

After their death, in some way a whisper of the tale began to
float about from one farm kitchen to another. How it got out no
one knew, but one thing I know, and that is, that when, after
standing empty for a year or two, the house was let again, the
farmer and his wife, on a certain night each year, used to see an
indistinct figure, all muffled up about the head, enter the kitchen
and stretch itself on the sconce, then in a few minutes a choked
kind of scream would sound through the room, and the figure
would disappear. The next night the same figure stepped from
the wool niche, glided noiselessly down the stairs, and disappeared in the ruins of the 'Nanny Horns.'

In the Court Of The Dragon

ROBERT W. CHAMBERS

Now for a very odd piece indeed, from a singular writer. Robert W. Chambers (1865–1933) was described in a magazine article in 1911 as 'the most popular writer in America': not bad for a man whose writing career had started in earnest only sixteen years before with a book in which he never again attempted to emulate. This was THE KING IN YELLOW (1895), from which comes 'In the Court of the Dragon'.

Chambers left his native New York in 1889 to study art in Paris, and his experiences led to his first book, IN THE QUARTER (1894), depicting various scenes among the artist's quarter of Paris. Then, almost out of the blue, came THE KING IN YELLOW, an original work that has inspired others but never been equalled, not even by its author. It was a book of short stories, set in France, all loosely connected by a mythical book of forbidden lore called 'The King in Yellow'. It is an uneven collection, almost unreadable in parts. One story, 'The Yellow Sign', has been a favourite with anthologists for years. This little item, rather overlooked for a long time, is dangerously close to being unintelligible, but repays a couple of readings.

The irony of Chambers' career is that, while THE KING IN YELLOW became a best seller and launched him on a phenomenal writing career, he never went back to horror, apart from one or two books such as THE MAKER OF MOONS (1896) and THE SLAYER OF SOULS (1920). He concentrated on spy stories, thrillers and society novels. While these earned him his undoubted reputation, macabre fiction enthusiasts now wonder just what would have been the outcome if Robert W. Chambers had devoted his forty-year writing career to producing more of the same as appeared in THE KING IN YELLOW.

ROBERT W. CHAMBERS

In the Court of the Dragon

I

'Oh Thou who burn'st in heart for those who burn
In Hell, whose fires thyself shall feed in turn;
How long be crying, "Mercy on them, God!"
Why, who art thou to teach and He to learn?'

In the Church of St. Barnabé vespers were over; the clergy left
the altar; the little choir-boys flocked across the chancel and
settled in the stalls. A Suisse in rich uniform marched down the
south aisle, sounding his staff at every fourth step on the stone
pavement; behind him came that eloquent preacher and good
man, Monseigneur C–.

My chair was near the chancel rail. I now turned towards the
west end of the church. The other people between the altar and
the pulpit turned too. There was a little scraping and rustling
while the congregation seated itself again; the preacher mounted
the pulpit stairs, and the organ voluntary ceased.

I had always found the organ-playing at St. Barnabé highly
interesting. Learned and scientific it was, too much so for my
small knowledge, but expressing a vivid if cold intelligence.
Moreover, it possessed the French quality of taste; taste reigned
supreme, self-controlled, dignified and reticent.

To-day, however, from the first choir I had felt a change for
the worse, a sinister change. During vespers it had been chiefly
the chancel organ which supported the beautiful choir, but now
and again, quite wantonly as it seemed, from the west gallery
where the great organ stands, a heavy hand had struck across the
church, at the serene peace of those clear voices. It was
something more than harsh and dissonant, and it betrayed no
lack of skill. As it recurred again and again, it set me thinking of
what my architect's books say about the custom in early times to
consecrate the choir as soon as it was built, and that the nave,

being finished sometimes half a century later, often did not get any blessing at all: I wondered idly if that had been the case at St. Barnabé, and whether something not usually supposed to be at home in a Christian church, might have entered undetected, and taken possession of the west gallery. I had read of such things happening too, but not in works on architecture.

Then I remembered that St. Barnabé was not much more than a hundred years old, and smiled at the incongruous association of mediaeval superstitions with that cheerful little piece of eighteenth century rococo.

But now vespers were over, and there should have followed a few quiet chords, fit to accompany meditation, while we waited for the sermon. Instead of that, the discord at the lower end of the church broke out with the departure of the clergy, as if now nothing could control it.

I belong to those children of an older and simpler generation, who do not love to seek for psychological subtleties in art; and I have ever refused to find in music anything more than melody and harmony, but I felt that in the labyrinth of sounds now issuing from that instrument there was something being hunted. Up and down the pedals chased him, while the manuals blared approval. Poor devil! whoever he was, there seemed small hope of escape!

My nervous annoyance changed to anger. Who was doing this? How dare he play like that in the midst of divine service? I glanced at the people near me: not one appeared to be in the least disturbed. The placid brows of the kneeling nuns, still turned toward the altar, lost none of their devout abstraction, under the pale shadow of their white headdress. The fashionable lady beside me was looking expectantly at Monseigneur C–. For all her face betrayed, the organ might have been singing an Ave Maria.

But now, at last, the preacher had made the sign of the cross, and commanded silence. I turned to him gladly. Thus far I had not found the rest I had counted on, when I entered St. Barnabé that afternoon.

I was worn out by three nights of physical suffering and mental trouble: the last had been the worst, and it was an exhausted body, and a mind benumbed and yet acutely sensitive, which I had brought to my favourite church for healing. For I had been reading 'The King in Yellow'.

'The sun ariseth; they gather themselves together and lay them down in their dens.' Monseigneur C–. delivered his text in a calm voice, glancing quietly over the congregation. My eyes turned, I knew not why, towards the lower end of the church. The organist was coming from behind his pipes, and passing along the gallery on his way out, I saw him disappear by a small door that leads to some stairs which descend directly to the street. He was a slender man, and his face was as white as his coat was black. 'Good riddance!' I thought, 'with your wicked music! I hope your assistant will play the closing voluntary.'

With a feeling of relief, with a deep calm feeling of relief, I turned back to the mild face in the pulpit, and settled myself to listen. Here at last, was the ease of mind I longed for.

'My children,' said the preacher, 'one truth the human soul finds hardest of all to learn; that it has nothing to fear. It can never be made to see that nothing can really harm it.'

'Curious doctrine!' I thought, 'for a Catholic priest. Let us see how he will reconcile that with the Fathers.'

'Nothing can really harm the soul,' he went on, in his coolest, clearest tones, 'because–'

But I never heard the rest; my eye left his face. I knew not for what reason, and sought the lower end of the church. The same man was coming out from behind the organ, and was passing along the gallery *the same way.* But there had not been time for him to return, and if he had returned, I must have seen him. I felt a faint chill, and my heart sank; and yet, his going and coming were no affair of mine. I looked at him: I could not look away from his black figure and his white face. When he was exactly opposite to me, he turned and sent across the church, straight into my eyes, a look of hate, intense and deadly: I have never seen any other like it; would to God I might never see it again! Then he disappeared by the same door through which I had watched him depart less than sixty seconds before.

I sat and tried to collect my thoughts. My first sensation was like that of a very young child badly hurt, when it catches its breath before crying out.

To suddenly find myself the object of such hatred was exquisitely painful: and this man was an utter stranger. Why should he hate me so? Me, whom he had never seen before? For the moment all other sensation was merged in this one pang: even fear was subordinate to grief, and for that moment I never doubted; but in the next I began to reason, and a sense of the incongruous came to my aid.

As I have said, St. Barnabé is a modern church. It is small and well lighted; one sees all over it almost at a glance. The organ gallery gets a strong white light from a row of long windows in the clere-story, which have not even coloured glass.

The pulpit being in the middle of the church, it followed that, when I was turned toward it, whatever moved at the west end could not fail to attract my eye. When the organist passed it was no wonder that I saw him; I had simply miscalculated the interval between his first and his second passing. He had come in that last time by the other side-door. As for the look which had so upset me, there had been no such thing, and I was a nervous fool.

I looked about. This was a likely place to harbour supernatural horrors! That clear-cut, reasonable face of Monsiegneur C–, his collected manner, and easy, graceful gestures, were they not just a little discouraging to the notion of a gruesome mystery? I glanced above his head, and almost laughed. That flyaway lady, supporting one corner of the pulpit canopy, which looked like a fringed damask table-cloth in a high wind, at the first attempt of a basilisk to pose up there in the organ loft, she would point her gold trumpet at him, and puff him out of existence! I laughed to myself over this conceit, which, at the time, I thought very amusing, and sat and chaffed myself and everything else, from the old harpy outside the railing, who had made me pay ten centimes for my chair, before she would let me in (she was more like a basilisk, I told myself, than was my organist with the anaemic complexion): from that grim old dame, to, yes, alas! to Monseigneur C–, himself. For all devoutness had fled. I had never yet done such a thing in my life, but now I felt a desire to mock.

As for the sermon, I could not hear a word of it, for the jingle in my ears of

> 'The skirts of St. Paul has reached.'
> Having preached us those six Lent lectures,
> More unctuous than ever he preached:'

keeping time to the most fantastic and irreverent thoughts.

It was no use to sit there any longer: I must get out of doors and shake myself free from this hateful mood. I knew the rudeness I was committing but still I rose and left the church.

A spring sun was shining on the rue St. Honoré, as I ran down the church steps. On one corner stood a barrow full of yellow jonquils, pale violets from the Riviera, dark Russian violets, and white Roman hyacinths in a golden cloud of mimosa. The street was full of Sunday pleasure-seekers. I swung my cane and laughed with the rest. Someone overtook and passed me. He never turned, but there was the same deadly malignity in his white profile that there had been in his eyes. I watched him as long as I could see him. His lithe back expressed the same menace; every step that carried him away from me seemed to bear him on some errand connected with my destruction.

I was creeping along, my feet almost refusing to move. There began to dawn in me a sense of responsibility for something long forgotten. It began to seem as if I deserved that which he threatened: it reached a long way back – a long, long way back. It had lain dormant all these years: it was there though, and presently it would rise and confront me. But I would try to escape; and I stumbled as best I could into the rue de Rivioli, across the Place de la Concorde and on to the Quai. I looked with sick eyes upon the sun, shining through the white foam of the fountain, pouring over the backs of the dusky bronze river-gods, on the far-away Arc, a structure of amethyst mist, on the countless vistas of grey stems and bare branches faintly green. Then I saw him again coming down one of the chestnut alleys of the Cours la Reine.

I left the river side, plunged blindly across to the Champs Elysées and turned towards the Arc. The setting sun was sending its rays along the green sward of the Rond-point: in the full glow he sat on a bench, children and young mothers all about him. He was nothing but a Sunday lounger, like the others, like myself. I said the words almost aloud, and all the while I gazed on the malignant hatred of his face. But he was not looking at me. I crept past and dragged my leaden feet up the Avenue. I knew that every time I met him brought him nearer to the accomplishment of his purpose and my fate. And still I tried to save myself.

The last rays of sunset were pouring through the great Arc. I passed under it, and met him face to face. I had left him far down the Champs Elysées, and yet he came in with a stream of people who were returning from the Bois de Boulogne. He came so close that he brushed me. His slender frame felt like iron inside its loose black covering. He showed no signs of haste, nor of fatigue, nor of any human feeling. His whole being expressed but one thing: the will, and the power to work me evil.

In anguish I watched him, where he went down the broad crowded Avenue, that was all flashing with wheels and the trappings of horses, and the helmets of the Garde Republicaine.

He was soon lost to sight; then I turned and fled. Into the Bois, and far out beyond it – I know not where I went, but after a long while as it seemed to me, night had fallen, and I found myself sitting at a table before a small café. I had wandered back into the Bois. It was hours now since I had seen him. Physical fatigue, and mental suffering had left me no more power to think or feel. I was tired, so tired! I longed to hide away in my own den. I resolved to go home. But that was a long way off.

I live in the Court of the Dragon, a narrow passage that leads from the rue de Rennes to the rue du Dragon.

It is an 'Impasse,' traversable only for foot passengers. Over the entrance on the rue de Rennes is a balcony, supported by an iron dragon. Within the court tall old houses rise on either side, and close the ends that give on the two streets. Huge gates, swung back during the day into the walls of the deep archways, close this court, after midnight, and one must enter then by ringing at certain small doors on the side. The sunken pavement collects unsavoury pools. Steep stairways pitch down to doors that open on the court. The ground-floors are occupied by shops of second-hand dealers, and by iron workers. All day long the place rings with the clink of hammers, and the clang of metal bars.

Unsavoury as it is below, there is cheerfulness, and comfort, and hard, honest work above.

Five flights up are the ateliers of architects and painters, and the hiding-places of middle-aged students like myself who want to live alone. When I first came here to live I was young, and not alone.

I had to walk awhile before any conveyance appeared, but at last, when I had almost reached the Arc de Triomphe again, an empty cab came along and I took it.

From the Arc to the rue de Rennes is a drive of more than half an hour, especially when one is conveyed by a tired cab horse that has been at the mercy of Sunday fête makers.

There had been time before I passed under the Dragon's wings, to meet my enemy over and over again, but I never saw him once, now refuge was close at hand.

Before the wide gateway a small mob of children were playing. Our concierge and his wife walked about among them with their black poodle, keeping order; some couples were waltzing on the side-walk. I returned their greetings and hurried in.

All the inhabitants of the court had trooped out into the street. The place was quite deserted, lighted by a few lanterns hung high up, in which the gas burned dimly.

My apartment was at the top of a house, half way down the court, reached by a staircase that descended almost into the street, with only a bit of passage-way intervening. I set my foot on the threshold of the open door, the friendly, old ruinous stairs rose before me, leading up to rest and shelter. Looking back over my right shoulder, I saw *him*, ten paces off. He must have entered the court with me.

He was coming straight on, neither slowly, nor swiftly, but straight on to me. And now he was looking at me. For the first time since our eyes encountered across the church they met now again, and I knew that the time had come.

Retreating backward, down the court, I faced him. I meant to escape by the entrance on the rue du Dragon. His eyes told me that I never should escape.

It seemed ages while we were going, I retreating, he advancing, down the court in perfect silence; but at last I felt the shadow of the archway, and the next step brought me within it. I had meant to turn here and spring through into the street. But the shadow was not that of an archway; it was that of a vault. The great doors on the rue. du Dragon were closed. I felt this by the blackness which surrounded me, and at the same instant I read it in his face. How his face gleamed in the darkness, drawing swiftly nearer! The deep vaults, the huge closed doors, their cold iron clamps were all on his side. The thing which he had threatened had arrived: it gathered and bore down on me from the fathomless shadows; the point from which it would strike was his infernal eyes. Hopeless, I set my back against the barred doors and defied him.

There was a scraping of chairs on the stone floor, and a rustling as the congregation rose. I could hear the Suisse's staff in the south aisle, preceding Monseigneur C– to the sacristy.

The kneeling nuns, roused from their devout abstraction, made their reverence and went away. The fashionable lady, my neighbour, rose also, with graceful reserve. As she departed her glance just flitted over my face in disapproval.

Half dead, or so it seemed to me, yet intensely alive to every trifle, I sat among the leisurely moving crowd, then rose too and went toward the door.

I had slept through the sermon. Had I slept through the sermon? I looked up and saw him passing along the gallery to his place. Only his side I saw; the thin bent arm in its black covering looked like one of the devilish, nameless instruments which lie in the disused torture chambers of mediaeval castles.

But I had escaped him, though his eyes had said I should not. *Had* I escaped? That which gave him the power over me came back out of oblivion, where I had hoped to keep it. For I knew him now. Death and the awful abode of lost souls, whither my weakness long ago had sent him – they had changed him for every other eye, but not for mine. I had recognized him almost from the first; I had never doubted what he was come to do; and now I knew that while my body sat safe in the cheerful little church, he had been hunting my soul in the Court of the Dragon.

I crept to the door; the organ broke out overhead with a blare. A dazzling light filled the church, blotting the altar from my eyes.

The people faded away, the árches, the vaulted roof vanished. I raised my seared eyes to the fathomless glare, and I saw the black stars hanging in the heavens: and the wet winds from the Lake of Hali chilled my face.

And now, far away, over leagues of tossing cloud-waves, I saw the moon dripping with spray; and beyond, the towers of Carcosa rose behind the moon.

Death and the awful abode of lost souls, whither my weakness long ago had sent him, had changed him for every other eye but mine. And now I heard *his voice*, rising, swelling, thundering through the flaring light, and as I fell, the radiance increasing, increasing, poured over me in waves of flame. Then I sank into the depths, and I heard the King in Yellow whispering to my soul: 'It is a fearful thing to fall into the hands of the living God!'

The Old House in Vauxhall Walk

MRS J.H. RIDDELL

The life of Mrs J.H. Riddell (1832–1906) went from rags to riches, and back to rags again. It was a tragic existence, but in the face of personal and family illness and appalling poverty, Charlotte Riddell produced some of the finest Victorian ghost stories, a fine tribute to a now forgotten talent.

In 1946, the noted anthologist Herbert van Thal reprinted Mrs Riddell's classic book WEIRD STORIES *(1884) and remarked: 'Connoisseurs of the ghost story will find here tales that should come up to their highest expectations; it is strange that their quality and skill should have been unrecognised so long.' Even stranger is her neglect since 1946, which was only slightly ameliorated by reprints of some of her stories in the early 1970s. Perhaps this story will help; it is certainly a fine example of the skills of Mrs Riddell, and a portrait of poverty made all the more accurate by her own experiences.*

MRS J.H. RIDDELL

The Old House in Vauxhall Walk

'Houseless – homeless – hopeless!'

Many a one who had before him trodden that same street must have uttered the same words – the weary, the desolate, the hungry, the forsaken, the waifs and strays of struggling humanity that are always coming and going, cold, starving and miserable, over the pavements of Lambeth Parish; but it is open to question whether they were ever previously spoken with a more thorough conviction of their truth, or with a feeling of keener self-pity, than by the young man who hurried along Vauxhall Walk one rainy winter's night, with no overcoat on his shoulders and no hat on his head.

A strange sentence for one-and-twenty to give expression to – and it was stranger still to come from the lips of a person who looked like and who was a gentleman. He did not appear either to have sunk very far down in the good graces of Fortune. There was no sign or token which would have induced a passer-by to imagine he had been worsted after a long fight with calamity. His boots were not worn down at the heels or broken at the toes, as many, many boots were which dragged and shuffled and scraped along the pavement. His clothes were good and fashionably cut, and innocent of the rents and patches and tatters that slunk wretchedly by, crouched in doorways, and held out a hand mutely appealing for charity. His face was not pinched with famine or lined with wicked wrinkles, or brutalised by drink and debauchery, and yet he said and thought he was hopeless, and almost in his young despair spoke the words aloud.

It was a bad night to be about with such a feeling in one's heart. The rain was cold, pitiless and increasing. A damp, keen wind blew down the cross streets leading from the river. The fumes of the gas works seemed to fall with the rain. The roadway was muddy; the pavement greasy; the lamps burned dimly; and that dreary district of London looked its very gloomiest and worst.

Certainly not an evening to be abroad without a home to go to, or a sixpence in one's pocket, yet this was the position of the young gentleman who, without a hat, strode along Vauxhall Walk, the rain beating on his unprotected head.

Upon the houses, so large and good – once inhabited by well-to-do citizens, now let out for the most part in floors to weekly tenants – he looked enviously. He would have given much to have had a room, or even part of one. He had been walking for a long time, ever since dark in fact, and dark falls soon in December. He was tired and cold and hungry, and he saw no prospect save of pacing the streets all night.

As he passed one of the lamps, the light falling on his face revealed handsome young features, a mobile, sensitive mouth, and that particular formation of the eyebrows – not a frown exactly, but a certain draw of the brows – often considered to bespeak genius, but which more surely accompanies an impulsive organisation easily pleased, easily depressed, capable of suffering very keenly or of enjoying fully. In his short life he had not enjoyed much, and he had suffered a good deal. That night, when he walked bareheaded through the rain, affairs had come to a crisis. So far as he in his despair felt able to see or reason, the best thing he could do was to die. The world did not want him; he would be better out of it.

The door of one of the houses stood open, and he could see in the dimly lighted hall some few articles of furniture waiting to be removed. A van stood beside the curb, and two men were lifting a table into it as he, for a second, paused.

'Ah,' he thought, 'even those poor people have some place to go to, some shelter provided, while I have not a roof to cover my head, or a shilling to get a night's lodging.' And he went on fast, as if memory were spurring him, so fast that a man running after had some trouble to overtake him.

'Master Graham! Master Graham!' this man exclaimed, breathlessly; and, thus addressed, the young fellow stopped as if he had been shot.

'Who are you that know me?' he asked, facing round.

'I'm William; don't you remember William, Master Graham?

And, Lord's sake, sir, what are you doing out a night like this without your hat?'

'I forgot it,' was the answer; 'and I did not care to go back and fetch it.'

'Then why don't you buy another, sir? You'll catch your death of cold; and besides, you'll excuse me, sir, but it does look odd.'

'I know that,' said Master Graham grimly, 'but I haven't a halfpenny in the world.'

'Have you and the master, then —' began the man, but there he hesitated and stopped.

'Had a quarrel? Yes, and one that will last us our lives,' finished the other, with a bitter laugh.

'And where are you going now?'

'Going! Nowhere, except to seek out the softest paving stone, or the shelter of an arch.'

'You are joking, sir.'

'I don't feel much in a mood for jesting either.'

'Will you come back with me, Master Graham? We are just at the last of our moving, but there is a spark of fire still in the grate, and it would be better talking out of this rain. Will you come, sir?'

'Come! Of course I will come,' said the young fellow, and, turning, they retraced their steps to the house he had looked into as he passed along.

An old, old house, with long, wide hall, stairs low, easy of ascent, with deep cornices to the ceilings, and oak floorings, and mahogany doors, which still spoke mutely of the wealth and stability of the original owner, who lived before the Tradescants and Ashmoles were thought of, and had been sleeping for longer than they, in St. Mary's churchyard, hard by the archbishop's palace.

'Step upstairs, sir,' entreated the departing tenant; 'it's cold down here, with the door standing wide.'

'Had you the whole house, then, William?' asked Graham Coulton, in some surprise.

'The whole of it, and right sorry I, for one, am to leave it; but nothing else would serve my wife. This room, sir,' and with a little conscious pride, William, doing the honours of his late residence, asked his guest into a spacious apartment occupying the full width of the house on the first floor.

Tired though he was, the young man could not repress an exclamation of astonishment.

'Why, we have nothing so large as this at home, William,' he said.

'It's a fine house,' answered William, raking the embers together as he spoke and throwing some wood upon them; 'but, like many a good family, it has come down in the world.'

There were four windows in the room, shuttered close; they had deep, low seats, suggestive of pleasant days gone by; when, well-curtained and well-cushioned, they formed snug retreats for the children, and sometimes for adults also; there was no furniture left, unless an oaken settle beside the hearth, and a large mirror let into the panelling at the opposite end of the apartment, with a black marble console table beneath it, could be so considered; but the very absence of chairs and tables enabled the magnificent proportions of the chamber to be seen to full advantage, and there was nothing to distract the attention from the ornamented ceiling, the panelled walls, the old-world chimney-piece so quaintly carved, and the fire-place lined with tiles, each one of which contained a picture of some scriptural or allegorical subject.

'Had you been staying on here, William,' said Coulton, flinging himself wearily on the settee, 'I'd have asked you to let me stop where I am for the night.'

'If you can make shift, sir, there is nothing as I am aware of to prevent you stopping,' answered the man, fanning the wood into a flame. 'I shan't take the key back to the landlord till to-morrow, and this would be better for you than the cold streets at any rate.'

'Do you really mean what you say?' asked the other eagerly. 'I should be thankful to lie here; I feel dead beat.'

'Then stay, Master Graham, and welcome. I'll fetch a basket of coals I was going to put in the van, and make up a good fire, so that you can warm yourself; then I must run round to the other house for a minute or two, but it's not far, and I'll be back as soon as ever I can.'

'Thank you, William; you were always good to me,' said the young man gratefully. 'This is delightful,' and he stretched his numbed hands over the blazing wood, and looked round the room with a satisfied smile.

'I did not expect to get into such quarters,' he remarked, as his friend in need reappeared, carrying a half-bushel basket full of coals, with which he proceeded to make up a roaring fire. 'I am sure the last thing I could have imagined was meeting with anyone I knew in Vauxhall Walk.'

'Where were you coming from, Master Graham?' asked William curiously.

'From old Melfield's. I was at his school once, you know, and he has now retired, and is living upon the proceeds of years of robbery in Kennington Oval. I thought, perhaps he would lend me a pound, or offer me a night's lodging, or even a glass of wine; but, oh dear, no. He took the moral tone, and observed he could have nothing to say to a son who defied his father's authority. He gave me plenty of advice, but nothing else, and showed me out into the rain with a bland courtesy, for which I could have struck him.'

William muttered something under his breath which was not a blessing, and added aloud:

'You are better here, sir, I think, at any rate. I'll be back in less than half an hour.'

Left to himself, young Coulton took off his coat, and shifting the settle a little, hung it over the end to dry. With his handkerchief he rubbed some of the wet out of his hair; then, perfectly exhausted, he lay down before the fire and, pillowing his head on his arm, fell fast asleep.

He was awakened nearly an hour afterwards by the sound of someone gently stirring the fire and moving quietly about the room. Starting into a sitting posture, he looked around him, bewildered for a moment, and then, recognising his humble friend, said laughingly:

'I had lost myself; I could not imagine where I was.'

'I am sorry to see you here, sir,' was the reply; 'but still this is better than being out of doors. It has come on a nasty night. I brought a rug round with me that, perhaps, you would wrap yourself in.'

'I wish, at the same time, you had brought me something to eat,' said the young man, laughing.

'Are you hungry, then, sir?' asked William, in a tone of concern.

'Yes; I have had nothing to eat since breakfast. The governor and I commenced rowing the minute we sat down to luncheon, and I rose and left the table. But hunger does not signify; I am dry and warm, and can forget the other matter in sleep.'

'And it's too late now to buy anything,' soliloquised the man; 'the shops are all shut long ago. Do you think, sir,' he added, brightening, 'you could manage some bread and cheese?'

'Do I think – I should call it a perfect feast,' answered Graham Coulton. 'But never mind about food to-night, William; you have had trouble enough, and to spare, already.'

William's only answer was to dart to the door and run downstairs. Presently he reappeared, carrying in one hand bread and cheese wrapped up in paper, and in the other a pewter measure full of beer.

'It's the best I could do, sir,' he said apologetically. 'I had to beg this from the landlady.'

'Here's to her good health!' exclaimed the young fellow gaily, taking a long pull at the tankard. 'That tastes better than champagne in my father's house.'

'Won't he be uneasy about you?' ventured William, who, having by this time emptied the coals, was now seated on the inverted basket, looking wistfully at the relish with which the son of the former master was eating his bread and cheese.

'No,' was the decided answer. 'When he hears it pouring cats and dogs he will only hope I am out in the deluge, and say a good drenching will cool my pride.'

'I do not think you are right there,' remarked the man.

'But I am sure I am. My father always hated me, as he hated my mother.'

'Begging your pardon, sir; he was over fond of your mother.'

'If you had heard what he said about her to-day, you might find reason to alter your opinion. He told me I resembled her in mind as well as body; that I was a coward, a simpleton, and a hypocrite.'

'He did not mean it, sir.'

'He did, every word. He does think I am a coward, because I – I –' and the young fellow broke into a passion of hysterical tears.

'I don't half like leaving you here alone,' said William,

glancing round the room with a quick trouble in his eyes; 'but I have no place fit to ask you to stop, and I am forced to go myself, because I am night watchman, and must be on at twelve o'clock.'

'I shall be right enough,' was the answer. 'Only I mustn't talk any more of my father. Tell me about yourself, William. How did you manage to get such a big house, and why are you leaving it?'

'The landlord put me in charge, sir; and it was my wife's fancy not to like it.'

'Why did she not like it?'

'She felt desolate alone with the children at night,' answered William, turning away his head; then added, next minute; 'Now, sir, if you think I can do no more for you, I had best be off. Time's getting on. I'll look round to-morrow morning.'

'Good night,' said the young fellow, stretching out his hand, which the other took as freely and frankly as it was offered. 'What should I have done this evening if I had not chanced to meet you?'

'I don't think there is much chance in the world, Master Graham,' was the quiet answer. 'I do hope you will rest well, and not be the worse for your wetting.'

'No fear of that,' was the rejoinder, and the next minute the young man found himself all alone in the Old House in Vauxhall Walk.

II

Lying on the settle, with the fire burnt out, and the room in total darkness, Graham Coulton dreamed a curious dream. He thought he awoke from deep slumber to find a log smouldering away upon the hearth, and the mirror at the end of the apartment reflecting fitful gleams of light. He could not understand how it came to pass that, far away as he was from the glass, he was able to see everything in it; but he resigned himself to the difficulty without astonishment, as people generally do in dreams.

Neither did he feel surprised when he beheld the outline of a female figure seated beside the fire, engaged in picking something out of her lap and dropping it with a despairing gesture.

He heard the mellow sound of gold, and knew she was lifting

and dropping sovereigns. He turned a little so as to see the person engaged in such a singular and meaningless manner, and found that, where there had been no chair on the previous night, there was a chair now, on which was seated an old, wrinkled hag, her clothes poor and ragged, a mob cap barely covering her scant white hair, her cheeks sunken, her nose hooked, her fingers more like talons than aught else as they dived down into the heap of gold, portions of which they lifted but to scatter mournfuly.

'Oh! my lost life,' she moaned, in a voice of the bitterest anguish. 'Oh! my lost life – for one day, for one hour of it again!'

Out of the darkness – out of the corner of the room where the shadows lay deepest – out from the gloom abiding near the door – out from the dreary night, with their sodden feet and the wet dripping from their heads, came the old men and the young children, the worn women and the weary hearts, whose misery that gold might have relieved, but whose wretchedness it mocked.'Round that miser, who once sat gloating as she now sat lamenting, they crowded – all those pale, sad shapes – the aged of days, the infant of hours, the sobbing outcast, honest poverty, repentant vice; but one low cry proceeded from those pale lips – a cry for help she might have given, but which she withheld.

They closed about her, all together, as they had done singly in life; they prayed, they sobbed, they entreated; with haggard eyes the figure regarded the poor she had repulsed, the children against whose cry she had closed her ears, the old people she had suffered to starve and die for want of what would have been the merest trifle to her; then, with a terrible scream, she raised her lean arms above her head, and sank down – down – the gold scattering as it fell out of her lap, and rolling along the floor, till its gleam was lost in the outer darkness beyond.

Then Graham Coulton awoke in good earnest, with the perspiration oozing from every pore, with a fear and an agony upon him such as he had never before felt in all his existence, and with the sound of the heart-rending cry – 'Oh! my lost life' – still ringing in his ears.

Mingled with all, too, there seemed to have been some lesson for him which he had forgotten, that, try as he would, eluded his memory, and which, in the very act of waking, glided away.

He lay for a little thinking about all this, and then, still heavy with sleep, retraced his way into dreamland once more.

It was natural, perhaps, that, mingling with the strange fantasies which follow in the train of night and darkness, the former vision should recur, and the young man ere long found himself toiling through scene after scene wherein the figure of the woman he had seen seated beside a dying fire held principal place.

He saw her walking slowly across the floor munching a dry crust – she who could have purchased all the luxuries wealth can command; on the hearth, contemplating her, stood a man of commanding presence, dressed in the fashion of long ago. In his eyes there was a dark look of anger, on his lips a curling smile of disgust, and somehow, even in his sleep, the dreamer understood it was the ancestor to the descendant he beheld – that the house put to mean uses in which he lay had never so far descended from its high estate, as the woman possessed of so pitiful a soul, contaminated with the most despicable and insidious vice poor humanity knows, for all other vices seem to have connection with the flesh, but the greed of the miser eats into the very soul.

Filthy of person, repulsive to look at, hard of heart as she was, he yet beheld another phantom, which, coming into the room, met her almost on the threshold, taking her by the hand, and pleading, as it seemed, for assistance. He could not hear all that passed, but a word now and then fell upon his ear. Some talk of former days; some mention of a fair young mother – an appeal, as it seemed, to a time when they were tiny brother and sister, and the accursed greed for gold had not divided them. All in vain; the hag only answered him as she had answered the children, and the young girls, and the old people in his former vision. Her heart was as invulnerable to natural affection as it had proved to human sympathy. He begged, as it appeared, for aid to avert some bitter misfortune or terrible disgrace, and adamant might have been found more yielding to his prayer. Then the figure standing on the hearth changed to an angel, which folded its wings mournfully over its face, and the man, with bowed head, slowly left the room.

Even as he did so the scene changed again; it was night once more, and the miser wended her way upstairs. From below,

Graham Coulton fancied he watched her toiling wearily from step to step. She had aged strangely since the previous scenes. She moved with difficulty; it seemed the greatest exertion for her to creep from step to step, her skinny hand traversing the balusters with slow and painful deliberateness. Fascinated, the young man's eyes followed the progress of that feeble, decrepit woman. She was solitary in a desolate house, with a deeper blackness than the darkness of night waiting to engulf her.

It seemed to Graham Coulton that after that he lay for a time in a still, dreamless sleep, upon awakening from which he found himself entering a chamber as sordid and unclean in its appointments as the woman of his previous vision had been in her person. The poorest labourer's wife would have gathered more comforts around her than that room contained. A four-poster bedstead without hangings of any kind – a blind drawn up awry – an old carpet covered with dust, and dirt on the floor – a rickety washstand with all the paint worn off it – an ancient mahogany dressing table, and a cracked glass spotted all over – were all the objects he could at first discern, looking at the room through that dim light which oftentimes obtains in dreams.

By degrees, however, he perceived the outline of someone lying huddled on the bed. Drawing nearer, he found it was that of the person whose dreadful presence seemed to pervade the house. What a terrible sight she looked, with her thin white locks scattered over the pillow, with what were mere remnants of blankets gathered about her shoulders, with her claw-like fingers clutching the clothes, as though even in sleep she was guarding her gold!

An awful and a repulsive spectacle, but not with half the terror in it of that which followed. Even as the young man looked he heard stealthy footsteps on the stairs. Then he saw first one man and then his fellow steal cautiously into the room. Another second, and the pair stood beside the bed, murder in their eyes.

Graham Coulton tried to shout – tried to move, but the deterrent power which exists in dreams only tied his tongue and paralysed his limbs. He could but hear and look, and what he heard and saw was this: aroused suddenly from sleep, the woman started, only to receive a blow from one of the ruffians, whose fellow followed his lead by plunging a knife into her breast.

Then, with a gurgling scream, she fell back on the bed, and at the same moment, with a cry, Graham Coulton again awoke, to thank heaven it was but an illusion.

III

'I hope you slept well, sir.' It was William, who, coming into the hall with the sunlight of a fine bright morning streaming after him, asked this question: 'Had you a good night's rest?'

Graham Coulton laughed, and answered:

'Why, faith, I was somewhat in the case of Paddy, "who could not slape for dhraming." I slept well enough, I suppose, but whether it was in consequence of the row with my dad, or the hard bed, or the cheese – most likely the bread and cheese so late at night – I dreamt all the night long, the most extraordinary dreams. Some old woman kept cropping up, and I saw her murdered.'

'You don't say that, sir?' said William nervously.

'I do, indeed,' was the reply. 'However, that is all gone and past. I have been down in the kitchen and had a good wash, and I am as fresh as a daisy, and as hungry as a hunter; and, oh, William, can you get me any breakfast?'

'Certainly, Master Graham, I have brought round a kettle, and I will make the water boil immediately. I suppose, sir' – this tentatively – 'you'll be going home to-day?'

'Home!' repeated the young man. 'Decidedly not. I'll never go home again till I return with some medal hung to my coat, or a leg or arm cut off. I've thought it all out, William. I'll go and enlist. There's a talk of war; and, living or dead, my father shall have reason to retract his opinion about my being a coward.'

'I am sure the admiral never thought you anything of the sort, sir,' said William. 'Why, you have the pluck of ten!'

'Not before him,' answered the young fellow sadly.

'You'll do nothing rash, Master Graham; you won't go 'listing, or aught of that sort, in your anger?'

'If I do not, what is to become of me?' asked the other. 'I cannot dig – to beg I am ashamed. Why, but for you, I should not have had a roof over my head last night.'

'Not much of a roof, I am afraid, sir.'

'Not much of a roof!' repeated the young man. 'Why, who could desire a better? What a capital room this is,' he went on, looking around the apartment, where William was now kindling a fire; 'one might dine twenty people here easily!'

'If you think so well of the place, Master Graham, you might stay here for a while, till you have made up your mind what you are going to do. The landlord won't make any objection, I am very sure.'

'Oh! nonsense; he would want a long rent for a house like this.'

'I daresay; *if he could get it*,' was William's significant answer.

'What do you mean? Won't the place let?'

'No, sir. I did not tell you last night, but there was a murder done here, and people are shy of the house ever since.'

'A murder! What sort of a murder? Who was murdered?'

'A woman, Master Graham – the landlord's sister; she lived here all alone, and was supposed to have money. Whether she had or not, she was found dead from a stab in her breast, and if there ever was any money, it must have been taken at the same time, for none ever was found in the house from that day to this.'

'Was that the reason your wife would not stop here?' asked the young man, leaning against the mantleshelf, and looking thoughtfully down on William.

'Yes, sir. She could not stand it any longer; she got that thin and nervous no one would have believed it possible; she never saw anything, but she said she heard footsteps and voices, and then when she walked through the hall, or up the staircase, someone always seemed to be following her. We put the children to sleep in that big room you had last night, and they declared they often saw an old woman sitting by the hearth. Nothing ever came my way,' finished William, with a laugh; 'I was always ready to go to sleep the minute my head touched the pillow.'

'Were not the murderers discovered?' asked Graham Coulton.

'No, sir; the landlord, Miss Tynan's brother, had always lain under the suspicion of it – quite wrongfully, I am very sure – but he will never clear himself now. It was known he came and asked her for help a day or two before the murder, and it was also known he was able within a week or two to weather whatever trouble had been harassing him. Then, you see, the money was never found; and, altogether, people scarce knew what to think.'

'Humph!' ejaculated Graham Coulton, and he took a few turns up and down the apartment. 'Could I go and see this landlord?'

'Surely, sir, if you had a hat,' answered William, with such a serious decorum that the young man burst out laughing.

'That is an obstacle, certainly,' he remarked, 'and I must make a note do instead. I have a pencil in my pocket, so here goes.'

Within half an hour from the dispatch of that note William was back again with a sovereign; the landlord's compliments, and he would be much obliged if Mr. Coulton could 'step round.'

'You'll do nothing rash, sir,' entreated William.

'Why, man,' answerd the young fellow, 'one may as well be picked off by a ghost as a bullet. What is there to be afraid of?'

William only shook his head. He did not think his young master was made of the stuff likely to remain alone in a haunted house and solve the mystery it assuredly contained by dint of his own unassisted endeavours. And yet when Graham Coulton came out of the landlord's house he looked more bright and gay than usual, and walked up the Lambeth road to the place where Wiliam awaited his return, humming an air as he paced along.

'We have settled the matter,' he said. 'And now if the dad wants his son for Christmas, it will trouble him to find him.'

'Don't say that, Master Graham, don't,' entreated the man, with a shiver; 'maybe after all it would have been better if you had never happened to chance upon Vauxhall Walk.'

'Don't croak, William,' answered the young man; 'if it was not the best day's work I ever did for myself I'm a Dutchman.'

During the whole of that afternoon, Graham Coulton searched diligently for the missing treasure Mr. Tynan assured him had never been discovered. Youth is confident, and self-opinionated, and this fresh explorer felt satisfied that, though others had failed, he would be successful. On the second floor he found one door locked, but he did not pay much attention to that at the moment, as he believed if there was anything concealed it was more likely to be found in the lower than the upper part of the house. Late into the evening he pursued his researches in the kitchen and cellars and old-fashioned cupboards, of which the basement had an abundance.

It was nearly eleven, when, engaged in poking about amongst the empty bins of a wine cellar as large as a family vault, he suddenly felt a rush of cold air at his back. Moving, his candle was instantly extinguished, and in the very moment of being left in darkness he saw, standing in the doorway, a woman, resembling her who had haunted his dreams overnight.

He rushed with outstretched hands to seize her, but clutched only air. He relit his candle, and closely examined the basement, shutting off communication with the ground floor ere doing so. All in vain. Not a trace could he find of living creature – not a window was open – not a door unbolted.

'It is very odd,' he thought, as, after securely fastening the door at the top of the staircase, he searched the whole upper portion of the house, with the exception of the one room mentioned.

'I must get the key of that to-morrow,' he decided, standing gloomily with his back to the fire and his eyes wandering about the drawing-room, where he had once again taken up his abode.

Even as the thought passed through his mind, he saw standing in the open doorway a woman with white dishevelled hair, clad in mean garments, ragged and dirty. She lifted her hand and shook it at him with a menacing gesture, and then, just as he was darting towards her, a wonderful thing occurred.

From behind the great mirror there glided a second female figure, at the sight of which the first turned and fled, uttering piercing shrieks as the other followed her up the stairs.

Sick almost with terror, Graham Coulton watched the dreadful pair as they fled upstairs past the locked room to the top of the house.

It was a few minutes before he recovered his self-possession. When he did so, and searched the upper apartments, he found them totally empty.

That night, ere lying down before the fire, he carefully locked and bolted the drawing-room door; before he did more he drew the heavy settle in front of it, so that if the lock were forced no entrance could be effected without considerable noise.

For some time he lay awake, then dropped into a deep sleep, from which he was awakened suddenly by a noise as if of something scuffling stealthily behind the wainscot. He raised himself on his elbow and listened, and, to his consternation, beheld seated at the opposite side of the hearth the same woman he had seen before in his dreams, lamenting over her gold.

The fire was not quite out, and at the moment shot up a last tongue of flame. By the light, transient as it was, he saw that the figure pressed a ghostly finger to its lips, and by the turn of his head and the attitude of its body seemed to be listening.

He listened also – indeed, he was too much frightened to do aught else; more and more distinct grew the sounds which had aroused him, a stealthy rustling coming nearer and nearer – up and up it seemed, behind the wainscot.

'It is rats,' thought the young man, though, indeed, his teeth were almost chattering in his head with fear. But then in a moment he saw what disabused him of that idea – *the gleam of a candle or lamp through a crack in the panelling.* He tried to rise, he strove to shout – all in vain; and, sinking down, remembered nothing more till he awoke to find the grey light of an early morning stealing through one of the shutters he had left partially unclosed.

For hours after his breakfast, which he scarcely touched, long after William had left him at mid-day, Graham Coulton, having in the morning made a long and close survey of the house, sat thinking before the fire, then, apparently having made up his mind, he put on the hat he had bought, and went out.

When he returned the evening shadows were darkening down, but the pavements were full of people going marketing, for it was Christmas Eve, and all who had money to spend seemed bent on shopping.

It was terribly dreary inside the old house that night. Through the deserted rooms Graham could feel that ghostly semblance was wandering mournfully. When he turned his back he knew she was flitting from the mirror to the fire, from the fire to the mirror; but he was not afraid of her now – he was far more afraid of another matter he had taken in hand that day.

The horror of the silent house grew and grew upon him. He could hear the beating of his own heart in the dead quietude which reigned from garret to cellar.

At last William came; but the young man said nothing to him of what was in his mind. He talked to him cheerfully and hopefully enough – wondered where his father would think he had got to, and hoped Mr. Tynan might send him some Christmas pudding. Then the man said it was time for him to go, and, when Mr. Coulton went downstairs to the hall-door, remarked the key was not in it.

'No,' was the answer, 'I took it out to-day, to oil it.'

'It wanted oiling,' agreed William, 'for it worked terribly stiff.' Having uttered which truism he departed.

Very slowly the young man retraced his way to the drawing-room, where he only paused to lock the door on the outside; then taking off his boots he went up to the top of the house, where, entering the front attic, he waited patiently in darkness and in silence.

It was a long time, or at least it seemed long to him, before he heard the same sound which had aroused him on the previous night – a stealthy rustling – then a rush of cold air – then cautious footsteps – then the quiet opening of a door below.

It did not take as long in action as it has required to tell. In a moment the young man was out on the landing and had closed a portion of the panelling on the wall which stood open; noiselessly he crept back to the attic window, unlatched it, and sprung a rattle, the sound of which echoed far and near through the deserted streets, then rushing down the stairs, he encountered a man who, darting past him, made for the landing above; but perceiving that way of escape closed, fled down again, to find Graham struggling desperately with his fellow.

'Give him the knife – come along,' he said savagely; and next instant Graham felt something like a hot iron through his shoulder, and then heard a thud, as one of the men, tripping in his rapid flight, fell from the top of the stairs to the bottom.

At the same moment there came a crash, as if the house was falling, and faint, sick, and bleeding, young Coulton lay insensible on the threshold of the room where Miss Tynan had been murdered.

When he recovered he was in the dining-room, and a doctor wsa examining his wound.

Near the door a policeman stiffly kept guard. The hall was full of people; all the misery and vagabondism the streets contain at that hour was crowding in to see what had happened.

Through the midst two men were being conveyed to the station-house; one, with his head dreadfully injured, on a stretcher, the other handcuffed, uttering frightful imprecations as he went.

After a time the house was cleared of the rabble, the police took possession of it, and Mr. Tynan was sent for.

'What was that dreadful noise?' asked Graham feebly, now seated on the floor, with his back resting against the wall.

'I do not know. Was there a noise?' said Mr. Tynan, humouring his fancy, as he thought.

'Yes, in the drawing-room, I think; the key is in my pocket.'

Still humouring the wounded lad, Mr. Tynan took the key and ran upstairs.

When he unlocked the door, what a sight met his eyes! The mirror had fallen – it was lying all over the floor shivered into a thousand pieces; the console table had been borne down by its weight, and the marble slab was shattered as well. But this was not what chained his attention. Hundreds, thousands of gold pieces were scattered about, and an aperture behind the glass contained boxes filled with securities and deeds and bonds, the possession of which had cost his sister her life.

'Well, Graham, and what do you want?' asked Admiral Coulton that evening as his eldest born appeared before him, looking somewhat pale but otherwise unchanged.

'I want nothing,' was the answer, 'but to ask your forgiveness. William has told me all the story I never knew before; and, if you let me, I will try to make it up to you for the trouble you have had. I am provided for,' went on the young fellow, with a nervous laugh; 'I have made my fortune since I left you, and another man's fortune as well.'

'I think you are out of your senses,' said the Admiral shortly.

'No, sir, I have found them,' was the answer; 'and I mean to strive and make a better thing of my life than I should ever have done had I not gone to the Old House in Vauxhall Walk.'

'Vauxhall Walk! What is the lad talking about?'

'I will tell you, sir, if I may sit down,' was Graham Coulton's answer, and then he told this story.

The Drunkard's Death

CHARLES DICKENS

If any author ever captured the essence of early Victorian life as he saw it, it must have been Charles Dickens (1812–1870). Born in poverty, the son of a well-paid but spendthrift navy payclerk, Dickens found himself taken away from school at the age of twelve and sent to work in a factory. This experience scarred him for life. It showed him at first-hand just what life was like for the poor of Victorian England, and he never forgot. After starting work at the age of fifteen as a clerk in a solicitor's office, he finally ended up as a reporter in the courts, and it was in this job that he started writing. In 1832 he began sending articles and stories to the papers and magazines, which were collected together into his first book SKETCHES BY BOZ *(1836). This led to* THE PICKWICK PAPERS *which became the most popular serialised work in the country and Dickens was a best seller from then on.*

Dickens never forgot that early taste of poverty; it coloured much of his work and some of his experiences eventually found their way in novel form into DAVID COPPERFIELD *(1850). He used his success to draw the attention of the public to the life of the poor, in a society that was largely indifferent to their fate.*

Charles Dickens had another, perhaps more potent, fixation. As his biographer Philip Collins points out: 'the themes of crime, evil and psychological abnormality recurred throughout his novels; a great celebrator of life, he was also obsessed with death.'

His fascination with death led him to introduce it into nearly every book he wrote. It could be sentimental – like the death of Smike in NICHOLAS NICKLEBY *– or it could be brutal and horrifying – like the deaths of Nancy and Bill Sikes in* OLIVER TWIST. *Death and poverty: Dickens showed them both again and again.*

In 'The Drunkard's Death', which comes from SKETCHES BY BOZ, *we find these twin obsessions brought together for perhaps the first time in the author's career. This is among the first things he ever wrote and has remained fairly neglected for years. While Dickens' youthful zeal sometimes lets him apply the effects with a shovel, it is still a grim tale with a tragic ending – a nightmare indeed.*

CHARLES DICKENS
The Drunkard's Death

We will be bold to say, that there is scarcely a man in the constant habit of walking, day after day, through any of the crowded thoroughfares of London, who cannot recollect among the people whom he 'knows by sight,' to use a familiar phrase, some being of abject and wretched appearance whom he remembers to have seen in a very different condition, whom he has observed sinking lower and lower by almost imperceptible degrees, and the shabbiness and utter destitution of whose appearance, at last, strike forcibly and painfully upon him, as he passes by. Is there any man who has mixed much with society, or whose avocations have caused him to mingle, at one time or other, with a great number of people, who cannot call to mind the time when some shabby, miserable wretch, in rags and filth, who shuffles past him now in all the squalor of disease and poverty, was a respectable tradesman, or a clerk, or a man following some thriving pursuit, with good prospects, and decent means; – or cannot any of our readers call to mind from among the list of their *quondam* acquaintance, some fallen and degraded man, who lingers about the pavement in hungry misery – from whom every one turns coldly away, and who preserves himself from sheer starvation, nobody knows how? Alas! such cases are of too frequent occurrence to be rare items in any man's experience; and but too often arise from one cause – drunkenness, – that fierce rage for the slow, sure poison, that oversteps every other consideration; that casts aside wife, children, friends, happiness, and station; and hurries its victims madly on to degradation and death.

Some of these men have been impelled by misfortune and misery, to the vice that has degraded them. The ruin of worldly expectations, the death of those they loved, the sorrow that slowly consumes, but will not break the heart, has driven them wild; and they present the hideous spectacle of madmen, slowly dying by their own hands. But, by far the greater part have wilfully, and with open eyes, plunged into the gulf from which the man who once enters it never rises more, but into which he sinks deeper and deeper down, until recovery is hopeless.

Such a man as this, once stood by the bed-side of his dying wife, while his children knelt around, and mingled low bursts of grief with their innocent prayers. The room was scantily and meanly furnished; and it needed but a glance at the pale form from which the light of life was fast passing away, to know that grief, and want, and anxious care, had been busy at the heart for many a weary year. An elderly female with her face bathed in tears, was supporting the head of the dying woman – her daughter – on her arm. But it was not towards her that the wan face turned; it was not her hand that the cold and trembling fingers clasped; they pressed the husband's arm; the eyes so soon to be closed in death, rested on his face; and the man shook beneath their gaze. His dress was slovenly and disordered, his face inflamed, his eyes blood-shot and heavy. He had been summoned from some wild debauch to the bed of sorrow and death.

A shaded lamp by the bed-side cast a dim light on the figures around, and left the remainder of the room in thick, deep shadow. The silence of night prevailed without the house, and the stillness of death was in the chamber. A watch hung over the mantelshelf; its low ticking was the only sound that broke the profound quiet, but it was a solemn one, for well they knew, who heard it, that before it had recorded the passing of another hour, it would beat the knell of a departed spirit.

It is a dreadful thing to wait and watch for the approach of death; to know that hope is gone, and recovery impossible; and to sit and count the dreary hours through long, long, nights – such nights as only watchers by the bed of sickness know. It chills the blood to hear the dearest secrets of the heart, the pent-up, hidden secrets of many years, poured forth by the unconscious helpless being before you; and to think how little the reserve, and cunning of a whole life will avail, when fever and delirium tear off the mask at last. Strange tales have been told in the wanderings of dying men; tales so full of guilt and crime, that those who stood by the sick person's couch have fled in horror and affright, lest they should be scared to madness by what they heard and saw; and many a wretch has died alone, raving of deeds, the very name of which, has driven the boldest man away.

But no such ravings were to be heard at the bed-side by which the children knelt. Their half-stifled sobs and moanings alone broke the silence of the lonely chamber. And when at last the mother's grasp relaxed; and turning one look from the children to their father, she vainly strove to speak, and fell backwards on the pillow, all was so calm and tranquil that she seemed to sink to sleep. They leant over her; they called upon her name, softly at first, and then in the loud and piercing tones of desperation. But there was no reply. They listened for her breath, but no sound came. They felt for the palpitation of the heart, but no faint throb responded to the touch. That heart was broken, and she was dead!

The husband sunk into a chair by the bed-side, and clasped his hands upon his burning forehead. He gazed from child to child, but when a weeping eye met his, he quailed beneath its look. No word of comfort was whispered in his ear, no look of kindness lighted on his face. All shrunk from, and avoided him; and when at last he staggered from the room, no one sought to follow, or console the widower.

The time had been, when many a friend would have crowded round him in his affliction, and many a heartfelt condolence would have met him in his grief. Where were they now? One by one, friends, relations, the commonest acquaintance even, had fallen off from and deserted the drunkard. His wife alone had clung to him in good and evil, in sickness and poverty; and how had he rewarded her? He had reeled from the tavern to her bedside, in time to see her die.

He rushed from the house, and walked swiftly through the streets. Remorse, fear, shame, all crowded on his mind. Stupefied with drink, and bewildered with the scene he had just witnessed, he re-entered the tavern he had quitted shortly before. Glass succeeded glass. His blood mounted, and his brain whirled round. Death. Every one must die, and why not *she*. She was too good for him, her relations had often told him so. Curses on them! Had they not deserted her, and left her to while away the time at home? Well she was dead, and happy perhaps. It was

better as it was. Another glass – one more! Hurrah! It was a
merry life while it lasted; and he would make the most of it.

Time went on; the three children who were left to him, grew
up, and were children no longer; – the father remained the same
– poorer, shabbier, and more dissolute-looking, but the same
confirmed and irreclaimable drunkard. The boys had, long ago,
run wild in the streets, and left him; the girl alone remained, but
she worked hard, and words or blows could always procure him
something for the tavern. So he went on in the old course, and a
merry life he led.

One night, as early as ten o'clock – for the girl had been sick
for many days, and there was, consequently, little to spend at the
public-house – he bent his steps homewards, bethinking himself
that if he would have her able to earn money, it would be as well
to apply to the parish surgeon, or, at all events, to take the trouble
of inquiring what ailed her, which he had not yet thought it worth
while to do. It was a wet December night; the wind blew piercing
cold, and the rain poured heavily down. He begged a few half-
pence from a passer by, and having bought a small loaf (for it was
his interest to keep the girl alive, if he could); he shuffled
onwards, as fast as the wind and rain would let him.

At the back of Fleet Street, and lying between it, and the
waterside, are several mean and narrow courts, which form a
portion of Whitefriars; it was to one of these, that he directed his
steps.

The alley into which he turned, might, for filth and misery,
have competed with the darkest corner of this ancient sanctuary
in its dirtiest and most lawless time. The houses, varying from
two stories in height to four, were stained with every indescribable hue that long exposure to the weather, damp, and rottenness
can impart to tenements composed originally of the roughest and
coarsest materials. The windows were patched with paper, and
stuffed with the foulest rags; the doors were falling from their
hinges; poles with lines on which to dry clothes, projected from
every casement, and sounds of quarrelling or drunkenness
issued from every room.

The solitary oil lamp in the centre of the court had been blown
out, either by the violence of the wind or the act of some
inhabitant who had excellent reasons for objecting to his

residence being rendered too conspicuous; and the only light which fell upon the broken and uneven pavement, was derived from the miserable candles that here and there twinkled in the rooms of such of the more fortunate residents as could afford to indulge in so expensive a luxury. A gutter ran down the centre of the alley – all the sluggish odours of which had been called forth by the rain; and as the wind whistled through the old houses, the doors and shutters creaked upon their hinges, and the windows shook in their frames, with a violence which every moment seemed to threaten the destruction of the whole place.

The man whom we have followed into this den, walked on in the darkness, sometimes stumbling into the main gutter, and at others into some branch repositories of garbage which had been formed by the rain, until he reached the last house in the court. The door, or rather what was left of it, stood ajar, for the convenience of the numerous lodgers; and he proceeded to grope his way up the old and broken stair, to the attic storey.

He was within a step or two of his room door, when it opened, and a girl, whose miserable and emaciated appearance was only to be equalled by that of the candle which she shaded with her hand, peeped anxiously out.

'Is that you, father?' said the girl.

'Who else should it be?' replied the man gruffly. 'What are you trembling at? It's little enough that I've had to drink to-day, for there's no drink without money, and no money without work. What the devil's the matter with the girl?'

'I am not well father – not at all well,' said the girl, bursting into tears.

'Ah!' replied the man, in the tone of a person who is compelled to admit a very unpleasant fact, to which he would rather remain blind, if he could. 'You must get better somehow, for we must have money. You must go to the parish doctor, and make him give you some medicine. They're paid for it, damn 'em. What are you standing before the door for? Let me come in, can't you?' 'Father,' whispered the girl, shutting the door behind her, and placing herself before it, 'William has come back.'

'Who!' said the man, with a start.

'Hush,' replied the girl, 'William; brother William.'

'And what does he want?' said the man, with an effort at composure— 'money? meat? drink? he's come to the wrong shop for that, if he does. Give me the candle – give me the candle, fool – I ain't going to hurt him.' He snatched the candle from her hand, and walked into the room.

Sitting on an old box, with his head resting on his hand, and his eyes fixed on a wretched cinder fire that was smouldering on the hearth, was a young man of about two-and-twenty, miserably clad in an old coarse jacket and trousers. He started up when his father entered.

'Fasten the door, Mary,' said the young man hastily — 'Fasten the door. You look as if you didn't know me, father. it's long enough, since you drove me from home; you may well forget me.'

'And what do you want here, now?' said the father, seating himself on a stool, on the other side of the fireplace. 'What do you want here, now?'

'Shelter,' replied the son, 'I'm in trouble; that's enough. If I'm caught I shall swing; that's certain. Caught I shall be, unless I stop here; that's *as* certain. And there's an end of it.'

'You mean to say, you've been robbing, or murdering, then?' said the father.

'Yes, I do,' replied the son. 'Does it surprise you, father?' he looked steadily in the man's face, but he withdrew his eyes, and bent them on the ground.

'Where's your brothers?' he said, after a long pause.

'Where they'll never trouble you,' replied his son: 'John's gone to America, and Henry's dead.'

'Dead!' said the father, with a shudder, which even he could not repress.

'Dead,' replied the young man. 'He died in my arms – shot like a dog, by a game-keeper. He staggered back, I caught him, and his blood trickled down my hands. It poured out from his side like water. He was weak, and it blinded him, but he threw himself down on his knees, on the grass, and prayed to God, that if his mother was in Heaven, He would hear her prayers for pardon for her youngest son. "I was her favourite boy, Will," he said, "and I am glad to think, now, that when she was dying, though I was a young child then, and my little heart was almost bursting, I knelt down at the foot of the bed, and thanked God for having made me so fond of hèr as to have never once done anything to bring the tears into her eyes. Oh, Will, why was she taken away, and father left!" There's his dying words, father,' said the young man; 'make the best you can of 'em. You struck him across the face, in a drunken fit, the morning we ran away; and here's the end of it.'

The girl wept aloud; and the father, sinking his head upon his knees, rocked himself to and fro.

'If I am taken,' said the young man, 'I shall be carried back into the country, and hung for that man's murder. They cannot trace me here, without your assistance, father. For aught I know, you may give me up to justice; but unless you do, here I stop, until I can venture to escape abroad.'

For two whole days, all three remained in the wretched room, without stirring out. On the third evening, however, the girl was worse than she had been yet, and the few scraps of food they had were gone. It was indispensably necessary that somebody should go out; and as the girl was too weak and ill, the father went, just at nightfall.

He got some medicine for the girl, and a trifle in the way of pecuniary assistance. On his way back, he earned sixpence by holding a horse; and he turned homewards with enough money to supply their most pressing wants for two or three days to come. He had to pass the public-house. He lingered for an instant, walked past it, turned back again, lingered once more, and finally slunk in. Two men whom he had not observed, were on the watch. They were on the point of giving up their search in despair, when his loitering attracted their attention; and when he entered the public-house, they followed him.

'You'll drink with me, master,' said one of them, proffering him a glass of liquor.

'And me too,' said the other, replenishing the glass as soon as it was drained of its contents.

The man thought of his hungry children, and his son's danger. But they were nothing to the drunkard. He *did* drink; and his reason left him.

'A wet night, Warden,' whispered one of the men in his ear, as he at length turned to go away, after spending in liquor one-half of the money on which, perhaps, his daughter's life depended.

'The right sort of night for our friends in hiding, Master Warden,' whispered the other.

'Sit down here,' said the one who had spoken first, drawing him into a corner. 'We have been looking arfter the young un. We came to tell him, it's all right now, but we couldn't find him 'cause we hadn't got the precise direction. But that ain't strange, for I don't think he know'd it himself, when he come to London, did he?'

'No, he didn't,' replied the father.

The two men exchanged glances.

'There's a vessel down at the docks, to sail at midnight, when it's high water,' resumed the first speaker, 'and we'll put him on board. His passage is taken in another name, and what's better than that, it's paid for. It's lucky we met you.'

'Very,' said the second.

'Capital luck,' said the first, with a wink to his companion.

'Great,' replied the second, with a slight nod of intelligence.

'Another glass here; quick' – said the first speaker. And in five minutes more, the father had unconsciously yielded up his own son into the hangman's hands.

Slowly and heavily the time dragged along, as the brother and sister, in their miserable hiding-place, listened in anxious suspense to the slightest sound. At length, a heavy footstep was heard upon the stair; it approached nearer; it reached the landing; and the father staggered into the room.

The girl saw that he was intoxicated, and advanced with the candle in her hand to meet him; she stopped short, gave a loud scream, and fell senseless on the ground. She had caught sight of the shadow of a man, reflected on the floor. They both rushed in, and in another instant the young man was a prisoner, and handcuffed.

'Very quietly done,' said one of the men to his companion, 'thanks to the old man. Lift up the girl, Tom – come, come, it's no use crying, young woman. It's all over now, and can't be helped.'

The young man stooped for an instant over the girl, and then turned fiercely round upon his father, who had reeled against the wall, and was gazing on the group with drunken stupidity.

'Listen to me, father,' he said, in a tone that made the drunkard's flesh creep. 'My brother's blood, and mine, is on your head: I never had kind look, or word, or care, from you, and alive or dead, I never will forgive you. Die when you will, or how, I will be with you. I speak as a dead man now, and I warn you, father, that as surely as you must one day stand before your Maker so surely shall your children be there, hand in hand, to cry for judgment against you.' He raised his manacled hands in a threatening attitude, fixed his eyes on his shrinking parent, and slowly left the room; and neither father nor sister ever beheld him more, on this side of the grave.

When the dim and misty light of a winter's morning penetrated into the narrow court, and struggled through the begrimed window of the wretched room, Warden awoke from his heavy sleep, and found himself alone. He rose, and looked round him; the old flock mattress on the floor was undisturbed; every thing was just as he remembered to have seen it last; and there were no signs of any one, save himself, having occupied the room during the night. He inquired of the other lodgers, and of the neighbours; but his daughter had not been seen or heard of. He rambled through the streets, and scrutinized each wretched face among the crowds that thronged them, with anxious eyes. But his search was fruitless, and he returned to his garret when night came on, desolate and weary.

For many days he occupied himself in the same manner, but no trace of his daughter did he meet with, and no word of her reached his ears. At length he gave up the pursuit as hopeless. He had long thought of the probability of her leaving him, and endeavouring to gain her bread in quiet, elsewhere. She had left him at last to starve alone. He ground his teeth, and cursed her!

He begged his bread from door to door. Every halfpenny he could wring from the pity or credulity of those to whom he addressed himself, was spent in the old way. A year passed over his head; the roof of a jail was the only one that had sheltered him for many months. He slept under archways, and in brickfields – any where, where there was some warmth or shelter from the cold and rain. But in the last stage of poverty, disease, and houseless want, he was a drunkard still.

At last, one bitter night, he sank down on a door-step faint and ill. The premature decay of vice and profligacy had worn him to the bone. His cheeks were hollow and livid; his eyes were sunken, and their sight was dim. His legs trembled beneath his weight, and a cold shiver ran through every limb.

And now the long-forgotten scenes of a misspent life crowded thick and fast upon him. He thought of the time when he had a home – a happy, cheerful home – and of those who peopled it, and flocked about him then, until the forms of his elder children seemed to rise from the grave, and stand about him – so plain, so clear, and so distinct they were that he could touch and feel them. Looks that he had long forgotten were fixed upon him once more; voices long since hushed in death sounded in his ears like the music of village bells. But it was only for an instant. The rain beat heavily upon him; and cold and hunger were gnawing at his heart again.

He rose, and dragged his feeble limbs a few paces further. The street was silent and empty; the few passengers who passed by, at that late hour, hurried quickly on, and his tremulous voice was lost in the violence of the storm. Again that heavy chill struck through his frame, and his blood seem to stagnate beneath it. He coiled himself up in a projecting doorway, and tried to sleep.

But sleep had fled from his dull and glazed eyes. His mind wandered strangely, but he was awake, and conscious. The well-known shout of drunken mirth sounded in his ear, the glass was at his lips, the board was covered with choice rich food – they were all before him: he could see them all, he had but to reach out his hand, and take them – and, though the illusion was reality itself, he knew that he was sitting alone in the deserted street, watching the rain-drops as they pattered on the stones; that death was coming upon him by inches – and that there were none to care for or help him.

Suddenly, he started up, in the extremity of terror. He had heard his own voice shouting in the night air, he knew not what, or why. Hark! A groan! – another! His senses were leaving him: half-formed and incoherent words burst from his lips; and his hands sought to tear and lacerate his flesh. He was going mad, and he shrieked for help till his voice failed him.

He raised his head, and looked up the long dismal street. He recollected that outcasts like himself, condemned to wander day and night in those dreadful streets, had sometimes gone distracted with their own loneliness. He remembered to have heard many years before that a homeless wretch had once been found in a solitary corner, sharpening a rusty knife to plunge into his own heart, preferring death to that endless, weary, wandering to and fro. In an instant his resolve was taken, his limbs received new life; he ran quickly from the spot, and paused not for breath until he reached the river-side.

He crept softly down the steep stone stairs that lead from the commencement of Waterloo Bridge, down to the water's level. He crouched into a corner, and held his breath, as the patrol passed. Never did prisoner's heart throb with the hope of liberty and life half so eagerly as did that of the wretched man at the prospect of death. The watch passed close to him, but he remained unobserved; and after waiting till the sound of footsteps had died away in the distance, he cautiously descended, and stood beneath the gloomy arch that forms the landing-place from the river.

The tide was in, and the water flowed at his feet. The rain had ceased, the wind was lulled, and all was, for the moment, still and quiet – so quiet that the slightest sound on the opposite bank, even the rippling of the water against the barges that were moored there, was distinctly audible to his ear. The stream stole languidly and sluggishly on. Strange and fantastic forms rose to the surface, and beckoned him to approach; dark gleaming eyes peered from the water, and seemed to mock his hesitation, while hollow murmurs from behind, urged him onwards. He retreated a few paces, took a short run, desperate leap, and plunged into the river.

Not five seconds had passed when he rose to the water's surface – but what a change had taken place in that short time, in all his thoughts and feelings! Life– life – in any form, poverty, misery, starvation – anything but death. He fought and struggled with the water that closed over his head, and screamed in agonies of terror. The curse of his own son rang in his ears. The shore – but one foot of dry ground – he could almost touch the step. One hand's breadth nearer, and he was saved – but the tide bore him onward, under the dark arches of the bridge, and he sank to the bottom.

Again he rose, and struggled for life. For one instant – for one brief instant – the buildings on the river's banks, the lights on the bridge through which the current had borne him, the black water, and the fast flying clouds, were distinctly visible – once more he sank, and once again he rose. Bright flames of fire shot up from earth to heaven, and reeled before his eyes, while the water thundered in his ears, and stunned him with its furious roar.

A week afterwards the body was washed ashore, some miles down the river, a swollen and disfigured mass. Unrecognised and unpitied, it was borne to the grave; and there it has long since mouldered away!

Luella Miller

MARY E. WILKINS-FREEMAN

Holding a place as she does in the leading ranks of American regional authors, Mary Eleanor Wilkins-Freeman has gained lasting recognition more for her New England stories than her tales of the supernatural. Born in Massachusetts in 1852, she started her writing career with poetry but, while employed as secretary to the novelist Oliver Wendell Holmes, she fell under the influence of the fiction market and started writing novels and short stories herself. Before her death in 1930, she produced a dozen novels and over two hundred short stories. Several volumes of her tales are worth finding, among them SILENCE *(1898),* CINNAMON ROSES *(1901),* THE POT OF GOLD *(1892) and the late volume* A FAR AWAY MELODY *(1922). Her best ghost stories were all in* THE WIND IN THE ROSE BUSH *(1903), from which comes 'Luella Miller'. This is a vampire story but of a kind you won't have read before. Forget about the blood and the stakes; Luella Miller's vampirism was of another kind altogether but no less deadly, and no less scary.*

MARY E. WILKINS-FREEMAN
Luella Miller

Close to the village street stood the one-storey house in which Luella Miller, who had an evil name in the village, had dwelt. She had been dead for years, yet there were those in the village who, in spite of the clearer light which comes on a vantage-point from a long-past danger, half believed in the tale which they had heard from their childhood. In their hearts, although they scarcely would have owned it, was a survival of the wild horror and frenzied fear of their ancestors who had dwelt in the same age with Luella Miller. Young people even would stare with a shudder at the old house as they passed, and children never played around it as was their wont around an untenanted building. Not a window in the old Miller house was broken: the panes reflected the morning sunlight in patches of emerald and blue, and the latch of the sagging front door was never lifted, although no bolt secured it. Since Luella Miller had been carried out of it, the house had had no tenant except one friendless old soul who had no choice between that and the far-off shelter of the open sky. This old woman, who had survived her kindred and friends, lived in the house one week, then one morning no smoke came out of the chimney, and a body of neighbours, a score strong, entered and found her dead in her bed. There were dark whispers as to the cause of her death, and there were those who testified to an expression of fear so exalted that it showed forth the state of the departing soul upon the dead face. The old woman had been hale and hearty when she entered the house, and in seven days she was dead; it seemed that she had fallen a victim to some uncanny power. The minister talked in the pulpit with covert severity against the sin of superstition; still the belief prevailed. Not a soul in the village but would have chosen the almshouse rather than that dwelling. No vagrant, if he heard the tale, would seek shelter beneath that old roof, unhallowed by nearly half a century of superstitious fear.

There was only one person in the village who had actually known Luella Miller. That person was a woman well over eighty, but a marvel of vitality and unextinct youth. Straight as an arrow, with the spring of one recently let loose from the bow of life, she moved about the streets, and she always went to church, rain or shine. She had never married, and had lived alone for years in a house across the road from Luella Miller's.

This woman had none of the garrulousness of age, but never in all her life had she ever held her tongue for any will save her own, and she never spared the truth when she essayed to present it. She it was who bore testimony to the life, evil, though possibly wittingly or designedly so, of Luella Miller, and to her personal appearance. When this old woman spoke – and she had the gift of description, although her thoughts were clothed in the rude vernacular of her native village – one could seem to see Luella Miller as she had really looked. According to this woman, Lydia Anderson by name, Luella Miller had been a beauty of a type rather unusual in New England. She had been a slight, pliant sort of creature, as ready with a strong yielding to fate and as unbreakable as a willow. She had glimmering lengths of straight, fair hair, which she wore softly looped round a long, lovely face. She had blue eyes full of soft pleading, little slender, clinging hands, and a wonderful grace of motion and attitude.

'Luella Miller used to sit in a way nobody else could if they sat up and studied a week of Sundays,' said Lydia Anderson, 'and it was a sight to see her walk. If one of them willows over there on the edge of the brook could start up and get its roots free of the ground, and move off, it would go just the way Luella Miller used to. She had a green shot silk she used to wear, too, and a hat with green ribbon streamers, and a lace veil blowing across her face and out sideways, and a green ribbon flyin' from her waist. That was what she came out bride in when she married Erastus Miller. Her name before she was married was Hill. There was always a sight of 'l's' in her name, married or single. Erastus Miller was good lookin', too, better lookin' than Luella. Sometimes I used to think that Luella wa'n't so handsome after all. Erastus just about worshipped her. I used to know him pretty well. He lived next door to me, and we went to school together. Folks used to say he was waitin' on me, but he wa'n't. I never thought he was except once or twice when he said things that some girls might have suspected meant somethin'. That was before Luella came here to teach the district school. It was funny how she came to get it, for folks said she hadn't any education, and that one of the big girls, Lottie Henderson, used to do all the teachin' for her, while she sat back and did embroidery work on a cambric pocket-handkerchief. Lottie Henderson was a real smart girl, a splendid scholar, and she just set her eyes by Luella, as all the girls did. Lottie would have made a real smart woman, but she died when Luella had been here about a year – just faded away and died: nobody knew what ailed her. She dragged herself to that schoolhouse and helped Luella teach till the very last minute. The committee all knew how Luella didn't do much of the work herself, but they winked at it. It wa'n't long after Lottie died that Erastus married her. I always thought he hurried it up because she wa'n't fit to teach. One of the big boys used to help her after Lottie died, but he hadn't much government, and the school didn't do very well, and Luella might have had to give it up, for the committee couldn't have shut their eyes to things much longer. The boy that helped her was a real honest, innocent sort of fellow, and he was a good scholar, too. Folks said he overstudied, and that was the reason he was took crazy the year after Luella married, but I don't know. And I don't know what made Erastus Miller go into consumption of the blood the year after he was married: consumption wa'n't in his family. He just grew weaker and weaker, and went almost bent double when he tried to wait on Luella, and he spoke feeble, like an old man. He worked terrible hard till the last trying to save up a little to leave Luella. I've seen him out in the worst storms on a wood-sled – he used to cut and sell wood – and he was hunched up on top lookin' more dead than alive. Once I couldn't stand it: I went over and helped him pitch some wood on the cart – I was always strong in my arms. I wouldn't stop for all he told me to, and I guess he was glad enough for the help. That was only a week before he died. He fell on the kitchen floor while he was gettin' breakfast. He always got the breakfast and let Luella lay abed. He did all the sweepin' and the washin' and the ironin' and most of the cookin'. He couldn't bear to have Luella lift her finger, and she let him do for her. She lived like a queen for all the work she did. She didn't even do her sewin'. She said it made her shoulder ache to sew, and poor Erastus's sister Lily used to do all her sewin'. She said it made her shoulder ache to sew, and poor Erastus's sister Lily used to do all her sewin'. She wa'n't able to, either; she was never strong in her back, but she did it beautifully. She had to, to suit Luella, she was so dreadful particular. I never saw anythin' like the fagottin' and hemstitchin' that Lily Miller did for Luella. She made all Luella's weddin' outfit, and that green silk dress, after Maria Babbit cut it. Maria she cut it for nothin', and she did a lot more cuttin' and fittin' for nothin' for Luella, too. Lily Miller went to live with Luella after Erastus died. She gave up her home, though she was real attached to it and wa'n't a mite afraid to stay alone. She rented it and she went to live with Luella right away after the funeral.'

Then this old woman, Lydia Anderson, who remembered Luella Miller, would go on to relate the story of Lily Miller. It seemed that on the removal of Lily Miller to the house of her dead brother, to live with his widow, the village people first began to talk. This Lily Miller had been hardly past her first youth, and a most robust and blooming woman, rosy-cheeked, with curls of strong, black hair overshadowing round, candid temples and bright dark eyes. It was not six months after she had taken up her residence with her sister-in-law that her rosy colour faded and her pretty curves became wan hollows. White shadows began to show in the black rings of her hair, and the light died out of her eyes, her features sharpened, and there were pathetic lines at her mouth, which yet wore always an expression of utter sweetness and even happiness. She was devoted to her sister; there was no doubt that she loved her with her whole heart, and was perfectly content in her service. It was her sole anxiety lest she should die and leave her alone.

'The way Lily Miller used to talk about Luella was enough to make you mad and enough to make you cry,' said Lydia Anderson. 'I've been in there sometimes toward the last when she was too feeble to cook and carried her some blanc-mange or custard – somethin' I thought she might relish, and she'd thank me, and when I asked her how she was, say she felt better than she did yesterday, and asked me if I didn't think she looked better, dreadful pitiful, and say poor Luella had an awful time

takin' care of her and doin' the work – she wa'n't strong enough
to do anythin' – when all the time Luella wa'n't liftin' her finger
and poor Lily didn't get any care except what the neighbours
gave her, and Luella eat up everythin' that was carried in for
Lily. I had it real straight that she did. Luella used to just sit and
cry and do nothin'. She did act real fond of Lily, and she pined
away considerable, too. There was those that thought she'd go
into a decline herself. But after Lily died, her Aunt Abby Mixter
came, and then Luella picked up and grew as fat and rosy as
ever. But poor Aunt Abby begun to droop just the way Lily had,
and I guess somebody wrote to her married daughter, Mrs. Sam
Abbot, who lived in Barre, for she wrote her mother that she
must leave right away and come and make her a visit, but Aunt
Abby wouldn't go. I can see her now. She was a real good-
lookin' woman, tall and large, with a big, square face and a high
forehead that looked of itself kind of benevolent and good. She
just tended out on Luella as if she had been a baby, and when
her married daughter sent for her she wouldn't stir one inch.
She'd always thought a lot of her daughter, too, but she said
Luella needed her and her married daughter didn't. Her
daughter kept writin' and writin', but it didn't do any good.
Finally she came, and when she saw how bad her mother looked,
she broke down and cried and all but went on her knees to have
her come away. She spoke her mind out to Luella, too. She told
her that she'd killed her husband and everybody that had
anythin' to do with her, and she'd thank her to leave her mother
alone. Luella went into hysterics, and Aunt Abby was so
frightened that she called me after her daughter went. Mrs. Sam
Abbot she went away fairly cryin' out loud in the buggy, the
neighbours heard her, and well she might, for she never saw her
mother again alive. I went in that night when Aunt Abby called
for me, standin' in the door with her little green-checked shawl
over her head. I can see her now. "Do come over here, Miss
Anderson," she sang out, kind of gasping for breath. I didn't stop
for anythin'. I put over as fast as I could, and when I got there,
there was Luella laughin' and cryin' all together, and Aunt Abby
trying to hush her, and all the time she herself was white as a
sheet and shakin' so she could hardly stand. "For the land sakes,
Mrs. Mixter," says I, "you look worse than she does. You ain't fit

to be up out of your bed."

' "Oh, there ain't anythin' the matter with me," says she. Then she went on talkin' to Luella. "There, there, don't, don't, poor little lamb," says she. "Aunt Abby is here. She ain't goin' away and leave you. Don't, poor little lamb."

' "Do leave her with me, Mrs. Mixter, and you get back to bed," says I, for Aunt Abby had been layin' down considerable lately, though somehow she contrived to do the work.

' "I'm well enough," says she. "Don't you think she had better have the doctor, Miss Anderson?"

' "The doctor," says I, "I think *you* had better have the doctor. I think you need him much worse than some folks I could mention." And I looked right straight at Luella Miller laughin' and cryin' and goin' on as if she was the centre of all creation. All the time she was actin' so – seemed as if she was too sick to sense anythin' – she was keepin' a sharp lookout as to how we took it out of the corner of one eye. I see her. You could never cheat me about Luella Miller. Finally I got real mad and I run home and I got a bottle of valerian I had, and I poured some boilin' hot water on a handful of catnip, and I mixed up that catnip tea with most half a wineglass of valerian, and I went with it over to Luella's. I marched right up to Luella, a-holdin' out of that cup, all smokin'. "Now," says I, "Luella Miller, *you swaller this!*"

' "What is – what is it, oh, what is it?" she sort of screeches out. Then she goes off a-laughin' enough to kill.

' "Poor lamb, poor little lamb," says Aunt Abby, standin' over her, all kind of tottery, and tryin' to bathe her head with camphor.

' "*You swaller this right down,*" says I. And I didn't waste any ceremony. I just took hold of Luella Miller's chin and I tipped her head back, and I caught her mouth open with laughin', and I clapped that cup to her lips, and I fairly hollered at her: "Swaller, swaller, swaller!" and she gulped it right down. She had to, and I guess it did her good. Anyhow, she stopped cryin' and laughin' and let me put her to bed, and she went to sleep like a baby inside of half an hour. That was more than poor Aunt Abby did. She lay awake all that night and I stayed with her, though she tried not to have me; said she wa'n't sick enough for watchers. But I stayed, and I made some good cornmeal gruel and I fed her a teaspoon every little while all night long. It seemed to me as if she was jest dyin' from bein' all wore out. In the mornin' as soon as it was light I run over to the Bisbees and sent Johnny Bisbee for the doctor. I told him to tell the doctor to hurry, and he come pretty quick. Poor Aunt Abby didn't seem to know much of anythin' when he got there. You couldn't hardly tell she breathed, she was so used up. When the doctor had gone, Luella came into the room lookin' like a baby in her ruffled nightgown. I can see her now. Her eyes were as blue and her face all pink and white like a blossom, and she looked at Aunt Abby in the bed sort of innocent and surprised. "Why," says she, "Aunt Abby ain't got up yet?"

' "No, she ain't," says I, pretty short.

' "I thought I didn't smell the coffee," says Luella.

' "Coffee," says I. "I guess if you have coffee this mornin' you'll make it yourself."

' "I never made the coffee in all my life," says she, dreadful astonished. "Erastus always made the coffee as long as he lived, and then Lily she made it, and then Aunt Abby made it. I don't believe I *can* make the coffee, Miss Anderson."

' "You can make it or go without, jest as you please," says I.

' "Ain't Aunt Abby goin' to get up?" says she.

' "I guess she won't get up," says I, "sick as she is." I was gettin' madder and madder. There was somethin' about that little pink-and-white thing standin' there and talkin' about coffee, when she had killed so many better folks than she was, and had jest killed another, that made me feel 'most as if I wished somebody would up and kill her before she had a chance to do any more harm.

' "Is Aunt Abby sick?" says Luella, as if she was sort of aggrieved and injured.

' "Yes," says I, "she's sick, and she's goin' to die, and then you'll be left alone, and you'll have to do for yourself and wait on yourself, or do without things." I don't know but I was sort of hard, but it was the truth, and if I was any harder than Luella Miller had been I'll give up. I ain't never been sorry that I said it. Well, Luella, she up and had hysterics again at that, and I jest let her have 'em. All I did was to bundle her into the room on the other side of the entry where Aunt Abby couldn't hear her, if she

wa'n't past it – I don't know but she was – and set her down hard
in a chair and told her not to come back into the other room, and
she minded. She had her hysterics in there till she got tired.
When she found out that nobody was comin' to coddle her and
do for her she stopped. At least I suppose she did. I had all I
could do with poor Aunt Abby tryin' to keep the breath of life in
her. The doctor had told me that she was dreadul low, and give
me some very strong medicine to give to her in drops real often,
and told me real particular about the nourishment. Well, I did as
he told me real faithful till she wa'n't able to swaller any longer.
Then I had her daughter sent for. I had begun to realize that she
wouldn't last any time at all. I hadn't realized it before, though I
spoke to Luella the way I did. The doctor he came, and Mrs.
Sam Abbot, but when she got there it was too late; her mother
was dead. Aunt Abby's daughter just give one look at her mother
layin' there, then she turned sort of sharp and sudden and looked
at me.

' "Where is she?" says she, and I knew she meant Luella.

' "She's out in the kitchen," says I. "She's too nervous to see
folks die. She's afraid it will make her sick."

'The Doctor he speaks up then. He was a young man. Old
Doctor Park had died the year before, and this was a young
fellow just out of college. "Mrs. Miller is not strong," says he,
kind of severe, "and she is quite right in not agitating herself."

' "You are another, young man; she's got her pretty claw on
you," thinks I, but I didn't say anythin' to him. I just said over to
Mrs. Sam Abbot that Luella was in the kitchen, and Mrs Sam
Abbot she went out there, and I went, too, and I never heard
anythin' like the way she talked to Luella Miller. I felt pretty hard
to Luella myself, but this was more than I ever would have dared
to say. Luella she was too scared to go into hysterics. She jest
flopped. She seemed to jest shrink away to nothin' in that
kitchen chair, with Mrs. Sam Abbot standin' over her and talkin'
and tellin' her the truth. I guess the truth was most too much for
her and no mistake, because Luella presently actually did faint
away, and there wa'n't any sham about it, the way I always
suspected there was about them hysterics. She fainted dead away
and we had to lay her flat on the floor, and the Doctor he came
runnin' out and he said somethin' about a weak heart dreadful

fierce to Mrs. Sam Abbot, but she wa'n't a mite scared. She faced him jest as white as even Luella was layin' there lookin' like death and the Doctor feelin' of her pulse.

' "Weak heart," says she, "weak heart; weak fiddlesticks! There ain't nothin' weak about that woman. She's got strength enough to hang onto other folks till she kills 'em. Weak? It was my poor mother that was weak: this woman killed her as sure as if she had taken a knife to her."

'But the Doctor he didn't pay much attention. He was bendin' over Luella layin' there with her yellow hair all streamin' and her pretty pink-and-white face all pale, and her blue eyes like stars gone out, and he was holdin' onto her hand and smoothin' her forehead, and tellin' me to get the brandy in Aunt Abby's room, and I was sure as I wanted to be that Luella had got somebody else to hang onto, now Aunt Abby was gone, and I thought of poor Erastus Miller, and I sort of pitied the poor young Doctor, led away by a pretty face, and I made up my mind I'd see what I could do.

'I waited till Aunt Abby had been dead and buried about a month, and the Doctor was goin' to see Luella steady and folks were beginnin' to talk; then one evenin', when I knew the Doctor had been called out of town and wouldn't be round, I went over to Luella's. I found her all dressed up in a blue muslin with white polka dots on it, and her hair curled jest as pretty, and there wa'n't a young girl in the place could compare with her. There was somethin' about Luella Miller seemed to draw the heart right out of you, but she didn't draw it out of *me*. She was settin' rocking in the chair by her sittin'-room window, and Maria Brown had gone home. Maria Brown had been in to help her, or rather to do the work, for Luella wa'n't helped when she didn't do anythin'. Maria Brown was real capable and she didn't have any ties; she wa'n't married, and lived alone, so she'd offered. I couldn't see why she should do the work any more than Luella; she wa'n't any too strong; but she seemed to think she could and Luella seemed to think so, too, so she went over and did all the work — washed, and ironed, and baked, while Luella sat and rocked. Maria didn't live long afterward. She began to fade away just the same fashion the others had. Well, she was warned, but she acted real mad when folks said anythin': said Luella was a

poor, abused woman, too delicate to help herself, and they'd
ought to be ashamed, and if she died helpin' them that couldn't
help themselves she would – and she did.

' "I s'pose Maria has gone home," says I to Luella, when I had
gone in and sat down opposite her.

' "Yes, Maria went half an hour ago, after she had got supper
and washed the dishes," says Luella, in her pretty way.

' "I suppose she has got a lot of work to do in her own house
to-night," says I, kind of bitter, but that was all thrown away on
Luella Miller. It seemed to her right that other folks that wa'n't
any better able than she was herself should wait on her, and she
couldn't get it through her head that anybody should think it
wa'n't right.

' "Yes," says Luella, real sweet and pretty, "yes, she said she
had to do her washin' to-night. She has let it go for a fortnight
along of comin' over here."

' "Why don't she stay home and do her washin' instead of
comin' over here and doin' *your* work, when you are just as well
able, and enough sight more so, than she is to do it?" says I.

'Then Luella she looked at me like a baby who has a rattle
shook at it. She sort of laughed as innocent as you please. "Oh, I
can't do the work myself, Miss Anderson," says she. "I never did.
Maria *has* to do it."

'Then I spoke out: "Has to do it!" says I. "Has to do it! She
don't have to do it, either. Maria Brown has her own home and
enough to live on. She ain't beholden to you to come over here
and slave for you and kill herself."

'Luella she jest set and stared at me for all the world like a
doll-baby that was so abused that it was comin' to life.

' "Yes," says I, "she's killin' herself. She's goin' to die just the
way Erastus did, and Lily, and your Aunt Abby. You're killin' her
jest as you did them. I don't know what there is about you, but
you seem to bring a curse," says I. "You kill everybody that is fool
enough to care anythin' about you and do for you."

'She stared at me and she was pretty pale.

' "And Maria ain't the only one you're goin' to kill," says I.
"You're goin' to kill Doctor Malcom before you're done with
him."

'Then a red colour came flamin' all over her face. "I ain't goin' to kill him, either," says she, and she begun to cry.

' "Yes, you be! says I. Then I spoke as I had never spoke before. You see, I felt it on account of Erastus. I told her that she hadn't any business to think of another man after she'd been married to one that had died for her: that she was a dreadful woman; and she was, that's true enough, but sometimes I have wondered lately if she knew it – if she wa'n't like a baby with scissors in its hand cuttin' everybody without knowin' what it was doin'.

'Luella she kept gettin' paler and paler, and she never took her eyes off my face. There was somethin' awful about the way she looked at me and never spoke one word. After awhile I quit talkin' and I went home. I watched that night, but her lamp went out before nine o'clock, and when Doctor Malcom came drivin' past and sort of slowed up he see there wa'n't any light and he drove along. I saw her sort of shy out of meetin' the next Sunday, too, so he shouldn't go home with her, and I begun to think mebbe she did have some conscience after all. It was only a week after that that Maria Brown died – sort of sudden at the last, though everybody had seen it was comin'. Well, then there was a good deal of feelin' and pretty dark whispers. Folks said the days of witchcraft had come again, and they were pretty shy of Luella. She acted sort of offish to the Doctor and he didn't go there, and there wa'n't anybody to do anythin' for her. I don't know how she did get along. I wouldn't go in there and offer to help her – not because I was afraid of dyin' like the rest, but I thought she was just as well able to do her own work as I was to do it for her, and I thought it was about time that she did it and stopped killin' other folks. But it wa'n't very long before folks began to say that Luella herself was goin' into a decline jest the way her husband, and Lily, and Aunt Abby and the others had, and I saw myself that she looked pretty bad. I used to see her goin' past from the store with a bundle as if she could hardly crawl, but I remembered how Erastus used to wait and 'tend when he couldn't hardly put one foot before the other, and I didn't go out to help her.

'But at last one afternoon I saw the Doctor come drivin' up like mad with his medicine chest, and Mrs. Babbit came in after supper and said that Luella was real sick.

' "I'd offer to go in and nurse her," says she, "but I've got my children to consider, and mebbe it ain't true what they say, but it's queer how many folks that have done for her have died."

'I didn't say anythin', but I considered how she had been Erastus's wife and how he had set his eyes by her, and I made up my mind to go in the next mornin', unless she was better, and see what I could do; but the next mornin' I see her at the window, and pretty soon she came steppin' out as spry as you please, and a little while afterward Mrs. Babbit came in and told me that the Doctor had got a girl from out of town, a Sarah Jones, to come there, and she said she was pretty sure that the Doctor was goin' to marry Luella.

'I saw him kiss her in the door that night myself, and I knew it was true. The woman came that afternoon, and the way she flew around was a caution. I don't believe Luella had swept since Maria died. She swept and dusted, and washed and ironed; wet clothes and dusters and carpets were flyin' over there all day, and every time Luella set her foot out when the Doctor wa'n't there there was that Sarah Jones helpin' of her up and down the steps, as if she hadn't learned to walk.

'Well, everybody knew that Luella and the Doctor were goin' to be married, but it wa'n't long before they began to talk about his lookin' so poorly, jest as they had about the others; and they talked about Sarah Jones, too.

'Well, the Doctor did die, and he wanted to be married first, so as to leave what little he had to Luella, but he died before the minister could get there, and Sarah Jones died a week afterward.

'Well, that wound up everything for Luella Miller. Not another soul in the whole town would lift a finger for her. There got to be a sort of panic. Then she began to droop in good earnest. She used to have to go to the store herself, for Mrs. Babbit was afraid to let Tommy go for her, and I've seen her goin' past and stoppin' every two or three steps to rest. Well, I stood it as long as I could, but one day I see her comin' with her arms full and stoppin' to lean against the Babbit fence, and I run out and took her bundles and carried them to her house. Then I went home and never spoke one word to her though she called after me dreadful kind of pitiful. Well, that night I was taken sick with a chill, and I was sick as I wanted to be for two weeks. Mrs. Babbit had seen me run out to help Luella and she came in and told me I was goin' to die on account of it. I didn't know whether I was or not, but I considered I had done right by Erastus's wife.

'That last two weeks Luella she had a dreadful hard time, I guess. She was pretty sick, and as near as I could make out nobody dared go near her. I don't know as she was really needin' anythin' very much, for there was enough to eat in her house and it was warm weather, and she made out to cook a little flour gruel every day, I know, but I guess she had a hard time, she that had been so petted and done for all her life.

'When I got so I could go out, I went over there one morning. Mrs. Babbit had just come in to say she hadn't seen any smoke and she didn't know but it was somebody's duty to go in, but she couldn't help thinkin' of her children, and I got right up, though I hadn't been out of the house for two weeks, and I went in there, and Luella she was layin' on the bed, and she was dyin'.

'She lasted all that day and into the night. But I sat there after the new doctor had gone away. Nobody else dared to go there. It was about midnight that I left her for a minute to run home and get some medicine I had been takin', for I begun to feel rather bad.

'It was a full moon that night, and just as I started out of my door to cross the street back to Luella's, I stopped short, for I saw something.'

Lydia Anderson at this juncture always said with a certain defiance that she did not expect to be believed, and then proceeded in a hushed voice:

'I saw what I saw, and I know I saw it, and I will swear on my death bed that I saw it. I saw Luella Miller and Erastus Miller, and Lily, and Aunt Abby, and Maria, and the Doctor, and Sarah, all goin' out of her door, and all but Luella shone white in the moonlight, and they were all helpin' her along till she seemed to fairly fly in the midst of them. Then it all disappeared. I stood a minute with my heart poundin', then I went over there. I thought of goin' for Mrs. Babbit, but I thought she'd be afraid. So I went alone, though I knew what had happened. Luella was layin' real peaceful, dead on her bed.'

This was the story that the old woman, Lydia Anderson, told, but the sequel was told by the people who survived her, and this is the tale which has become folklore in the village.

Lydia Anderson died when she was eighty-seven. She had continued wonderfully hale and hearty for one of her years until about two weeks before her death.

One bright moonlight evening she was sitting beside a window in her parlour when she made a sudden exclamation, and was out of the house and across the street before the neighbour who was taking care of her could stop her. She followed as fast as possible and found Lydia Anderson stretched on the ground before the door of Luella Miller's deserted house, and she was quite dead.

The next night there was a red gleam of fire athwart the moonlight and the old house of Luella Miller was burned to the ground. Nothing is now left of it except a few old cellar stones and a lilac bush, and in summer a helpless trail of morning glories among the weeds, which might be considered emblematic of Luella herself.

A Psychological Experiment

RICHARD MARSH

Reputedly inspired by the success of DRACULA, THE BEETLE
*(1897) by Richard Marsh (1847–1915) is probably the only work by
this prolific and talented author of which most people will have heard.
Yet Marsh wrote over seventy successful books in the Victorian era and
these were printed and reprinted right up into the 1920s.*

*Richard Marsh started his writing career at the age of twelve, selling
stories to boy's magazines, and he wrote for a living as soon as he was
able. His work spanned detective stories, humour, adventure tales and
ghost stories.*

*In the space of three years, Marsh published his best four collections
of weird short stories, starting with* MARVELS AND MYSTER-
IES *and* THE SEEN AND THE UNSEEN, *both in 1900, and
the next two years publishing* BOTH SIDES OF THE VEIL
(1901) and BETWEEN THE DARK AND THE DAYLIGHT
(1902).

'A Psychological Experiment' comes from THE SEEN AND
THE UNSEEN, *and is a neat little story (some might say too neat) of
mounting terror with some very odd things going on.*

RICHARD MARSH

A Psychological Experiment

The conversation had been of murders and of suicides. It had almost seemed as if each speaker had felt constrained to cap the preceding speaker's tale of horror. As the talk went on, Mr. Howitt had drawn farther and farther into a corner of the room, as if the subject were little to his liking. Now that all the speakers but one had quitted the smoking-room, he came forward from his corner, in the hope, possibly, that with this last remaining individual, who, like himself, had been a silent listener, he might find himself in more congenial society.

'Dreadful stuff those fellows have been talking!'

Mr. Howitt was thin and he was tall. He seemed shorter than he really was, owing to what might be described as a persistent cringe rather than a stoop. He had a deferential, almost frightened air. His pallid face was lighted by a smile which one felt might, in a moment, change into a stare of terror. He rubbed his hands together softly, as if suffering from a chronic attack of nerves; he kept giving furtive glances around the room.

In reply to Mr. Howitt's observation the stranger nodded his head. There was something in the gesture, and indeed in the man's whole appearance, which caused Mr. Howitt to regard him more attentively. The stranger's size was monstrous. By him on the table was a curious-looking box, about eighteen inches square, painted in hideously alternating stripes of blue and green and yellow; and although it was spring, and the smoking-room was warm, he wore his overcoat and a soft felt hat. So far as one could judge from his appearance, seated, he was at least six feet in height. As to girth, his dimensions were bewildering. One could only guess wildly at his height. To add to the peculiarity of his appearance, he wore a huge black beard, which not only hung over his chest, but grew so high up his cheeks as almost to conceal his eyes.

164

Mr. Howitt took the chair which was in front of the stranger. His eyes were never for a moment still, resting, as they passed, upon the bearded giant in front of him, then flashing quickly hither and thither about the room.

'Do you stay in Jersey long?'

'No.'

The reply was monosyllabic, but, though it was heard so briefly, at the sound of the stranger's voice Mr. Howitt half rose, grasped the arm of his chair, and gasped. The stranger seemed surprised.

'What's the matter?'

Mr. Howitt dropped back on to his seat. He took out his handkerchief to wipe his forehead. His smile, which had changed into a stare of terror on its reappearance, assumed a sickly hue.

'Nothing. Only a curious similarity.'

'Similarity? What do you mean?'

Whatever Mr. Howitt might mean, every time the stranger opened his mouth it seemed to give him another shock. It was a moment or two before he regained sufficient control over himself to enable him to answer.

'Your voice reminds me of one which I used to hear. It's a mere fugitive resemblance.'

'Whose voice does mine remind you of?'

'A friend's.'

'What was his name?'

'His name was – C – C – Cookson.'

Mr. Howitt spoke with a perceptible stammer.

'Cookson? I see.'

There was silence. For some cause, Mr. Howitt seemed on a sudden to have gone all limp. He sat in a sort of heap on his chair. He smoothed his hands together, as if with unconscious volition. His sickly smile had degenerated into a fatuous grin. His shifty eyes kept returning to the stranger's face in front of him. It was the stranger who was the next to speak.

'Did you hear what those men were talking about?'

'Yes.'

'They were talking of murders.'

'Yes.'

'I heard rather a curious story of a murder as I came down to Weymouth in the train.'

'It's a sort of talk I do not care for.'

'No. Perhaps not; but this was rather a singular tale. It was about a murder which took place the other day at Exeter.'

Mr. Howitt started.

'At Exeter?'

'Yes; at Exeter.'

The stranger stood up. As he did so, one realised how grotesquely unwieldy was his bulk. It seemed to be as much as he could do to move. The three pockets in the front of his overcoat were protected by buttoned flaps. He undid the buttons. As he did so the flaps began to move. Something peeped out. Then hideous things began to creep from his pockets – efts, newts, lizards, various crawling creatures. Mr. Howitt's eyes ceased to stray. They were fastened on the crawling creatures. The hideous things wriggled and writhed in all directions over the stranger. The huge man gave himself a shake. They all fell from him to the floor. They lay for a second as if stupefied by the fall. Then they began to move to all four quarters of the room. Mr. Howitt drew his leg under his chair.

'Pretty creatures, aren't they?' said the stranger. 'I like to carry them about with me wherever I go. Don't let them touch you. Some of them are nasty if they bite.'

Mr. Howitt tucked his long legs still further under his chair. He regarded the creatures which were wriggling on the floor with a degree of aversion which was painful to witness. The stranger went on.

'About this murder at Exeter, which I was speaking of. It was a case of two solicitors who occupied offices together on Fore Street Hill.'

Mr. Howitt glanced up at the stranger, then back again at the writhing newts. He rather gasped than spoke.

'Fore Street Hill?'

'Yes – they were partners. The name of one of them was Rolt – Andrew Rolt. By the way, I like to know with whom I am talking. May I inquire what your name is?'

This time Mr. Howitt was staring at the stranger with wide-open eyes, momentarily forgetful even of the creatures which were actually crawling beneath his chair. He stammered and he stuttered.

'My name's – Howitt. You'll see it in the hotel register.'

'Howitt? – I see – I'm glad I have met you, Mr. Howitt. It seems that this man, Andrew Rolt, murdered his partner, a man named Douglas Colston.'

Mr. Howitt was altogether oblivious of the things upon the floor. He clutched at the arms of his chair. His voice was shrill.

'Murdered! How do they know he murdered him?'

'It seems they have some shrewd ideas upon the point, from this.'

The stranger took from an inner pocket of his overcoat what proved, when he had unfolded it, to be a double-crown poster. He held it up in front of Mr. Howitt. It was headed in large letters, 'MURDER! £100 REWARD.'

'You see, they are offering £100 reward for the apprehension of this man, Andrew Rolt. That looks as if someone had suspicions. Here is his description: Tall, thin, stoops; has sandy hair, thin on top, parted in the middle; restless grey eyes; wide mouth, bad teeth, thin lips; white face; speaks in a low, soft voice; has a nervous trick of rubbing his hands together.' The stranger ceased reading from the placard to look at Mr. Howitt. 'Are you aware, sir, that this description is very much like you?'

Mr. Howitt's eyes were riveted on the placard. They had followed the stranger as he read. His manner was feverishly strained.

'It's not. Nothing of the sort. It's your imagination. It's not in the least like me.'

'Pardon me, but the more I look at you the more clearly I perceive how strong is the resemblance. It is you to the life. As a detective' – he paused, Mr. Howitt held his breath – 'I mean supposing I were a detective, which I am not' – he paused again, Mr. Howitt gave a gasp of relief – 'I should feel almost justified in arresting you and claiming the reward. You are so made in the likeness of Andrew Rolt.'

'I'm not. I deny it! It's a lie!'

Mr. Howitt stood up. His voice rose to a shriek. A fit of trembling came over him. It constrained him to sit down again. The stranger seemed amused.

'My dear sir! I entreat you to be calm. I was not suggesting for one moment that you had any actual connection with the miscreant Rolt. The resemblance must be accidental. Did you not tell me your name was Howitt?'

'Yes; that's my name, Howitt – William Howitt.'

'Any relation to the poet?'

'Poet?' Mr. Howitt seemed mystified; then, to make a dash at it, 'Yes; my great-uncle.'

'I congratulate you, Mr. Howitt, on your relationship. I have always been a great admirer of your great-uncle's works. Perhaps I had better put this poster away. It may be useful for future reference.'

The stranger, folding up the placard, replaced it in his pocket. With a quick movement of his fingers he did something which detached what had seemed to be the inner lining of his overcoat from the coat itself – splitting the garment, as it were, and making it into two. As he did so, there fell from all sides of him another horde of crawling creatures. They dropped like lumps of jelly on to the floor, and remained for some seconds, a wriggling mass. Then, like their forerunners, they began to make incursions towards all the points of the compass. Mr. Howitt, already in a condition of considerable agitation, stared at these ungainly forms in a state of mind which seemed to approach to stupefaction.

'More of my pretty things, you perceive. I'm very fond of reptiles. I always have been. Don't allow any of them to touch you. They might do you an injury. Reptiles sometimes do.' He turned a little away from Mr. Howitt. 'I heard some particulars of this affair at Exeter. It seems that these two men, Rolt and Colston, were not only partners in the profession of the law, they were also partners in the profession of swindling. Thorough-paced rogues, both of them. Unfortunately, there is not a doubt of it. But it appears that the man Rolt was not only false to the world at large, he was false even to his partner. Don't you think, Mr. Howitt, that it is odd that a man should be false to his partner?'

The inquiry was unheeded. Mr. Howitt was gazing at the crawling creatures which seemed to be clustering about his chair.

'Ring the bell!' he gasped. 'Ring the bell! Have them taken away!'

'Have what taken away? My pretty playthings? My dear sir, to touch them would be dangerous. If you are very careful not to move from your seat, I think I may guarantee that you will be safe. You did not notice my question. Don't you think it odd that a man should be false to his partner?'

'Eh? – Oh! – Yes; very.'

The stranger eyed the other intently. There was something in Mr. Howitt's demeanour which, to say the least of it, was singular.

'I thought you would think it was odd. It appears that one night the two men agreed that they would divide spoils. They proceeded to do so then and there. Colston, wholly unsuspicious of evil, was seated at a table, making up a partnership account. Rolt, stealing up behind him, stupefied him with chloroform.'

'It wasn't chloroform.'

'Not chloroform? May I ask how you know?'

'I – I guessed it.'

'For a stranger, rather a curious subject on which to hazard a guess, don't you think so? However, allowing your guess, we will say it was not chloroform. Whatever it was it stupefied Colston. Rolt, when he perceived Colston was senseless, produced a knife – like this.'

The stranger flourished in the air a big steel blade, which was shaped like a hunting-knife. As he did so, throwing his overcoat from him on to the floor, he turned right round towards Mr. Howitt. Mr. Howitt stared at him voiceless. It was not so much at the sufficiently ugly weapon he was holding in his hand at which he stared, as at the man himself. The stranger, indeed, presented an extraordinary spectacle. The upper portion of his body was enveloped in some sort of oilskin – such as sailors wear in dirty weather. The oilskin was inflated to such an extent that the upper half of him resembled nothing so much as a huge ill-shaped bladder. That it was inflated was evident, with something, too, that was conspicuously alive. The oilskin writhed and twisted, surged and heaved, in a fashion that was anything but pleasant to behold.

'You look at me! See here!'

The stranger dashed the knife he held into his own breast, or he seemed to. He cut the oilskin open from top to bottom. And there gushed forth, not his heart's blood, but an amazing mass of hissing, struggling, twisting serpents. They fell, all sorts and sizes, in a confused, furious, frenzied heap, upon the floor. In a moment the room seemed to be alive with snakes. They dashed hither and thither, in and out, round and round, in search either of refuge or revenge. And, as the snakes came on, the efts, the newts, the lizards, and the other creeping things, in their desire to escape them, crawled up the curtains, and the doors, and the walls.

Mr. Howitt gave utterance to a sort of strangled exclamation. He retained sufficient presence of mind to spring upon the seat of his chair, and to sit upon the back of it. The stranger remained standing, apparently wholly unmoved, in the midst of the seeming pandemonium of creepy things.

'Do you not like snakes, Mr. Howitt? I do! They appeal to me strongly. This is part of my collection. I rather pride myself on the ingenuity of the contrivance which enables me to carry my pets about with me wherever I may go. At the same time you are wise in removing your feet from the floor. Not all of them are poisonous. Possibly the more poisonous ones may not be able to reach you where you are. You see this knife?' The stranger extended it towards Mr. Howitt. 'This is the knife with which, when he had stupefied him, Andrew Rolt slashed Douglas Colston about the head and face and throat like this!'

The removal of his overcoat, and, still more, the vomiting forth of the nest of serpents, had decreased the stranger's bulk by more than one-half. Disembarrassing himself of the remnants of his oilskins, he removed the soft felt hat, and, tearing off his huge black beard, stood revealed as a tall, upstanding, muscularly-built man, whose head and face and neck were almost entirely concealed by strips of plaster, which crossed and recrossed each other in all possible and impossible directions.

There was silence. The two men stared at each other. With a gasp Mr. Howitt found his voice.

'Douglas!'

'Andrew!'

'I thought you were dead.'

'I am risen from the grave.'

'I am glad you are not dead.'

'Why?'

Mr. Howitt paused as if to moisten his parched lips.

'I never meant to kill you.'

'In that case, Andrew, your meaning was unfortunate. I do mean to kill you – now.'

'Don't kill me, Douglas.'

'A reason, Andrew?'

'If you knew what I have suffered since I thought I had killed you, you would not wish to take upon yourself the burden which I have had to bear.'

'My nerves, Andrew, are stronger than yours. What would crush you to the ground would not weigh on me at all. Surely you knew that before.' Mr. Howitt fidgeted on the back of his chair. 'It was not that you did not mean to kill me. You lacked the courage. You gashed me like some frenzied cur. Then, afraid of your own handiwork, you ran to save your skin. You dared not wait to see if what you had meant to do was done. Why, Andrew, as soon as the effects of your drug had gone, I sat up. I heard you running down the stairs, I saw your knife lying at my side, all stained with my own blood – see, Andrew, the stains are on it still! I even picked up this scrap of paper which had fallen from your pocket on to the floor.'

He held out a piece of paper towards Mr. Howitt.

'It is the advertisement of an hotel – Hotel de la Couronne d'Or, St. Helier's, Jersey. I said to myself, I wonder if that is where Andrew is gone. I will go and see. And I will find him and I will kill him. I have found you, and behold, your heart has so melted within you that already you feel something of the pangs of death.' Mr. Howitt did seem to be more dead than alive. His face was bloodless. He was shivering as if with cold.

'These melodramatic and, indeed, slightly absurd details' – the stranger waved his hand towards the efts, and newts, and snakes, and lizards – 'were planned for your especial benefit. I was aware what a horror you had of creeping things. I take it, it is constitutional. I knew I had but to spring on you half a bushel or so of reptiles, and all the little courage you ever had would vanish. As it has done.'

The stranger stopped. He looked, with evident enjoyment of his misery, at the miserable creature squatted on the back of the chair in front of him. Mr. Howitt tried to speak. Two or three times he opened his mouth, but there came forth no sound. At last he said, in curiously husky tones –

'Douglas?'

'Andrew?'

'If you do it they are sure to have you. It is not easy to get away from Jersey.'

'How kind of you, Andrew, and how thoughtful! But you might have spared yourself your thought. I have arranged all that. There is a cattle-boat leaves for St. Malo in half an hour on the tide. You will be dead in less than half an hour – so I go in that.'

Again there were movements of Mr. Howitt's lips. But no words were audible. The stranger continued.

'The question which I have had to ask myself has been, how shall I kill you? I might kill you with the knife with which you endeavoured to kill me.' As he spoke, he tested the keenness of the blade with his fingers. 'With it I might slit your throat from ear to ear, or I might use it in half a hundred different ways. Or I might shoot you like a dog.' Producing a revolver, he pointed it at Mr. Howitt's head. 'Sit quite still, Andrew, or I may be tempted to flatten your nose with a bullet. You know I can shoot straight. Or I might avail myself of this.'

Still keeping the revolver pointed at Mr. Howitt's head, he took from his waistcoat pocket a small syringe.

'This, Andrew, is a hypodermic syringe. I have but to take firm hold of you, thrust the point into one of the blood-vessels of your neck, and inject the contents; you will at once endure exquisite tortures which, after two or three minutes, which will seem to you like centuries, will result in death. But I have resolved to do myself, and you, this service, with neither of the three.'

Again the stranger stopped. This time Mr. Howitt made no attempt to speak. He was not a pleasant object to contemplate. As the other had said, to judge from his appearance he already seemed to be suffering some of the pangs of death. All the manhood had gone from him. Only the shell of what was meant to be a man remained. The exhibition of his pitiful cowardice afforded his whilom partner unqualified pleasure.

'Have you ever heard of an author named De Quincey? He wrote on murder considered as a fine art. It is as a fine art I have had to consider it. In that connection I have had to consider three things: 1. That you must be killed. 2. That you must be killed in such a manner that you shall suffer the greatest possible amount of pain. 3 – and not the least essential – That you must be killed in such a manner that under no circumstances can I be found guilty of having caused your death. I have given these three points my careful consideration, and I think that I have been able to find something which will satisfy all the requirements. That something is in this box.'

The stranger went to the box which was on the table – the square box which had, as ornamentation, the hideously alternating stripes of blue and green and yellow. He rapped on it with his knuckles. As he did so, from within it there came a peculiar sound like a sullen murmur.

'You hear? It is death calling to you from the box. It awaits its prey. It bids you come.'

He struck the box a little bit harder. There proceeded from, it, as if responsive to his touch, what seemed to be a series of sharp and angry screeches.

'Again! It loses patience. It grows angry. It bids you hasten. Ah!'

He brought his hand down heavily upon the top of the box. Immediately the room was filled with a discord of sounds, cries, yelpings, screams, snarls, the tumult dying away in what seemed to be an intermittent, sullen roaring. The noise served to rouse the snakes, and efts, and lizards to renewed activity. The room seemed again to be alive with them. As he listened, Mr. Howitt became livid. He was, apparently, becoming imbecile with terror.

His aforetime partner, turning to him, pointed to the box with outstretched hands.

'What a row it makes! What a rage it's in! Your death screams out to you, with a ravening longing – the most awful death that a man can die. Andrew – to die! and such a death as this!'

Again he struck the box. Again there came from it that dreadful discord.

'Stand up!'

Mr. Howitt looked at him, as a drivelling idiot might look at a

keeper whom he fears. It seemed as if he made an effort to frame
his lips for the utterance of speech. But he had lost the control of
his muscles. With every fibre of his being he seemed to make a
dumb appeal for mercy to the man in front of him. The appeal
was made in vain. The command was repeated.

'Get off your chair, and stand upon the floor.'

Like some trembling automaton Mr. Howitt did as he was
told. He stood there like some lunatic deaf mute. It seemed as if
he could not move, save at the bidding of his master. That
master was careful not to loosen, by so much as a hair's-breadth,
the hold he had of him.

'I now proceed to put into execution the most exquisite part of
my whole scheme. Were I to unfasten the box and let death loose
upon you, some time or other it might come out – these things do
come out at times – and it might then appear that the deed had,
after all, been mine. I would avoid such risks. So you shall be
your own slayer, Andrew. You shall yourself unloose the box,
and you shall yourself give death its freedom, so that it may work
on you its will. The most awful death that a man can die! Come
to me, here!'

And the man went to him, moving with a curious, stiff gait,
such as one might expect from an automaton. The creatures
writhing on the floor went unheeded, even though he trod on
them.

'Stand still in front of the box.' The man stood still. 'Kneel
down.'

The man did hesitate. There did seem to come to him some
consciousness that he should himself be the originator of his own
violation. There did come to his distorted visage an agony of
supplication which it was terrible to witness.

The only result was an emphasised renewal of the command.
'Kneel down upon the floor.'

And the man knelt down. His face was within a few inches of
the painted box. As he knelt the stranger struck the box once
more with the knuckles of his hand. And again there came from
it that strange tumult of discordant sounds.

'Quick, Andrew, quick, quick! Press your finger on the spring!
Unfasten the box!'

The man did as he was bid. And, in an instant, like a

conjurer's trick, the box fell all to pieces, and there sprang from it, right into Mr. Howitt's face, with a dreadful noise, some dreadful thing which enfolded his head in its hideous embraces.

There was silence.

Then the stranger laughed. He called softly –

'Andrew!' All was still. 'Andrew!' Again there was none that answered. The laughter was renewed.

'I do believe he's dead. I had always supposed that the stories about being able to frighten a man to death were all apocryphal. But that a man could be frightened to death by a thing like this – a toy!'

He touched the creature which concealed Mr. Howitt's head and face. As he said, it was a toy. A development of the old-fashioned jack-in-the-box. A dreadful development, and a dreadful toy. Made in the image of some creature of the squid class, painted in livid hues, provided with a dozen long, quivering tentacles, each actuated by a spring of its own. It was these tentacles which had enfolded Mr. Howitt's head in their embraces.

As the stranger put them from him, Mr. Howitt's head fell, face foremost, on to the table. His partner, lifting it up, gazed down at him.

Had the creature actually been what it was intended to represent it could not have worked more summary execution. The look which was on the dead man's face as his partner turned it upwards was terrible to see.

A Derelict

J.A. BARRY

Many Victorian anthologies demonstrate the popularity of tales of the sea in this era, and here is a superbly atmospheric tale of the ocean by a man who spent twelve years sailing round the world.

John Arthur Barry (1850–1911) went to sea from his native Torquay at the age of thirteen and after twelve years in the Merchant Marine, left to prospect for gold in Australia. He obviously didn't do too well at this, for he is next reported as a station manager in the bush before finally settling in Sydney in the early 1880s. His first literary contribution appeared in The Times *in 1884 and his first book was published in Australia nine years after that. Oddly enough, this first book was one of the few ever to deal with a mythical Australian monster,* STEVE BROWN'S BUNYIP *(1893).*

Barry's archetypal sea story book, IN THE GREAT DEEP *(1895), was probably his best. I have selected from this 'A Derelict' in which Barry, as William Hope Hodgson was to later, writes of an encounter with a derelict vessel. Unlike Hodgson, however, Barry's derelict is probably much nearer to the nasty reality of many of those Victorian hulks and the reason for their abandonment.*

J.A. BARRY

A Derelict

'Take the glass, Mr Staunton, your eyes are younger than mine, and tell me what you make of her.'

The speaker was the master of the British ship *Minnehaha*, just thirty days out from London to Algoa Bay, and at that moment lying becalmed about two degrees south of the Equator, with a great deal more easting in her longitude than she had any business with. Indeed, we should not have been very much surprised, owing to the set of a current the ship had got into, and the incessant calms experienced of late, to sight the African coast at any minute. Taking the telescope from the captain's hand, and resting it on the ratlines of the mizzen rigging, I had a long look at the distant object, which had since daybreak been exciting our curiosity.

That it was a ship of some kind or other, and a big one, there was no doubt; and presently, as she floated into the field of the glass, I could see that, whilst she appeared very high out of the water, she had nothing standing aloft above her topmasts, and, as far as I could make out, no sail of any kind set, nor any signals flying.

'Ah,' remarked the captain, 'a derelict, I expect, and one, in this part of the sea into which our singular bad fortune has brought us, of no recent making. If you don't mind losing your watch below you can take two or three hands in the quarter-boat, or perhaps the gig will be lighter, and board her. It's just possible there may be some poor wretch on her still. We shall, worse luck, be drifting closer to you all the time. I shouldn't be much astonished to find ourselves at anchor off some infernal swamp, with the ship full of fever and mosquitoes, if this kind of thing lasts much longer,' and so saying, the skipper went below, with a sigh of weariness, and a glance around at the monotonous scene, familiar for so long, the bleaching decks and spars, the drooping, listless canvas, with everywhere the deadly sameness of oily-looking, greenish-blue water.

I was the second mate of the *Minnehaha*, and the hard routine of my profession had not as yet in those days wholly knocked the romance out of me, so that it was with not a little feeling of eager anticipation for the adventure that I waited for the bell to strike eight, and my relief to turn out.

'Fair and easy, my boy,' said the first officer as he, at length, stood yawning by my side after having taken a long squint at the stranger; 'take my advice, and have breakfast before you start. It's a long pull, and the sun will be out strong by the time you're halfway. I'm of the old man's opinion that she's been knocking about for some time, months perhaps. A foreigner, I should imagine, by the cut of her, and likely enough, grass on her decks a foot long.'

After breakfast, myself, the boatswain, and two of the able seamen – the latter, in spite of the long pull before them, as happy as schoolboys at the prospect of a holiday and a change from the weary ship – set off on our visit to the derelict.

It was now about nine o'clock, and before we had gone one mile out of the four that we had judged the distance at, the men's clothes were wet through with perspiration.

I had brought a small beaker of water, two bottles of ship's rum, and some eatables with us; so, after a good draught of six-water grog all round, the boatswain and myself gave the two seamen a spell at the oars; and soon the mysterious ocean wanderer loomed up large ahead of us. As we drew nearer we saw that she was a ship of fully 1400 tons, nearly twice the size of our own little clipper, and that she had originally been painted white with a yellow streak.

At last we were alongside, and, as the men ceased rowing, we all gazed with something of awe up at the desolate, forsaken thing. She was an immense height out of the water, and her sides – weatherbeaten, blistered, for the most part bare of paint, and with long streaks of iron rust straggling down them – towered above us, grim, forbidding, and uncanny.

As we slowly paddled round her we saw that in one place the sea had made a clean breach through her bulwarks on either side. Strips of her topsails and courses were still hanging from the yards, and, as we came athwart her bows, the rotting bolt-ropes of some of her head-sails swung to and fro under the bowsprit with every little lurch she gave. Aft we noticed the davit-falls and tackles, all fagged out and minus the lower blocks, drooping down just as they had been left when the boats deserted her to let her wander about the ocean, the sport and plaything of every little breeze that blew. It was indeed a melancholy sight, and to a sailor more especially, of all men!

No name was on her stern, only the broad, blank, yellow streak continued.

'I think, sir,' remarked the boatswain, a fine old seaman named Dyson, 'that she's a Portugee or somethin' o' the kind, an' she may have been deserted for years by the look of her. My eye, she's light an' no mistake! In ballast, I s'pose. No name ahead or astern, either,' continued he, glancing suspiciously up at the old-fashioned quarter-galleries, which gave her such a cumbrous look aft. 'I don't like her nohow, an' I don't care how soon we all gets aboard the little *Minnie* agen.'

'Come, come, Dyson,' said I laughingly, 'it would never do for us to go back without overhauling her. We'll have a snack here in the boat and then we'll take a look aboard this big castaway.'

We were by this time again under the bows, and one of the sailors putting up his boathook and dragging away a portion of the canvas which hung down, disclosed to view the derelict's figurehead, a piece of magnificent carving, representing a woman in three-quarter length, clad in flowing classical drapery, and whose features seemed to look down upon us with an expression of solemn sadness, whilst one arm, slightly raised, pointed to the dark sky overhead. It was a masterpiece of the sculptor's art, such as I had never dreamed of seeing placed on the bows of a ship, and was doubtless meant for the Madonna. And, strangely enough, the paint, so worn and abraded everywhere else, still showed on the figure above us in almost all its pristine whiteness. Perhaps the overhanging canvas had protected it.

'Good Lord!' ejaculated the old boatswain presently, as we all stared at the nobly gracious, but sorrowful features. 'Did ever mortal man see such a figgerhead as that! I never did; and forty year an' more I've been a-roamin' about amongst every sort o' craft as sails. I almost begins to believe, sir, as this old derelick's been a sort o' floatin' gospel-house – that is,' he quickly qualified, 'so long as I looks at that bit o' work there.'

Evidently many a great sea, tall as she was, had swept her fore and aft, without, however, doing much damage beyond making the two rents in her thick bulwarks mentioned above. The hatchways were closely battened down, and the main one, which we could see had been fitted with gratings, was now secured with inch planks fastened to the deck by stout iron bolts.

All about the decks, in the scuppers everywhere, in confused bunches, lay the running rigging, just as the seas of the last gale she had encountered had washed it; but of the wreck of the missing spars there was no sign.

The deck planking was covered thickly with a kind of dry, mossy substance that crackled beneath our tread, showing that, at one time, the vessel's decks had been, perhaps, for weeks under water.

I had just shut down the lid of the signal-locker, in which I had been vainly searching amongst a bundle of mouldering bunting for some colour which might denote the nationality of the derelict, when I was startled by a loud shout from below. Hastily descending, I found my three companions grouped together in front of the main entrance to the cuddy, and evidently in a state of high excitement.

'Let's get away, Brown,' one of the seamen was saying; 'I've had enough of this cussed old hooker!'

'What's the matter, Dyson?' I asked of the bo'sun, who stood wiping his forehead with his neckerchief, and looking rather scared.

'Matter enough, sir, in there,' replied he, pointing to the dark cabin entrance. 'We just stepped in, an' Brown struck a light, when, who should we see, when we turns round, but Old Nick hisself, leanin' against the mizzenmast, an' grinnin' at us like one o'clock!'

'Nonsense!' I exclaimed angrily. 'I'm ashamed of you, bo'sun, I am indeed! The idea of you talking such rubbish!' and, stepping into the cabin, which was almost in darkness, I struck a match from the open box in my hand, and looked around. I must confess that, as I did so, I heartily excused the boatswain and his mates their terror, for, although I did not budge an inch, I was scarcely less frightened myself for a minute or two.

Exactly facing me, and not more than a foot away, supported, apparently, by the casing of the mizzenmast, was a human skeleton, gleaming whitely in the feeble light of the match.

The men were now close at my heels, and telling the other seaman, whose name was Johnson, to go up on the poop, clear away the sail, and open the main skylight and booby-hatch, I struck some more matches, and proceeded farther along the large saloon.

Presently down came a flood of glorious sunshine, streaming into the cabin, illumining with its rays the poor skeleton – lashed to the mast, as we soon discovered, by many turns of the chain main-tack – and revealing a scene of confusion and disorder almost indescribable.

The stateroom doors were all either shattered to pieces by bullets, dozens of which were embedded in the woodwork round about, or, wrenched altogether from their hinges, were lying on the floor, which was littered with all kinds of female and male wearing apparel, broken bottles, papers, straw, crockery, cutlery, and all the usual paraphernalia of a big ship's saloon and pantry, and, to boot, the contents of its passengers' luggage.

Mould, damp, and mildew were everywhere; and everywhere, spite of open doors and skylights, was a fœtid, rotting, nauseous odour that seemed to hang thickly about and defy dispersal.

We searched the berths, but they were all empty, and then, as if by mutual consent, we found ourselves once more facing the grim emblem of mortality that grinned at us from its iron bonds.

'What do you think of it, Dyson?' I asked at length.

'Lashed there alive, sir,' muttered the old boatswain, as he pointed to the bony arms of the skeleton, which, as I now observed, were indeed tied back behind the mast, 'an' for the Lord knows how long, carried about the sea. I never did hear tell of such a thing,' he went on, 'but my mind misdoubted somethin' was wrong, spite o' the pretty figgerhead, when I sees how the craft's name had been a-wiped out. There's been rum doin's aboard here, sir; but I can't get the hang o' the thing rightly.'

'I wouldn't stay a night aboard her,' here put in Johnson, 'if anybody could give me a hundred pounds down in solid coined gold.'

'Same here, matey,' chimed in Brown; 'I don't think I ever got such a bad scare afore, an' who knows what might happen to a feller in the dark night-time.'

The papers strewn about the saloon floor were mostly, as I soon discovered, blank leaves of log-books, and the greater number were simply parcel-wrappers. Not one scrap of writing or print even rewarded my search, and I began to think that everything had been carefully gone over before. At this moment, and just as the boatswain and myself were on our knees gingerly turning over some of the clothing, most of which had evidently at one time been of rich and costly material, we were startled by Brown's voice shouting down the skylight, 'Mr Staunton, sir, the ship's signalling us; and there's a big squall comin'!' We hastily ran out on deck and up the poop ladder. There, abeam, was the *Minnehaha* busily clearing up and stowing her light sails; whilst, just beyond her, the sky was black as night. From her peak hung the ensign, which, even as we looked, blew out flat, a small square of bright colour against the dark background of wind, rain, and sea, which was coming along like a racehorse. Now she fired three guns in quick succession, and before the echoes of the last one had died away, we were in the boat, and pulling like madmen away from the derelict.

We had scarcely gone a hundred yards before I saw that it was too late. The squall would be upon us ere we could cover a quarter of the distance to the *Minnehaha*. For a moment I hesitated, then shouting, 'Back, men, for your lives!' I brought the rudder hard over, and in a few minutes more we were scrambling up the derelict's side. Bringing the remainder of the provisions and the waterkeg on board, we passed our boat astern. Not a bit too soon had we gained shelter, for, already, not more than a cable's length away, roared the furious squall, coming with a rush of wind and white water heavy enough to have swamped the stoutest boat that ever floated.

It struck the old derelict fairly abeam, heeling her over, over, over, till I really thought she was going to turn turtle with us altogether. But she was probably used to this kind of thing, for in a minute or two, during which her lower yardarms ploughed great white furrows in the water, she righted, and slowly turning her stern to the wind, began to make a little headway. I ran to the wheel to help her if I could, but found it completely useless, the rudder chains and blocks being simply masses of rust.

The sea was fast getting up, and spray was beginning to fly over the tall bulwarks of the pitching, lurching derelict, whose timbers creaked and groaned complainingly, while all sorts of strange noises came up from her hold, noises of something rolling, bounding, and clattering from side to side of the ship at every wild stagger that she gave.

As we listened wonderingly to all this racket, an exclamation from the boatswain made me turn my eyes to where, bringing with her a still stronger wind, the *Minnehaha* was bearing straight down upon us, foaming along under three close-reefed topsails and fore and mizzen staysails.

As the *Minnehaha* drew closer we could distinctly see the figures of the crew as they crowded along the weather-rail and waved their hats to us by way of encouragement. The captain and the chief officer were standing by the wheel, looking anxiously up at the huge, wallowing prison in which we had allowed ourselves to be entrapped.

Presently, seeing that we were determined, involuntarily on our part, God knows, to cut the running out for him, our captain set his maintopsail, braced his yards up, and kept away on our weather-bow, with, for our comfort, the 'rendezvous' flag flying at the mizzen-peak.

It was by this getting well on in the afternoon, and the squall had grown into a roaring gale, which howled and screeched through our rigging, banging the swinging yards about, and hooting and whistling around the tenantless forecastle and along the wet decks, like some wild and evil spirit, as the ship of death and mystery wallowed and tottered and slid over the great waves, coming to and falling off at her own sweet will and pleasure, but, somehow, always just in the nick of time.

Casting a last look at the *Minnehaha*, now fast fading away on the murky horizon, I stumbled aft to see to the boat, altogether forgotten in the absorbing interest of watching the manœuvres of our own vessel.

As might have been expected, she was gone, not a vestige of her anywhere to be seen, with the exception of the loose painter, which I mechanically hauled in, and to the end of which the drawn ringbolt out of the gig's bows was still attached.

The men said very little. That grim sight in the cabin and the incessant and inexplicable noises that pervaded the vessel had taken a lot of heart out of them, and I knew that, with the kind of night that was before us, a light of some sort was an imperative necessity.

'Bo'sun,' I said, 'forage around for oil. There must be some in her somewhere. It's stuff that doesn't rot. I saw a swing-lamp in the saloon; we'll light that and any others we may find.'

And then what I had expected came to pass.

'Beggin' your pardon, sir,' said Johnson, 'me an' Brown here would sooner stay on deck all night than go back into that there saloon for one single hour.'

'Please yourself, lads,' I said; 'she is bound to broach-to through the night with a sea like this on, and I reckon, if you're not both overboard, we'll soon have you in the cabin with us.'

The words were scarcely out of my mouth when Dyson shrieked out, 'Into the rigging for your lives!' and in less time than it takes to write it we were half-way up the mainshrouds. Looking aft, I saw a huge wall of water overhanging the poop. The derelict's way seemed suddenly stopped, as if she saw the futility of attempting to escape, then down fell the avalanche with a noise like thunder, burying everything beneath it and roaring away for'ard till it found an exit through the broken bulwarks. But that her deck-fittings, skylights, galley, etc, were of most exceptional strength, they must all have gone; and, assuredly, had we been a few minutes later in gaining our place of refuge, we should have been swept away like four straws into the seething wilderness around us. After this the derelict, appearing to think that she had done enough scudding for one night, hove herself to in a kind of a way, but any ship less high out of the water would have been swamped over and over again. There was no more talk about not going into the cabin; and presently in one of the after-lockers we had the luck to find a drum of oil, besides several lamps, including a big riding light, so that soon we had the saloon quite brightly illuminated.

Very fortunately, as it now turned out, when leaving the *Minnehaha*, the steward had packed away a more than ample supply of provisions, and these, having been stowed away in one of the top bunks of the saloon berths, had escaped the general wetting. Bringing everything to the table, I, first giving each man a glass of rum, served out all round a biscuit, a slice of pork, and a lump of cheese. Rescue was so uncertain that I thought it best to husband our resources as much as possible. There might be food left on the derelict, and water also, but, again, there might not be a scrap or drop of anything. The men's spirits rose considerably after this repast; though, for the matter of that, all our glances wandered irresistibly, now and again, to the gaunt, woeful figure that, half in shadow, half in a bright light, seemed to preside at the head of the table.

There are few men nowadays more stubbornly superstitious than your average merchant-seaman, and it would have taken very little indeed to have frightened Brown and Johnson completely out of their wits, half believing already, as they did, that they were on board of an enchanted, haunted vessel on which they were doomed to roam the seas for evermore; and so catching is terror that whilst Dyson was not much less scared than the pair, I myself was beginning to feel the effect of their pale, frightened faces and sudden starts of alarm. As we moved on in a body out on to the deck, the lamp casting uncertain quivering patches of white light on the slippery, discoloured planking, we felt, as we hung on to stanchions, corners, anything we could get hold of, that the gale was increasing in violence, although the sea was not quite so high as before; the wind blowing with such terrific force at times as to keep it down in a sheet of dazzling foam, off which it every minute hurled pieces at us that cut and stung our flesh as if they had been snowballs.

At length, exhausted and half-blinded, we gained the poop, and, with infinite trouble and difficulty, succeeded in lashing the massive copper lantern about half-way up the mizzen-rigging, whence it cast a flickering streak of light, now on the foam-flecked water, now on the ship, as she lay sometimes in a deep gully, at others nearly on her beam-ends at the summit of a monstrous roller. The night was black as pitch, and the shrieking of the gale, the rush and roar of water on the main-deck, with, aloft, the creaking and working of the spars, made such an incessant hurly-burly that speech was impossible, and we were all glad to find ourselves back in the saloon, to which the lights imparted at least a semblance of security, although at times a stream of water would glide in over the high wash-boards at each of the three doors. The din, too, here was muffled and subdued, coming only on the ears as a combined, sullen, ceaseless roar.

'That she's a furriner is certain,' said Dyson presently, as we recovered a little from our exertions. 'Most likely a Spanisher or a Portugee, an' it's many a long year since she was builded. They don't make 'em like that nowadays, sir,' pointing, as he spoke, to the huge beams and stanchions that made themselves visible here and there about the saloon. 'But where she's from, or where bound to when they left her, I can't give a notion.'

'I am as much at fault as yourself, bo'sun,' I answered. 'But maybe we'll find out a little more about her when daylight comes. Did you ever come across a derelict before, Dyson?' I asked.

'Yes, sir,' he replied. 'When I was in the old *Neptune*, packet-ship, across the Western Ocean, we boarded a derelict, as they calls 'em. A Quebecer she was – a timber drogher. Nothin' on her but a big half-starved Newfoundland dog. But she was a honest, fair, an' above-board derelict, she were, not like this no-name furriner;' and the boatswain, casting around a look expressive of the most intense disgust, continued –

'What but some murderin', bloody-minded dago would ever ha' thought o' lashin' a man – like enough it's the skipper himself – to his own mizzenmast! By Gosh! sir, it beats all I ever heerd tell on. Eat alive, too, as like as not, by the rats. Why, when me and Johnson there went into the midship-house arter the oil the place was a-swarmin' with 'em.'

This news threw light on a subject which had puzzled me not a little. I had particularly noticed how perfectly clean and bare every bone of the skeleton was, and I knew that it must have taken a very long period of time unaided to have completed such a process, most likely many years, years in which the masts, yards, and standing-gear of the ship, if not herself, would inevitably suffer decay from dry-rot and neglect; whilst, on the contrary, with the exception of the exposed canvas and some of the running-gear, everything was comparatively strong and well-preserved.

'God Almighty protect us!' at this moment exclaimed Dyson. 'What *is* them unearthly noises down below?'

There was a long lull in the gale as the boatswain spoke, at the same time starting to his feet, and the derelict giving two or three sharp rolls, there came distinctly to our ears from the hold a sound as of many people thumping with mallets at the ship's sides. Then there would be a pause, broken by a long, sliding, crashing noise, as if a whole shoal of crockery had fetched way to leeward with the roll.

'It's only the ballast shifting, bo'sun,' I said, as we listened.

'No, sir,' he answered, 'that noise comes from the 'tween decks – an' ballast ain't usually carried there.'

'Well, then,' I replied impatiently, 'it's some of the cargo, passengers' luggage, or something of the kind. We'll take the hatches off in the morning, and see what all the row's about down there.'

The two seamen had, for some time past, been fast asleep at the saloon table, their heads between their arms, and their bodies swaying and jerking uncomfortably with every wild movement of the vessel.

'I'd feel more easy in my mind, sir,' said the boatswain presently, 'if I knowed what this craft carried for cargo in her 'tween decks. The lazarette hatch is just be-aft the table there. S'pose, sir, you an' me takes a light an' goes down. Mebbe, as in a good many ships, there's only a gratin' rigged up to divide the storeroom from the 'tween decks, an' we'll be able to get a look through.'

To tell the truth, I had not by this time any too much stomach for the adventure; but I was not going to be outdone in courage by one whom I had more than once mentally accused of pusillanimity, so, unhooking one of the wildly-swinging lamps, I made my way to the extreme end of the long saloon. The small hatch was firmly secured by a cross-bar and staple of iron. As I glanced back down the dim vista of the cabin whilst Dyson was busy with the fastenings, I thought I had never set eyes on a drearier, more eerie scene; scarcely lit up as it was by the single swaying lamp, right under which were the two uneasily-shifting bodies of the sleepers; on each hand the long range of empty, yawning staterooms, the floor and table all littered with rubbish and wet with sea water, whilst at the farther end, only just visible in the feeble light, stood the swathed skeleton.

My nerves are, I believe, fairly strong, but what with the time, and the surroundings that I had just been taking in, I own that when Dyson, at last, with a wrench, pulled off the hatch, disclosing a dark square hole up which ascended in double intensity the rank, fœtid odour I have before spoken of – I own, I say, that I hesitated, and half hoped that the boatswain, the proposer of the excursion, would take the light from my hand and lead the way.

But he did no such thing. So, lowering the lamp, I set my foot on the board rung of the ladder thus disclosed to view, and cautiously descended, closely followed by Dyson.

My appearance was heralded by the scampering of thousands of small feet, mingled with shrill squeaks of alarm and rage. I thought of the skeleton, and shivered as I listened.

Landing safely on the lower deck, and placing my lamp on an iron tank near by, I gazed curiously around.

And truly there was enough to excite anyone's curiosity!

Instead of the usual grating, a solid bulkhead of great thickness stretched right across from one side of the ship to the other.

Casks, cases, baskets of all sizes and descriptions lay scattered around, most of them open and their contents mouldy, decaying, and gnawed, strewing the place.

But the object which at once arrested our attention was a large brass gun – an 18-pounder, Dyson said – which, mounted on its carriage, with all its tackling complete, was pointed for'ard through a large opening in the bulkhead.

Catching up my lamp, I was tumbling towards this opening, or port-hole, when the boatswain, grabbing me by the shoulder, stammered in a horror-stricken voice, pointing to the 'tween decks, where still the noises continued with every movement of the vessel, 'Dead men's bones, as sure as there's a God above us! Look here, sir,' he continued, holding up to the light a large, bulbous, conical object of a reddish colour, 'this is grapeshot!'

'Well?' I asked.

'Don't you see, sir?' replied the boatswain, 'there's been awful goings-on here! A coolie ship, or somethin' o' the kind, an' the whole cargo on 'em mowed down with shot in the 'tween decks there, an' the bodies left to the rats. No wonder there's rows when, perhaps, six or seven hundred skeletons gets a-rollin' an'

smashin' about in a sea like this! Nothin' else but a floatin'
slaughter-house; sure's my name's John Dyson!'

But, unconvinced, I passed on towards the muzzle of the
cannon, and, stooping, peered through the aperture, which was
jagged and splintered as if hurriedly-cut with an axe.

As I gazed, the vessel gave a sharp, sudden hoist to port, and a
heap of something came sliding, rattling, and crashing just
beneath me.

Lowering my lamp, as it sped swiftly by on the smooth deck, I
saw that it was indeed a confused heap of bones, glistening white
as ivory. As I followed them with my eyes disappearing into the
darkness of the wings, five or six round objects came bounding
singly along, one of which hit me a sharp blow on the side of the
head, whilst another knocked the lamp out of my hands clear
away into the black void beyond me, not before, however, I had
recognized the thing with its grinning jaws and empty sockets. It
was a human skull.

I am not ashamed to confess that I now altogether lost my
presence of mind under this grim bombardment, and hastily
turning, I staggered and stumbled towards where a feeble gleam
of light showed the position of the ladder and the hatchway.

Quick as I was, the boatswain was up before me, and if ever
two thoroughly scared men looked into each other's pale faces, it
was the pair of us as we regained our old places in the saloon,
fronting the still slumbering seamen.

'Coolies, you said, bo'sun,' I remarked, as soon as I had in
some measure collected my scattered wits, 'what would a coolie
ship be doing hereabouts?'

'Who's to tell, Mr Staunton, sir,' rejoined Dyson, 'where she
fust come from? She might ha' been bound round the Horn to
Valparaiser or the Chinchis. An' then, when this here wholesale
slaughterin' takes place, an' the crew mutinies an' battens the
Chinkies, an' perhaps the passengers too, for all we knows, down
in the 'tween decks; what does they do but gets the gun into the
lazarette there, an' shoves the grape into the poor devils, on the
idea that dead men tells no tales. I mayn't ha' got altogether the
right drift o' the thing, but I can't see no other. An',' continued
the boatswain, 'this here derelick, high out o' the water, an' as
strong as a castle, might ha' come right across here on her own

hook with her cussed loading o' rats an' skeletons. Dash me!' he exclaimed, 'if I think I ever got such a turn as when I hears that lamp a-gettin' knocked out o' your hand by one o' them bouncin' bones.'

'Why, Dyson,' I retorted indignantly, 'you were half-way up the ladder almost before I made a start.'

'Well, sir,' replied he, with a half-laugh, 'I reckon neither of us lost much time. And anyways, I'm glad we knows the reason now of that infarnal rumpus down there; though I must say I never did think it was as bad's it is. I'll just go up on the poop an' get a mouthful o' fresh air, an' see if the light's a-burnin'.'

Awaking the two seamen, but saying nothing to them of our adventure, we all went on deck.

The light was still burning, but very dimly. However, as the dawn was beginning to break, that was of little moment.

All that remained was to wait and hope that the *Minnehaha* was not very far away. Nor was she. For, when the daylight fully broke, ascending into the mizzen-top, I saw, about three miles away, hove-to under a topsail and couple of staysails, our own little ship; and the comfort and relief the sight afforded me would be hardly appreciated by anyone who had not spent such a night as I had. It was wonderful how she had contrived so well to keep in touch with us. But, as we afterwards discovered, it was our riding light in the rigging that did it. With their night-glasses, her look-outs had scarcely lost sight of us for five minutes together.

I cheered and waved my hat to the anxious watchers below, who heartily responded.

A few minutes later, the *Minnehaha*, with her yards just checked, ran down close to us, riding easily over the billows, at times perched like some great bird right on the summit of one; then, with a long, slow, heaving slide, leaning over till the morning sun shone on her bright copper, she would swoop down the steep green incline and be for a moment lost to view, with the exception of her royal yards just showing above the watery mountain-tops, till, presently, she again ascended, a glorious fabric, instinct with life and grace and human skill in her every motion.

'I wonders, now,' said the boatswain, as we stood holding on to the mizzen-rigging and watching her, 'how the old man means to get us out of this fix.'

However, that it was the captain's intention to lower a boat we soon discovered, although how she would approach close enough to the storm-swept derelict to be of any service to us passed our comprehension. We now saw, so close was the *Minnehaha*, the hands lie aft in a body, and almost before we realised what was going on, the lifeboat, so called from her being built in watertight compartments and her double bows, was in the water full of men, and pulling towards us. More often out of than in sight, as the great waves hid her in their valleys, on she came gallantly, making for the derelict's stern, where we stood ready with lines to heave to her.

I could see the first officer, as he hung on with all his might to the long, powerful steering-oar, bareheaded, with the angry spray flying like hail over himself and the crew.

Now a huge billow lifted the boat nearly level with the derelict's quarter-gallery, only escaping destruction by a miracle of skilful steering. At this moment Dyson hove his line, for so close were we that they could almost have touched us with their oars, yet in a trice they were a hundred yards away on the quarter.

Hauling in our line, we found attached to it the end of a new one, to which was made fast a life-buoy.

'Oh, that's it, is it?' exclaimed Dyson, as he unbent the half-rotten rope we had hove from the derelict. 'It's risky, but the old man's right. It's the only way.'

Whilst saying this the boatswain had got into the buoy, to which, of course, another line from the boat, as well as ours, was attached. We waved our hats to those in the lifeboat as a signal, and Dyson, watching his chance, sprang overboard, and, half pulled, half swimming as we rapidly paid out line, was at length dragged safely into the boat.

Being a capital swimmer, I had decided to go last, and, after seeing the two seamen in safely, I hauled back the buoy and in my turn leaped over the taffrail, and though, being without the saving check exerted by the inboard line, I was carried a long way to leeward and half smothered by being dragged by those in the boat through the tops of the waves, instead of being allowed to make my own way over them, I had the satisfaction at length of feeling myself pulled by a dozen strong arms into the boat, in the stern-sheets of which I laid gasping and draining.

In less than half an hour we all stood, little the worse for our adventure, on board of our own vessel, along whose decks, before the davit-tackles had been well made fast, sounded the sharp orders, 'Reefs out of the top'sls!' 'Loose foresail and mainsail!' 'Set the main-to'gall'ns'l!'

Our story, as may be imagined, excited no end of comment and conjecture from those on board of the *Minnehaha*, and many were the yarns spun that passage, both in saloon and forecastle.

Duly recorded, too, was the occurrence in the official log-book, extracts from which, in course of time, appeared in *Lloyd's* and a few other nautical journals; but, so far as I was able to learn, without doing anything towards clearing up the mystery of the wandering vessel, which, with the gruesome remnants of her ill-fated occupants, is possibly, even yet, drifting, ever drifting, becalmed or tempest-tossed, perhaps not far from where we first sighted her, perhaps now in distant seas, with still the beautiful image, pointing heavenward, before her; still bound to her mast, with its bonds of iron, the grim skeleton; still, in windy weather, clattering along her hold those others, fated only to disclose their terrible secret when the sea shall give up its dead.

Elsewhere in his books, J. A. Barry reports the true story of the *Napoleon Canavero*, which sailed from Macao in April 1866, bound for Peru, carrying 600 coolies. The crew mutinied and slaughtered the coolies in just the manner described here. Truth is indeed stranger than fiction. ED.

The Haunted Mill

OR

The Ruined Home

JEROME K. JEROME

There's very little one can say about the next item. If I tell you it comes from the pen of the author of THREE MEN IN A BOAT *(1889) it will give you some idea of what to expect. Jerome K. Jerome (1859–1927) was one of the Victorian era's great humorists. The son of a clergyman, his career embraced periods as a schoolmaster, an actor and a journalist. In the latter capacity, he was co-founder with Robert Barr, another contributor to this volume, of* The Idler, *a successful magazine.*

The work in question which follows comes from an incredible book, TOLD AFTER SUPPER *(1891). Published by the Leadenhall Press, on thick blue paper, it was illustrated on almost every page by K.M. Skeaping.* TOLD AFTER SUPPER *consisted of Jerome sending up almost every ghost story in sight, while at the same time inventing a few of his own – and then sending* them *up. That ghost story literature survived the experience speaks volumes for its stamina.*

This selection from the book is made up of two pieces run together. The first half is the book's introduction, worthy of resurrection in itself and also setting the tone for the following tale, one of those told by the various guests in Jerome's book who each recount a seasonal Yuletide ghost story. Charles Dickens must have spun in his grave.

JEROME K. JEROME

Introductory

I begin this way, because it is the proper, orthodox, respectable way to begin, and I have been brought up in a proper, orthodox, respectable way, and taught to always do the proper orthodox, respectable thing; and the habit clings to me.

Of course, as a mere matter of information it is quite unnecessary to mention the date at all. The experienced reader knows it was Christmas Eve, without my telling him. It always is Christmas Eve, in a ghost story.

Christmas Eve is the ghosts' great gala night. On Christmas Eve they hold their annual fête. On Christmas Eve everybody in Ghostland who *is* anybody – or rather, speaking of ghosts, one should say, I suppose, every nobody who *is* any nobody – comes out to show himself or herself, to see and to be seen, to promenade about and display their winding-sheets and grave-clothes to each other, to criticize one another's style, and sneer at one another's complexion.

'Christmas Eve parade,' as I expect they themselves term it, is a function, doubtless, eagerly prepared for and looked forward to throughout Ghostland, especially by the swagger set, such as the murdered Barons, the crime-stained Countesses, and the Earls who came over with the Conqueror, and assassinated their relatives, and died raving mad.

Hollow moans and fiendish grins are, one may be sure, energetically practised up. Blood-curdling shrieks and marrow-freezing gestures are probably rehearsed for weeks beforehand. Rusty chains and gory daggers are overhauled, and put into good working order; and sheets and shrouds, laid carefully by from the previous year's show, are taken down and shaken out, and mended, and aired.

Oh, it is a stirring night in Ghostland, the night of December the twenty-fourth!

Ghosts never come out on Christmas night itself, you may

have noticed. Christmas Eve, we suspect, has been too much for them; they are not used to excitement. For about a week after Christmas Eve, the gentleman ghosts, no doubt, feel as if they were all head, and go about making solemn resolutions to themselves that they will stop in next Christmas Eve; while the lady spectres are contradictory and snappish, and liable to burst into tears and leave the room hurriedly on being spoken to, for no perceptible cause whatever.

Ghosts with no position to maintain – mere middle-class ghosts – occasionally, I believe, do a little haunting on off-nights: on All Hallows Eve, and at Midsummer; and some will even run up for a mere local event – to celebrate, for instance, the anniversary of the hanging of somebody's grandfather, or to prophesy a misfortune.

He does love prophesying a misfortune, does the average British ghost. Send him out to prognosticate trouble to somebody, and he is happy. Let him force his way into a peaceful home, and turn the whole house upside down by foretelling a funeral, or predicting a bankruptcy, or hinting at a coming disgrace, or some other terrible disaster, about which nobody in their senses would want to know sooner than they could possible help, and the prior knowledge of which can serve no useful purpose whatsoever, and he feels that he is combining duty with pleasure. He would never forgive himself if anybody in his family had a trouble and he had not been there for a couple of months beforehand, doing silly tricks on the lawn or balancing himself on somebody's bedrail.

Then there are, besides, the very young, or very conscientious ghosts with a lost will or an undiscovered number weighing heavy on their minds, who will haunt steadily all the year round; and also the fussy ghost, who is indignant at having been buried in the dust-bin or in the village pond, and who never gives the parish a single night's quiet until somebody has paid for a first-class funeral for him.

But these are the exceptions. As I have said, the average orthodox ghost does his one turn a year, on Christmas Eve and is satisfied.

Why on Christmas Eve, of all nights in the year, I never could myself understand. It is invariably one of the most dismal of nights to be out in – cold, muddy, and wet. And besides, at Christmas time, everybody has quite enough to put up with in the way of a houseful of living relations, without wanting the ghosts of any dead ones mooning about the place, I am sure.

There must be something ghostly in the air of Christmas – something about the close, muggy atmosphere that draws up the ghosts, like the dampness of the summer rains brings out the frogs and snails.

And not only do the ghosts themselves always walk on Christmas Eve, but live people always sit and talk about them on Christmas Eve. When ever five or six English-speaking people meet round a fire on Christmas Eve, they start telling each other ghost stories. Nothing satisfies us on Christmas Eve but to hear each other tell authentic anecdotes about spectres. It is a genial, festive season, and we love to muse upon graves, and dead bodies, and murders, and blood.

There is a good deal of similarity about our ghostly experiences; but this of course is not our fault but the fault of the ghosts, who never will try any new performances, but always will keep steadily to the old, safe business. The consequence is that, when you have been at one Christmas Eve party, and heard six people relate their adventures with spirits, you do not require to hear any more ghost stories. To listen to any further ghost stories after that would be like sitting out two farcical comedies, or taking in two comic journals; the repetition would become wearisome.

There is always the young man who was, one year, spending the Christmas at a country house, and, on Christmas Eve, they put him to sleep in the west wing. Then in the middle of the night, the room door quietly opens and somebody – generally a lady in her night-dress – walks slowly in, and comes and sits on the bed. The young man thinks it must be one of the visitors, or some relative of the family, though he does not remember having previously seen her, who, unable to go to sleep, and feeling lonesome, all by herself, has come into his room for a chat. He has no idea it is a ghost: he is so unsuspicious. She does not speak, however; and, when he looks again, she is gone!

The young man relates the circumstance at the breakfast-table next morning, and asks each of the ladies present if it were she who was his visitor. But they all assure him that it was not, and the host, who has grown deadly pale, begs him to say no more about the matter, which strikes the young man as a singularly strange request.

After breakfast the host takes the young man into a corner, and explains to him that what he saw was the ghost of a lady who had been murdered in that very bed, or who had murdered somebody else there – it does not really matter which: you can be a, ghost by murdering somebody else or by being murdered yourself, whichever you prefer. The murdered ghost is, perhaps, the more popular; but, on the other hand, you can frighten people better if you are the murdered one, because then you can show your wounds and do groans.

Then there is the sceptical guest – it is always 'the guest' who gets let in for this sort of thing by-the-bye. A ghost never thinks much of his own family: it is 'the guest' he likes to haunt who after listening to the host's ghost story, on Christmas Eve, laughs at it, and says that he does not believe there are such things as ghosts at all; and that he will sleep in the haunted chamber that very night, if they will let him.

Everybody urges him not to be reckless, but he persists in his foolhardiness, and goes up to the Yellow Chamber (or whatever colour the haunted room may be) with a light heart and a candle, and wishes them all goodnight, and shuts the door.

Next morning he has got snow-white hair.

He does not tell anybody what he has seen: it is too awful.

There is also the plucky guest, who sees a ghost, and knows it is a ghost, and watches it, as it comes into the room and disappears through the wainscot, after which, as the ghost does not seem to be coming back, and there is nothing, consequently, to be gained by stopping awake, he goes to sleep.

He does not mention having seen the ghost to anybody, for fear of frightening them – some people are so nervous about ghosts, – but determines to wait for the next night, and see if the apparition appears again.

It does appear again, and, this time, he gets out of bed, dresses himself and does his hair, and follows it; and then discovers a secret passage leading from the bedroom down into the beer-cellar – a passage which, no doubt, was not unfrequently made use of in the bad days of yore.

After him comes the young man who woke up with a strange sensation in the middle of the night, and found his rich bachelor uncle standing by his bedside. The rich uncle smiled a weird sort of smile and vanished. The young man immediately got up and looked at his watch. It had stopped at half-past four, he having forgotten to wind it.

He made inquiries the next day, and found that, strangely enough, his rich uncle, whose only nephew he was, had married a widow with eleven children at exactly a quarter to twelve, only two days ago.

The young man does not attempt to explain the extraordinary circumstance. All he does is to vouch for the truth of his narrative.

And, to mention another case, there is the gentleman who is returning home late at night, from a Freemasons' dinner, and who, noticing a light issuing from a ruined abbey, creeps up, and looks through the keyhole. He sees the ghost of a 'grey sister' kissing the ghost of a brown monk, and is so inexpressibly shocked and frightened that he faints on the spot, and is discovered there the next morning, lying in a heap against the door, still speechless, and with his faithful latch-key clasped tightly in his hand.

All these things happen on Christmas Eve, they are all told of on Christmas Eve. For ghost stories to be told on any other evening than the evening of the twenty-fourth of December would be impossible in English society as at present regulated. Therefore, in introducing the sad but authentic ghost stories that follow hereafter, I feel that it is unnecessary to inform the student of Anglo-Saxon literature that the date on which they were told and on which the incidents took place was – Christmas Eve.

Nevertheless, I do so.

JEROME K. JEROME

The Haunted Mill

OR

The Ruined Home

(Mr Coombes's Story)

Well, you all know my brother-in-law, Mr Parkins (began Mr Coombes, taking the long clay pipe from his mouth, and putting it behind his ear: we did not know his brother-in-law, but we said we did, so as to save time), and you know of course that he once took a lease of an old mill in Surrey, and went to live there.

Now you must know that, years ago, this very mill had been occupied by a wicked old miser, who died there, leaving – so it was rumoured – all his money hidden somewhere about the place. Naturally enough, every one who had since come to live at the mill had tried to find the treasure; but none had ever succeeded, and the local wiseacres said that nobody ever would, unless the ghost of the miserly miller should, one day, take a fancy to one of the tenants, and disclose to him the secret of the hiding-place.

My brother-in-law did not attach much importance to the story, regarding it as an old woman's tale, and, unlike his predecessors, made no attempt whatever to discover the hidden gold.

'Unless business was very different then from what it is now,' said my brother-in-law, 'I don't see how a miller could very well have saved anything, however much of a miser he might have been: at all events, not enough to make it worth the trouble of looking for it.'

Still, he could not altogether get rid of the idea of that treasure.

One night he went to bed. There was nothing very extraordinary about that, I admit. He often did go to bed of a night. What *was* remarkable, however, was that exactly as the clock of the village church chimed the last stroke of twelve, my brother-in-law woke up with a start, and felt himself quite unable to go to sleep again.

Joe (his Christian name was Joe) sat up in bed, and looked around.

At the foot of the bed something stood very still, wrapped in shadow.

It moved into the moonlight, and then my brother-in-law saw that it was the figure of a wizened little old man, in knee-breeches and a pig-tail.

In an instant the story of the hidden treasure and the old miser flashed across his mind.

'He's come to show me where it's hid,' thought my brother-in-law; and he resolved that he would not spend all this money on himself but would devote a small percentage of it towards doing good to others.

This apparition moved towards the door: my brother-in-law put on his trousers and followed it. The ghost went downstairs into the kitchen, glided over and stood in front of the hearth, sighed and disappeared.

Next morning, Joe had a couple of bricklayers in, and made them haul out the stove and pull down the chimney, while he stood behind with a potato-sack in which to put the gold.

They knocked down half the wall, and never found so much as a four-penny bit. My brother-in-law did not know what to think.

The next night the old man appeared again, and again led the way into the kitchen. This time, however, instead of going to the fireplace, it stood more in the middle of the room, and sighed there.

'Oh, I see what he means now,' said my brother-in-law to himself; 'it's under the floor. Why did the old idiot go and stand up against the stove, so as to make me think it was up the chimney?'

They spent the next day in taking up the kitchen floor; but only thing they found was a three-pronged fork, and the handle of that was broken.

On the third night, the ghost reappeared, quite unabashed, and for a third time made for the kitchen. Arrived there, it looked up at the ceiling and vanished.

'Umph! he don't seem to have learned much sense where he's been to,' muttered Joe, as he trotted back to bed; 'I should have thought he might have done that at first.'

Still, there seemed no doubt now where the treasure lay, and the first thing after breakfast they started pulling down the ceiling. They got every inch of the ceiling down, and they took up the boards of the room above.

They discovered about as much treasure as you would expect to find in an empty quart pot.

On the fourth night, when the ghost appeared, as usual, my brother-in-law was so wild that he threw his boots at it; and the boots passed through the body, and broke a looking-glass.

On the fifth night, when Joe awoke, as he always did now at twelve, the ghost was standing in a dejected attitude, looking very miserable. There was an appealing look in its sad eyes that quite touched my brother-in-law.

'After all,' he thought, 'perhaps the silly chap's doing his best. Maybe he has forgotten where he really did put it, and is trying to remember. I'll give him another chance.'

The ghost appeared grateful and delighted at seeing Joe prepare to follow him, and led the way into the attic, pointed to the ceiling, and vanished.

'Well, he's hit it this time, I do hope,' said my brother-in-law; and next day they set to work to take the roof off the place.

It took them three days to get the roof thoroughly off, and all they found was a bird's nest; after securing which they covered up the house with tarpaulins, to keep it dry.

You might have thought that would have cured the poor fellow of looking for treasure. But it didn't.

He said there must be something in it all, or the ghost would never keep on coming as it did; and that, having gone so far, he would go on to the end, and solve the mystery, cost what it might.

Night after night, he would get out of his bed and follow that spectral old fraud about the house. Each night, the old man would indicate a different place; and, on each following day, my brother-in-law would proceed to break up the mill at the point indicated, and look for the treasure. At the end of three weeks, there was not a room in the mill fit to live in. Every wall had been pulled down, every floor had been taken up, every ceiling had

had a hole knocked in it. And then, as suddenly as they had begun, the ghost's visits ceased; and my brother-in-law was left in peace, to rebuild the place at his leisure.

'What induced the old image to play such a silly trick upon a family man and a ratepayer?' Ah! that's just what I cannot tell you.

Some said that the ghost of the wicked old man had done it to punish my brother-in-law for not believing in him at first; while others held that the apparition was probably that of some deceased local plumber and glazier, who would naturally take an interest in seeing a house knocked about and spoilt. But nobody knew anything for certain.

An Unexpected Journey

J.H. PEARCE

J.H. Pearce received glowing reviews for his short story book DROLLS FROM SHADOWLAND *(1893). The New York* Mail and Express *said it contained 'genius of an uncommon kind'; the* Boston Traveller *described the stories as 'beautiful to read from their deep imagination and haunting in their allegorical depth'; in Britain the* Illustrated London News *commented: 'his is imagination of a fine kind'. Yet, for all this praise, and that afforded his other work in this vein* TALES OF THE MASQUE *(1894), Pearce faded into obscurity after what appears to be his last work* THE DREAMER'S BOOK *(1905).*

Joseph Henry Pearce was born in 1856 and his writing career started in 1891 with the novel ESTHER PENTREATH. *He wrote several Cornish novels, and all told published nine books in fourteen years.*

'An Unexpected Journey' comes from DROLLS FROM SHADOWLAND, *and is an atmospheric vignette on a familiar theme. In Mr Pearce's capable hands, it carries extra weight.*

J.H. PEARCE

An Unexpected Journey

The performance was over: the curtain had descended and the spectators had dispersed.

There had been a slight crush at the doors of the theatre, and what with the abrupt change from the pleasant warmth and light of the interior to the sharp chill of the night outside, Preston shivered, and a sudden weakness smote him at the joints.

The crowd on the pavement in front of the theatre melted away with unexampled rapidity, in fact, seemed almost to waver and disappear as if the *mise en scène* had changed in some inexplicable way.

A hansom drove up, and Preston stepped into it heavily, glancing drowsily askance at the driver as he did so.

Seated up there, barely visible in the gloom, the driver had an almost grisly aspect, humped with waterproof capes, and with such a lean, white face. Preston, as he glanced at him, shivered again.

The trap-door above him opened softly, and the colourless face peered down at him curiously.

'Where to, sir?' asked the hollow voice.

Preston leaned back wearily. 'Home,' he replied.

It did not strike him as anything strange or unusual, that the driver asked no questions but drove off without a word. He was very weary, and he wanted to rest.

The sleepless hum of the city was abidingly in his ears, and the lamps that dotted the misty pavements stared at him blinkingly all along the route. The tall black buildings rose up grimly into the night; the faces that flitted to and fro along the pavements, kept ever sliding past him, melting into the darkness; and the cabs and 'buses, still astir in the streets, had a ghostly air as they vanished in the gloom.

Preston lay back, weary in every joint, a drowsy numbness settling on his pulse. He had faith in his driver: he would bring him safely home.

204

Presently they were at one of the wharves beside the river: Preston could hear the gurgle of the water around the piles.

Not this way had he ever before gone homeward. He looked out musingly on the swift, black stream.

'Just in time: we can go down with the tide,' said a voice.

Preston would have uttered some protest, but this sluggishness overpowered him: it was as if he could neither lift hand nor foot. The inertia of indifference had penetrated into his bones.

Presently he was aware that he had entered a barge that lay close against the wharf, heaving on the tide. And, as if it were all a piece of the play, the lean old driver, with his dead-white face, had the oars in his hands and stood quietly facing him, guiding the dark craft down the stream.

The panorama of the river-bank kept changing and shifting in the most inexplicable manner, and Preston was aware of a crowd of pictures ever coming and going before his eyes: as if some subtle magician, standing behind his shoulder, were projecting for him, on the huge black screen of night, the most marvellous display of memories he had ever contemplated. For they were all memories, or blends of memories, that now rose here on the horizon of his consciousness. There was nothing new in essentials presented to him: but the grouping was occasionally novel to a fault.

The dear old home – the dear old folks! Green hills, with the little white-washed cottage in a dimple of them, and in the foreground the wind-fretted plain of the sea. The boyish games – marbles and hoop-trundling – and the coming home at dusk to the red-lighted kitchen, where the mother had the tea ready on the table and the sisters sat at their knitting by the fire.

The dear, dear mother! how his pulse yearned towards her! there were tears in his eyes as he thought of her now. Yet, all the same, the quiet of his pulse was profound.

And there was the familiar scenery of his daily life: the ink-stained desks, the brass rails for the books, the ledgers and bank-books, and the files against the walls; and the faces of his fellow-clerks (even the office boy) depicted here before him to the very life.

The wind across the waters blew chilly in his face: he shivered, a numbness settling in his limbs.

His sweet young wife, so loving and gentle – how shamefully he had neglected her, seeking his own pleasure selfishly – there she sat in the familiar chair by the fireside with dear little Daisy dancing on her knee. What a quiet, restful interior it was! He wondered: would they miss him much if he were dead? . . . Above all, would little Daisy understand what it meant when some one whispered to her *'favee is dead'*?

The wavering shadows seemed to thicken around the boat. And the figure at the oars – how lean and white it was: and yet it seemed a good kind of fellow, too, he thought. Preston watched it musingly as the stream bore them onward: the rushing of the water almost lulling him to sleep.

Were they sweeping outward, then, to the unknown sea?

It was an unexpected journey . . . . . And he had asked to be taken *home!*

Presently the air grew full of shapes: shadowy shapes with mournful faces; shapes that hinted secrets, with threatenings in their eyes.

If a man's sins, now, should take to themselves bodies, would it not be in some such guise as this they would front and affright him at dead of night?

Preston shivered, sitting there like a mere numb lump.

How much of his wrong-doing is forgiven to a man – and how much remembered against him in the reckoning?

How awful this gruesome isolation was becoming!

Was it thus a man went drifting up to God?

The figure at the oars was crooning softly. It was like the lullaby his mother used to sing to him when he was a child.

There was a breath of freer air – humanity lay behind them – they were alone with Nature on the vast, dim sea.

The numbness crept to the roots of his being. He had no hands to lift; he had no feet to move. His heart grew sluggish: there was a numbness in his brain.

Death stood upright now in the bow before him: and in the east he was aware of a widening breadth of grey.

Would the blackness freshen into perfect day for him . . . . or would the night lie hopelessly on him for ever? . . . .

The figure drew near – and laid its hand across his eyes . . . .

★   ★   ★

'Thrown out of the hansom, and the wheels went over him, sir. He was dead in less than five minutes, I should think.'

'Cover his face . . . . and break it gently to his wife.'

The Page-Boy's Ghost

THE COUNTESS OF MUNSTER

Wilhelmina Fitzclarence, the Countess of Munster (1830–1906) started writing late in life, producing her first book DORINDA *at the age of fifty-nine. The daughter of the twelfth Earl of Cassillia, Wilhelmina had married her cousin, the second Earl of Munster, in 1855. He died in 1901, and three years later she published her autobiography* MY MEMORIES AND MISCELLANIES. *They had seven children but only two survived her.*

The Countess was a keen animal lover and there are several pets to be found in her collection GHOSTLY TALES *(1896) from which this story is taken. The Countess of Munster's stories are, to my mind, among the best of the late Victorian era. They are plainly written, they make no allowances for the fashion of the day, and they proceed to the point with admirable haste. In the nicest possible way, compare this story with that of Mrs Banks, and see the differing literary styles that went to make up Victorian ghostly tales.*

THE COUNTESS OF MUNSTER
The Page-Boy's Ghost

In the month of March of the year 1894, I, accompanied by my niece, Clara (who is young, pretty, and, moreover, a very clever and practical hospital nurse), went with my cousin Mrs Oliver in search of a house for the latter lady, who was about to settle in Bath.

The house-agent, of course, told us of many residences likely to suit our requirements, and amongst others, there was one especially – situated in 'Granville Crescent.' Cards were given us to view the house, and one lovely morning we three ladies started for that purpose.

When we arrived at the door, we found it was a corner house, which had been added to according to the owner's convenience, and was consequently rather a rambling building, although not large.

After viewing the basement and dining rooms, we proceeded upstairs. I had not been noticing my niece for some minutes, having, of course, been thoroughly occupied with my cousin, looking over the rooms, their furniture, etc.; but suddenly I felt a tug at my sleeve, and turning, I saw Clara looking ghastly pale, and evidently much disturbed.

'Dearest Aunt,' she gasped, rather than whispered, 'do come away!'

'Why, Clara!' I said, 'what has happened? Are you ill?'

'Oh, Auntie,' she reiterated, 'come away! Tell Mrs Oliver not to take the house – for it is haunted! *Don't you hear them?*'

'Hear *them!*' I repeated, and laughed merrily. 'What! You!' I added, 'a nurse – and so well known for practical common sense, and frightened at ghosts!'

But I was struck, all the same, by the expression of her face; it was so wistful, so terrified! All her lovely colour was gone. She was as unlike her bright, laughing little self as it was possible to conceive.

In spite of her beseeching looks, however, I felt I *must* accompany my cousin upstairs; and after a few minutes, Clara (who had kept close to me, evidently dreading to be left alone) once more timidly caught hold of my arm, and whispered in awe-stricken tones:

'Auntie, come away from this dreadful house! I tell you it is haunted! Oh! don't you hear them? Wherever we go footsteps are dogging us. For God's sake, Auntie, come away!'

I was rather provoked at her persistency, and all the more so when, upon my insisting on further explorations, she positively refused to be of the party, and ran down the stairs and out of the house, in an extremity of terror! After having seen everything, we also (i.e., Mrs Oliver and myself) left the house, and discovered Clara walking up and down outside, like some uneasy spirit.

She proceeded again to implore my cousin not to take the house, for, she said, she had never experienced such a sensation before – and she *knew* it was haunted!

Mrs Oliver thereupon, to Clara's enormous relief, told her that the house did not suit her, and that she did not mean to take it; but for the space of quite three weeks, subsequent to our visit to Granville Crescent, Clara told me she constantly felt she was being followed, and always was aware of footsteps (sometimes in front of, and sometimes behind her), whenever and wherever she walked! The whole thing, however, eventually passed out of our minds, till it was recalled some months later thus:

My cousin, the same Mrs Oliver called upon me one day, stating she had received a letter from a relative of hers, begging her to visit a friend of his who had taken a house in Granville Crescent, and who, having no friends or acquaintances there, began to find Bath lonely.

'Will you come with me?' asked my cousin; 'for I don't know the lady – besides which, I really think (from the address given me by my brother-in-law) that it is no other than Clara's "haunted house" in which they have taken up their abode!'

'Oh! do let us go and see!' I exclaimed; and we started together.

Directly we got to the house we both exclaimed: 'Just as we thought! It *is* Clara's "haunted house"! Now we shall hear something about it worth hearing!'

Mrs Oliver laughed, and said: 'Well, we won't alarm the inmates, supposing *they* have heard or seen nothing!'

So we rang, and waited.

After waiting some minutes – 'Did you knock as well as ring?' I asked.

'No, I don't think I did! but I will do so now.'

Mrs Oliver knocked, and rang again, and again we waited. Then we both knocked, and rang violently; but no one came to the door.

We tried to look in at the windows, but in vain! Thick muslin curtains effectually hid the view; then we peered down into the area, – but it seemed untenanted.

'There must be a mistake in the address,' I suggested, and we were on the point of giving up any further efforts, when a woman of the 'caretaker' genus, came up from the area of one of the neighbouring houses, looked mysterious, and approaching me near enough to be just audible, said in a stage-whisper: 'That 'ouse is h-empty!'

She then hastily descended once more into the darkness below, not pausing for one moment, but tearing down the steps as though some unseen and dreaded pursuer were on her track. After violently slamming and locking the area door, she returned to her chair at the basement window, and watched us intently; to note (apparently) the effect of her oracular words.

We stood there for a few minutes, but as no signs of entreaty could persuade her to come out to us again, we were constrained to depart without any explanation; and curiously enough, we did not connect the circumstances in any way with Clara's impressions about the house! We simply thought some mistake had been made concerning the address, which was very dull of us!

When my cousin got home, she wrote at once to her relation, saying she had not neglected his request, but that he must have given her the wrong address, or number, as no one lived in the house he had indicated; but that if he would rectify the mistake, she would gladly call again on his friend, when she hoped she should be more successful.

A few days later my cousin again appeared, in a state of great excitement. She brought with her a letter from the lady we had so fruitlessly sought to see, which fully explained the extraordinary circumstance.

After a few civil regrets over her loss of Mrs Oliver's visit, she wrote: 'We went to Granville Crescent, the house having been strongly recommended to us by the agent; but what we went through there it is impossible to describe! Indeed, we packed up and left very soon – in fact, in a few days; – being content and happy rather to sacrifice our rent (if needs be) than to subject ourselves to mysterious terrors, and possible dangers. Besides, our exodus was scarcely optional; for none of the servants would stay – and really we could not be surprised, *for neither could we!* "And why?" I can hear you ask.

'Well – listen! We were followed *all day* by an invisible something! Whether we went up or downstairs, a footstep either followed or preceded us. If we walked across the room, someone was ever at our side; if we sat down, we felt a presence. We knew we were never alone. But – *at night!* Ah! that was worse still! The house was full of crooked passages, and one night I came suddenly round a corner, and face to face with the attenuated figure of an emaciated-looking page-boy, who stood quite still and looked at me. He had long thin hands, with very white fingers, and one hand he held behind him as though he held, and were concealing, something which trailed behind him. I screamed for one of the servants, but by the time they came the figure had disappeared.

'My sister also saw him; she met him at the bottom of the stairs; he appeared suddenly – looking at her over the banisters, and she fell down in a faint.

'Wherever there was a curtained door-way, or a sudden turn in any passage, one never felt sure of not meeting the pale, haggard-looking page, with his one long white hand in front, while the other was concealed behind him trailing something on the ground.

'At last we got thoroughly terrified, and left! We wrote to the agent, after leaving, and reproached him, feeling sure he must have known something about the apparition.

'He acknowledged that some months before, a miserable page-boy had committed suicide in the house, by hanging himself with a rope, to the stair-banisters. And he added in the letter, "he supposed he must haunt the building, trailing the rope."

'We all wished the agent had told us this story before we had entered the house! For he evidently knew a great deal; but he did not insist upon his rent!'

The lady ended her letter by saying that after her departure, someone sent her a local-newspaper, giving a full account of the suicide, and of the coroner's inquest.

Mysterious Maisie

WIRT GERRARE

Wirt Gerrare was the curious nom-de-plume *adopted by William Oliver Greener (1862 – 1935) for the bulk of his literary output. Greener was a historian and expert on small arms who wrote two textbooks on guns and shooting at the turn of the century. Under his own name, he seems to have published just two books, both spy stories, but under the name Gerrare he turned out a small but widely varied range of titles. His first book* RUFIN'S LEGACY *appeared in 1892 and his last published work appears to have been* THE EXPLOITS OF JO SALIS, A BRITISH SPY *(1905). In between he published books on the history of Moscow, spying in Port Arthur, sharpshooting, and a futuristic novel* THE WARSTOCK *(1898).*

'Mysterious Maisie' comes from PHANTASMS *(1895), which appeared under the Gerrare pseudonym. Subtitled 'Original stories illustrating posthumous personality and character' it was published by an obscure London firm. It was notable for carrying a unique sales advertisement. Described as 'the sole edition', it stated on the flyleaf that copies of it would be unobtainable after 31 March 1895. It would be interesting to find out just how many extra copies of this odd little book that advertisement managed to sell. It is certainly one of the rarest items in the macabre fiction collector's list.*

PHANTASMS *was a loosely connected series of tales of ghosts and hauntings, all 'investigated' by two psychic detectives. In general, the two investigators were introduced by the author merely to top and tail the stories, as in 'Mysterious Maisie'. What I like about this story is the sheer exuberance of its special effects. Very few tales of this era carried such gruesome passengers, or indeed, carried such shocking hints of diabolical scheming. I think you'll enjoy meeting Wirt Gerrare's Miss Mure.*

WIRT GERRARE

Mysterious Maisie

Dear Mr Vesey – It is very good of you to interest yourself in my behalf in our quest for 'Mysterious Maisie' – so we have named the kind creature – and I lose no time in giving you not only all the facts concerning her visits, but many details of my sister's strange experiences. For the best of reasons I cannot add to the particulars now given; you have the whole story, and nothing extraneous to it, save such slight embellishments as my sister herself has written in her letters and journal, and some explanatory comments by myself to references which would be unintelligible to a stranger.

I will preface the story by stating that my sister Laura was seventeen when our father died; in our straitened circumstances, and with mother's health failing, it was needful that she should at once earn her living. She was not fitted for teaching, and had she been so, I think my experiences as assistant mistress of a High School were well enough known to her to act as an efficient repellant from embarking upon a like career. She was accomplished, fond of literature, painted a little, played well, and was of such a kindly disposition that she seemed eminently fitted for the post of companion to an elderly or invalid lady, and we were glad to accept a situation of this kind for her. True it was obtained through an agency, but the references were quite satisfactory, and such enquiries as we could make brought replies which reassured us, and we were confident that Laura would quickly gain the affection of all with whom she came in contact. My sister at that time was *very* pretty; she had a really beautiful face, but she was *petite*, very slight, very fragile; a delicately nurtured child, but full of verve, and not wanting in courage. She was not unduly timorous, nor was she over imaginative, and so truthful in all she said, and honest in all she did, that I accept as actual fact every statement she has made, exaggerated though those accounts may appear, and extraordinary as they undoubtedly are.

215

But to the story. My sister wrote in her journal, under the date of October 22nd, 1889:

"Arrived safely at Willesden Junction at 4.33; after waiting nearly half-an-hour, took the train to —, reaching that station in less than twenty minutes; took a 'four-wheeler' to Miss Mure's. The streets had a very dingy appearance, — is a dowdy suburb. Soon we turned down a winding lane, very badly fenced, not many houses in it, they were all old and were built on one side of the road; plenty of trees, nearly all of them bare of leaves. The car stopped in a wider road just out of the lane; the house looks old and badly kept from the outside; it stands back about twelve yards from the road. The garden in front is very badly kept – I have not yet seen that at the back – it is walled in, with iron palisades on the top of the wall, and ivy and other creepers grow over the fence as well as over the house. The front gate is in an iron arch, and was locked. The maid, whose name is Agnes, was a long time answering our appeal; then, when she saw who it was, she went back into the house for the key, so the cabman put my box on the footway, I paid him, and he drove away. I did not at all like the look of the house or the garden, and the cold flagstones with which the walk from the gate to the front door is paved are very ugly and cheerless. Agnes locked the gate again before we went into the house. In the little hall it was so dark I could not see anything, but when the door was shut, and we opened another leading to the stairs, I felt that the front door was lined with sheet iron. Every time I see such a door I think of the house in which Bill Sikes made his last stand, but I do not want to frighten myself. My room is large; it has a four-post bedstead with green rep hangings, a chest-upon-chest, an old closed press, and some old-fashioned chairs. The only lights are candles, the window is small, overgrown with a creeper from which the leaves are fast falling, and is barred with five iron bars and some ornamental scroll work. There are very curious prints on the wall, and some designs, which I cannot make out, on the ceiling. In the walls there are three doors, not counting the one in use; one of those has no bolts, but is locked. I have placed my box against it.

'I have not seen Miss Mure. Agnes tells me she does not wish to see me until tomorrow. I have had tea in the front room downstairs. It is a long, narrow room, with three tall and very narrow windows looking into the front garden, and a smaller window at the side, by the fire-place, also looking out upon the garden. There is a door leading to the drawing-room, which is at the back of the house. The room seemed to be very dark, but perhaps that was due to the dismal light out of doors, and the thick growth of trees and shrubs in front. When the candles were lit – we have no gas nor lamps – I saw that the room had a papered ceiling, a dirty, cream-coloured ground, with an open floral design in blue. The walls are panelled half way, the upper half is covered with an ornamental net reaching up to the cornice; at the back of the netting the wall is plastered over with canvas, which some time was painted stone colour. There are no pictures in the room. It is not home-like or cosy, and I do not admire the style; but I have never seen anything like it before, perhaps it will be better when I am accustomed to it; at present there is an air of mystery about the house and its inmates.

'Since I wrote the above I have had a talk with Agnes. I hope nothing she told me was true. She is a strange woman; but she says she has been here over fourteen years, so I cannot think things are so bad as she represents them to be. If her idea was to frighten me, she failed; I do not believe her silly tales. At first I was amused at her talk, for she speaks the true cockney dialect, and with a peculiar inflexion, very different to the accent habitual to people of the Midlands. I think Agnes is good-natured, but it was cruel to attempt to frighten me with silly superstitions; she is very ignorant if she does not know that all she said is false. I hope Miss Mure is more enlightened, otherwise my sojourn here will not be pleasant. I judge them to be funny people; they must be eccentric, or they would not keep a crocodile for a pet.

'Agnes says that my room is called the dragon room, from the pattern upon the ceiling. I am to go later into "Caduceus", but she persuaded Miss Mure to let me have the larger room at first, as being more homelike. I wonder what "Caduceus" is like! There are seven bedrooms – some of them must be very small – and one over the back kitchen; in that Agnes sleeps, and it is reached by different stairs.

'After her silly tales about hauntings, I asked her why she did not keep a dog. She replied that she had tried several times to get one to stay, but they all ran away. "They sees 'em, and they won't stop. Why there's Draysen's bull terrier, what'll kill anythin' livin'; when 'e came with the meat one day. I 'ticed him in through the side entrance, and put him in the back garden. He were right savage when I shut the door on him, but 'e no sooner turned round and looked the otherway than his tail dropped, and he whined that awful I were glad to let 'im out there and then. But we must ha' summut, so we've got Sivvy."

'For answer, Agnes commenced to explain that Miss Mure is a spiritualist, and constantly attended by a lot of spiritual companions, so that dogs and other animals dread her. At this I laughed heartily. Agnes was not offended, but she said I evidently knew very little of such matters. We were then silent for a few minutes, and I heard mumblings and acratchings. "Is that Sivvy?" I asked laughingly. "No," she replied very seriously, "they're at it agen," by they meaning the spirits, I suppose; but after listening she said it was the "sooterkin," at which I was, of course, as wise as before. I shall have to enlarge my vocabulary very considerably before understanding the inmates of this house. Sivvy frightened me much more than any ghost is likely to do. She is a huge crocodile, nearly four feet in length, and she ran, or rather waddled, straight towards me as soon as the door to the kitchen was opened; she hissed the whole time, and sent one of the chairs spinning by a blow from her tail. Agnes had ready a rough and much torn Turkish towel, which she threw over Sivvy's head; the reptile snapped savagely at it, and got its teeth entangled in the threads, and being also blindfolded by the towel, was quiet until Agnes seized its snout with her left hand, and taking its right thigh in her other, lifted it from the floor. It then commenced to lash savagely with its tail, and if Agnes was not badly hurt by the blows, she must be destitute of feeling; but it was only for an instant, for she slipped the reptile into a tank underneath the side-table by the window. She looked hot and flurried when the business was over, but she gave me to understand that the vicious thing was always loose in the outer kitchen, and that I must not presume to pass that way unless she accompanied me. She said also that Sivvy was in and out of the tank in her kitchen all night; a significant hint that neither I nor Miss Mure must venture beyond our own quarters after Sivvy's supper time.

'I did not sleep very well last night. Someone was in and out of my room several times, but they did not reply to my challenge, and as they did not molest me, no harm is done. I expect it was Agnes, trying to convince me of the truth of her ghost stories. I saw Miss Mure just after twelve o'clock today. She is an ogress. I think she is harmless, for she is nearly blind, but she is dreadful to look upon; very big, very stout, with a great fat face and tremendous cheeks and neck. She speaks in a very snappy, peremptory manner, but what she has said so far has not been disagreeable. My chief duty it appears is to read to her in the afternoons. We commenced today; she has a large number of books, but they are very old and about many curious things. Some of them are in black letter, which is very hard to read; some are in Latin, which I can read, but cannot understand. Miss Mure says, so much the better. When she tries to read she has to bring the volume quite close to her nose, and then runs along the line. It must be very trying work for her, but it is quite comical to see. We finished by reading in a book called *Certaine Secret Wonders of Nature*, and I had to copy out the following description of a monster, for Miss Mure said she knew where that was one just like it, only it was nearly six months old; she seemed very much interested in the description, which she has learned by heart.

> ' "Begotten of honourable parents, yet was he most horrible, deformed and fearefull, having his eyes of the colour of fire, his mouth and his nose like to the snoute of an Oxe, wyth an Horne annexed thereunto like the Trumpe of an Elephant; all hys back shagge-hairde like a dogge, and in place where other men be accustomed to have brests, he had two heads of an Ape, having above his navell marked the eies of a cat, and joyned to his knee and armes foure heades of a dog, with a grenning and fearefull countenance. The palmes of his feet and handes were like to those of an Ape; and among the rest he had a taile turning up so high, that the height thereof was half an elle; who after he had lived foure houres died.'

'A fortnight has passed since I last wrote in my journal. I have had two letters from my sister Maggie, and one from mother; both complain that they have not heard from me save by the note advising my arrival. I have given three letters to Agnes to post for me, today I found them on the dresser in her kitchen. I am not allowed to go out of the house at all; first one excuse and then another is made, but I shall soon see whether or not any attempt will be made to keep me prisoner here. Two people have been at different times to see Miss Mure, but the interviews have been private. There is very little variety in the life we lead, and our reading is confined to the same class of book. I have become quite learned respecting goblin-land. I should know much more if I understood better the Latin books I have to read, but they are printed in such strange type and with so many abbreviations, that I have to concentrate my attention upon the words, not the sense. How different this world to the one about which I used to read, and in which I used to live! This is one peopled by demons, phantoms, vampires, ghouls, boggarts, and nixies. Names of things of which I knew nothing are now so familiar that the creatures themselves appear to have real existence. The *Arabian Nights* are not more fantastic than *our* gospels; and Lempriére would have found ours a more marvellous world to catalogue than the classical mythical to which he devoted his learning. Ours is a world of luprachaun and clurichaune, deev and cloolie, and through the maze of mystery I have to thread my painful way, now learning how to distinguish oufe from pooka, and nis from pixy; study long screeds upon the doings of effreets and dwergers, or decipher the dwaul of delirious monks who have made homunculi from refuse. Waking or sleeping, the image of some uncouth form is always present to me. What would I not give for a volume by the once despised 'A. L. O. E' or prosy Emma Worboise? Talk of the troubles of Winifred Bertram or Jane Eyre, what are they to mine? Talented authoresses do not seem to know that however terrible it may be to have as a neighbour a mad woman in a tower, it is much worse to have to live in a kitchen with a crocodile. This elementary fact has escaped the notice of writers of fiction; the re-statement of it has induced me to reconsider my decision as to the most longed-for book; my choice now is the *Swiss Family Robinson*. In it I have no doubt I should find how to make even the crocodile useful, or how to kill it, which would be still better.

'It is a month to-day since I left home. It seems a year. I am conscious of a great change in myself; this cooped-up life, the whole of my time passed in the company of people for whom I have no affection, and my thoughts engaged with things to which

I have a natural aversion, have altered my character. That this change was desired by my employer I am certain. The atmosphere of mystery and unreality which pervades this house has broken my nerve. The trifling irregularities at which I used to laugh now oppress me; the dream faces, the scrapings, the waving of the bed-curtains, the footsteps and the scurrying, which disturb my rest, I cannot attribute to my imagination. Until a week or so ago I felt strong enough to dismiss them as absurdities, now I do not know what to think. I see strange forms disappearing from the rooms as I enter them; creatures, like to nothing in the heaven above or in the earth beneath, trip across the landing as I mount the stairs to my chamber; small headless beasts creep through the skirting-board on the corridor to hide themselves from my gaze, and these matters now affect me greatly. In the words of Job, 'Fear came upon me, and trembling, which made all my bones to shake. Then a spirit passed before my face; the hair of my flesh stood up: it stood still, but I could not discern the form thereof.' I am quite in the power of Miss Mure; she takes my hand in hers, and I know not how the time passes, but I feel weak and listless; even the letters from Maggie and mother do not interest me; they are in answer to letters I do not remember to have written. There has been one gathering here for the performance of the rites of the higher mystery. I was present, but I remember very little of them; one great horror excluded all others. A thing they brought here, half human, half— I know not what. I was in the front room downstairs when it arrived. It stood on two splayed feet outside the front gate when I first saw it, and its hand was grasped by a sad-looking, demure little man, with white hair, and wearing large blue spectacles. *Its* face was hidden by a dark silk pocket handkerchief tucked in under the edge of a heavy cloth cap, and it made uncouth noises, and tugged at the bars of the gate like a wild beast in a cage. At the *séance* we were in semi-darkness; at the table it was placed right opposite me, and the cap and handkerchief were removed – but it would be wicked to describe what was disclosed – neither God nor demon could have made that horror! Its keeper stood at the back of it, and he had taken from the black handbag he carried a short, stiff stick with a pear-shaped end, with which he energetically cudgelled the horror about the elbows when it tried to get across the table to me; apparently the only thing it sought to do. Strange shapes flitted about in the gloom, harsh noises were made, there was some weird chanting and hysterical sobbing; the sooterkin was brought from its warm-lined hatching-box, and twitched two tentacles sluggishly after the manner of a moribund jelly-fish; but my attention was riveted on the horror before whom I crouched. Since the *séance* I have had more leisure, and have hardly seen Miss Mure, who is engaged in preparations for some other orgie; thus I have time, and now some inclination, to write once more.

'Agnes tells me that I am soon to go into "Caduceus," a small room at the back of the house. It looks out upon that corner of the garden which is a dense tangle of shrub and bramble. It is at the angle nearest to a low building which has been built on a piece of land cut off from the garden. The building, Agnes says, is the mortuary for this district, and it is only when there are bodies there that Miss Mure convenes a meeting. The girl who came to the last *séance* and sat at my side is, Agnes informs me, a successful sorceress. Only a short time ago she was robust, stout, and healthy; now she is like a walking corpse, and she draws her strength from those of her acquaintance who do not shun her. If Agnes is to be believed, this Miss Buimbert must be a sort of soul vampire, sucking the spirituality from every person who allows her to approach within range of her influence. I was doubtful whether she was in reality a person or only the phantom of one; it has become so hard to me now to distinguish the actual from the seemingly real. I know that the headless forms and curious creatures which are ever flitting before me, and disappearing at my approach, are but illusions or phantasms conjured by Miss Mure to make an impression upon me, and it is to her that I owe the visitations of intangible visionary monsters who disturb my rest with groans, and make my waking moments horrible by their hideous grimaces and threatening gestures. I know the horror was real, for it had to be admitted by the front gate, and the impress left by its clubbed feet was visible for days on the clayey side walk outside the entrance gate. The sooterkin is real, for I have touched the brown skin of its boneless body, and seen the impression of its short, flabby, rounded limbs in the soft cotton wool of its bed.

'I know the phantoms cannot harm me, and I pray earnestly for preservation from all ill, and that I may be delivered from this place.

'Why was I brought here? For what unholy purpose am I necessary to these people that they guard me so jealously? Perhaps Agnes may be induced to give me some indication of my fate.

'Three days have passed since I wrote in my journal; an event has happened which has increased the mystery of this place. Yesternight, about ten o'clock, a car drew up at the front gate. I was in the front room and peeped through the blind. As Agnes passed the door to answer the knock she turned the key of the room and made me a prisoner. She admitted three men, and a fourth stood on the flags between the door and the gate. I had ample opportunity for examining him closely. A coarse, ruffianly-looking, burly man, a drover or butcher, or one following some brutalizing calling, I judged, from his appearance and his manner whilst standing and walking. Dark hair, a short beard, and a raucous voice. After admitting the men Agnes went hurriedly to her kitchen, and locked and barred the door, and soon I heard the hiss and the clattering of furniture which followed "Sivvy's" entrance into the front kitchen.

'The three men went upstairs, and in a few moments the stillness of the house was broken by the shrill shrieks of a female; the screams were accompanied by sounds of a scuffle and overturned furniture, then the noise partly subsided, but the struggle had not ceased. I heard the heavy breathing of the men, and seemed to see the efforts made by the woman they were dragging to the stairs. There were gasps and short cries as they brought her downstairs, and a short but sharp struggle in the hall. Then the burly man stepped within, and soon the four re-appeared in front, half carrying half dragging a struggling woman. Her light hair flew in disorder, as she twisted and bent to free herself. It was with diffculty they forced her into the car, and I saw her arms waving in helplessness as the captors endeavoured to enter the vehicle. I saw, too, that something had been tied over her mouth, and the last thing I noticed on her thin forearm, from which the dress had been torn, was a freshly-made scratch two or more inches in length, from which the blood was still trickling. Three of the men, including the burly drover, having entered the vehicle, the fourth rang our bell, then mounted the seat by the driver, and as they drove away I saw them pulling down the blinds to the windows of the car.

'Agnes went out at once and locked the gate, then bolted and barred the door and came to me. She appeared to have been drinking heavily, and answered my earnestly-put questions in an incoherent manner. If I am to believe her there have been several girls engaged at different times as companions to Miss Mure, and none of them have escaped; some have died, others have been taken away after residing here a long time. What am I to do? I will see Miss Mure tomorrow and demand some explanation of what I have seen and heard; and I have told Agnes to tell Miss Mure when she first sees her tomorrow that I must have an interview.

'I did not sleep at all last night, for I could not dismiss from my mind the scene I had witnessed, and what with speculating upon the fate of the unhappy creature forcibly taken away, and forebodings of ill to myself, I passed a most wretched time.

'Somewhat to my surprise Miss Mure expressed her willingness to see me at once. She was at breakfast when I entered her bedroom, feeling very nervous, and not quite knowing what to say. I told her that I did not like the place, and wished to go home; that she had no confidence in me, and did not even let me know who were the inmates of the house. To this she replied that she was sorry that I was not comfortable, that Agnes should have instructions to give me greater attention, and that any delicacy I might express a liking for should be obtained for me. As to not knowing who were the inmates of the house, she could not understand to whom I referred. No one was there, or had been there, but herself, myself, and Agnes. When I told her of what I had seen, she said it was all imagination; she knew nothing of anyone having been there, and surely she would have heard had there been any such struggle as I described. I told her that the footprints on the footway outside the gate, and the marks of the carriage wheels, were still to be seen distinctly, so that I was sure I had not deceived myself. She said it was cruel of me to mention such evidence, as I knew she was so afflicted that she could not see the marks herself; and even were the marks there, as I said, she was not responsible, for they were not upon her premises, and what people did outside our gates was beyond our control. The neighbourhood had greatly deteriorated since she first resided there. Had they not forced her to give up the most delightful portion of the garden for the erection of a public mortuary? A thing which so incensed her that she had entirely neglected the "beautiful pleasure grounds" since, and allowed the gardens to run wild, for she never used them now, and she only hoped that the authorities would allow her to enjoy possession of her house unmolested for the few years that remained to her. Then I complained of the crocodile. To this the answer was that I need not go near it. Siva – that is its correct name – was to be kept in the kitchen; it was a strange pet, but Agnes wished to keep it, and as long as she kept it in her own quarters she was to be allowed to do so. If it was once found in any other part of the house it was to go; Agnes knew that, and I need not fear that it would be allowed to pass the threshold of the kitchen. Then I said that I did not like the "horror", and I could not, and would not, stay if it ever came again. She replied that it was impertinent of me to attempt to dictate to her as to whom she should or should not invite as guests to her house, and that she would not submit to my dictation; no harm had been done to me, I had experienced no rudeness, and she was sure that none of her acquaintance would insult me. I then told her that I had heard that none of the persons who had previously filled the post I occupied had received any wages; that I was too poor to stay there if not paid, and that my only object on leaving home was to earn something to help to support my mother, as my sister's salary was insufficient, and that I should be pleased to be able to send them something at once. She listened in silence, but veritably stormed her reply. I had been listening to "idle kitchen tales," for she always paid when the money was due, my first quarter's salary was not payable until Christmas. I should have it then, unless she sent me about my business before, and she would like to know if there were any other preposterous claims I wished to make. To this I replied somewhat hotly that I had not made any preposterous claims, that I had simply asked for an advance of money as a favour and for the purpose I stated; that I certainly did wish for greater liberty; that I had never been outside the door since the day I came, that I wanted greater freedom for writing and posting my letters, and that I could not consent to remain in her service unless she showed greater confidence in me, and informed of the object she had in view when compelling my attendance at such meetings as the *séance* at which I had assisted. She said that she was pleased I had spoken out boldly, for she now felt no diffidence in making our relative positions plain to me. She wished me to remember that she stood *in loco parentis*, and therefore could not allow me to wander about alone, for the neighbourhood was not one of the kind in which a young girl could do so with impunity. But I was not to imagine that it was by her wish that I was confined to the premises. On fitting occasions, and as opportunities offered, we should drive and walk out together. As to the writing of letters I was, and always had been, quite free to write when I liked and whatever I wished to either my mother or my sister, and so far from having tampered with my correspondence she was only too pleased to know that my letters had been delivered to me personally by the postman. I sadly mistrusted her, but she was sure it was because I did not know her sufficiently well, and as proof of the kindly interest she took in my welfare, and that of my mother and sister, she would be pleased to advance me, there and then, five pounds on account of my first quarter's salary if I would undertake to send it at once, writing only a few lines to say why it had been sent, and in her presence putting the money in the envelope, sealing it and taking it directly to the gate, and giving it to any boy who might be playing in the locality to post in the letter box which we could see about a hundred yards distant. She knew it must be tiresome to a young girl to have no companion but Agnes, so, if my mother was agreeable, I might at Christmas spend a few days with friends in London; or, if that could not be arranged, I might invite anyone to spend some time with me in her house; she would always be ready to grant me facilities to receive or visit any friend of whom my mother might approve. As to the object of her studies and work, she was gratified that I showed any interest in them. I was possessed of sufficient intelligence, she thought, to form some idea of her work from the books I had read to her. She was engaged in researches of a kind not understood by many, and she admitted that the methods it was necessary to adopt were not always pleasant; indeed they were viewed with such suspicion by the authorities that it was advisable to work in secret, or at any rate in such a manner as would excite but little suspicion. She concluded, "I liked you, dear, from the time I first saw your portrait, and I hope some day you will be an earnest worker in the cause to which I have devoted my life."

'I made haste to apologise fully, and gladly availed myself of her offer to make the remittance. I thought how pleased dear mother and Maggie would be to receive my first earnings, and I took the five sovereigns to Agnes to get changed into a note by one of the tradesmen. Then I wrote my letter, and submitted it to Miss Mure, who at once approved it, though it took her some time to read it. When Agnes brought up the note I took the number and date, at Miss Mure's suggestion, and also the name of the last owner, "H. Fletcher," scrawled on the back, and stated them upon the receipt I gave her; then in her presence and in that of Agnes I put the note and the letter in the envelope, sealed it with black wax, and at once went with Agnes to the front gate to find a boy to post it. At Miss Mure's suggestion we stayed there, and watched him take it to and drop it in the box, then gave him another penny when he came back. I never was so pleased as when I saw the boy drop the letter in. I felt quite content to remain with Miss Mure, and I told Agnes so. She did not say anything. I added that though we had no friends in London, a friend of mine had, and no doubt I should have an invitation from them, and leave for a few days at Christmas. "Oh no, you won't!" said Agnes. "I've been here fourteen year last Febry, and it ain't the fust time I've seen this trick played. Don't I remember poor Miss Jo? Why, 'er stood here just as you, she talked about goin' 'ome in a fortnight; but 'er took bad and died; and 'er went 'ome from the mortrey, 'er did. The missis ain't never so dangerous as when her's nice, that's it, miss. It ain't her fault, but I'm sorry for yer, I am."

'No sooner were we back in the house than Miss Mure called me. I hastened to her, and she held out to me the note I had sent in the letter, and laughingly asked me why I had forgotten to enclose it. There it was, the number and the name both corresponded with those I had taken of the one I was sure I had enclosed to mother. "Have you sent the real note or only the phantom?" she asked. I was too confused to reply. "Well, we will wait until we hear from your home," she said with a smile, and motioned me to leave the room.

'I have had a long talk with Agnes; she refused to say anything about the event of the other evening, but says I shall "see what I shall see." I cannot make out at all what became of the other girls; but as to my fate, Agnes makes no secret of what she believes is in store for me. "If I was you, miss, I should pray. I should; it can't do no harm to you, and it'll make yer 'appy. Why don't I pray? It ain't much use prayin' when the copper 'ave 'is 'and on yer shoulder, is it? I 'adn't. If I'd gone to quod it'd only been for life at the wust. But Agnes Coley'd had one taste, and her d'ain't want two, so 'er chivvied the beak, and 'as 'er liberty – livin' alone in a cellar with a bloomin' crocerdile, that's what 'er's doin".'

' "But I have not 'chivvied the beak",' and I am here,' I argued.

' " 'Course yer 'aven't. It's yer fate, that' all. You won't be here for a couple o' bloomin' stretches fightin' for yer livin' with a stinkin' crocerdile. You'll be a hangel long afore that."

' "But, Agnes, tell me why must I be an angel? If what you tell me is true, I do not think poor Miss Mure and her friends want angels, they seem to choose such very opposite characters for their acquaintance."

' "Look 'ere, miss, 't ain't that missis wants yer to become a hangel; yer'll become a hangel 'cause it's yer nature."

' "I do not understand you."

' "Well, see 'ere. S'pose – only s'pose a' course – s'pose that there thing yer call the 'orror were to come here, and be put in 'Salymandy,' and you in 'Caduceus,' with only a bit a' tishy paper a dividin' yer room from his 'n. Don't yer think yer'd soon be a hangel thin?"

'I shuddered.

' "Yer'd better pray, miss; though it ain't for the likes o' me to tell *you* to pray – if I'd a pray'd for fourteen year instead o' carryin' on as I've been doin' – but there, it ain't no use cryin' over spilt milk.'

' "But why should the horror be brought here at all?"

' "You ask that? Well, I should 'ave thought you'd a knowed. There was poor Miss Jo, a nice girl she was, and she used to tell me that what the hinner cercle was after was the makin' o' summat different to 'omunclusses, and as how, when all things was properishus, they'd try agen and agen until they did get somethin' fresh. We was great in mandrakes in them days, miss, and some hawful things I've seen in this house. Poor Miss Jo, 'er *was* a dear good girl, just like yerself; but I found her 'alf dead in 'Caduceus,' and the dwerger what used to be here ain't been nigh since that. You do put me in mind o' Miss Jo, miss, you do."

'I did not quite understand Agnes at first, but soon the import of much I had read to Miss Mure seemed clear to me.

'You pretend to like me, Agnes, I said. Why did you not help Miss Jo, if you liked her as you say you did?'

' "That's it, miss, I ain't no good. When the time is properishus I could no more stir a finger to help yer than Sivvy could if yer tumbled in a vat o' bilin' oil."

' "Then if you believe that, and wish to help me, let me escape from here at once." I clung to her arm, for I felt a fear I had never before experienced.

' "No, miss, that wouldn't save yer, and it'd be worse than death to me. I 'ain't live 'ere fourteen year for nothin'. I've 'erd all that before. Yer a brave girl, you are, braver than Miss Jo, but I s'pose it'll be the same with you as with the rest."

'We were silent for some time.

' "Agnes, will you tell me – will you let me know – if that thing ever comes here again?"

' "I can't promise, miss."

' "If only I could get a few days I could escape," I said in despair.

' "No, yer couldn't. There was that Miss Vanover who got out of a Russian prison, trying for months to escape from 'ere, and 'er never could. Besides, 'ow do you know 'e ain't here now? What would you do if you met 'im on the stairs to-night?"

'I screamed.

' "Be quiet, or I'll let Sivvy in. You'd better go to bed now."

' "Oh, do help me, Agnes!" I pleaded.

' "And 'aven't I helped yer? 'Aven't I warned yer of yer fate? Ain't it because I like you I've told yer what I 'ave? You do what I told you."

'I came upstairs, and have written, and now feel more trustful. Surely mother's prayers will avail with the good God, and His angels will guard me.

'I slept soundly that night, but the last two days my terror has increased. I notice just those indications of a forthcoming meeting which immediately preceded the last *séance*, and the passages we have read in the books of magic have prepared me for the attempt which I feel certain will be made. Agnes has taken me, for the first time, into "Caduceus," and shewn me the window bars which were bent by Miss Jo in her frantic endeavours to escape, and I have peeped into the adjoining cupboard, "Salamander," which is arranged more like a stall for a beast than a bedroom for a human creature. It is divided by the flimsiest of partitions from "Caduceus," and there is a door communicating which *I* could easily break down. I have a letter from mother acknowledging the receipt of my remittance,* and containing some words of encouragement which I shall lay to heart. I showed the letter to Miss Mure, and read it to her. She smiled and said she hoped I was now satisfied. Unfortunately I am not.

'Last night I sustained another shock. I was again in that downstairs room where I spend so much of my time, fearing to see that horror once more, yet always on the lookout for it; it would be still worse if it came to the house unknown to me. A two-wheeled cart of funny shape, like that used for delivering pianofortes, stopped at the gate. Four men were on it. I recognised the tread of one at once, he was the burly, butcher-like man who had waited on the flags when the woman was dragged away. I was again locked in the room by Agnes, who however did not retreat to her kitchen, but fetched lights, and the men brought from the vehicle a large coffin. Their burden seemed heavy. They spoke in low whispers, and once inside the house the door was shut. They they conveyed the coffin upstairs, and I heard their irregular tramp across the landing. From the manner in which the coffin was handled I knew that it was not empty.

---

*No money was received and no acknowledgement sent. – MAGGIE GLEIG.

'Did it contain the corpse of the woman whom less than a week ago I had seen forcibly dragged from the house? Or was it intended for me? Did it contain the living horror, smuggled thus into the house so that I should not know of its coming?

'The men were not long upstairs, and soon descended and drove away. Agnes went straight to her kitchen without unfastening the door of the room in which I was. I called and knocked, but obtained no reply.

'It was nearly midnight when the door communicating with the drawing-room opened, and Miss Mure beckoned to me to follow her. We went upstairs, and she told me that my room had been changed. I was to sleep henceforth in "Caduceus," whither my things had already been conveyed.

"She showed me into the room and left me there with less than a half inch of candle, locking the door upon me. I at once attempted to barricade the flimsy door which divided my room from the "pen," but the result was unsatisfactory. Then I looked for my Bible, but none of my books appeared to have been brought into the room. It did not take long to search the small apartment, and my things were so few that the books must have been left behind purposely. There was no bedstead in the room, but in its place was a long settle like a boxed-in bath or water cistern, and of the top of this a straw mattress was laid and the bed made; a long curtain, hanging over a pole swung above the middle of the bed in the French fashion, hid the want of a bedstead. Suddenly it occurred to me that the coffin had been placed in the locker under my bed. For some minutes I was too frightened at the thought to do more than stare blankly at the bed. When I commenced to lift up the palliasse the candle gave a warning flicker, and I was in utter darkness before I could make even a cursory examination of the locker. Left without light and with the apartment in disorder, I sat in a half dazed condition on the first chair into which I could drop; straining my eyes to see further into the darkness and and my ears to catch a sound from the next room. In a short time I succeeded in frightening myself completely. I heard, or thought I heard, the peculiar grunting of the horror, and I flung myself against the door from my room, hoping to break it down, but the effort was useless, and I again sank helplessly into the chair. It was whilst listening breathlessly

for the sounds I so well remembered, that my attention was
distracted by a sigh, as the soughing of the wind, from the box
bed before me. I looked in that direction, and in the pitchy
blackness saw a bright white figure, first its head projecting
through the lid of the box, or the bottom of the bed, then slowly
it arose – a corpse fully dressed out in its grave clothes, with livid
face, fallen jaw, and wide-open glassy eyes staring vacantly
before it. Very many strange things I had seen since staying at
Miss Mure's, but no spectre so struck me with terror as did this
one. I felt that I could not stay there with it. I sprang up, and
whilst my gaze was riveted upon it fell back towards the door of
"Salamander" and groped for the fastenings. The door yielded
to my pressure, and scrambling over my box I entered the little
pen or cupboard, which was associated in my mind with the thing
I most dreaded. In the delirium of terror I felt that I must reach
Agnes, but I had sufficient sense to clutch at the bed coverlet as I
escaped from my room. The door from "Salamander" was
unlocked, and without stopping to think I sped along the corridor
and hurried downstairs, groping my way more slowly in the less
known hall and passages leading to the kitchen. The door had no
lock – in this very old part of the house a drop latch was the only
fastening – and by working away perseveringly the stop peg
Agnes stuck in above the latch would drop out. I knew Siva
would be near, and had the coverlet ready to throw over her, but
when I gently opened the door and peered in I saw Siva was
perched half on a chair and half on the kitchen table still and
dumb, whilst before the fire there stood the figure of a man from
whom the skin had been removed. It was like an anatomical
figure designed to show the muscles; its grinning face, prominent teeth, and colourless scalp were doubly horrible in the glow
of the dying fire. As it turned its head to look at me the last spark
of hope died in my heart, and with a loud scream I fell forward
on the floor and fainted.

'When I recovered consciousness I was again on the bed in
"Caduceus." The light of a foggy morning showed that the room
was empty, and some untouched breakfast was on a tray by my
bedside. Was the adventure of last night a dream or a reality?

'I arose and went at once downstairs and wrote up my journal.
When I went there again, in the dusk of the early evening, a

young woman was sitting in an obscure corner: I bowed to her, and took up my accustomed position at the front window. She crossed over to me, and sat by my side. I felt pleased that she did so, and soon we commenced a conversation. I learned that her name was Maisie, and she told me that she understood my fears, and that in time I should be free of them. Her face seemed familiar, her voice was sweet, and manner gentle and subdued. I could learn nothing concerning Miss Mure, and Maisie told me that she could never see me in her presence, but she would be in that room frequently, and possibly she could come to me occasionally in my new room.

'I told her of my dread of that room, and of the great fear I entertained that the cupboard next to it would be tenanted by the creature who was sometimes brought there. She told me it was wrong to anticipate trouble, the danger was less real than I imagined. I spoke of what I had seen from that window, and she shuddered when I described the struggles of the woman who had been dragged away. I commenced to tell her of what I had seen brought back the night before, but she prevented me with an impatient gesture. I dropped the subject, but soon the thoughts which were uppermost in mind were again the topic of my tale, and I told her of the spectre I had seen arise from beneath my bed. She arose abruptly, and, with a sad wave of the hand, left the room by the door leading to the passage. I remained there musing, and hoping that she would soon return. The darkness and loneliness became oppressive. I sought Agnes, but I dared not speak to her of Maisie, and as we had little to say to each other, she went to bed early.

'That night I barely slept at all, the remembrance of my adventures the night before, or the too vivid nature of my dream, prevented slumber. I may have dozed several times, but I had no sleep until daylight broke, when I fell into a troubled slumber. When in the afternoon I again entered the downstairs room Maisie was there. Her presence cheered me; she said but little, and all too soon she went. I am pleased with the companionship of Maisie; sometimes I find her in my bedroom, but there she is always more sad than when downstairs, and I barely notice her coming and going. She glides in and out as a ghost might. My manner, likely enough, is the same. Today, when I looked in the mirror, I was horrified at my appearance. My face is pallid as death, and set in its frame of hay-coloured hair, and with two violet eyes shining like burning coals, I doubt whether it would not frighten a visitor as much as any real spectre could do.

'Something tells me I am not long for this world; I think of mother and Maggie, and burst into tears. They will miss me. If it were not for them I think I should like to be at rest; but when I think about it "a strange perplexity creeps coldly on me, like a fear to die." I have talked about this to Maisie, and she answered peremptorily that I must not die here. "You know not what it means to die in this place." I looked at her earnestly. Was she real? The words of Dryden came imperatively into my mind—

> ' "Oh! 't is a fearful thing to be no more.
> Or if it be, to wander after death;
> To walk, as spirits do, in brakes all day;
> And when the darkness comes, to glide in paths
> That lead to graves; and in the silent vault,
> Where lies your own pale shroud, to hover o'er it,
> Striving to enter your forbidden corpse."

'I looked tearfully at Maisie; she did not reply, but her face was ineffably sad. As I cried piteously, "Oh, Maisie! Maisie!" she left the room hastily.

'I saw her again when I went to my room; her face was still troubled, but she drew me towards her affectionately, and we talked together for a long time of love, and trust, and of beauty. The pale moonlight shone into the room, and by its faint glimmer Maisie's face seemed truly beautiful; but for the first time I noticed that her hands were coarse, and that upon the wrist of one there was the scratch I had seen on the arm of the woman who had been dragged from the house on that terrible evening a fortnight ago. She smiled when she saw that I noticed the scar, but offered no explanation. It seemed to alter the thread of our discourse, for she talked to me of my position in the house, of the heavy work *she* had to do on the morrow. It would be best for me to go, if I really wished. I told her how I dreaded the next meeting, and how anxious I was to escape. For some minutes she was silent; she then said it would be hard to part from me, but tomorrow, if I would trust her, she would show me how to escape. I was to follow her in silence, soon after midnight, and must promise not to speak to her. I expressed my readiness to do all that she wished, and commenced at once to think out my plans for getting my things together in readiness. She said that she was tired, and with my permission would rest for a time on my bed. She lay down, and after looking at her for a time I turned away and watched the moon and the slowly-floating clouds. I must have dozed, for when I again looked for her I found that she had disappeared.

'When I awoke in the morning it was already late, but I should have slept on had not the noise of strange footsteps on the landing disturbed me. I dressed hastily, and upon leaving my room was in time to see two men dragging the coffin from under my bed through a door in the wooden partition which divided the room from the landing. I waited and saw that it was taken to the *séance* room.

'Agnes has been in a very bad temper all day. Siva has been thrust out into the garden, and lurks about in the bushes. The house has been reeking with strange odours, and the preparations for the meeting tonight are now completed. I do so hope Maisie will not fail me, and that I shall leave this house tonight for ever. I have not seen Miss Mure, nor did I expect to. Masie has not been here, and I am waiting patiently at the window, looking out for the arrival of that most fearful of all things which attends the meeting of the black magicians. I feel that if I see it again I shall never more write in this, my journal. It is at the gate, gripped tightly by the old man with blue spectacles. Adieu!

'East Sheen,
'*December 14th*

'Dearest mother – Mr Frank's telegramme has informed you that I have left Miss Mure's. That the why and wherefore of my conduct may be understood without inconvenient explanations by word of mouth when I see you, I send you the journal I have kept since I went there, and when I tell you that I have promised one to whom I owe my life that I will never speak of my experiences while with those dreadful people, I know that both Maggie and yourself will accept this account as final, and so far complete as I am able to make it . . . At the *séance* I was pleased to

see Maisie sitting opposite me in the seat which the horror had
occupied on the last occasion. On the table between us was the
coffin, open, and containing Maisie herself. The other Maisie,
the living one, smiled at me as she saw my wondering face. The
monster still had its face covered, and was tolerably still. I kept
my gaze fixed upon Maisie during the performance of the
preliminary rites. Later, when the face of the horror was
uncovered, it whined piteously, and moved about the room as a
ferret which has escaped from a rat-hole, sniffing and creeping,
but avoiding the seat on which Maisie sat, and towards which it
was evident its keeper wished to direct it. Then it clambered on
to the table, and threw itself upon the body in the coffin. Maisie
at once arose, and crossing to where I was gazing in the
stupefaction of fascination upon the horror, she touched me
lightly on the shoulder, and I turned and followed her from the
room. We went downstairs and through the kitchens, then along
an old, little-used passage leading to a stable-yard. In this there
was a door locked from the inside, the key still in the lock. Maisie
indicated that I was to open the door, and we passed out into a
passage leading to the pathway by the mortuary. We were free.
She then made me promise never to speak of what had happened
to me, and told me to hasten towards town. I looked behind me,
and saw her pale, wistful face still watching me. How I reached
here I can tell you fully. It was all so strange. In the thick London
fog the men and creatures all loomed upon me suddenly, and
took seemingly strange shapes. I became frightened, but
struggled on to the address I had determined to reach. More I
will never tell until Maisie shall have released me from the
promise I made.'

Nothing has shaken my sister's resolution. Miss Mure has
now left the house, and resides with a relative. Agnes, we
learned, has joined her friends in Australia. Whether the mystery
is fact or fiction I may never know, but my sister is often
strangely affected since her return to us. She starts in her sleep,
is often found weeping, is timorous, and will not be alone after
dusk. Even when she is with us, and we are as merry as we know
how to be, her face will suddenly become clouded, and she will
shrink as though some great horror were before her, and oft

times she will raise her hands as though to screen from view something which terrifies her, and sends her sobbing to mother or myself.

A CATALOG OF SELECTED
DOVER BOOKS
IN ALL FIELDS OF INTEREST

A CATALOG OF SELECTED DOVER
BOOKS IN ALL FIELDS OF INTEREST

CONCERNING THE SPIRITUAL IN ART, Wassily Kandinsky. Pioneering work by father of abstract art. Thoughts on color theory, nature of art. Analysis of earlier masters. 12 illustrations. 80pp. of text. 5⅜ x 8½.   0-486-23411-8

CELTIC ART: The Methods of Construction, George Bain. Simple geometric techniques for making Celtic interlacements, spirals, Kells-type initials, animals, humans, etc. Over 500 illustrations. 160pp. 9 x 12. (Available in U.S. only.)   0-486-22923-8

AN ATLAS OF ANATOMY FOR ARTISTS, Fritz Schider. Most thorough reference work on art anatomy in the world. Hundreds of illustrations, including selections from works by Vesalius, Leonardo, Goya, Ingres, Michelangelo, others. 593 illustrations. 192pp. 7⅛ x 10¼.   0-486-20241-0

CELTIC HAND STROKE-BY-STROKE (Irish Half-Uncial from "The Book of Kells"): An Arthur Baker Calligraphy Manual, Arthur Baker. Complete guide to creating each letter of the alphabet in distinctive Celtic manner. Covers hand position, strokes, pens, inks, paper, more. Illustrated. 48pp. 8¼ x 11.   0-486-24336-2

EASY ORIGAMI, John Montroll. Charming collection of 32 projects (hat, cup, pelican, piano, swan, many more) specially designed for the novice origami hobbyist. Clearly illustrated easy-to-follow instructions insure that even beginning papercrafters will achieve successful results. 48pp. 8¼ x 11.   0-486-27298-2

BLOOMINGDALE'S ILLUSTRATED 1886 CATALOG: Fashions, Dry Goods and Housewares, Bloomingdale Brothers. Famed merchants' extremely rare catalog depicting about 1,700 products: clothing, housewares, firearms, dry goods, jewelry, more. Invaluable for dating, identifying vintage items. Also, copyright-free graphics for artists, designers. Co-published with Henry Ford Museum & Greenfield Village. 160pp. 8¼ x 11.   0-486-25780-0

THE ART OF WORLDLY WISDOM, Baltasar Gracian. "Think with the few and speak with the many," "Friends are a second existence," and "Be able to forget" are among this 1637 volume's 300 pithy maxims. A perfect source of mental and spiritual refreshment, it can be opened at random and appreciated either in brief or at length. 128pp. 5⅜ x 8½.   0-486-44034-6

JOHNSON'S DICTIONARY: A Modern Selection, Samuel Johnson (E. L. McAdam and George Milne, eds.). This modern version reduces the original 1755 edition's 2,300 pages of definitions and literary examples to a more manageable length, retaining the verbal pleasure and historical curiosity of the original. 480pp. 5³⁄₁₆ x 8¼.   0-486-44089-3

ADVENTURES OF HUCKLEBERRY FINN, Mark Twain, Illustrated by E. W. Kemble. A work of eternal richness and complexity, a source of ongoing critical debate, and a literary landmark, Twain's 1885 masterpiece about a barefoot boy's journey of self-discovery has enthralled readers around the world. This handsome clothbound reproduction of the first edition features all 174 of the original black-and-white illustrations. 368pp. 5⅜ x 8½.   0-486-44322-1

STICKLEY CRAFTSMAN FURNITURE CATALOGS, Gustav Stickley and L. & J. G. Stickley. Beautiful, functional furniture in two authentic catalogs from 1910. 594 illustrations, including 277 photos, show settles, rockers, armchairs, reclining chairs, bookcases, desks, tables. 183pp. 6½ x 9¼. 0-486-23838-5

AMERICAN LOCOMOTIVES IN HISTORIC PHOTOGRAPHS: 1858 to 1949, Ron Ziel (ed.). A rare collection of 126 meticulously detailed official photographs, called "builder portraits," of American locomotives that majestically chronicle the rise of steam locomotive power in America. Introduction. Detailed captions. xi+ 129pp. 9 x 12. 0-486-27393-8

AMERICA'S LIGHTHOUSES: An Illustrated History, Francis Ross Holland, Jr. Delightfully written, profusely illustrated fact-filled survey of over 200 American lighthouses since 1716. History, anecdotes, technological advances, more. 240pp. 8 x 10¾. 0-486-25576-X

TOWARDS A NEW ARCHITECTURE, Le Corbusier. Pioneering manifesto by founder of "International School." Technical and aesthetic theories, views of industry, economics, relation of form to function, "mass-production split" and much more. Profusely illustrated. 320pp. 6⅛ x 9¼. (Available in U.S. only.) 0-486-25023-7

HOW THE OTHER HALF LIVES, Jacob Riis. Famous journalistic record, exposing poverty and degradation of New York slums around 1900, by major social reformer. 100 striking and influential photographs. 233pp. 10 x 7⅞. 0-486-22012-5

FRUIT KEY AND TWIG KEY TO TREES AND SHRUBS, William M. Harlow. One of the handiest and most widely used identification aids. Fruit key covers 120 deciduous and evergreen species; twig key 160 deciduous species. Easily used. Over 300 photographs. 126pp. 5⅜ x 8½. 0-486-20511-8

COMMON BIRD SONGS, Dr. Donald J. Borror. Songs of 60 most common U.S. birds: robins, sparrows, cardinals, bluejays, finches, more—arranged in order of increasing complexity. Up to 9 variations of songs of each species.
Cassette and manual 0-486-99911-4

ORCHIDS AS HOUSE PLANTS, Rebecca Tyson Northen. Grow cattleyas and many other kinds of orchids—in a window, in a case, or under artificial light. 63 illustrations. 148pp. 5⅜ x 8½. 0-486-23261-1

MONSTER MAZES, Dave Phillips. Masterful mazes at four levels of difficulty. Avoid deadly perils and evil creatures to find magical treasures. Solutions for all 32 exciting illustrated puzzles. 48pp. 8¼ x 11. 0-486-26005-4

MOZART'S DON GIOVANNI (DOVER OPERA LIBRETTO SERIES), Wolfgang Amadeus Mozart. Introduced and translated by Ellen H. Bleiler. Standard Italian libretto, with complete English translation. Convenient and thoroughly portable—an ideal companion for reading along with a recording or the performance itself. Introduction. List of characters. Plot summary. 121pp. 5¼ x 8½. 0-486-24944-1

FRANK LLOYD WRIGHT'S DANA HOUSE, Donald Hoffmann. Pictorial essay of residential masterpiece with over 160 interior and exterior photos, plans, elevations, sketches and studies. 128pp. 9¼ x 10¾. 0-486-29120-0

THE CLARINET AND CLARINET PLAYING, David Pino. Lively, comprehensive work features suggestions about technique, musicianship, and musical interpretation, as well as guidelines for teaching, making your own reeds, and preparing for public performance. Includes an intriguing look at clarinet history. "A godsend," *The Clarinet,* Journal of the International Clarinet Society. Appendixes. 7 illus. 320pp. 5⅜ x 8½. 0-486-40270-3

HOLLYWOOD GLAMOR PORTRAITS, John Kobal (ed.). 145 photos from 1926-49. Harlow, Gable, Bogart, Bacall; 94 stars in all. Full background on photographers, technical aspects. 160pp. 8⅜ x 11¼. 0-486-23352-9

THE RAVEN AND OTHER FAVORITE POEMS, Edgar Allan Poe. Over 40 of the author's most memorable poems: "The Bells," "Ulalume," "Israfel," "To Helen," "The Conqueror Worm," "Eldorado," "Annabel Lee," many more. Alphabetic lists of titles and first lines. 64pp. 5³⁄₁₆ x 8¼. 0-486-26685-0

PERSONAL MEMOIRS OF U. S. GRANT, Ulysses Simpson Grant. Intelligent, deeply moving firsthand account of Civil War campaigns, considered by many the finest military memoirs ever written. Includes letters, historic photographs, maps and more. 528pp. 6⅛ x 9¼. 0-486-28587-1

ANCIENT EGYPTIAN MATERIALS AND INDUSTRIES, A. Lucas and J. Harris. Fascinating, comprehensive, thoroughly documented text describes this ancient civilization's vast resources and the processes that incorporated them in daily life, including the use of animal products, building materials, cosmetics, perfumes and incense, fibers, glazed ware, glass and its manufacture, materials used in the mummification process, and much more. 544pp. 6⅛ x 9¼. (Available in U.S. only.) 0-486-40446-3

RUSSIAN STORIES/RUSSKIE RASSKAZY: A Dual-Language Book, edited by Gleb Struve. Twelve tales by such masters as Chekhov, Tolstoy, Dostoevsky, Pushkin, others. Excellent word-for-word English translations on facing pages, plus teaching and study aids, Russian/English vocabulary, biographical/critical introductions, more. 416pp. 5⅜ x 8½. 0-486-26244-8

PHILADELPHIA THEN AND NOW: 60 Sites Photographed in the Past and Present, Kenneth Finkel and Susan Oyama. Rare photographs of City Hall, Logan Square, Independence Hall, Betsy Ross House, other landmarks juxtaposed with contemporary views. Captures changing face of historic city. Introduction. Captions. 128pp. 8¼ x 11. 0-486-25790-8

NORTH AMERICAN INDIAN LIFE: Customs and Traditions of 23 Tribes, Elsie Clews Parsons (ed.). 27 fictionalized essays by noted anthropologists examine religion, customs, government, additional facets of life among the Winnebago, Crow, Zuni, Eskimo, other tribes. 480pp. 6⅛ x 9¼. 0-486-27377-6

TECHNICAL MANUAL AND DICTIONARY OF CLASSICAL BALLET, Gail Grant. Defines, explains, comments on steps, movements, poses and concepts. 15-page pictorial section. Basic book for student, viewer. 127pp. 5⅜ x 8½. 0-486-21843-0

THE MALE AND FEMALE FIGURE IN MOTION: 60 Classic Photographic Sequences, Eadweard Muybridge. 60 true-action photographs of men and women walking, running, climbing, bending, turning, etc., reproduced from rare 19th-century masterpiece. vi + 121pp. 9 x 12. 0-486-24745-7

CATALOG OF DOVER BOOKS

LIGHT AND SHADE: A Classic Approach to Three-Dimensional Drawing, Mrs. Mary P. Merrifield. Handy reference clearly demonstrates principles of light and shade by revealing effects of common daylight, sunshine, and candle or artificial light on geometrical solids. 13 plates. 64pp. 5⅜ x 8½. 0-486-44143-1

ASTROLOGY AND ASTRONOMY: A Pictorial Archive of Signs and Symbols, Ernst and Johanna Lehner. Treasure trove of stories, lore, and myth, accompanied by more than 300 rare illustrations of planets, the Milky Way, signs of the zodiac, comets, meteors, and other astronomical phenomena. 192pp. 8⅜ x 11. 0-486-43981-X

JEWELRY MAKING: Techniques for Metal, Tim McCreight. Easy-to-follow instructions and carefully executed illustrations describe tools and techniques, use of gems and enamels, wire inlay, casting, and other topics. 72 line illustrations and diagrams. 176pp. 8¼ x 10⅞. 0-486-44043-5

MAKING BIRDHOUSES: Easy and Advanced Projects, Gladstone Califf. Easy-to-follow instructions include diagrams for everything from a one-room house for bluebirds to a forty-two-room structure for purple martins. 56 plates; 4 figures. 80pp. 8¾ x 6⅜. 0-486-44183-0

LITTLE BOOK OF LOG CABINS: How to Build and Furnish Them, William S. Wicks. Handy how-to manual, with instructions and illustrations for building cabins in the Adirondack style, fireplaces, stairways, furniture, beamed ceilings, and more. 102 line drawings. 96pp. 8¾ x 6⅜. 0-486-44259-4

THE SEASONS OF AMERICA PAST, Eric Sloane. From "sugaring time" and strawberry picking to Indian summer and fall harvest, a whole year's activities described in charming prose and enhanced with 79 of the author's own illustrations. 160pp. 8¼ x 11. 0-486-44220-9

THE METROPOLIS OF TOMORROW, Hugh Ferriss. Generous, prophetic vision of the metropolis of the future, as perceived in 1929. Powerful illustrations of towering structures, wide avenues, and rooftop parks–all features in many of today's modern cities. 59 illustrations. 144pp. 8¼ x 11. 0-486-43727-2

THE PATH TO ROME, Hilaire Belloc. This 1902 memoir abounds in lively vignettes from a vanished time, recounting a pilgrimage on foot across the Alps and Apennines in order to "see all Europe which the Christian Faith has saved." 77 of the author's original line drawings complement his sparkling prose. 272pp. 5⅜ x 8½. 0-486-44001-X

THE HISTORY OF RASSELAS: Prince of Abissinia, Samuel Johnson. Distinguished English writer attacks eighteenth-century optimism and man's unrealistic estimates of what life has to offer. 112pp. 5⅜ x 8½. 0-486-44094-X

A VOYAGE TO ARCTURUS, David Lindsay. A brilliant flight of pure fancy, where wild creatures crowd the fantastic landscape and demented torturers dominate victims with their bizarre mental powers. 272pp. 5⅜ x 8½. 0-486-44198-9

Paperbound unless otherwise indicated. Available at your book dealer, online at **www.doverpublications.com**, or by writing to Dept. GI, Dover Publications, Inc., 31 East 2nd Street, Mineola, NY 11501. For current price information or for free catalogs (please indicate field of interest), write to Dover Publications or log on to **www.doverpublications.com** and see every Dover book in print. Dover publishes more than 500 books each year on science, elementary and advanced mathematics, biology, music, art, literary history, social sciences, and other areas.